:r

Copying recordings is illegal. All recorded items
are hired entirely at hirer's own risk

Swindon
BOROUGH COUNCIL

6 906 668 000

Visit www.dorindabalchin.com
to find out more about the author and her works

Prologue

What had woken him? Paul Hetherington lay still for a moment, wondering what could have disturbed his deep, dreamless sleep. There was a certain chill to the room that had not been there before, and he glanced over towards the open window. The thick heavy curtains hung unmoving, no wind finding its way in through there to raise the hairs on his arms and to make the skin on the back of his neck crawl. He listened intently. No sound, nothing but the steady ticking of the clock in its ancient oak casing. The springs in the old four-poster creaked and complained as he rolled over and looked towards the fireplace, cold and empty now that it was summer; yet as the temperature continued to fall, he wished that he had laid a fire before retiring. Something was wrong. He did not know what it was, or how he knew, but there was something indefinably different about the room, and he felt a strange uneasiness. He did not want to augment the feeling by naming it fear, yet he knew that the beating of his heart, the knotting in his stomach and the cold which now seemed to reach his very bones, was something beyond the normal, the expected.

Paul sat up, drawing the old patchwork counterpane tightly around his shoulders as he leant back against the heavy wooden headboard and allowed his eyes to search the room, exploring every nook and cranny for ... something. What was that deeper shadow beside the door? Had it been there before? He wracked his brain, trying to see in his mind's eye what had stood there when he went to bed, what it was that could create such a shadow, but he could think of nothing. His hand was shaking as he reached out towards the bedside light, knocking over his glass of water in the process, yet he did not seem to notice, his whole attention was focused on the shadow behind the door. He could swear that it had moved. Was it bigger now? It seemed to be moving across the room towards him, and he switched on the lamp, certain in that second that its light would reveal nothing out of the ordinary and he would laugh at his fears. The warm yellow light flooded the room and the shadow solidified, no longer an indistinct and insubstantial mass, but the form of a woman.

'Who the hell are you, and what are you doing in my room!' Paul's cry rent the silence, anger and fear causing the adrenalin to flow as he tensed ready to spring towards the intruder.

The woman stepped forward, the movement causing her long black dress to rustle like tiny creatures amongst dry leaves. Paul found himself shivering uncontrollably as his eyes were drawn to her face. He could not tell how old she was, some indeterminate age between thirty and sixty, her skin lined and cracked as though she had been out in all weathers, yet it did not have the colour of someone who lived their life in the open. Her skin was dark blue, almost black; dark brown eyes bulged from the deep sockets; blue, bloodless lips were stretched in a grim line. Wisps of grey hair escaped from a thick plait which hung over her shoulder. The deep pools of her eyes stared at him and Paul shivered, not with the cold but with fear. His mouth was dry as he struggled to get the words out, to challenge the intruder in his home, his bedroom, his place of safety and security.

'I said, who are you and what are you doing here?'

The woman frowned as she looked at him, her head tilted slightly to one side as her eyes hungrily devoured his features. 'Does this house belong to thee now?' The voice that issued from the blue and seemingly lifeless lips was cold and harsh, as though drawn forth through unimaginable pain and suffering. Somehow she seemed to belong there, in that room, in that house, in a way that Paul felt he did not, and he found himself nodding at her question.

'Yes. This is my house. Now tell me who you are, and what you are doing here.'

It was as if she could not hear his questions, or chose to ignore them, he did not know which, for she continued with her own relentless train of thought as she stepped closer to the bed and leant forward to scrutinise his features. 'What is it that they call thee?'

'My name is Hetherington. Paul Hetherington. Now who the devil are you? You have no right to be here! I'm going to call the police.' He was beginning to feel more in control of himself as the shock of finding a stranger in his bedroom began to recede before his growing anger. She was only an old lady, for God's sake! Why was he so afraid to confront her? Throwing back the covers he climbed out of bed and stood before her.

'Now, you're coming downstairs with me while I call the police. I don't know what you're doing here. Maybe the old owners let you wander around freely, but this is my house now, and you are not welcome.'

He found that he was looking down at her. The woman was small, barely five feet tall, and he felt ridiculous at having been afraid of her, and feeling ridiculous made him angry. He did not like to be made a fool of by anyone. He reached out a hand to take her by the arm and guide her downstairs to the phone in the hall, but the old woman shook her head.

'Hetherington. Not Hardwycke.'

Paul frowned. 'What do you mean?'

'You are not a Hardwycke?'

'That's right. My name is Hetherington. Now come with me.'

Paul reached out and placed his hand on her arm, or at least where her arm appeared to be, but there was nothing there. He saw his fingers pass through the air where her body should have been, and a strange icy coldness gripped him to the core. A tingling sensation began at his fingertips and travelled up his arm until he felt every hair on his body standing on end, as though he had experienced an electric shock. With a cry of fear he stepped back, afraid of what he could see but could not feel. The old woman laughed.

'Do not fear me, sir, for I do not come here looking for thee. I have waited many years for Hardwycke to return to this house and face me. No matter that you are not he, I can wait many more years. As many as it takes.' A humourless smile twisted her thin lips. 'He will return, and I will be waiting.'

Paul trembled with fear as he watched the woman turn and walk, no glide, across the room towards the door. He expected her to stop to open the door but she just continued, not even the thick wooden door seemed to be strong enough to stand up to her insubstantial frame as she glided through it and out of his sight.

The temperature in the room began to rise rapidly at the woman's departure, but Hetherington was unaware of it as he stood shivering in the middle of the room, wondering if buying this house had been such a good idea after all.

Chapter 1

Present day

The battered estate car pulled in at the side of the road and drew to a halt. Putting the car into neutral, Robert Hardwick wound down the window and breathed the clean fresh air of the countryside deeply, his eager gaze taking in the view which unfolded before him. To his right, a low stone wall bordered lush green pastureland dotted with the white cotton-wool shapes of sheep. The pasture was framed by two broad swathes of trees which swept down to a small lake and beyond, drawing the eye towards the Manor house which nestled in a fold of land just below the brow of the hill. The house was protected on all sides from severe weather, yet open to the views down the valley towards the distant spires of the colleges of Oxford, which punctuated the skyline like so many stalagmites.

The early afternoon sun bathed the facade of the building and reflected from its windows. The warm yellow stone seemed to radiate a feeling of permanence, of a belonging to this place which went beyond time and space. The house was meant to be here, the curve of the hillside and the sweeping trees like the arms of a protecting deity holding it close and safe, its foundations fixed firmly to the bedrock of the land. Rob smiled. The view – the house, the land, the trees, the sheep – this spoke to him of history. This was what he would have seen if he had travelled along this road three or four hundred years earlier. What stories this place could tell! Taking a deep breath he put the car into gear and moved off down the road. He was going to like it here, he just knew it. This was going to be less of a job and more of the fulfilment of a dream.

Half a mile further down the road, the huge iron gates of Marston Manor stood wide in welcome. Rob swung his car onto the sweeping gravel drive which led through the trees of the broad-leaved woodland towards the house, hidden from sight at the moment but still drawing him on towards his destiny. He drove slowly, the only sound the gravel crunching beneath his tyres. So quiet, so peaceful, so beautiful. As the car rounded the first bend Rob stopped, strangely angered by what he saw. In a clearing to his left clustered a group of caravans, lines of washing connecting them like obscene parodies of carnival bunting. Four horses were tethered to one side and grazed the close-cropped grass while a crowd of scruffy urchins ran between them, laughing and screaming. The smoke from a large wood fire in the centre of the site rose lazily into the still summer air, drifting towards the cluster of parked vehicles – powerful cars to haul the caravans, old lorries which had seen better days, dirty vans

– and beyond them a pile of rubbish. As he drove slowly past Rob saw old beds, discarded fridges, heaps of metal and wood, old tyres. An ugly scene. The more so after his idyllic view of the Manor house only moments before. This was not right. These people did not belong here, he felt it deep inside with an unshakeable certainty. Surely Paul Hetherington would not allow this? As he pulled away a large, scruffy black dog broke from the trees and pursued his car, barking and snapping, its flag of a tail waving wildly. Rob put his foot down causing a shower of gravel to be kicked up by the wheels. The dog yelped as the stones stung its flesh, veering off into the trees, still barking madly.

Rob felt a tension in his shoulders as his hands gripped the wheel tightly. 'Bloody travellers.' He glanced back through the mirror, but the campsite had been lost by the curve of the drive and he was in clean fresh woodland again. He frowned for a moment, then shrugged. He would obviously not be able to complete his job with the travellers there, but that was not his problem. He would concentrate on the house and outbuildings, the old gardens, the core of the estate which gave it its heart. The problem of the travellers was someone else's, not his, and he would not let it spoil his introduction to Marston Manor.

At last the sweeping drive brought him out of the trees, and he could see the house once more. Breathing deeply, Rob calmed his raw nerves, putting all thoughts of the travellers' camp out of his mind as he drew to a halt in front of the sweep of steps which led up to the enormous oak door. Leaving his car beside the four-wheel drive vehicle which dominated the driveway, he looked down towards the lake and the road beyond, to the place where he had stopped such a short time before to view the house. He could see now why it had been sited here. The lines of trees were not quite parallel, but widened out as they swept past the lake and on towards the road, opening up a vista of the English countryside which had not changed for centuries. This was permanence, stability. Rob felt a strange feeling of belonging, as though this place drew him to itself, as though he were a part of it already. He felt a rush of adrenalin, eager to get to work, to find out about the people and events which had shaped this place, and which would become his life for the foreseeable future.

Rob turned back to the door and smiled to see an ancient bell pull. Grasping the warm iron work in his hand he pulled, then waited for the sound of the bell which would have called forth the servants in the past. To his annoyance the old bell pull had been connected to a modern electric buzzer which rent the air with its shrillness. He cringed. That would have to go.

There were no sounds from the house. Perhaps no one was home. He looked at his watch. 1.30. Admittedly he was a little early, but surely there should be someone there to meet him? Ringing the bell again, he turned his back to the building to drink in the view once more, and was unaware of the door opening. He started at the sound of the voice.

'Hi. You must be Rob Hardwick. Come in.'

Rob turned to peruse the man who had greeted him. He was about the same age as Rob, possibly a little older. Thirty-four? Five? Taller than Rob, he had mousy hair and grey eyes which smiled a welcome though held deep within them a hint of flint as though this was not a man to be crossed. Broad shoulders filled the dark blue polo shirt worn with a pair of faded jeans and Reebok trainers. Rob smiled.

'Yes. That's right. I'm here to see Mr Hetherington. Is he home?'

The man held out his hand and grinned. 'I'm Paul Hetherington.'

Rob took the proffered hand, the grip strong and sure. 'Sorry. I was expecting someone...'

'Older? More conservative?' Paul smiled, and Rob found himself responding.

'Well, maybe. It's good to meet you, Mr Hetherington.'

'Paul, please. Now do come in.' He led the way into the hall as he spoke, and Rob allowed his gaze to wander over the old paintings, antique furniture, suits of armour. An unusual collection, he thought, something would definitely have to be done about them; but he did not have time to view them properly as Paul led him through to the library which opened off of the hall.

'Please sit down, Rob. I may call you Rob?' He indicated a comfortable leather chair as he spoke, and Rob sat down with a nod of acceptance at the use of his name. 'What do you think of the house so far?'

'Well, from the outside it's magnificent. It's rare to find a place like this which hasn't been changed and altered over the years by successive generations. Looking at it, you can imagine what it would have looked like during the Civil War. And this library is incredible.' He allowed his gaze to wander over the shelves of books, their faded leather bindings speaking of their age. 'There's a wonderful atmosphere in here which can be utilised.'

'So you think my idea will work?' Paul's eyes were lit with excitement as he seated himself opposite Rob, who nodded his agreement.

'Yes. I've read your proposal in detail and I think it has great potential, but there will be lots of things which will need changing in the house if it is to truly work.'

'Such as?'

'Well, the hall for a start. You have some fine antiques in there, but they're from all sorts of periods and don't go together. If this is going to be a re-creation of a Manor house during the period of the Civil War then it needs a more cohesive identity. Take a look at this library, for instance.'

Paul perused the room. 'I thought you liked it?'

'Oh, I do,' Rob agreed, 'but look at it. Old leather bound books and a few paperbacks on the same shelves. If it's going to work, everything must fit in. We have to be careful to ensure that nothing is out of place.'

'That's your job, if you still want it.'

Rob beamed. 'Yes. Definitely. The Civil War has always been the period of history which grips me; it was my specialism at university. To be able to work on something like this is a dream come true for me.'

'Good. That's what my sources said, and why I approached you in the first place. I've got so many plans for the place, but to do something like this is way out of my league.' He grinned. 'I made my money on the Stock Market, which enabled me to buy this place with plenty left over for any work that needs doing. It needs to be good, Rob, if we are to attract all the different kinds of people I want to come here.'

'Such as?'

'Well, your bog-standard tourist for a start. Someone who is interested in history but doesn't know much, so needs it all laid out for them on a plate. I want them to be able to see and feel and hear and smell a Manor during the Civil War. I want characters in costume about the place to make it feel real to them. Then I want to re-enact battles. That should draw the crowds. Roundheads and Cavaliers fighting out there in front of the house.' He waved a hand in the general direction of the lake as he spoke, his enthusiasm spilling from him. 'Then there are the educational opportunities. We won't get so many tourists out of season so I want to set up an educational facility to encourage school visits, to let the kids dress up and do things, to feel that they are living in the past.'

'You really have a passion for history, don't you, Paul, wanting to pass it on to others like that. That's how I feel too.'

Paul shook his head. 'Not quite. I am interested in history up to a point, but this isn't about what others can get out of it. It's what I can get.'

'Which is?'

'Money. This is a business venture, Rob. That's why it needs to be so true to life. It's the best way to attract the crowds. Who knows? Maybe we can even encourage some TV or Hollywood directors to film here. That would really put us on the map.'

Rob frowned. 'Money is all well and good, Paul, but it can't stand in the way of authenticity.'

'Oh, I agree. That's why the historical aspect is yours, and I won't interfere. I shall be focussing on the business side of things.'

'How much freedom will I have in my work?'

'As much as you like. You come up with the ideas, cost them, present them to me. If they're viable then you can go ahead with them. You come highly recommended, Rob. I will trust your judgment. But don't let me down.'

Rob noticed the steely edge to the voice. This was a man who knew what he wanted and how to get it. But as long as he did not dictate to Rob then he could work with him. 'I won't let you down.'

Paul grinned as he stood and held out his hand. 'You'll not regret this, Rob. Welcome aboard.'

***

'The historian seems okay. I think he'll be able to give me what I want.'

The older man turned his weather-beaten features towards Paul. 'He knows his stuff then?'

'Yes. He recognised a lot of the irrelevant furniture which has been collected over the years and needs replacing. And he seems very keen on the educational aspects.'

Jim Brand scratched at his short-cropped hair. 'So what's he up to now?'

'Oh, he's put his stuff up in his room and is taking a look around the house. Getting the feel of things, he says. Obviously there'll be rooms that won't be on display, private areas where I'll stay when I'm in the area. It will be fun to have friends over for the odd weekend when we are closed to the public. We can have some themed parties.'

Jim laughed. 'Not much money in them.'

Paul was silent for a moment, then grinned. 'Could be, Jim. Could be.'

The two men made their way down towards the barn and outbuildings, empty now of life but peopled in Paul's imagination with costumed figures and farm animals.

'How long since these buildings were last used?'

'The previous owners used the barn as a garage and storage area, so it's in pretty good condition. The rest of the buildings haven't been used for some years, but it won't take much to get them back into order. Then there's the stables, of course. As you know I've got a couple of horses in there, so they're well kept.'

Paul turned to his estate manager. He knew what was what, he knew the estate like the back of his hand and, more importantly, he lived in the twenty-first century and was open to new ideas. Paul was glad he'd kept him on when he bought the Manor, his experience working for the previous owners would be invaluable.

'As I said, you can keep your horses there for as long as you like. They'll make good additions to the stock once we open.'

Jim laughed. 'There had to be an ulterior motive there! Seriously though, I don't see why you don't ride one of them some time, you're more than welcome.'

Paul shook his head ruefully. 'No, the closest I get to nature is on the golf course!' He was thoughtful for a moment. 'I wonder if Rob rides? It might help him to get to know the area better.'

'Well, he can ride my horses any time he likes; they could do with the exercise. Ask him. If he wants an early ride, I'll be going out at about six tomorrow morning.'

'Six!' Paul laughed. 'I'll see what he says, but don't hold your breath!'

'It's strange his name being Hardwick, isn't it?'

Paul turned to his companion. 'What do you mean?'

'Well, what with the Hardwycke's owning the place for so long.'

'Did they?'

'Didn't you know? The Hardwycke family built this place and were here during the Civil War. It just seems strange that the man you hire to research it all is a Hardwick too.'

'Hardwycke.' Paul shivered. 'Do you know anything about their history?'

Jim shrugged. 'Not much. Me, I'm more interested in the land and the animals. Estate manager and gamekeeper. Not much interested in history.'

Paul chewed thoughtfully on his lower lip. Perhaps Jim was the one to ask. He was pretty down to earth and wouldn't say anything to anyone else, even if he thought Paul a little strange. Coming to a decision, he stopped beside the barn door and turned to face his companion.

'Any history of ghosts in the house?'

He expected Jim to laugh and say no, there were no legends of hauntings. Instead the older man frowned. 'Why do you ask?'

'Well, is the place haunted or not?'

Jim shrugged. 'I've never seen anything, but there are stories about an old woman being seen wandering about the place at night. Some of the locals swear that she is searching for revenge, but they don't know from whom or why. Personally, I'll believe it when I see it.'

'I'm not one for the paranormal either,' Paul began, 'but I don't think it would be hard to convince me. On my first night in the house I woke up to find a little old woman in my room. She asked me my name and when she found out it was Hetherington she said I wasn't the one she was waiting for, but she could wait as long as necessary.' He shivered. 'I think it must have been the ghost.'

Jim laughed. 'How can you tell? Did she walk through a wall or something?'

'Yes.'

'Shit! Maybe the old place is haunted after all! Did she say who she was waiting for?'

'Yes. Hardwycke.'

'And you've just hired a Hardwick? Interesting. Are you going to tell him?'

'I don't know. Maybe it was just a dream; you know, moving into an old house, feeling tired, affected by the atmosphere. Perhaps I dreamt the whole thing.' He was quiet for a moment, then smiled. 'I might tell Hardwick, though; it should fuel his historian's curiosity. I think I'll...'

'What the hell is that!'

'What?'

'Over there!' Jim was walking swiftly towards his old battered land rover as he spoke. 'See, above the trees by the road?'

Paul looked. Clouds of oily black smoke were beginning to rise above the trees in the still summer air, hanging there like a portent of evil. 'It's those bloody travellers!' Paul climbed in beside Jim as he spoke. 'Come on, let's get down there!'

The car bounced down the drive, taking the corners at speed, then screeched to a halt on the edge of the camp, waves of gravel being thrown up by the wheels. The vehicle had barely come to a halt when Paul climbed out.

'What the hell is going on here?'

'Surely that's bloody obvious, even to a toffee-nosed git like you.'

Paul perused the man who had spoken. He was in his mid-forties with long brown hair tied back in a ponytail, two days' stubble shadowing his cheeks and chin. An old tyre was clutched in his hand, and there was a pile of others beside him. Paul looked at the fire. Flames licked at the heap of black rubber, causing clouds of black smoke to roil into the air, leaving an acrid taste in his mouth. He looked back at the man with the tyre.

'And who the hell are you?'

'My name's Patrick Cowan, if it's any business of yours. My friends call me Paddy, but you can call me Mr Cowan.'

The group of travellers who had gathered around him began to laugh as he swung his arm and flung the tyre onto the fire.

'I don't give a shit what your name is.' Paul moved to stand between the man and the fire. 'This is my land and you have no business to be here. I've tried to ignore you for the past couple of days since you arrived, but this is going too far. You're polluting my land with this and I've had enough. I expect you, and all your rubbish, to be gone by first thing tomorrow.'

Cowan looked him up and down. 'So you're the new owner, are you? We'd heard that the old lot had gone. Well, for your information we stay here every year and we ain't movin' just 'cause you take a dislike to us.'

Paul turned to Jim, who had climbed out of the car and was standing in a carefully relaxed manner beside the driver's door. 'Jim?'

'A group of travellers camped here last year. I recognise some of them, but not this bloke. The lot we had last year only stayed a week or two then went. They caused no trouble and left no mess.'

'And we'll be no trouble. As long as you leave us alone.'

'Then put the fire out.'

Cowan grinned. 'I said there'd be no trouble if you left us alone. Tellin' us what to do ain't leavin' us alone now, is it?'

This raised another laugh from his audience and he turned to them with a mock bow.

'This is my land and you have no rights here. I want you gone by tomorrow. Understand?'

'Piss off.'

Paul stepped towards Cowan, who raised his fists and adopted a fighting stance. 'Want to take me on, nancy boy?'

'Paul, I wouldn't recommend it.' Jim's voice was soft, and when Paul turned to face him he indicated the rest of the travellers with a nod of his head. The women and children had stepped back, leaving a row of men in a semi-circle around Paul and Cowan. Paul had to admit to himself that this was neither the time nor place to confront Cowan.

'You just go on back to your big posh house and leave us here.' Cowan grinned. 'Come on you lot, let's get on with it.'

As Paul retreated towards the land rover the travellers began to throw more tyres onto the fire. He clenched his fists and gritted his teeth in an effort not to lose control. No one spoke to him like that and got away with it. Cowan may have won this round, but Paul Hetherington would be victorious in the end. Opening the door of the land rover he muttered at Jim.

'And where were you when I needed you?'

The older man inclined his head towards the bed of the vehicle where his hand rested on a shotgun. 'Providing back-up.'

Once Paul was in the car Jim joined him, revved the engine and swung round to head back up the drive to the house.

'They can't get away with this!' Paul's voiced hissed angrily between his teeth. 'When I get back I'll phone the police and get them thrown off.'

Jim shrugged. 'You can try, but it's not that easy. Their sort always seem to have the law on their side these days.'

'We'll see, Jim. We'll see.'

Rob found himself back in the library. The old house certainly had an atmosphere, and the rooms which Paul said he wanted for public display had great potential. This was going to be a very enjoyable job. Running his hands over the cracked leather spines of some of the books on the shelves he felt their age, as though they were talking to him. He took one down at random. He loved the texture of the binding, the smell of the old paper; there was so much here that could tell him of the past and he hoped that he would have time to study it all. As his gaze wandered around the room his eyes fell on the bulk of an old family Bible displayed on a small lectern beneath the window. Crossing the room, he laid his hands on the warm leather, feeling its age. The leather was cracked and worn from exposure to the sun through the window. He determined that it should be restored, then kept safely away from the sun's harmful rays. The brass bindings of the enormous book were shiny with age, the once beautiful engraving now worn thin by the touch of devout hands over the centuries. He smiled to himself. If only people realised how much history was contained in a Bible like this. Undoing the clasps which held it shut, he lifted the heavy cover and let out a satisfied sigh as he saw the delicate writing in ink, once black but now faded to grey-blue with age. The handwriting changed every few entries as the head of the household came and went. This was what history was about. Rob touched the page almost reverently. Real families. Real people. Here was the record of their births and deaths, their loves and marriages; this was what the past was really about.

A word caught his eye and he leaned forward to have a closer look. No, he had not been mistaken. This was the Hardwycke family Bible. With a dry mouth and heart beating wildly, he began to read.

Thomas Hardwycke married Mary Sutter this day 24th October 1623.
This Bible shall be the record of our family over the generations. I pray God's blessing on our marriage and our future life together.

Rob began to read eagerly. The beginning of a family history, what more did this book have to tell? The next entry spoke of the building of a new Manor house for the family, and he realised that this gave him the date for the building of Marston Manor, begun in 1623 and completed in 1625. He smiled at the entry recording the first-born son of Thomas and Mary.

Although the house is not yet complete, it is our wish that our children be born here. For that reason we lived in the finished rooms for some weeks until the good Lord blessed us with the safe birth of a son and heir.

Thomas Hardwycke born this day 15th January 1625.
The Lord be praised for his goodness.

Rob continued to read. Two more sons, Charles and Simon, and two daughters, Mary and Elizabeth. Little Mary only lived for two days, and Charles for a brief four and a half months, but the others reached adult hood. As he read on, Rob charted their history and that of their children and grandchildren down through the years, the centuries, until he read one entry and his heart missed a beat. Taking a deep breath he read it again, but there was no mistake.

Charles David Hardwycke born this day 9th April 1843

He read the remaining entries. Then read them again. There was no further mention of Charles David Hardwycke in the Bible. No marriage. No death. He seemed to have disappeared into thin air.

Rob found that his heart was beating wildly as he rested his hands on the table and breathed deeply in an effort to regain control. Charles David Hardwycke. He had searched for that name in the records of Oxfordshire for years, and now here it was. With a sudden grin that lit his face he took out his mobile phone and dialled swiftly.

It rang, and rang.

'Come on. Come on.'

He was about to give up when finally there was an answer.

'Hello?'

'Caroline, it's me.'

'Rob? What are you doing calling me at this time of day? I've got patients waiting. Can't this wait till tonight?'

'No. Sorry love, but this is important.'

'It had better be.' Caroline was obviously annoyed, but Rob did not recognise the tone of voice, he was so wrapped up with his news.

'You'll never guess what I've found! It's brilliant!'

There was a lightening of the tone on the other end of the line. 'Okay Rob, I've got five minutes. What is it this time?'

Rob had the decency to grin.

'Sorry love, I do tend to go a little over the top with my finds, don't I. But this is something special. You know I've researched my family history and can't get back beyond the marriage of Charles to Sarah Bell in Faringdon? The only clue was that Charles came from Oxford, and I've searched all the records there. But I didn't search all of the villages outside.'

'So?'

'So, I'm at Marston Manor and guess what! The house was built by the Hardwycke family, and there's a Bible tracing their family history. There's a Charles David Hardwycke, spelt with 'y' and an 'e' on the end, who was born on 9ᵗʰ April 1843 then disappears from the family record. My ancestor was Charles David Hardwick from Oxford, who was 22 when he married Sarah Bell on 1ˢᵗ June 1865.'

'What are you trying to say, Rob?'

'It must be the same person. It's too much of a coincidence.'

'What about the spelling?'

'What?'

'Hardwycke with a 'y' and an 'e'. You don't have them.'

'Oh, plenty of mistakes like that were made when records were written in the past. They didn't put the letters in the register, so the family stopped using them. Isn't this brilliant! I think I've found the branch of my family that I've been looking for. And can now trace it right back to 1623! The research I do about this house in the Civil War will be about my own ancestors! Isn't that great!'

'Yes, darling, it's great. Now can I get back to work?'

Rob laughed. 'Sorry, love. Of course. I'll call you again later.'

'And preferably not at work.'

'Okay, okay. I'll try to control myself in future and not call you at work.'

It was Caroline's turn to laugh. 'You'll never stick to it. But that's what I love about you, you're so impulsive!'

'And I thought it was my charming bedside manner.'

'I'm the doctor here, not you. But your manner *in* bed is pretty appealing. Now, let me get back to work!'

'Okay. I'll call later. I love you.'

'And I love you too.'

Rob switched off and pocketed his phone. Charles David Hardwick! Paul Hetherington was never going to believe this!

As Rob ran his hand over the Bible once more he felt a sudden chilling of the air. Somewhere behind him he could have sworn that he heard someone whispering the name Hardwick, but when he turned there was no one there.

***

Rob was sitting at the kitchen table with a mug of coffee in his hand as he perused the plans of the house. The door behind him slammed. He turned to see who it was.

'Bloody travellers.'

'Anything wrong, Paul?'

'Anything wrong? You should see the mess they're making down there. Burning tyres. I ask you. What's the point? I'm sure they're doing it just to annoy me.'

'They seem to have succeeded.'

Paul proceeded to make a mug of coffee, banging kettles and mugs around in his anger. 'Of course they've pissed me off. What gives them the right to camp on my land? I was fairly lenient about that. Thought they'd be gone in a week or two. But now they're creating a mess that will take ages to fix. And it's right on the drive. We can't have that when this place opens.'

'But you've got plenty of time, Paul. You won't be able to open up before next year, so you've got time to get rid of them.'

'That's beside the point. I don't want bastards like that Cowan on my land.'

'Who?'

'Patrick Cowan. He seems to be their leader. No-one, and I mean *no-one*, speaks to me like that and gets away with it.'

Paul's anger was palpable, and Rob wondered how he could calm him down.

'Have you tried calling the police?'

'Yes. They say that there's nothing they can do. It's my land for God's sake, and they're trespassing on it and making a mess, but there's nothing the police can do. The police will only get involved if they cause a great deal of damage. But how do they define that? Something has to be done, Rob. I don't know what, but I'll think of something.'

Rob sipped his coffee as he watched his employer filling a mug. The man was obviously very tense; the best thing he could do at the moment would be to distract him from all thoughts of the travellers.

'I found something very interesting in the library.'

'Yes?' Paul turned towards him as he spoke. 'Valuable?'

'Not financially, no. But valuable to me.'

'Explain.'

'Well, I found out that this Manor was built by the Hardwycke family.'

'Funny you should mention that. I was talking to Jim, my estate manager, about that and was going to tell you this evening.'

'Well, it's not just a coincidence that my name is Hardwick.'

'What do you mean?'

Rob grinned. He still could hardly believe that what he was about to tell Paul was true, but all the evidence pointed to the fact.

'Well, the Bible in the library records the family history up to the end of the First World War. It mentions a younger son called Charles David who seems to have disappeared in the mid nineteenth century.'

'So what?'

'So, I can trace my family back to a Charles David Hardwick from this area who was born in the same year as the younger son of the family.'

'What are you saying?'

'I think, no I'm ninety nine point nine percent certain, that I'm descended from the Hardwyckes who built Marston Manor. The family we are researching is my family. This house is my ancestral home.'

'You're not planning to claim it back, are you?'

Rob laughed. 'Good Lord, no! It's just that it's all so personal now. I can't wait to find out more about them. When we set up this place as a Civil War Manor, I will actually be able to see how my ancestors lived. Isn't that something?'

'It should at least ensure that you do a good job.'

'Cynic!'

Paul sat down at the table and grinned. 'Sorry. It's just those damned travellers who've put me on edge. Do you really think that you are related to these Hardwyckes? Only...'

'Only what?'

Paul frowned at Rob's question. 'Well, it's a bit difficult really. You see I saw, or dreamt I saw, an old woman who said she was looking for Hardwycke. Jim thinks it might be the Manor ghost.'

Rob laughed. 'I don't believe in ghosts! What did this 'ghost' want Hardwycke for?'

Paul shrugged. 'I don't know. The local legend is that she's seeking revenge. Perhaps for something your family did in the past?' He grinned suddenly. 'Are you sure you want to stay here? She might visit you in your bed, like she did me.'

Rob laughed. 'Just my luck, then, that it's an old woman. Why couldn't it be someone young and nubile?'

Paul joined in the laughter. 'You're right. Why is it that ghosts are always old and wrinkled, and seeking revenge? I must have been dreaming when I saw what I thought I saw, so don't worry about anything. This house is as safe as they come.'

'Who said I was worried!'

The two men laughed and turned their attention to the plans once more, all thoughts of the ghost searching for Hardwycke banished from their minds.

***

Rob placed his book on the bedside table and turned out the light, lying back with a contented sigh. The social history of the Civil War period was like a maze, with its mixture of puritan simplicity and Royalist decadence. He would enjoy unravelling the threads and weaving them into a tapestry of his own, peopled with characters in authentic period costumes, each with their own stories to tell. He could already see in his mind's eye the rich splendour of the Cavaliers at the Manor, and the poverty of the workers on the estate, some of whom no doubt must have been Roundheads, who would have hoped for a change in their circumstances if the king should lose the war.

Rob looked towards the open window, drinking in the peaceful scene of the stables and outbuildings bathed in moonlight. He smiled as he closed his eyes and drifted towards a sleep which he knew would be visited by dreams of his ancestors living in the Manor, sleeping in this very room, seeing this very scene through the open window.

Rob was not sure if he had slept at all, for the moon had barely moved in her course across the heavens when he became aware of a cool breeze blowing across him. He shivered as he pulled the counterpane over his body, curious at the sudden change in the temperature. He could see through the window that the sky was still cloudless and there was no wind to move the branches of the trees, and he wondered where the breeze had come from. Maybe the fireplace? If so it would need blocking off if he was ever to get a good night's sleep.

Rob turned over to see if there was any evidence of a draught from the fireplace, then froze at the sight which greeted him. Standing in the far corner of the room was a woman. She was small and bent, giving the impression of years of toil. The dark pools of her eyes gazed at him from a face creased with age, the creases augmented by the deep frown which furrowed her brow. More startling was the colour of the face, a deep bluish purple, as though the woman was suffocating, struggling for oxygen. Then she spoke.

'So, thou hast returned.'

Rob felt icy fingers of fear course down his spine at the sound of the cracked voice issuing from her bloodless lips. He shook his head.

'I don't know who you are, but I've never been here before.' He licked his dry lips. Was this the apparition that Paul had seen? Was he seeing a ghost for the first time in his life? He fervently wished that it was not so, and that she was just some mad intruder who had found her way into the house.

The old woman stepped a little closer, still frowning; then her eyes cleared and she nodded. 'Oh, I know thee, Hardwycke. How could it be that I would ever forget thy face.'

'You must be mistaken.' Rob inched further up the bed as he spoke, wanting to put as much distance as possible between himself and the old crone. 'I told you, I've never been here before.'

'Truly it was long ago, but thou cannot have forgotten, Hardwycke.'

'How do you know my name?'

'The Hardwycke family did us a great wrong.' Slowly she raised a hand and pointed a bent and arthritic finger accusingly at him. 'We were innocents, but because of thee we endured the punishment for crimes which we did not commit.'

'I don't know what you're talking about!'

'Thou must remember, Hardwycke, or thou must fervently seek out and learn the truth of my words. For it is thee who will pay for the crimes of thy family. And for thine own.'

Rob's mind was in turmoil. Was he dreaming? Was this all real? If so, was she a living breathing person, or a ghost from the long distant past destined to forever haunt this house and this family? He wanted to get up, to run from the apparition, but he would have to pass her to get to the door and his fear held him still. He decided that she must be some local madwoman roaming the place; he could not accept that she was a ghost seeking revenge for something which he knew nothing about. He forced all the confidence which he could muster into his voice as he confronted her.

'What crimes? What are you talking about? You're nothing but a crazed old woman!'

The temperature in the room plummeted, as though his words had angered her and caused her to lash out in some strange supernatural way. Rob was frozen to the core and shivered as her voice rose in anger.

'If I am crazy then the fault is thine!' She stepped forward, her finger still held unwaveringly pointed at Rob's chest. Her words were filled with venom, and Rob cowered before her anger. 'No-one could endure what was done to us by thee and remain sane! Thou wast there at the end, Hardwycke. Did it amuse thee? Didst thou laugh to see the handiwork of thy family?'

Robs mind was filled with a terrible confusion. He wanted to clasp his hands over his ears to shut out the sound of her voice, but found that he could not move. He cried out despairingly. 'I don't understand!'

'Oh, thou wilt before the end, Hardwycke. And when thou doth understand, and when thou doth remember, I shall have my revenge on thee. And all thy family.'

'Revenge for what?'

'For what thou didst to me. But most of all for what thou didst to her!' The woman's eyes hardened as she spoke, and Rob saw a deep pain reflected in the impenetrable depths.

'To who?'

It was as though the ghost had not heard him as she cried out with all the pain and anguish of centuries of waiting. 'She was the brightest and best of us, the heart of me. She ... we will be avenged when thou burnest in hell!'

With that the woman turned and walked away. Rob's heart missed a beat as he watched her pass through the wall as though it were not there. With fumbling hand he turned on the bedside light and sat shivering, although the temperature in the room had now returned to normal. He had never known such fear in his life. Somehow, deep in the depths of his soul, he knew that what she said was connected to him in some indefinable way, and that the only way for him to rid himself of the ghost was to find out how, and why, their lives were inextricably linked over the centuries.

Drawing up his knees to his chest, Rob wrapped his arms around them then rested his chin on his arms. Slowly calming his fears, he stared at the place where she had disappeared, and settled down to wait for morning.

Chapter 2

Rob gently stroked the muzzle of the tall bay gelding. He had always found being with horses soothing, and that was what he wanted this morning. He supposed that he must have slept during the night, for he had been woken by the sound of birdsong coming from the yard. He had lain for some moments nursing a headache reminiscent of a hangover, although he had drunk nothing the night before. Then he had remembered and sat up with a jolt, swiftly scanning all corners of the room, fearful that the ghost might have returned. But the room was as he had first seen it — bathed in the gentle glow of dawn and with an atmosphere of calm and peace. Rising swiftly, Rob had quickly dressed and made his way down to the stables.

There was the sound of footsteps crossing the yard and Rob turned to see Jim Brand approaching.

'Morning, Rob. I must admit that when I said you could take one of the horses out for an early ride, I didn't expect you to be up this early!'

'Morning, Jim.' Rob smiled ruefully. 'I hadn't intended to be up this early, but I didn't sleep too well last night so it seemed like a good idea. There's nothing like an early morning ride to blow away the cobwebs.'

'You're right there, but I'm sorry I can't join you today as I have to be in London early this morning on business. Do you feel confident enough to go out on your own? Tully here can be a handful for inexperienced riders, but if you know what you're doing and let him know who's in charge he's as gentle as a lamb.'

'Tully?'

Jim grinned. 'Yep. After Jethro Tull — and before you say anything, I do not mean the band!'

Rob laughed. 'Of course not. With your love of the land I would guess he's named after Jethro Tull, inventor of the seed drill, among other things.'

'You certainly do know your history.'

'Tull was around during the period I'm interested in. A fascinating time.' He continued to stroke the horse as he spoke. 'I'm sure Tully and I will get along just fine.'

'Well, there are plenty of footpaths and bridleways around here, mostly on Paul's land, so just feel free to ride and explore.'

'Thanks, though I won't go too far this morning. Tully and I need time to get to know each other. Don't we boy?' The horse whickered and the two men laughed.

'Sounds like he agrees with you! Well, I must be off or I'll miss my train. See you later, Rob. And enjoy your ride!'

'Thanks, Jim, I'm sure I will.'

***

Half an hour later, Rob rode Tully at a gentle walk through the orchard. The apples on the trees were small and green, still months away from ripeness, but he could see that it would be a good harvest. He looked closely at the trees – mainly high-yielding modern varieties – it would be fun to try to find some of the older English types and replant the part of the orchard closest to the house, where the visitors would go. In a few years they could be walking beneath Ashmead's Kernel apple trees, just as the locals had done back in the seventeenth century. There was certainly some scope for developing other fruit trees from the period as well. Rob smiled at the prospect of the research that lay ahead. Tully suddenly shook his head and began to prance skittishly sideways, bringing Rob swiftly back to the present.

'Settle down boy. What's upset you?' Rob spoke gently to the horse as he steadied his seat and softly played the reins. Tully settled quickly and stood still, head held high, gazing intensely through the trees. Rob turned to look in the same direction and saw a young woman walking slowly through the orchard, emerging from a low mist which quickly dissipated behind her. Her hand was held out to her side so that her fingers brushed the warm bark of the trees as she passed. Rob had the strangest feeling that she belonged there. Maybe it was her clothes, the bodice and the long brown skirt from under which her bare feet trod gently in the dew dampened grass. Or maybe it was her long brown hair, the same shade as a newly ripened chestnut, which fell over her shoulders in waves. Rob guessed that she came from the travellers' camp. Many of the New Age travellers liked to dress in old-fashioned clothing. They often seemed incongruous in the busy streets of English towns, but here in the woodland, with no sound save the birds and the restless movement of Tully's feet in the long grass, it seemed as though he had stepped back in time to a bygone age.

The young woman looked up, her hazel eyes meeting his of a deeper brown hue. For a moment they looked at each other and Rob felt a tightening in his chest, a strange breathlessness, a light-headedness, along with a clarity of vision which enabled him to absorb every fine nuance and detail of her being. Then she smiled.

A smile came unbidden to Rob's lips as he unthinkingly turned the horse and urged him towards the young woman. For a moment Tully resisted, then suddenly all resistance was gone and he stepped eagerly forward, light footed and nimble, towards the girl who waited beneath the trees.

'Hi. You're out early!' The words sounded banal to Rob's ears and he cringed, but the girl just smiled.

'As indeed art thou.'

Rob laughed. 'True. It's been a long time since I was able to ride out and enjoy a morning such as this.'

'It has also been long for myself. Overlong.' There was a wistfulness in her expression which Rob found endearing. The young woman could not have been much more than sixteen or seventeen years old, and Rob smiled.

'Time can pass slowly for someone of your age.'

His comment was greeted with laughter, a light delicate sound which seemed so unique, yet so familiar, to Rob. 'Yes, time does indeed pass slowly for one such as myself.'

'Are you from the camp?'

'Camp, sir?'

'The travellers, in the woods?'

'My home is indeed in the woods, sir.'

'For goodness sake, don't call me sir! I'm not that much older than you!' Rob found himself dismounting as he spoke. 'If you are to call me anything, then my name is Rob. Short for Robert.'

'Robert.' Her eyes were thoughtful, then she smiled again. 'Robert. I like that.'

'Then you can call me Robert if you like, though no-one apart from my mother has done that since I left school!'

'Thank you, Robert. It is an honour.'

'You're welcome ... ?'

'Rebekah.'

Rebekah! Why did that name sound so familiar? He had never known anyone by that name before, but he knew in some unfathomable way that the name belonged to her, was a part of her in the same way that the sun was what it described, or a rose, or the sea. Rob frowned at the unaccustomed way his thoughts were drifting. He was not usually one to go all mystical like this. What was it about this girl that affected him so? It was as though he had known her all his life, yet they had only just met. Unsure of himself, Rob inclined his head towards the travellers' camp.

'May I walk some of the way with you?'

'Indeed you may, Robert. If that is your wish.'

Rob found her unique turn of phrase and the unusual accent, which he could not quite place, strangely endearing. He smiled as he led Tully off through the trees, Rebekah taking her place on the other side of the horse as though she belonged there. As they walked, she lifted a hand to stroke the powerful neck. The horse nickered softly.

'He likes you.'

'I have always had a love for animals, for the outdoors, for plants and for all that the Good Lord has given to us.'

'Animals recognise that affinity, and respond to it.'

'Unlike people.'

'That's a strange thing to say.'

Rebekah was quiet for a moment, then sighed. 'Not so strange, Robert. Do the people up at the big house feel an affinity for the people living in the woods?'

'Well no, I suppose not. But then the travellers in the woods have hardly been very friendly.' He was silent for a moment, then 'I'm sorry if I've offended you or your family.'

'No, Robert. I am not offended for it is ever the way. People do not seek to know that which they do not understand. If they did, then the problem would be insignificant and of no concern to anyone.'

'You may be right there.' He stopped walking and turned towards Rebekah, gently pushing Tully away so that his eyes could meet hers. 'You have a pretty wise head on those young shoulders.'

'Wisdom comes with experience, not with age, Robert.' She frowned at him. 'You do not know of what I speak?'

'No, I'm afraid I haven't had much experience with travellers, although the troubles between them and the locals where they settle are always in the news.'

'Perhaps one day I shall talk with you of my experiences, but not now.'

'Why not?' But as he spoke Rob realised deep inside that she was right, he was not ready for what she had to tell him. He felt a shiver of apprehension. How did he know that?

'This is going to sound strange, Rebekah, but I feel that I know you from somewhere. And that's not a pick-up line!'

'A pick-up line?'

'Yes, you know, I'm not trying to ask you out or anything. I'm much too old for you.'

The captivating laugh rang out again. 'It is not the body which tells the age, Robert, it is who we are inside. Be you but twenty years or fifty...'

'Fifty! God I hope I don't look that old! I'm thirty, Rebekah!'

'It is a manner of speech only, Robert; be you twenty or fif...' she inclined her head and smiled 'thirty, your character is the same and any outward sign of age insignificant.'

'If everyone thought like that the cosmetics firms would go out of business overnight!' Rebekah frowned in puzzlement and Rob looked sheepish. 'Sorry, here you are giving me mature advice way beyond your years and I'm the one acting like a seventeen...'

'Sixteen.'

'Sixteen year old. Although...' Rob smiled 'you certainly look more like eighteen or nineteen.'

'Age means nothing, Robert.' Rebekah turned and looked into the trees as she spoke. For a moment Rob thought he saw someone else there, but then realised that it must have been just a shadow cast by the early morning sun. Tully tossed his head nervously and tried to back away, pulling strongly on the reins so that Rob had to struggle to hold him. Rebekah reached out a gentle hand and the horse quietened, although his ears lay back against his skull and Rob knew that something had frightened him.

'I must go, Robert. May I speak with you again sometime?'

Rob nodded. 'I would like that.'

Without another word Rebekah turned and disappeared into the trees. Tully stopped his restless and frightened prancing and began to graze quietly as Rob laid a comforting hand on his withers.

They stood like this for minutes, the horse grazing contentedly and Rob lost in his thoughts. Who was this woman, girl really? And why did she seem so familiar to him? With a sudden movement Rob gathered the reins together, swiftly mounting Tully and galloping away through the trees in an attempt to clear his confused thoughts.

***

Rob stood at the library window, gazing out across the parklands to the distant spires of Oxford while, unbidden and unnoticed, his fingers caressed the warm leather of the great Bible on the table beside him. He was deep in thought, wondering about the young woman he had met in the orchard. She seemed too grounded, too pacific, to belong to the travellers; yet she had said that she came from the camp. Rob wondered how she had managed to keep her naturalness among such people. He found himself hoping that he would see her again.

'So Rob, where do we go from here?'

With a start, Rob pulled his thoughts back to the here and now as he turned to face Paul. 'What do you mean?'

'Plan of action. Business plan. You know.'

Rob nodded. 'Sure. I guess the question is what do you want to do first, and how authentic do you want it to be?'

'Completely authentic.'

'Well, does that mean antique furniture? That will cost a small fortune, if you can get everything, and it would be prone to damage in some of the public areas.'

'I get your point. There should be some authentic stuff, particularly in the display rooms which will be "look but don't touch".' He frowned. 'Can you get fake furniture for the period?'

Rob's nod was reassuring. 'Yes, of course. There are skilled craftsmen out there if you know where to look. Some carpenters and furniture restorers could make what you want in a way that is almost indistinguishable from the real thing. It would still be costly, but not as much as the authentic stuff.'

'You know I want to set up some sort of educational centre. What about in there?'

'It should be easy enough to find someone who can make fakes for kids to use.'

'Good. Make a list of what you want, and the costs, and I'll look at it.'

'For which rooms?'

Paul thought for a moment, then, 'The main hall, at least two of the main living rooms, a couple of bedrooms, all the corridors which people will move along. Then there's this library of course.'

'Don't forget the kitchens. Then there's the staff quarters to do, the stables and outbuildings, the...'

'Christ, Rob! I want to open next year! Can we do it by then?'

Rob noticed the edge in Paul's voice, reinforcing his earlier impression that this was a man who would not take kindly to hold ups. He smiled nervously.

'I think so. But you can always just open some of the rooms first and go on to do the rest later.'

'Okay'. Paul gazed thoughtfully at the plans of the building which he had spread on the large oak table earlier. 'First job for you is to decide exactly what rooms people will want to see, and devise a route between them. Next, look at each of those rooms and start getting the furniture.'

'I can get that started and have another team working on the outside buildings, if that's okay?'

'I told you, money's no object, as long as it gets the job done. What else will you need?'

'Obviously we'll have to re-decorate the rooms, not just put in furniture. Then we'll have to find our...' he frowned. 'I'm not sure what you'll call them. Staff? Characters? Actors? You know, people to dress up in period costume and play the part of the original inhabitants.'

'There are probably plenty of out-of-work actors who can do that.'

Rob grinned and nodded. 'I can get a friend who studied drama to do some workshops with them, and I'll coach them in everyday life from the period. Costumes should be fairly easy too, maybe a company that makes costumes for films?'

'Good idea. That would also give us a foot in the door when we're ready to offer our services as a film set.'

'Yes, but hold your horses on that one Paul, it's a couple of years away yet! Let's get the basics done first!'

Paul laughed. 'I'm impatient to spend my money, and to make more!' He looked at the plans again. 'So, where are you going to start?'

'That's easy. While I'm looking at the plans and deciding which rooms to use, I'll find all the authentic period furniture already in the building and allocate it, probably to the main hall and in here first. So that's where the decorating will start too. By the time that's all underway the rest of the planning will be in hand, and we can start on the other rooms.' He gazed around at the shelves of books. 'I'll start by going through this lot. One pile to keep and return here when the room is finished, the rest to be boxed up and dealt with later.'

'Which books will you keep?'

'Not too many, even a house like this would have had only a fairly small library back then, so we'll probably need to remove some of the shelves.' He frowned thoughtfully. 'I think there'll be almost enough books here, if not then we can make some dummies rather than spending time and money looking for originals.'

'Dummies?'

'Fake spines of books that are made to look authentic. If they go on the top shelves' no-one will notice.'

Paul laughed. 'I like your way of thinking!'

Rob grinned in return. 'You'd be surprised how often that's done! We'll keep all the good stuff, though, and some of it will need renovation work.'

'Renovation? Books?'

Rob nodded. 'Yes. Not too many. But there's this Bible for a start.' He laid his hand on the book as he spoke. 'See how it's been damaged by the sun? We can repair that.'

'You'll never get that looking like new again!'

Rob shook his head. 'I don't intend to, just some basic repairs and stop it deteriorating more. Books like this are historical documents in themselves and can tell us so much about the family who owned them. The Hardwyckes…'

'Great' interrupted Paul. 'Whatever you say. Look, I've got to be away for a few days on business. Why don't we look at your plans when I get back? But don't wait on me, okay? Get started on what you can, get things moving.'

Rob nodded. 'It will be my pleasure!'

'Great, I'll see you at the end of the week.' With that Paul turned and headed for the door, already dialling a number on his mobile. Rob grinned as he reached out to pick up the book. Family Bibles had been used so much more in the past. This one would have been read out to the family and servants by the head of the household and there was evidence of this continual use in the occasional slightly torn page, the worn leather where countless hands had rubbed it smooth. He would get this book to a good restorer; he wanted the binding kept as close as possible to its present condition to preserve the unique history of this family. Rob smiled. His family! The Bible would have to be kept out of the sunlight, preferably in a temperature and humidity-regulated glass case. Perhaps he would display it opened at the front page with its handwritten history, a perfect way to evoke the feeling of a past time and the continuity of history to the tourists who visited the Manor, and the authenticity of the characters in costume who would people the house and grounds.

Rob turned the heavy object in his hands and noticed that the binding was strained and damaged in places by a number of articles placed between the pages. He smiled happily. Family Bibles often contained personal mementos between the pages; there were still more hidden secrets about his ancestors in this book. Rob turned to a section of the Bible where the page edges looked uneven. Opening it carefully he found a postcard, one of the mass- produced ones sent by the troops from the trenches during the First World War. The words on it were faded, telling of a son's love for his family and eagerness to be home again, but nothing of the horror through which he was living. Beneath the card was a slip of paper, black-edged, a telegram whose words were faded almost to illegibility, but Rob did not really need to read it to know that it was a notification of loss, of a young man's body left somewhere in the fields of France for ever more.

Rob felt the loss personally, and was more subdued as he retrieved other family mementoes from between the pages – a lock of hair, a newspaper cutting whose increasing acidity with the passing years had left a ghost of itself upon the pages of the Psalms, a dried flower, brown now with age. This was what made history so beguiling to him. The personal, the real everyday life, not just that of the few elite who ruled the land.

Rob continued his inspection of the Bible and found a piece of paper slipped carefully down the spine. He frowned. This was not like the other items he had found, placed in the Bible for safe keeping, this had been deliberately hidden, concealed from prying eyes, and he wondered what its secret might be. He carefully opened the sheet of paper, hoping that it would not tear down the ancient folds, and laid it out before him.

The handwriting was faded but legible, and Rob began to read.

My darling Rebekah...

Rob took a quick inward breath. Rebekah. What a coincidence that he should meet a girl of the same name in the grounds of the Manor! He shook his head and smiled ruefully. Yes, a coincidence, now back to work!

My darling Rebekah, today is that day which I long hast dreaded. Today is the day I should have walked with thee into the church and made thee mine own in front of God and of witnesses. Today is the day on which my life should have begun anew, my life with thee forever beside me through the long years that lie ahead. But those years shall be long indeed, longer than I canst imagine, for I must take another to wife this morn, another shall walk beside me through all my days, and she shall be one with whom I can share nothing of my heart and mind as I have shared them with thee.

Abigail is a good woman, Rebekah, and if I had known thee not then perchance we could have been happy together, but how can I give myself to her knowing that it is thee I cherish? Thee, whom I crave during each long and lonely night?

Oh Rebekah! How my heart weeps! How it breaks! For not only have I lost thee, my one true love, but I know that if not for me thou wouldst still be here. If not for the foolishness of my youth thou wouldst still live close by, we would still be able to share our love, though it be secretive and hidden from the prying eyes of those who could never understand and could only condemn.

I pray that you were able to forgive me my love, for I shall never be able to forgive myself. My guilt will haunt me until the day that I shall meet with my Maker and seek his pardon and forgiveness for my wrongs. But know ye this, every day that I live shall be a penance, every hour I will try to live my life as you wouldst have me do, every minute I shall think of thee.

My darling Rebekah, this is the goodbye I was never allowed to speak. Forgive my past deeds and my betrayal of you as I now take Abigail to wife. There is nothing else that I am able to do and so I shall live the remainder of my days in utter hopelessness...

Rob felt his heart beating rapidly. His mind was full of questions as he walked to the window and gazed out at the gardens. Who had written this? Who were Rebekah and Abigail? Why must he marry one and not the other? What had he done that was so wrong? Rob felt the old familiar excitement at a story from history partially revealed, a story just waiting for him to research, and he was eager to get to work and discover just who these people were and what their story was. He smiled ruefully, the research would have to be a sideline while he was working on Paul Hetherington's project, but at least it would give him something to do in his spare time – if he had any! But where to start? Rob turned back to the desk and his eyes were drawn to the Bible. If the paper was hidden there then it must have been written by a member of the family. Returning to the desk he opened the Bible at the page containing the handwritten family history, somewhere in there would be the names he was searching for.

There was a Rebekah, born in 1653, and two Abigails. One, the sister of Rebekah, was born in 1657, the other Abigail was mother to both the girls. There were two other mentions of this Abigail, her marriage to Simon Hardwycke in December 1651 and her death in 1672. No other mentions. And the letter had to have been written by someone with access to the Bible. There was a Simon, the fifth child of Thomas and Mary who had built Marston Manor. This Simon had married Abigail and fathered the two girls. So the letter was almost certainly his, and written just after the Civil War ended. Rob could hardly believe his luck. Maybe some of this story would fit into what he planned to do with the house after all! Now he had justification to find out all he could about Simon and Abigail, and the enigmatic Rebekah.

***

Rob glanced at the table as he climbed into bed. The letter he had found in the Bible was there, where he had placed it after reading it once again. As he switched off the light and lay down he was smiling. Simon. Rebekah. Who were they? Perhaps their families were from opposing sides during the Civil War? Sir Thomas Hardwycke had been leader of the local Cavaliers, his eldest son had fought beside the King; perhaps then Rebekah's family had been Puritans? That was enough for the families to keep them apart. Rob sighed. If only he knew her surname; 'Rebekah' was so little to go on.

Chapter 3

April 1642

The woods were fresh and clean after the spring rains. Sunlight filtered down through the branches of the trees, some already wearing their cloak of fresh spring green, while others showed tiny buds waiting to burst forth with new life. The pony picked its way delicately along the pathway, carefully avoiding the puddles which mired its path. The boy on its back was smiling to himself. How he had hated being cooped up inside the Manor house during the rain. After a long cold winter, this opportunity to be out exploring was not to be missed.

As he rode he heard a rustling in the undergrowth to his left, and reined in to take a look. Maybe it was a rabbit. He could see the bushes moving; whatever it was, it was too big for a rabbit. A fox perhaps. If so he would tell his father, and they could come hunting this area another day. There was a sudden snuffling and snorting noise to his right and the boy turned in the saddle. Emerging stiff legged from the trees, the ridge of brittle hair at the nape of its neck standing on end, was a wild boar. The smile left the boy's face as he froze. He knew how unpredictable these animals could be, the slightest movement could make it charge. He hoped that the creature had been hunted before and was afraid of humans, then she might run.

The boy's hands began to shake and he felt real fear as he looked again at the boar. It was a female. Her udders were full of milk, which meant that her young must be somewhere in the vicinity. She would be aggressive, willing to do anything to protect them.

The rustling in the undergrowth to his left continued and the boy turned his head slowly. As he watched two, no three, young boar emerged from the bushes. He was directly between them and their mother, and knew that his best hope of escape was to remain perfectly still. As he was thinking this, the pony sensed danger and began to prance skittishly, fighting the reins as the boy struggled to control it. With a squeal of fear the pony reared, throwing the boy to the ground before galloping off down the path. The movement of the pony, and the cry of pain from the child as he landed heavily on the ground, finally goaded the sow into action. She bellowed a challenge and ran forwards to protect her young.

The boy tensed as he saw the huge beast charge towards him, tusks protruding from jowls dripping saliva. He knew that one thrust from those tusks could be fatal. He curled up into a ball, minimising his size and trying to look unthreatening. The sow however was not really interested in him; all she wanted to do was get back to her young. All her attention was focused on the piglets, so that when the huge feet came down onto the boy's ribs it was purely unintentional. As her great weight crushed the air from his lungs and he began to lose consciousness, the boy dimly saw the small family re-united and making off into the trees.

Then everything went dark.

***

Something cool wet his lips and he opened his eyes. Everything seemed blurred, out of focus. He frowned.

'Do not move for a moment. Just lie still and regain your breath.'

It sounded like a young girl, and the boy struggled again to focus on the figure leaning over him. Long brown hair framed a small oval face, and brown eyes gazed at him with concern. The boy tried to sit up and cried out in pain.

'I said not to move, master.' The voice was gentle, soothing. 'I do not think she gored you as I cannot see any more blood than that from your cuts and bruises, but I do think she stepped on you. Does your chest hurt?' The boy nodded. 'Roll to your side; then use your hands to push yourself up. Here, I will help,' she said as he felt a gentle hand on his shoulder.

It was a struggle. The boy was feeling breathless as he sat for a moment, hoping that the world would stop swimming and dancing before his eyes. The girl held a small flask to his lips and he felt again the cool, invigorating touch of the water. He drank gratefully.

'Thank you.' The world had stopped spinning, and he was able to focus on his Good Samaritan. She looked younger than him, perhaps seven years old, but she seemed to have a self-assurance beyond her years. He smiled at her concerned features. 'You have been very kind. Now I must go home.'

She shook her head, setting the brown curls dancing. 'I do not think so, master. It is too far for you to walk at present, and I do not know where your pony is.'

The boy sat upright and cried out in agony. As the pain finally subsided he was able to speak again. 'Was she hurt? My pony? Did the boar get her?'

For the first time the little girl smiled. 'No, master. The speed she was moving, the boar could never have caught up with her!'

The boy laughed, then laid an arm across his aching ribs with a groan. 'She is a swift pony. But where did she go?'

'I cannot say, master, but I would think she will find her way home, and then someone from the big house will come looking for you.'

'From the big house? How do you know…?'

'I have seen you about, master, riding with your father, or in the village. No doubt you have never noticed me, though.'

He shook his head. 'No. Sorry.'

She shrugged. 'It is no matter.'

'Who are you?'

'My name is Rebekah.'

'And I am Simon.'

'Indeed. As I said, I know who you are.'

Simon struggled to his feet. The pain was subsiding somewhat, but he knew that he was not yet in a fit state for the walk home. He looked at the woods surrounding them.

'Which is the swiftest way to go?'

Rebekah pointed to what appeared to be impenetrable undergrowth, then Simon saw a narrow track. 'My home is down there, just a minute's walk. That is how I saw what happened to you whilst I was picking herbs. If we go there, my mother will be able to give you something for the pain and bind your wounds. It will then be easier for you to go home.'

'Thank you.'

They made their way down the narrow track to a small clearing where Simon saw a hut, no bigger than his father's pigsty. To one side a cauldron hung over a fire, wood smoke curling around it as it rose into the air. Simon could smell the aroma of cooking vegetables and something else, maybe rabbit.

A woman was bent over the cauldron, stirring its contents. Her rough homespun skirt was damp about its hem from the grass; the once white blouse was grey from prolonged use, but perfectly clean, as was the cap on her head. The woman straightened as she heard them approach, knowing from the noise that her daughter was not alone; Rebekah moved as silently as a mouse, sometimes startling her mother with her sudden appearance. As she turned her eyes quickly took in the lad, his shiny green breeches and jacket covered in mud, the white stockings torn, the white lace collar slightly bloodied from a small cut to his forehead; one of his white lace cuffs was missing and the other hung muddied and torn. His long wavy locks fell in an unruly muddle on his shoulders.

'Rebekah, child. What little waif and stray have you found for me this time?' She was smiling in welcome as she stepped towards the two children. 'My, my. If it is not Master Simon Hardwycke. What have you done to yourself, young master?'

'My pony was frightened by a boar and threw me.' Simon hung his head a little at the admission.

'Do not worry about that, young sir. Many's the grown man been thrown by a horse confronted by such a beast. But are you injured?'

'She trod on his ribs, Mother. I think they are bruised, maybe even broken.'

Simon turned to look at Rebekah. 'How would you know that?'

Rebekah's mother laughed. 'She has learned her healing from me, sir. Usually it is rabbits, or foxes, or perhaps a young bird with a broken wing that she brings to me and asks me to heal. Today she has surely surpassed that! Now, come and sit by the fire and let me take a look at you.'

Simon was happy to comply. 'Thank you, Mistress...' He realised that he did not know her name.

'I am the Mistress Sawyer, young sir.'

'Thank you, Mistress Sawyer.'

As he was speaking Rebekah's mother undid the buttons on his jacket and gently helped him out of it, giving him an opportunity to observe her. It was clear to see that she was Rebekah's mother, the same eyes and hair, although with features some twenty years more mature. The brown eyes were kind and full of laughter, and Simon felt at ease with her. Feeling his ribs with expert fingers, Ann Sawyer nodded knowingly.

'I fear one may be broken, but the others only bruised. You were lucky, young sir.'

'I do not feel lucky.'

Rebekah laughed. 'You are lucky. My mother is an expert in herbs and healing. Everyone comes to her for a cure. She is the best person to help you after your fall.'

'Indeed I am. So you fetch me some of that willow bark, young Rebekah, whilst I bind his ribs.'

Rebekah disappeared into the hut as her mother took a length of homespun cloth from the clothesline and bound it tightly around Simon's chest. The child clenched his teeth against the pain.

'I know it hurts, but it is best to keep your ribs still.'

'Thank you.'

Rebekah re-appeared with some powdered willow bark, which she set to steep in a bowl of hot water beside the fire. Her mother gently washed the cut on Simon's forehead, applied a salve and smiled encouragingly.

''Tis but a small cut and will not scar your pretty features, young sir.'

Simon found himself blushing as Rebekah laughed gaily. Thankfully the young girl's attention was distracted from him by the sound of hooves on the path as a man appeared leading a very muddy pony, which nickered in greeting as it spied its master. The man was tall, well-built and obviously strong. Fine blond hair framed a weather-beaten face that spoke of hours out in the sun and wind and rain. There was a look of gentle surprise in his blue eyes.

'Well, well, what have we here? There I was about to tell you about a mysterious pony I found wandering along the path, a pony with no rider and no one in sight. And what do I find? It looks to me like you have found the rider already!'

'Indeed we have, Father.'

Rebekah ran to her father and quickly recounted the events of the afternoon. He turned to Simon.

'I am glad your injuries are no more than they are, young master, and that you are looking somewhat recovered.'

'That is thanks to your wife and daughter, Master Sawyer. And I must also thank you for finding my pony. I must admit that the thought of walking home was somewhat daunting. Now I can take my leave and ride home in comfort.'

'You can certainly ride home, but I will not permit you to go alone after such a fall.' Henry Sawyer smiled. 'I will accompany you in case you feel faint, or meet another adventure on the way.'

Simon was pleased to accept the offer, and with smiles and thanks to Mistress Sawyer and her daughter he mounted the pony to be led away by Henry. He turned as they entered the trees to see a smiling Rebekah waving goodbye. Simon raised his hand too, glad that his misfortune had brought them together.

***

Simon made his way gingerly down the staircase. His ribs had been re-bandaged by the doctor who said that they would soon mend, but it would be some time before he would be able to move comfortably. Simon smiled as he remembered his homecoming. His father had been called from the house to see Henry Sawyer leading the pony, and his relief at the safe return of his son was evident. Henry had refused any recompense for the help his family had given, insisting that any pennies which Sir Thomas offered should be placed in the poor box in the church. Simon had thanked his rescuer and entered the Manor house to the tender ministrations of his sister, almost thankful for the injuries which gentled his father's scolding for riding out alone. After a good night's sleep, Simon was now feeling somewhat better as he made his way towards the study. Just outside the door he stopped. He could hear his father's voice raised in anger.

'For the Lord's sake, man! He is the King! You know what that means. He was divinely appointed by God to rule over us. How dare a man such as Sir John lead soldiers of this land against him! It is treason! Nothing less!'

Simon opened the door a crack and peered inside. He could see his father, standing beside the window. His tall, slim frame was tense, as though he were ready to fight. The dark brown eyes flashed steel, matching the steely grey which had begun to fleck his black hair when he passed his fortieth year. Opposite him stood his protagonist, shorter in stature but no less athletic, auburn hair framing a pale face which showed a sprinkle of freckles across the bridge of the nose. Sir Francis Morrison. Simon frowned. He had known Sir Francis all of his life as the best friend of his father, yet today they faced each other in such anger that no friendship showed in their eyes.

'Do not be a fool, Thomas! The King was crowned in the name of God, but that does not mean that he was chosen by God to rule us! If that were the case, why have so many kings in the past died at the hand of rebellion? You know how the murderer of princes lost his crown to Henry, the Seventh of that name. If God had placed Richard on the throne as divine ruler, why did he then replace him?'

'Richard was a murderer; that is a mortal sin. God would allow none with such a stain on their soul to rule.'

Simon slipped silently into the room and stood with his back to the door, intrigued by what he was hearing.

'If you are right, and kings are divinely chosen and divinely deposed,' Francis argued, 'then what is happening now is a sign that God is displeased with the King, and that he must be more accommodating if he wishes to continue his reign in peace.'

Thomas looked horrified. 'Are you suggesting that we go to war? Yet another bloody conflict to tear this nation apart? How can you want such a thing, Francis? I have always known you to be such a man of peace!'

Francis threw up his arms in exasperation. 'That I am indeed, Thomas! But a man, and a country, can only take so much! When King Henry defeated Richard and came to the throne he claimed to rule by divine right, but at least he and his children worked with Parliament to achieve their aims, even if they did not always agree. But these Stuarts are a different mettle of men, they use Parliament only to grasp what they want, not for the betterment of the people. How many times has this king, and his father before him, dismissed Parliament so that they cannot help to guide him, and only recalled it again when he wanted more money? That is no way to treat a body of men chosen by the people!'

'And why did they dismiss Parliament, Francis?' Thomas had ceased to shout, was trying to explain his views more calmly, more rationally. 'Each time that Parliament was called to session and asked to raise taxes for the King's needs, they refused. Look at the Great Protestation! Parliament actually submitted a document to the King to assert their right to debate state affairs, and to advise him!'

'And why not? The power of the King, and the privileges of his lords, have been protected since the Great Charter was signed in the reign of King John. Over four hundred years, Thomas. Why do these Stuarts believe that they can undo four hundred years of history and the people will do nothing about it? The King has no right to rule this land without Parliament at his side. Yet he took nine of these men, men elected by the people, and imprisoned them because they stood against him.'

'That still does not give Sir John the right to lead the King's own forces against him.'

'Thomas. Why do you not at least try to understand? No one could lead His Majesty's forces against him if they were not willing to be led. Not only has the King created a rift with his Parliament, but his moves toward the Catholic Church are driving a wedge between him and the common people, too. He must stop what he is doing, Thomas. If he does not then any conflict in this land will be his doing.'

Thomas shook his head. 'That is not so, Francis. I will admit that the King's religious practices place him much closer to those of Henry the Eighth than to the Puritans who seem so popular in this land at present, but that does not make him a Papist.'

'Then why appoint a man who favours the Church of Rome as Archbishop of this land? Of the Church of England? Why force the Book of Common Prayer onto the Scottish Kirk? Surely he should have known that the Calvinists would be opposed? That move has led directly to the troubles we are facing now.'

Thomas nodded sadly. 'I will not disagree with you on that, Francis.' He stepped towards his old friend as he spoke. 'The last thing we needed was another war with the Scots. That we were forced to sign a truce at Berwick was a disgrace, but it would not have happened if Parliament had given the King the funds for war.'

Francis shook his head sadly. 'How could they? Parliament had not sat for eleven long years because the King forbade it.'

'He had dismissed Parliament because they would not grant him money. And what happened this time? We had been defeated by the Scots. The King asked for money to re-open that war, but Parliament refused yet again.'

'They said they would grant the money if he withdrew the ship tax.'

'But I have been trying to explain, and still you choose not to see, my dear Francis, that they have no right to refuse a divinely chosen king. They left him with no choice but to dismiss Parliament once again.'

'He did have a choice, Thomas, but he chose not to take it. If he had, then we could have equipped a full army, instead of the sorry lot that were sent north so poorly armed that the Scots took English land. That was a shame to us all.'

'Indeed it was.'

The two men looked at each other. Thomas smiled ruefully as Francis shook his head in exasperation.

'Francis, my oldest friend, what is to become of us? I see what happened as Parliament trying to take all that it could from its rightful ruler, you see it as men who had been missused trying to take back what was rightfully theirs. And they got it, did they not? They forced His Majesty to pass an Act allowing them to meet every five years before they would give him the money to push the damned Scots from our land. Perhaps if they had stopped there, things could have been allowed to settle. But to pass the Triennial Act allowing Parliament to meet without the King's command, and calling illegal the ship money which is so valuable to him, these were bound to raise the temperature of the disagreement.'

'Those actions were needed, Thomas.'

'I cannot agree. But even then we could have stepped back from the brink. In God's name, what made Parliament declare that they should be responsible for the defence of the realm and not the King? That is one prerogative of majesty which has been there from time immemorial. How can you deny a king his right to protect his people and not expect him to react? It is treasonous.'

'No man who supports Parliament wishes for talk of treason. They wish only for their rights.'

'But the King did not see it your way, else he would not have charged Pym and the rest with treason. How could Parliament then stand against the Attorney General and spirit those men away? From five men acting in treason, we suddenly moved to a whole parliament behaving in that manner.'

'But the people agreed; the people who had elected Parliament.'

'So much so that they have been declaring against His Majesty'. Thomas shook his head sadly. 'It is a shameful thing indeed that the King was forced to move his family to Hampton Court for safety. For safety from his own people!'

'It is not the first time that that has happened to an unpopular king.'

Thomas gazed sadly at his friend. 'Look at us. I am glad that we no longer shout our arguments at each other, that we speak more calmly, but we are still as far apart as ever, and it breaks my heart, my friend.'

Francis nodded. 'Mine too, Thomas. But I do not know what else to do. The queen has been sent to the Continent to raise money and arms for the King, to be used against his parliament. I do not know how we are going to be able to avoid war.'

'War is not inevitable, Francis. But you must see that the further parliament pushes His Majesty, the more likely war is. If Parliament does not want to fight, then why have they passed the Militia Ordinance? They have taken over what is virtually the only properly armed body in the country. Surely even you can see that this is a provocative act?'

Francis nodded sadly. 'I do not say that I agree with everything that Parliament has done, but I do believe that they have been forced into these actions by the King's intransigence.'

Sir Thomas was silent for a moment as he gazed at his friend, his eyes holding a deep sadness. Finally he spoke. 'We are on the brink, Francis, and if we do not step back now then there will be war. I cannot see how we can avoid it.'

'If war comes, I must declare for Parliament.'

Thomas nodded sadly. 'I know. Every word which you have spoken today has told me so. But I can do no other than declare for the King.' He walked across the room until he was no more than a pace away from Francis. 'You are my oldest and dearest friend, Francis, and though I disagree with what you say I call you friend still; and will do so until the end of my days. Is there nothing we can do? God forbid that we shall one day find ourselves face to face on the field of battle, for I have to put my King before all else and I cannot bear the thought of raising my hand against you.'

'I pray to God that it will not come to that, Thomas. But if we should find ourselves in such an evil situation then I shall not raise a hand against you.'

'Then that is the best that we can hope for.' Thomas held out his hand and Francis took it in his own. 'I wish you well, my friend, and pray that we may meet again in more peaceful times.'

'As do I, Thomas. But I fear that it may be many a long year before that happens, and I doubt that we shall meet again before then.'

With moist eyes, Thomas closed the final space between them and the two men embraced. As Francis finally stepped back he spoke softly. 'I will pray every day that God will keep you and yours safe.'

'And my prayers for your family will always be there. Goodbye, Francis.'

'Goodbye, Thomas.'

As Francis turned towards the door, the two men spied Simon for the first time. The boy looked shocked, afraid, and Thomas stepped towards him.

'How long have you been standing there, son?'

The boy frowned. 'Why is Sir Francis going to fight you, Father?'

Francis crossed the intervening space and fell to one knee in front of the boy. 'I will not fight your father, Simon. On my honour I promise that. But we disagree on politics and I am afraid that the people we support will be fighting each other, and we will have to fight with them. Do you understand?'

The boy shook his head and looked to Sir Thomas. 'Will you explain, Father?'

Thomas placed a gentle hand on his son's brown curls. 'I will try, Simon, but it is too much for a boy of ten to understand. Indeed, if you have been standing there for any length of time you will know that even Sir Francis and I do not understand.'

Sir Francis rose to his feet. 'Goodbye, my friend. I pray that this is all over before there is any need for young Simon to understand, or to become involved.'

'Goodbye, Francis. God go with you.'

At that Francis turned and left the room. Thomas knelt beside his son and enfolded him in his arms for a moment before leaning back and looking him in the eye. 'Come then, Simon. Let me try to explain…'

***

A week had passed since the confrontation in the library. Simon wanted to thank Henry Sawyer and his family for their help and, now that his ribs were much better, Sir Thomas had agreed that he could ride out to their cottage. Simon had raised no protest when his father had insisted that this time he must be accompanied by a groom.

As they rode into the clearing in the woods, Simon dismounted and handed the reins of his pony to John, taking in return the basket of food which cook had put together for him.

'You can take the horses to graze John, but do not go too far. I will want you to return when I call.'

'Yes, master.'

The groom dismounted and led the two animals to the edge of the clearing while Simon looked around. It was Sunday so he had hoped to find the family together rather than working. He was not disappointed. On seeing his young visitor, Henry Sawyer rose to his feet from where he was sitting on an overturned tree trunk, and stepped forward.

'Greetings, young master.'

'Good afternoon to you, Master Sawyer. Are the rest of your family here?'

'They are indeed. See, here they come now.' As he spoke Rebekah and her mother appeared at the edge of the clearing, carrying baskets full of herbs. When she saw Simon, Rebekah ran forward eagerly, placing her basket beside the door of the hut.

'Hello! How are you feeling?'

Simon smiled. 'Much better, thank you. And that is all because of your mother's kindness.' He turned as he spoke. 'I have come to thank you properly, Mistress Sawyer, for the aid which you rendered me. I hope that you will accept this as a token of my gratitude.'

Ann Sawyer took the basket from him and lifted a corner of the cloth which covered the contents. 'My goodness! Fresh bread, a cheese, some ham. Why, young master, this is too much!'

Simon smiled. 'It is no more than you deserve.'

'Then you must share some of this with us. Come along.'

Ann Sawyer led him to a rough-hewn bench where he sat, Rebekah by his side and Henry opposite. Ann brought some small beer in roughly turned wooden tumblers and sat with them.

'So, Simon, are your ribs healed?'

'Rebekah!' Ann's voice was reproving. 'You must not speak to the young master like that!'

'Please,' Simon's smile was disarming, 'can we not be friends, Mistress Sawyer? I would like to call Rebekah by her given name, and she may call me by mine.'

Ann looked at her husband. Henry shrugged. 'If that is what you want, young master, then so be it.'

Simon turned back to the child. 'Yes, Rebekah, my ribs are much better and soon will be fully mended.' He frowned. 'If truth be told, I have given little thought to my injuries over the last week. There have been too many other things to think about.'

'That sounds exciting!'

Simon shook his head. 'Intriguing perhaps is a better word. I found my father arguing with his oldest friend about the situation in our country. He has tried to explain it to me, but I still find myself mystified by many of the things he said.'

'What puzzles you, master?'

Simon took a notebook from his small leather satchel. 'See here, Master Sawyer. I have found things so confusing that I have written them down to try to make sense of it all, but without success.' He looked up shyly. 'Can you take a look, sir, and see if you can help me to understand?'

He held the book out but Henry refused to take it, shaking his head. 'I am not able to read, master. But if you tell me what troubles you, perhaps I can help.'

'Well...' the boy began hesitantly... 'Father told me that the King had tried to collect some of his arms from the city of Hull, but they had refused him so he is now in the city of York, and Sir John Hotham is opposing him.' The boy frowned. 'I do not understand how one of the King's liegemen can stand against him. And I do not understand how my father and Sir Francis, who are such good friends still, must act as enemies and may even fight each other in battle!'

'Everyone hopes that it will not come to war, master,' Henry began, 'but we have two groups of people with two very different ideas about how we should live our lives and how things should be done.'

'Can they not compromise?'

Henry smiled sadly. 'One group, consisting of the Puritans and Parliament, wish to do so but the King refuses to work with them.'

'But if he is the king, surely he can do whatever he likes?'

Henry turned to his daughter. 'That is what the King thinks. But others say that a king can never do what he likes. He should only do what is best for his people.'

'Are the two things not the same?'

'Yes, if you have a good king.' Henry frowned for a moment, then turned back to Simon. 'Can your father always do what he wants?'

'Yes.'

'Should he?'

Simon frowned. 'I do not know what you mean.'

'Well,' Henry continued, 'we all know that your father is a good man, but what if he were not? He could gamble and waste all of his money and property leaving his family destitute. Although he *could* do that, would it be *right* for him to do so?'

Simon shook his head vehemently. 'Of course not!'

'It is the same with the King. He can take money and land and whatever else he wants because he is king, but that does not mean that it is the best thing for his people, and that he should be allowed to do that.'

'I see. I think.'

'Well, almost twenty years ago the King signed a petition which Parliament put before him. It was to protect people like myself, as well as wealthy people and merchants, from paying taxes which Parliament had not agreed to.'

'Is that fair?'

'Well, let me give you an example. There is "ship money" which is a tax paid by merchants in the coastal towns to help with the upkeep of the Royal Navy, because the navy protects their ships and trade.'

'I suppose that makes sense.'

'Yes, but then the King said everyone in the country must pay it. Why should I, in the middle of my wood, pay for a navy I will never see?'

'Because it keeps you safe from invasion?'

Henry laughed. 'Well, young master, it seems as though you will make a politician when you are grown! The problem is, there are other taxes which we pay as well. We can only afford so much.'

Simon laughed. 'That makes sense too! How am I supposed to understand?'

'Well, it is not just about taxes. It is about our religion as well,' interrupted Ann.

'Are we not all Christians?' asked Rebekah.

'That we are,' her father agreed, 'but religion is the same as politics. You can have a faith where the people are involved, or one where things are imposed on them.'

'You mean like King and Parliament?'

Henry nodded at Simon. 'Exactly like that. England was Catholic until the time of the Tudors when we gained more freedom to worship, and the Church of England was created. Since then some people have wanted less control and more freedom.'

'My father mentioned the puritans. Is that what they want?'

'Yes, young master. We are Puritans.'

'But father said they were bad!'

Ann laid a hand on his arm. 'I am sure he meant that in the same way he meant that his friend was bad. It is the idea he is opposed to, not the person.'

'Good.' Simon was forceful. 'I would not want to be enemies with you! But why is religion such a problem?'

'The king has married a Catholic. What if he becomes a Catholic? What if his children give power to the Pope in England? We would not then be able to worship as we want to.'

'Surely the King should be able to worship as he wants to as well?'

'Yes, all men should have that freedom. But if he takes this country back to Rome then we shall lose our freedom to worship.'

Simon was silent for a moment. His eyes were troubled when they next met Henry's.

'It sounds as though the two sides are so very different that they can never work together.' He paused. 'If there is a war, will you join with Parliament, the same as Sir Francis?'

Henry Sawyer nodded gravely. 'That I will, young master.'

'Then we are enemies, for I will have to side with the King, like my father.'

Ann Sawyer shook her head sadly. 'I fear that, if war does come, there will be many a family that is divided father against son, brother against brother. You are free to choose your own way.'

Henry shook his head. 'That is not so, Ann, for he is just a boy. When he is a man he may choose other than his father, but as a boy he has no choice.'

'I pray that any conflict will be long over before he is old enough to make that choice, or go to war.'

Henry nodded towards his wife. 'Amen to that.'

'I do not really understand what you are talking about.'

Simon turned and smiled at Rebekah. 'You are only seven years old, the arguments are too much for you. I barely understand them, and I am ten!'

Henry laughed. 'Exactly! You are children. We shall allow no enmity or war to come between us, and we shall remain friends regardless, if I may be so bold as to count ourselves your friends, young sir.'

Simon smiled and nodded.

'Good!' Ann rose to her feet. 'Now let me get the food and we shall talk of pleasanter things!'

A chorus of assent greeted her words, but as Simon put his book back into his pocket he knew that there were many more thoughts, and fears, which he needed to record there.

Chapter 4

August 1642

'Have you heard the news?'

Simon's elder brother ran across the flowerbeds in his excitement and eagerness to reach his father and brother. Simon smothered a smile as he looked surreptitiously towards his father. Sir Thomas was glowering like a thundercloud.

'Thomas! For the Lord's sake calm down! And get your feet out of those gardens!' He shook his head sadly. 'Heaven knows what your mother would have thought, God rest her soul, to see you destroying the flowers she so loved!'

Thomas had the grace to hang his head sheepishly. 'Sorry, Father.' But his sorrow was shortlived and he raised his animated gaze to that of Sir Thomas. 'Have you heard the news?'

'What news? That the cow gave birth this morning? That the hay field needs mowing? Or that you have been on another visit to your tailor?'

Simon could no longer hide his mirth and laughed out loud as his brother glanced down at his new clothes, and the wide-brimmed hat he carried which sported a matching feather of deepest burgundy. Thomas grinned too, as he looked up to see the bright twinkle in his father's eye. The two looked so alike, indeed if one did not look too closely at the portrait of Sir Thomas, which hung in the hall and had been painted before his marriage, you might think that it was a picture of his eldest son.

'No, Father. This is serious. The King has raised his standard at Nottingham.'

Sir Thomas paled. 'Surely not, son. That would mean that he has declared war on Parliament!'

His eldest son nodded. 'Yes, Father. I have the news from a man who was in Nottingham. He has been sent by the King to bring the news to this part of his country. It seems that His Majesty believes Parliament has tried to humiliate him once too often. Parliament cannot keep pushing him round like this and not expect a response!' The tall young man reached down and ruffled the hair of his younger brother. 'I am off to war, Simon!'

'I pray that it will not come to that.'

Thomas shot a puzzled look at his father. 'Why not? Are you not for the King?

'Of course I am! But no sane man wishes for war. If it comes though, we will fight.'

'You mean I can fight too!' Simon was all excitement at the prospect, but his excitement was shortlived as his father shook his head.

'No, Simon, you are too young.' He turned his serious gaze to his namesake. 'War is not a game, my sons. People die. Sometimes men return home so badly maimed that maybe it were better if they had died. I will go and fight for my King. Thomas will help with the defence here and...'

'You mean I am not to fight?' The young man was incredulous.

Sir Thomas shook his head sadly. 'I do not want you to fight, for I fear losing you.' He scrutinised his son's face. 'You are so like your mother, Thomas. I could not bear to lose you as well.'

'But what of my duty?'

'And mine?' piped up Simon.

Sir Thomas placed a hand on Simon's shoulder. 'We all have our duty, son. This land is held by us for the King, so someone must stay to defend it. I hope that will be your brother whilst I go to fight; but if not then I shall stay while he goes to the King. You, my little one, have a duty to grow strong and true. When you reach manhood, then we shall decide what you must do.'

'The war may be over by then!'

His father nodded. 'I pray God that it is. I pray even more fervently that this raising of the standard will be the wakening call which this country needs. Parliament can want war no more than the King does. They have declared now, but maybe this openness will give them pause for thought so that they can talk and reach a solution to the problems which beset our beloved England.'

'Do you think they will?'

Sir Thomas furrowed his brow, then shook his head sadly. 'I fear not, Thomas. The King has a divine right to rule and he cannot give this up. Parliament must bow its knee to him, but they cannot accept that. I fear that war is inevitable. And if it comes, Thomas, no matter whether you ride with the King or stay here at home, you will be in danger. We all will be. This will be a civil war. Englishman against Englishman, neighbour against neighbour. I doubt that there will be one corner of this land which will be truly safe.'

Simon took pause in his jubilation at the thought of war. His father was all that he looked up to, all that he hoped to become. If he feared war, perhaps Simon should not wish for himself, or his brother, to go.

Chapter 5

November 1642

Simon raised his sword to parry. The move was easily evaded by Thomas as he swung his weapon down in a sweeping arc which landed against his brother's ribs.

'Keep your guard forward, Simon! A move like that in battle and you would be dead!'

'But I had to block you!'

Thomas lowered his sword and took Simon by the wrist, angling his hand so that the sword tip pointed down and slightly away from his body. 'That would block my weapon, but also leave you protected.'

Simon nodded. 'I see. Can we try again?'

Thomas raised his sword. 'Now, en garde.'

Simon adjusted his stance, raising his left hand for balance as he presented his sword and took up the traditional en garde position. Thomas stepped forward slowly then lunged quickly. Simon stepped back, taking a semi-circular parry and sliding down his brother's blade towards his chest. Thomas changed the angle of his wrist, pushing the attacking blade away before disengaging and lunging again. Simon beat the blade and stepped forward into the attack, halting with his point resting against Thomas's chest.

'Touché!'

Simon grinned. 'You let me get that hit.'

Thomas ruffled his younger brother's hair. 'Yes. You need to feel what it is like to make the movement correctly and get the hit. Your body will remember so that you do not have to.'

'Am I ready for battle yet?

Thomas shook his head. 'Do not even think of that, Simon. Even if you were an expert with the blade, which you are not yet, you do not have the strength or stamina to go to battle. You would not survive long. When you are full grown, then will be the time to think of battle.'

'But the war might be over by then!'

'I pray that it is!'

Simon frowned. 'You are only seven years older than me, and you survived the battle at Edgehill without a scratch. It must have been glorious and exciting! Why do you want the war to end?'

'Yes. It was glorious and exciting. But I also lost friends to the enemy. No sane man would want to go to war, and anyone involved in it will want it to end as soon as possible. But with us being the winning side, of course!'

'What was it like?'

Thomas was silent for a moment, then led his brother over to a bench where they sat down, the prospect of the Oxfordshire landscape opening out in front of them.

Thomas sighed. 'I know I am older than you, but I am only seventeen and inexperienced. Though please do not let Father know I said that, or he may not let me go back.' Thomas's face was grim. 'I have to admit that it all felt glorious before the battle. I was assigned to the General Horse led by the King's nephew, Prince Rupert. He is only twenty-two, so many people thought that he would not be able to lead us. But he soon proved them wrong! We were marching towards London. If we could take the city then that would be the end of the Parliamentarians and the war would be over. What we did not know as we marched was that the Earl of Essex was also making for London with his force.' Thomas laughed. 'We heard that he was taking his coffin with him, just in case he died in battle! That could hardly have inspired his troops!' Simon laughed, too, as Thomas continued. 'We were in the villages around Edgecote, getting ready to march on Banbury, when some of our forces clashed with the enemy on the evening of the twenty-second. Until then we had not realised that they were so close.'

Simon looked up at his brother in awe. 'What did you do?'

'The King had us range for battle on an escarpment so that we were ready for the enemy the next morning. Essex formed up in front of us, but clearly had no intention of attacking uphill.'

'What happened?'

'Prince Rupert wanted the Cavalry to lead a charge. He suggested that if we used sabres and rode the enemy down, we could overcome them before they reloaded.' His eyes took on a far-away look. 'We could see everything from up there on the hill. It was easy to see where the enemy were, and how they were disposed, which gave us a great advantage. Then the King finally arrived.' The young man turned to his younger brother. 'He looked magnificent! He wore a black velvet cloak lined with ermine, with his orders pinned to the breast! I tell you Simon, anyone who could have seen him that day would have been proud to fight for him!

'Prince Rupert looked even more dazzling, dressed in scarlet with silver lace. I was lucky enough to be with him when he approached the King. I was naïve about battle and thought everything would be simple, but I was wrong. Rupert wanted to form up on a broad front only six deep, instead of eight, which would lengthen our line and give increased firepower. Lindsey wanted the usual formation. There was quite a set-too.'

'What happened?'

'The King decided in the end. We followed Rupert's plan.'

'Which obviously worked!'

'They attacked first. At around three in the afternoon they started firing their cannon and we fired back.' He shook his head as though still finding it hard to believe what he had experienced. 'The noise was tremendous, and the damage when the shot hit the line...' He was silent for a moment, then 'I am glad that I am cavalry and not infantry.'

'Is that when you went into battle?'

Thomas nodded. 'We started out like any normal cavalry attack, at a walk, and then fired at the enemy. They expected us to turn and reload, but instead we drew our sabres and charged, ready to cut them down.' He smiled grimly. 'They were not expecting that, and turned tail and ran!'

'Hurrah!' cried Simon. 'The battle was won!'

'Hardly! We pursued the enemy and got caught up in the baggage train, so we missed much of what else happened before we were able to turn and re-join the battle. But we did win. I just wish we had moved on to London then. The war might be over now if we had.'

'Why did you not?'

'How am I to know? That was the King's decision. But maybe father will allow us to dine with His Majesty, then we may both find out.'

Simon's face was awe-struck. 'What do you mean? Dine with His Majesty?'

Thomas grinned. 'That is why I am here. I have already spoken with father and given him the message that the King will be taking luncheon here at Marston, tomorrow!'

***

The next twenty-four hours were hectic, the Manor a hive of activity as sheep and chickens were slaughtered, vegetables prepared, the main rooms cleaned until everything shone. Sir Thomas supervised everything with an exterior calm, although inside he was as agitated as the rest. He was well acquainted with the King, but this was the first time that he would play host. He was determined that everything would go well, despite the war. Indeed, he would like King Charles to forget about the war whilst at Marston, and take the opportunity to relax and rest a little before resuming the campaign. Yet he knew that the King could not forget that his people had risen against him. The thought must prey on his mind every minute of every day. So why was he coming to Marston? Sir Thomas realised that it must have something to do with the King's plans. He hoped that he would not fail his sovereign.

Simon spent the day in frenetic activity, chasing from one place to another to see if everything was ready, yet only managing to get in the way. Finally, his exasperated father sent him up onto the roof to act as lookout and report when the King's entourage was sighted. The boy could hardly contain his excitement as he waited. The King was coming to Marston! He would be in Simon's own home, eating in his own dining room! Would the King actually speak to him? Would he dare to answer? The more time passed the more nervous he became, until he did not know whether or not he was even looking forward to the King's visit any longer. At last, a little before noon, he spied a column of horsemen approaching, and raced down the stairs and into the library.

'He is here! He is here!' The boy skidded to a halt on the polished floor as Sir Thomas looked up from his papers.

'For the Lord's sake, Simon, calm down!'

Simon took a deep breath and tried to stand still as his father rose and walked over to him.

'Now, do you remember all that I told you?'

The boy nodded eagerly. 'Bow to the King. Do not speak to him unless he addresses me first. Call him "Your Majesty".'

'And?'

'And stay out of the way. Do not ask to join you for luncheon. Allow you and the King to be alone.'

His father nodded. 'Good.'

'Will Thomas be joining you for luncheon?'

'I do not know. Maybe. After all, he is part of the King's army.'

'But…'

'No buts, Simon.'

Simon sighed. 'Yes, Father.'

Sir Thomas smiled at his son. 'Now come along. Let me introduce you to your King.'

Thomas and his sister, Elizabeth, were already waiting on the steps as their father and younger brother joined them. At fifteen Elizabeth was developing into a young woman, although she still felt something of a child in her changing body. Like all the family she was slim, her tiny waist accentuating her blossoming bosom; chestnut hair framed the pale features of her heart-shaped face. Elizabeth's hazel eyes lifted nervously to her father as she clenched her hands in front of her. Sir Thomas laid a comforting hand on her shoulder.

'Do not worry, my dear. The King is unlikely to speak with you.'

Elizabeth nodded, although the smile she gave her father did not reach her eyes, which reflected her anxiety. Thomas also glanced nervously at his father, who smiled reassuringly.

'Just be yourself, Thomas. That is all His Majesty would wish.'

The young man nodded and turned to face the approaching group. As the horsemen cantered into the yard they quickly circled and set up a perimeter to guard the house and its occupants. Behind them came the King on an enormous black stallion. He sat easily on its back, controlling the prancing animal without a thought, and it was obvious to all why he had such a reputation as a hunter. A groom ran forward to take the horse as the King dismounted.

The first thing that struck Simon was his height. The King was much shorter than he had expected; even Thomas was an inch or two taller than the monarch. He was dressed in the finest silk and velvets, with a long feather in his broad-brimmed hat. To Simon's eyes he looked truly magnificent.

As the King's gaze turned towards them the three men on the steps executed sweeping bows whilst Elizabeth lowered herself into a curtsey.

'Your Majesty. Welcome to Marston Manor.'

The King stepped forward and waved a limp hand at Sir Thomas. 'Please s-s-stand.'

Simon was surprised to hear the slight stammer. That was something he associated with shyness, or nervousness. He had never anticipated that the King would have a speech impediment! King Charles was looking at Thomas.

'This is your son, Sir Thomas? Methinks I-I-I saw him on the field at Edgehill?'

'Yes, Your Majesty. Thomas. He is with the General Horse.'

'Ah, j-j-just so. And this young pup?'

He turned to Simon as he spoke, and the boy blushed.

'My youngest son, Your Majesty. Simon.'

The King smiled. 'Good-day to you, S-S-Simon.'

The young boy looked wide-eyed at his father who nodded encouragingly. Simon bowed again.

'Good-day, Your Majesty. Welcome to Marston Manor.'

The King smiled at Sir Thomas. 'Two excellent sons.'

'Thank you, Your Majesty. And my daughter, Elizabeth.'

The King inclined his head courteously towards the fifteen-year-old girl, but said nothing as Sir Thomas turned and led the way into the Manor. His two sons fell in behind as young Thomas turned to whisper to his sister.

'Go to the kitchens, Elizabeth. Make sure that everything is ready for when Father calls.'

She nodded and gratefully turned away, glad that she had an excuse not to be in the King's company for too long. The thought terrified her. Simon laid a hand on Thomas's sleeve as Elizabeth walked away and his older brother leant down towards him.

'What is his accent?' Simon whispered. 'He speaks strangely.'

Thomas frowned angrily. 'Shhh. How dare you criticise him? He speaks with a Scottish accent of course.' He replied in an equally subdued whisper.

'It was not a criticism, just an observation.'

'Then keep your observations to yourself if you want to keep your liberty!'

Simon hung his head in shame as they made their way into the library behind the King and their father. King Charles seated himself beside the roaring fire as the family ranged themselves in front of him. He looked thoughtfully at young Thomas.

'So, the General Horse is it?'

'Yes, Your Majesty.'

'And how d-d-did you fare at Edgehill?'

'I was lucky, Your Majesty, and sustained no injuries.'

'Lucky indeed.' The King turned towards Sir Thomas. 'I have never liked b-b-battle, but to fight my own people...' He shook his head sadly. 'So much blood and d-d-death, Sir Thomas. It broke my heart.'

'But they were the enemy!'

'Simon!'

The boy had the decency to hang his head. 'I am sorry, Father.'

The King waved a hand dismissively. 'Do not worry, child. I understand your thoughts. B-b-but it matters not that they were the enemy. It is hard to see men die, to hear the screams and cries of p-p-pain.' He looked at Sir Thomas sadly. 'It was thoughts of that carnage which held me back. Perhaps we should have p-p-pushed on to London as the Prince Rupert suggested, but I feared to see so many good Englishmen on yet another battlefield. Now it is too late. The c-c-city g-g-gates are held against us and the resolution of this conflict will not be swift.'

Young Thomas was eager to speak. The King saw it in his eyes for he waved an encouraging hand. 'You would speak, young man?'

'Only to say that we surely have the advantage, Your Majesty? Our cavalry is unbeatable under Prince Rupert, which should give us command of any battle field!'

The King nodded. 'Indeed, you speak truthfully. But our infantry is not so well-equipped. The cavalry can give a great advantage in b-b-battle, but if the infantry fails...' He left his sentence hanging, no need for him to finish the thought.

'But with God on our side, Your Majesty...'

The King nodded at Sir Thomas. 'Yes. God must have been with us at Edgehill. I would never ch-ch-choose to fight on the Sabbath, but it was forced upon us, and the Good Lord chose to bring us the victory.' He smiled. 'I also see God's hand on the actions of Sir Faithfull Fortesque.

His defecting to our side could not have come at a more opportune moment.'

Simon stood listening silently. To hear of the battle from the King's own lips! This was something he would remember for the rest of his life! He glanced across at his father who stood proudly in front of Charles, and at his brother who had already fought for the King. He took a deep breath and straightened his shoulders, proud of the part that his family were playing in the war.

The King was silent for a moment and Sir Thomas took the opportunity to offer him a glass of wine. Charles waved a dismissive hand. 'Later thank you, Sir Thomas. I have little time so I must discuss my p-p-plans with you before luncheon.'

Sir Thomas turned towards his sons. 'I think it time that you left us.'

'No, they may stay. What I have to say is no secret.' The King turned towards Sir Thomas. 'I shall m-m-make my headquarters here in Oxford. Close to London yet in no grave danger. It is also a city from where it will be easy to communicate with the rest of the country. Much of the army will be quartered with me there, whilst the rest seek out and destroy the enemy wherever p-p-possible.' He turned to Thomas. 'You, young man, shall re-join the cavalry under the c-c-command of my nephew.'

Thomas bowed low. 'It will be an honour, Your Majesty.'

'And you, Sir Thomas, will remain here.'

'Your Majesty?'

'I will need to have early warning if the enemy advance toward Oxford. I am placing my truest n-n-noblemen around the city to set up a defensive perimeter and to keep watch. It shall be your task to warn me if the enemy approaches from this direction, and to hold him off until more of my forces can reach you to help d-d-defend the western side of the city.' The King frowned. 'It is not an easy task I ask of you. I pray that for much of the time you will be sorely pressed to find anything to do, yet you must be ever vigilant, ever ready to fight to d-d-defend the city.'

Sir Thomas bowed low. 'It is an honour, Your Majesty.'

'Good. I shall billet some soldiers, and one or two artillery p-p-pieces here for your defence. If an attack does come, or an army marches this way, then you must send word immediately.'

'Indeed, Your Majesty.'

King Charles rose to his feet. 'Good. Now that is settled let us take luncheon, for I have others to see and wish to be in the city b-b-before nightfall.'

Chapter 6

Present day

Rob sat up and stretched lazily before swinging his feet out of bed and onto the floor. As his eyes fell on the old letter he smiled. What an incredible dream! It had felt as though he was actually there, experiencing the events he was dreaming of. Simon and Rebekah. Strange, though, that he had dreamt of them as children when the letter had obviously been written by an adult. How the mind plays tricks on you, he thought. The Rebekah in his dream could have been the childhood version of the Rebekah he had met in the woods the previous morning. As for Simon… He frowned slightly as he thought back to the boy in his dreams. The aristocratic Simon had been the spitting image of himself as a child, although the long hair typical of a cavalier had prevented him from realising this at first.

Rob picked up the letter, feeling the age of it speaking to him of the past. Of history. Of his history. Perhaps that was it. The excitement of finding out that Marston Manor was his own ancestral home must have set his subconscious on the path to the dream. Putting the letter down, Rob dressed quickly and hurried down to the library where he opened the Bible to the family page and read the dates once more. Simon had been born in July 1632. That would have meant that he would have been just a boy when war broke out. The same age as Simon in his dream. Rob felt a shiver run down his spine and he felt uneasy. How could he know about Simon as a child? The strange feeling disappeared as suddenly as it had come, and Rob grinned. The thrill of the new job, the excitement of finding his family after so many years of searching, his plans to re-create a replica Civil War Manor. No doubt his mind had been working overtime while he was sleeping, creating a backdrop for the project he was working on. He would speak to Caroline about it when he next saw her. After all, if anyone was to know how the mind can play tricks, it would be her.

As Simon closed the Bible he hoped that he would have another dream. The family seemed so real. And the King! He would use his subconscious imaginings to create seventeenth century Marston Manor, filling it with people in costumes to mirror the lives of the people in his imagination. Though he would not use the character who had appeared in his first dream, the evil woman who sought some sort of revenge. At thoughts of her the rooms seemed to grow cold as ice for a moment, and Rob shivered.

It had been a dream. Hadn't it?

***

'So, how come you're such an expert on the Civil War?' The two men were seated beneath the spreading branches of a huge chestnut tree, watching the sun as it fell closer to the horizon. Paul handed a beer to the historian as he spoke. The frosted glass was cool in his hand. Rob took a sip before replying.

'Do you know Faringdon?'

'The one in London, or the one near here?'

'Between here and Swindon.'

Paul shook his head. 'No, never been there. Why?'

'That's where I grew up.' Rob smiled. 'The town played a minor role in the Civil War, and when I was a child the Sealed Knot did a re-enactment of a battle there. It was amazing! Muskets and cannons and pikes. Camp sites with camp followers, all in costumes. Roundheads and Cavaliers. The smell of gunpowder and smoke. The noise. I was hooked!'

'Was Faringdon a major battle in the war?'

'No. But there were plenty of skirmishes over a number of years. The town held for the King and was attacked by the Roundheads. At one point Cromwell himself set up a battery on a hill overlooking the Manor house.'

Paul frowned thoughtfully. 'I wonder if there was a battle here?'

Rob shrugged. 'I don't know. And before you ask ... I do intend to find out. If there was, we can perhaps incorporate it into what we do here.'

'You mean a re-enactment?'

Rob nodded. 'Yes. I was thinking we could host one for the opening weekend. It will be spectacular, and something like that will always draw the crowds. If it can be based on an actual event, so much the better.'

Paul's eyes took on a far-away look. 'Would something like that cost a lot?'

Rob smothered a grin. Why was it that any conversation with Paul Hetherington always came down to money? He shrugged noncommittally.

'I'm not sure what the expenses would be. These re-enacters have all their own kit, but I'm not sure how much they'll charge to help cover their costs. I'll have to find out. The thing is though, that this will be a huge piece of marketing for us. The aim won't be to make a lot of money on the day, although I'm sure we can turn some sort of profit. The aim will be to get Marston Manor noticed. A good opening day, with plenty of publicity, will lead to lots of people wanting to visit in the weeks and months that follow.'

'So, how's the planning going on that?'

'Early days yet, Paul.' Rob took another sip of beer. 'If we pull out all the stops, the Manor could be ready for the spring. That way we will have a full season next year. I'll need to book the re-enactment now, but the rest of the planning for the battle can come later.'

Paul grinned. 'I like the idea. Make sure you get on to it straight away.'

'I'm ahead of you there. I'm meeting someone I know in the English Civil War Society the day after tomorrow.'

'Is that what people call the Sealed Knot?'

Rob shook his head. 'No, but it is similar. A friend of mine from university is a member. In fact he's one of the people responsible for organising battles. The perfect man for the job!'

Paul raised his glass in a toast. 'To the battle of Marston Manor!'

Rob laughed as he raised his glass in salute. 'To the battle!'

**

Rob lovingly stroked the smooth barrel of the flintlock.

'She's a beauty, isn't she?'

'She most certainly is, Dave.' Rob smiled. 'I wouldn't mind owning something like this one day.'

'There are plenty of replicas around. I could get you one tomorrow if you want.'

'Thanks, but no thanks. It's an original like this that I want.'

'You know, I've often wondered why you don't join us, Rob. You have such a love for the period; and such knowledge. You'd have a great time, and you'd be invaluable to us.'

Rob nodded. 'Maybe one day. For now, though, I've got too much on my plate. I told you about my new job helping to set up a Civil War Manor house didn't I?'

'Yes. Sounds exciting.'

'It is. And I could use your help.'

Dave Bullington raised a quizzical eyebrow. 'Me?'

'Yes. There's a couple of things. I know that you're heavily involved in the English Civil War Society and I want to book your lot to do a re-enactment for our opening day. Would you be interested?'

Dave grinned widely. 'Of course! Just let me know the date and I'll book you in. What do you want? A skirmish or the full battle?'

'My boss won't settle for anything less than a full battle. And I have to agree that it would be good for publicity. I don't know if there was any fighting at Marston Manor, but if there was we could try to re-create what happened there.'

'Do you want me to try to find out?'

'Could you?'

'Yes. Shouldn't be too difficult. There is a huge amount of information held by people in the different regiments, both ours and the Sealed Knot. I'll put out an enquiry and see what we can come up with. If there was fighting at Marston, somebody will know.' He replaced the flintlock in its glass case and locked the door before turning back to Rob. 'What was the other thing you wanted?'

'That's a bit more personal. We're going to staff the house with people in period costume. I had thought of using actors, but then wondered if any of your members, or people from the Sealed Knot, might be looking for work? I would be able to give them contracts to do just what they do at your meetings – camp followers, cooks, Royalists and parliamentarians, armourer, blacksmith, domestics. Basically, anything that can give a feel for what life was like in the seventeenth century.'

Dave scratched his head. 'Are you talking paid employment here?'

Rob nodded. 'Not necessarily full-time for everyone, but weekends and special occasions, and the odd educational session. Do you think anyone will be interested?'

Dave grinned. 'Are you kidding? I can already think of two or three who are out of work and would love this. Including me.'

'Oh, I wouldn't want you for that.'

'Why not?' Dave felt put out, and a frown furrowed his brow. Rob couldn't help but laugh.

'Because I want you to oversee the character actors, that's why. And it will pay much better!'

Dave joined in the laughter. 'Then you can count me in! Come and look at this.' Rob crossed the study and peered over his friends shoulder at the computer screen on his desk. 'This is our website. You can see the kind of people we will be able to supply. And the kind of activities. Musket and pike men, artillery, camp followers, drummers. Then there's a whole raft of civilian characters.' Dave turned to look over his shoulder at the historian. 'What do you think?'

'It's perfect! If you can start getting feelers out about Marston during the war, and anyone who might be interested working there now, I'll put together a scope of work for you. How's that sound?'

'I don't know who's more excited about this, Rob. You or me!' Dave grinned. 'I don't think I've looked forward to anything so much in a long time!'

'Great. I'll call you in a few days. Okay?'

'Sure. I'll be waiting.'

As Rob turned to go, a sudden thought struck him and he turned back. 'Say, Dave. You don't happen to know if King Charles ever visited Marston Manor, do you?'

'That's an easy one. You know my interest is in the King's governing from Oxford. He paid a short visit to Marston Manor in 1642. November I think. Didn't stay long as far as I can recall. Just some sort of planning meeting, although I don't know the details.'

Rob felt shivers run down his spine. November 1642. That was the date he dreamt King Charles visited the Manor. His vision blurred for a moment. It was almost as though he was there; could see the King again, hear his voice. He could almost feel again the excitement of a small boy meeting his sovereign for the first time. His hands shook and he stumbled slightly.

'Rob? Are you alright?'

At the sound of his friend's voice, the recollection of his dream faded. Rob's vision cleared and he found himself surrounded by seventeenth century costumes and weapons. For a moment he continued to feel disorientated. Then he realised that he was seeing his friend's collection of Civil War memorabilia. He turned to Dave, whose eyes were full of concern.

'Rob?'

Rob managed to give a weak smile. 'Sorry, Dave. A blinding headache just hit me from nowhere. I guess I'd better head for home.'

'Are you okay to drive?'

Rob nodded. 'Sure. See you in a few days.'

The historian turned and left, unaware of his friend's concerned look. How could his dream have been so accurate? What had happened to him at Marston? And what further secrets did the Manor hold?

***

The early evening air was warm and muggy. Grey clouds scudded across the sky and Rob thought there might be a thunderstorm later. Even Tully was restless and edgy as they made their way through the trees. The horse pranced skittishly and it took some skill for the rider to keep him heading in the right direction at a steady pace. The headache which had come on so suddenly in Dave's study had refused to go away. Rob had hoped that a ride might somehow clear his brain, but that now seemed unlikely as his head continued to throb.

As they reached the edge of the trees Rob reined in the horse and gazed down at the travellers' camp. He had set out without a thought for his destination, but after a while realised that he was heading for the encampment and had begun to direct Tully more consciously. Now, as he looked down at the caravans and motor-homes, he wondered why he had wanted to come here. The place was a mess. There were piles of rubbish, clothes hanging on lines, heaps of scrap metal. Rob could perfectly understand why Paul was so frustrated with these people, but he was pretty sure they would move on again soon and the site put back to nature long before the Manor opened for visitors.

As he watched a group of children playing, running and shouting as they chased between the trees, Rob found himself looking carefully at the women, as though trying to identify someone. With a sudden jolt he realised that he was looking for Rebekah. He frowned. Now why would he do that? He had only met the young woman once, and for just a short time. Why would he want to ride all the way out here just on the off chance of seeing her again? He couldn't answer his own question, and his frown deepened.

After a moment he became aware of the quiet, and realised that the children were no longer shouting. He focused on the camp again. Someone had seen him and now everyone there was looking at the man on the horse in the shadow of the trees. There were about twenty women and children, their faces hostile. Rob was glad to see that Rebekah was not among them. Somehow he could not see her as part of this inhospitable crowd. As he watched, the door of one of the motor-homes opened and Cowan stepped down. Seeing Rob, the traveller pulled himself up to his full height, glaring across the intervening space.

'What do you want?' The voice was angry, threatening.

'Just out to get some fresh air.'

'Well it's a big estate. Ride somewhere else.'

'I'm not doing any harm.'

Cowan laughed. 'Right, A little spy for that poncy git up at the big house. Just leave us alone.'

Rob sighed. 'I'm not sure what your problem is, but I'm going anyway. There are far more beautiful sights than your camp!'

As Rob turned to ride away he heard Cowan shout something, but was unable to distinguish the words. He didn't care. What he had intended to be a ride to clear his head had left him with a worse headache than before, and he certainly wasn't feeling relaxed. He rode towards the orchard, hoping that he wouldn't come across more of the travellers on his way.

The sound of birdsong and the breeze in the trees began to calm him. Even Tully had settled down, extending his stride and lowering his head in a relaxed walk. Still, each step the horse took caused Rob's head to throb, and he decided to dismount and walk for a while. There was the scent of rain in the air as he walked, one hand on the horse's flank, enjoying the warmth of its body and the rippling movement of its muscles. After a time they stopped so that Tully could graze. Rob held the reins loosely. He smiled as he watched a fox trot along the path. It stopped for a moment, raising its head and gazing into the distance, before turning away and disappearing into the undergrowth. Rob tried to see what had startled it, and saw a movement in the distance. He tensed for a moment. He was sure it was a woman in a long dress.

'Rebekah!' He called out without thinking, and was sure that the figure turned towards him. Pulling on the reins, Rob began to lead the horse towards the woman but she turned and stepped into the trees. Within seconds, she was gone.

Rob was glad that Paul was away on business. The headache had not cleared, in fact it seemed to be getting worse, and he couldn't face dinner and conversation. Taking a bottle of pain-killers and a large glass of whisky with him, Rob retired early to bed.

Chapter 7

October 1643

Simon was in the library when he heard the sound of horses. Without a second thought he abandoned his school books and ran to the window.

'Master Simon! You have not yet finished with your mathematics! Come and sit down!'

'But there are soldiers coming!'

James Ely sighed in exasperation. He knew that a mere tutor could not compete with the arrival of soldiers for the attention of an eleven year old boy. The rotund man in his late forties closed the books.

'What can you see?'

'Horses! It looks like cavalry. And I think that Thomas is with them!'

'Then you had better go and greet your brother.'

Simon needed no further encouragement as he raced from the room. The horses were just reining to a halt in the courtyard as the boy burst out onto the steps in time to see Thomas leap from his horse and throw the reins to a groom, who had come running.

'Put my horse away. Then show the rest of the men where to put their horses and find them lodging.'

His companions, thirty men from the King's cavalry, dismounted and began to lead their horses towards the stables.

'Thomas! You are returned!

'And you are still as observant as ever!' laughed Thomas as he made his way up the steps and into the hall, Simon trailing behind him. 'Where is father?'

'Here I am, son.' Sir Thomas came up the steps behind him. 'I was out in the pasture when I saw your arrival.' He smiled broadly at his first-born. The younger Thomas, now well past his eighteenth birthday, still had the smooth features of a young man, and still dressed in the flamboyant Royalist style. Yet his father noticed a maturity in his gaze which had not been there before, as though the boy had aged five years or more in the short while he had been away. He decided to say nothing and smiled his greeting. 'It is good to see you safe home!'

'It is good to be home, Father, although I am afraid my stay will not be over-long.'

'No matter. I notice you are not alone? Are you expecting trouble?'

Thomas shook his head.

'No, sir. His Majesty wanted to see Prince Rupert so the cavalry have been ordered to Oxford. I managed to persuade the prince that he will not need me there and to let me have a few days leave. My friends will join me here in that leave if you agree, Father? They are far from home and…'

'Of course they may stay for a few days.'

'Is Prince Rupert with you?'

Thomas smiled down at his brother's eager face. 'No, Simon. If he were with me do you think I would have sent him to stable his own horse?'

Sir Thomas laughed. 'Only if you cared nothing for promotion! I assume he has gone on to Oxford?'

'He left us at the entrance to the estate.'

'You mean he was just half a mile away?' Thomas nodded at Simon's question. 'Then why did you not invite him here? I would love to meet him! You have told me so much about him in your letters!'

'Prince Rupert has far more important things to do than to go out of his way to meet a small boy.'

'I am not small!'

Thomas looked at his brother. 'You have certainly grown some since last I saw you; that I will admit. You must have outgrown your pony by now.'

Simon turned to Sir Thomas. 'See, Father! I told you!'

Sir Thomas groaned. 'Thomas, your brother has been pestering me for a new horse so that he can train for the cavalry. He says his pony is too small.'

'It is!'

Thomas laughed, glad to be back with his family. 'Well, I can only stay for two days, and then I go to Oxford. I will look out for a suitable mount while I am there.'

Simon's eyes were wide with delight. 'Thank you, Thomas!'

'I am not promising anything,' his brother cautioned, 'but if I do find something suitable, and with Father's permission of course, I will purchase it for you.'

'Father?'

Sir Thomas looked at the eager face of his son, and smiled. 'I see that I am outnumbered!'

'Thank you! Thank you both!'

With that Simon ran off to find Elizabeth, to tell her that Thomas was going to buy him a horse.

Thomas could not see the surface of the table under the clutter of papers. He smiled indulgently as Simon explained it all.

'See, here are all of your letters. And here are my map and my notebook.'

The candle-light flickered over the papers as Thomas leaned closer. 'So, how do my letters fit in with everything?'

Simon opened his notebook. 'I started writing things in here a long time ago, to try to help me understand why we were going to war. Then I decided to write down how the war affected me.'

'Have you written a great deal?'

Simon shook his head. 'Apart from the King's visit nothing has happened to me that is worth writing about!'

Thomas laughed at his brother's frustrated features. 'Do not worry, Simon; you are better off out of it all!'

'But your letters are so exciting! Look!' He turned the pages in the book. 'Here I have written about some of the skirmishes you told me about, and the battles you took part in.'

'I am impressed.' Thomas thumbed through the pages. 'This is a very comprehensive report of the war.' He handed the book back to Simon. 'And the map?'

The boy grinned. 'Mr Ely says that I spend far too long thinking about the war instead of my studies, so he has incorporated that into my geography lessons! Look...' He pulled the map towards him as he spoke. 'See here, where I have marked the battles? I did them in different colours so we have Roundhead victories in blue here at Lichfield, Reading, Wakefield and Gainsborough. The red ones are our victories at Brentford, Ripple Field, Tewkesbury, Chewton Mendip, Chalgrove Field, Lansdowne Hill and Bristol.'

'And what is this?'

Simon smiled. 'Blue and red. We lost Lichfield and Gainsborough but then won them back again!'

'As I said, very impressive! Perhaps I should suggest that you join the King's staff?'

Simon laughed. 'If only that were possible!'

'Excuse me, Thomas. I do not want to disturb you but...'

Thomas turned towards the young cavalry officer at the door. 'You are not disturbing me, Matthew. What can I do for you?'

'We apprehended this gentleman sneaking towards the house. He says that he must speak to you, or your father, urgently.'

Only then did Thomas notice the drawn revolver and he frowned. 'Who is it?'

The man standing to Matthew's left took a step forward into the light. Simon gasped.

'Sir Francis! It must be eighteen months since I saw you last! What are you doing here? Surely you are with Parliament!'

At the young boy's words Matthew cocked his pistol and raised it towards the older man's head. Thomas raised a hand.

'No, Matthew. Lower your weapon. This man may have declared for Parliament but I do not believe that he is an enemy to this family.'

'That is so, Thomas. Did I not say as much to you, young Simon, when last we met?'

Simon nodded. 'You also said that we would not see you again until the war was over. What are you doing here?'

'A fair question, Simon.' Thomas turned to Sir Francis as he spoke. 'To what do we owe this...pleasure?'

Sir Francis sighed. 'This is not easy for me. I stand with Parliament, and will fight for them on the field of battle. As such I have a unit of their men billeted on my land.'

'Yes, we know this.'

'You were observed coming home, Thomas; and it was noted that Prince Rupert was with you. I swore to your father that I would not raise a hand against this family so I have come to warn you that they intend to attack at first light to capture, or kill, the Prince.'

'But he is not here!'

Sir Francis frowned. Simon's comment had been instinctive and so he did not doubt its truth.

'Not here?'

Thomas shook his head. 'No, he went on to the King at Oxford. You can call the attack off.'

Sir Francis shook his head. 'I am afraid not, Thomas. If I were to tell them that Rupert was in Oxford they would know that I had been here and count me traitor. I have already risked much coming here and dare not risk my family further.'

Thomas nodded. 'I understand.' He bowed to the older man. 'I thank you for your friendship and pray that no one finds out about your visit here. If I can offer you wine I shall call father and...'

'No, Thomas, as much as I would like to see my dear friend I can stay no longer. I pray that you have time to ready yourself before morning. And that you and your family remain safe.'

'If we do then it will be thanks to you, sir.'

Sir Francis smiled down at Simon. 'The understanding of this gets no easier, does it?'

Simon shook his head. 'Indeed not. But as father said last time you met, we pray for your family also.'

'Thank you for the warning, Sir Francis, and go in peace.' Thomas turned to his brother officer. 'Matthew, please escort Sir Francis safely from our land, then return here. I have work for you!'

Thin mist hung in the still air, the torsos of humans floating legless above it. Heavy dew lay on the branches of the trees and dripped onto the earth below. A damp and dreary pre-dawn in which all sound seemed muffled and indistinct. The family stood on the steps, wrapped warmly against the cold morning air.

'Are we ready, Thomas?'

'Yes, Father. Mortars have been set up on all sides of the house with the farmworkers behind them, armed with pikes.'

'I pray they will not get that far.' Elizabeth's face was white and troubled. Thomas reached out to place a comforting arm around her shoulders.

'Do not worry, sister. We have trained soldiers as well as the labourers, so you will not lack protection. There are eighteen soldiers up on the roof where they will have a commanding field of fire. They should be able to cut down any enemy before they get close. And see over there?' He pointed to a dark shadow, indistinct in the early morning light; a group of men positioned at the point where the sweeping drive entered the courtyard. 'I have six more soldiers there to hold back any frontal attack.'

Simon frowned. 'Six? It may be the lack of light, or the mist, but I am sure I can count seven.'

Sir Thomas nodded. 'You are right. Mr Ely has chosen to take his stand there also.'

'My tutor?'

Sir Thomas nodded. 'He supports the King, just like the rest of us. Even if he did not he is in just as much danger.'

'But he is old!'

Sir Thomas smiled grimly. 'No older than myself; and equally entitled to choose his own way in this matter.'

Simon gazed across the courtyard, a small frown furrowing his brow. He would never have suspected such an attitude of bravery from the small man. This war would certainly test the courage and honour of many people before it was over. He prayed that, when his time came, he would not be found wanting.

'What about you, Thomas? Will you be with Mr Ely?'

'No. Father will command the defence of the house from here while I take charge of the cavalry. We are small in number but should prove effective with the element of surprise. See, they wait for me in the orchard.'

Simon could make out the shapes of the horses in the dim dawn light; there was a shuffling of feet, and a snorting which raised clouds of warm air from the nostrils of the chargers.

'Where shall I be?'

Thomas looked down at his younger brother. 'In the nursery. With Elizabeth. As far away from the windows as it is possible to get.'

'But I will not be able to fight there!'

'That is the whole point, my boy.' Sir Thomas looked gravely at his younger son. 'This is not some game. We are all in real danger here, and we need to know that you and your sister are safe if we are to focus on our work.'

'Can I not just watch from here?'

'Most certainly not!' Thomas sighed. 'A musket ball does not know who is fighting and who just watching. It would not be safe.'

'But...'

'But nothing, Simon!' The boy was surprised by the harsh tone in his sister's voice, and turned towards her. 'This is not a game! Not only would you be in danger if you tried to fight, or watch from here, but so would father and Thomas. And anyone else near you who would be trying to keep you safe instead of focusing on themselves and the enemy. We will go to the nursery. And we will stay there until it is all over.'

'But how long will that be?'

'I do not know. I sent a rider to Oxford but it will be noon at the earliest before Prince Rupert will be able to get here to help us. With the enemy so close it would have been foolish of him to set out in the dark, so he will only now be leaving the King's headquarters.'

As Thomas was speaking Matthew cantered his horse into the courtyard, drawing to a halt in a shower of stones. The horse, sensing battle, pranced and champed at the bit.

'A medium sized cannon has been drawn into position. They have set it up on the driveway.'

'Can they reach us from there?'

Matthew turned towards Sir Thomas. 'Yes, sir. I estimate that they will be ready to fire in five minutes. Ten at most.'

'And the rest of their number?'

'A troop of muskets defending the cannon. Another troop of mainly pike men ready to advance. They greatly out-number us.'

'But we have the superior position. What about cavalry?'

'About the same number as ours, but I do not get the impression that they are as well trained.'

'Then we have the advantage there.'

Thomas's gaze swept the area, taking one final look at the disposition of his men. With a satisfied nod he turned back to Matthew.

'Get the men mounted. As soon as it is light enough we will make a flanking attack on the cannon. The ground is too uneven to attack in this half-light.'

With a nod Matthew wheeled his horse and rode into the orchard.

The four members of the family stood in silence for a moment, each wondering if they would all survive the morning, but none daring to express their fears. It was Sir Thomas who finally broke the strained silence.

'May God protect you all, my children.' He opened his arms wide and embraced the three young people. Each member of the family drew courage and strength from the others in the embrace, none of them wanting to be the first to break it. In the end it was Sir Thomas who drew back. 'Get to your men, Thomas, I can handle things here well enough.'

'Yes, Father.'

With a final encouraging smile to his younger siblings, Thomas turned and walked away.

Sir Thomas placed a kiss on the forehead of each of his younger children. 'Now get yourselves to the nursery. And keep your heads down!'

'Yes, Father.' Elizabeth took Simon's hand in hers as she spoke. 'I will take care of Simon, so you do not need to worry about us.'

'Thank you, Elizabeth. Your mother would have been proud of you. Of both of you.' He watched as the two young people made their way into the house and closed the door behind them. Stealing himself for the ordeal which lay ahead, Sir Thomas turned and made his way over to James Ely and the men waiting at the entrance to the courtyard. 'Well Mr Ely, I am glad to stand beside you, although this is not what I employed you for!'

The rotund man smiled nervously as he checked his musket. 'Nevertheless I am here, and we are ready.'

Sir Thomas perused the soldiers as they calmly awaited the attack. Although they had spent most of the war stationed at Marston, all were experienced soldiers and would not be facing the enemy for the first time. Each man held his flintlock casually, resting the almost five feet of its length against their bodies. With a range of up to three hundred yards they would be lethal on a battlefield against a mass of men, but were not always accurate against individuals. In a skirmish like this the enemy would be much closer before the muskets could be brought into play, leaving little time to reload.

'Are your weapons ready?'

The soldier closest to Sir Thomas nodded. 'All loaded, sir, but we will not prime them until the last minute. This damp air is going to cause problems with our powder.'

Sir Thomas nodded. 'At least you have flintlocks, which should give us an advantage. The flint should spark regardless of the weather while the flax serpents for the enemy's matchlocks may well be damp and not ignite the powder.'

'We can hope that it is so, sir.'

'Are you planning volley fire?'

'Yes, sir. We can fire slightly faster than the matchlocks but not by much. I hope that we will be able to get at least two, maybe even three, volleys off before they get close enough for hand to hand fighting.'

'If they get that close then we retreat behind the mortars and pikes. You will be able to fire effectively from there?'

'Yes, sir.'

'Then we are ready.'

Sir Thomas turned to face the direction of the anticipated attack, shoulders tensed nervously as he waited. The wait was not long.

With a sudden roar the enemy cannon hidden in the mist fired its first round, which fell short and wide to the left. Sir Thomas looked over at the orchard. The shadowy cavalry was still amongst the trees, waiting for more light. There would be no help from there for the time being. With long strides Sir Thomas made his way back to the mortars which flanked the front of the house.

'Can you see it?'

'No, sir. And if we could we would be unlikely to hit it from here.'

Sir Thomas nodded. 'Then make ready. If you can identify the flash when they next fire, and think that you can hit within ten yards of it, then return fire. You may not get the cannon but the gun crew and pike men are vulnerable. If not, wait until you can see the infantry approaching. Then fire at will.'

Sir Thomas looked down at the short barrelled, dumpy mortar. Small and easy to manoeuvre, one man alone could handle them, shooting the explosive shell high into the air so that it fell amongst the enemy and exploded on impact. They might be much smaller than the opposing cannon, but mortars had proved themselves to be the more destructive during the first months of the Civil War. A pile of shells lay on the gravel beside the gun. Sir Thomas's face was harsh as he looked from them out into the lightening day.

'If they seem to be getting too close then add stones to the barrel.'

The soldier nodded. 'Yes, sir.'

Neither needed to speak, they both knew how deadly the gravel would be, travelling at speed into the bodies of the enemy. It was not something Sir Thomas liked to contemplate, but he would do it if it was the only way they could force back the enemy and protect the Manor.

The enemy cannon roared again, this time the shot fell much closer to the house.

'They must have someone in the trees sending messages to let them know where they are hitting. They surely cannot see us from the cannon?'

'No, sir. But whoever is sending the information knows what he is doing. The next shot is likely to hit us.'

Sir Thomas nodded. 'Be ready.'

With that he turned and hurried back to join the soldiers.

The mist was dissipating with the coming dawn. It was now possible to see the shadowy mass of the enemy further down the drive, the cannon in their midst. As he watched, Sir Thomas saw the gun fire again. A puff of smoke and flames, followed by a roar as the weapon discharged. There was a loud crash behind the defenders and they turned to look at the house in time to see a small portion of the left corner crumble and fall in a cloud of dust and broken masonry. As Sir Thomas turned back towards the enemy the scent of gunpowder drifted towards him on the strengthening breeze, which began to tear the remaining mist to shreds.

The soldier next to him raised his musket. 'They heavily out-number us, sir.'

'Then do something about it and reduce their number.' Sir Thomas smiled grimly and the soldier nodded.

'Ready!'

As one the soldiers poured powder into their pans. Resting their guns on the low stone wall in front of them they took aim on the enemy.

'Fire!'

The soldiers pulled their triggers and the flint fell on the powder. There was a crackle of musket fire as two of the enemy fell, clutching wounds.

'Re-load!'

The soldiers poured gunpowder into the barrel of each musket and packed it down with a rod before dropping in the ball and, finally, ramming home the wadding to hold the ball in place. The cannon roared again as the soldiers raised their weapons.

'Fire!'

The volley of flintlock fire was answered with a volley from the enemy matchlocks. The defenders ducked behind the wall for protection as they began to reload, none of them wounded. A second volley came from the enemy. With their superior numbers they were able to have two ranks of soldiers, one firing whilst the other was re-loading, which gave them a distinct advantage.

With the defending muskets pinned down by the enemy infantry, the attacking cavalry made its way through its own lines, moving towards the house at a steady canter. The cannon roared again and there was the sound of falling masonry. Another hit to the Manor. The mortars at the house opened up, sending shot into the attacking cavalry. A few horses stumbled and fell, and the cavalry lost momentum for a moment before surging forward again as the guns began to re-load. Without warning a wave of horsemen galloped from the orchard to the flank of the attackers. Sabres flashed in the brightening sunshine as the horses crashed into the enemy.

'For the King! For the King!'

The cry echoed in the sudden silence as the muskets ceased to fire, neither side wanting to kill its own men in the crossfire. The attacking cavalry tried to wheel to their left to face the Royalists, but there was little space and they were travelling too fast. Pulling on the reins they forced their horses to sit on their haunches and spin round. One or two of the great beasts lost their footing on the damp grass and fell, taking their riders with them. The un-seated men struggled to move out of the way of the crashing hooves and flashing weapons, no longer a part of the fray.

Thomas felt exhilarated as he urged his horse onwards. Parry, cut, thrust, parry again. At times his blade sliced through thin air, but there were times, many times, when it met the resistance of flesh and bones. The neighing of the horses, the cries of the wounded, the shouts of the fighting men, all merged into unrecognisable chaos as the defending cavalry surged forward. The less experienced opposition was forced to a halt under the intense onslaught. No longer on the attack they fought a frantic defence as they wheeled their horses about and beat a hasty retreat towards their own lines.

Thomas led his men in close pursuit, taking one or two more of the enemy before they reached the parliamentarian forces. As the retreating cavalry cleared their own men Thomas saw the cannon fire again and the defensive ring of infantry around it readying their muskets. Sweeping his sabre to the right he turned his horse in the same direction.

'Back to the orchard!'

As the defenders wheeled their horses the muskets fired. Two horses fell and two more continued rider-less as the cavalry made it back to the shelter of the trees. Thomas led the way, weaving through the trees until they were close to the house once more and out of sight of the enemy. He looked round at his troop. The two rider-less horses had kept up with them, the herd instinct drawing them along with the rest. There were four men missing, of the remainder one cradled a hand missing two fingers whilst the others, apart from a few minor cuts, seemed to have weathered the attack. All had blood on their clothes, most of it not their own.

'Matthew.' The soldier rode forward as Thomas spoke. 'Take Adam to the house where someone can care for his hand.' Matthew nodded and took the reins from the injured man, leading his horse behind his own. 'Is there anyone else too injured to continue?' Thomas's question was met with silence. 'Good. We stay here for the time being until I can see how best we may be used. Stay alert, the enemy could be anywhere in these trees.'

Whilst Thomas was talking the enemy muskets fired again. Looking back he saw the pike-men beginning to advance under cover of the matchlocks. Turning towards the house Thomas could see his father shouting up to the soldiers on the roof, then to the men manning the mortars. The two mortars flanking the front of the building fired together, bringing down a handful of the attackers. As they began to re-load a volley of musket-fire came from the roof, and more of the attackers fell. The front line of the enemy paused, raised their muskets and fired before opening their ranks to allow the pike-men through.

'Get away from the window!'

Simon turned towards his sister as she spoke.

'You must come and see this! Those pikes are so long, I do not know how the soldiers can wield them!'

The cannon roared again and there was a crash to their right; another direct hit on the house.

'Simon! That cannon could hit this room next! You must get away from the window!'

Simon hardly heard his sister so excited was he by the scene opening up before him. He could see the cannon, actually see the men re-loading and firing! In a circle all around it were twenty or thirty pike-men, backs to the weapon and facing out so that any attacker would meet the gleaming blades on the end of the fifteen foot poles long before they could reach the men, or the cannon. The attacking pike-men were twenty yards from the wall where he could see his father and James Ely readying their weapons. The enemy fired another volley towards the roof, and Simon heard more musket-fire coming from above him. Some of the attackers stumbled and fell. His father and the defenders rose and fired into the confusion. More attackers fell.

'This is so exciting!'

'No, Simon. This is war. Those men out there are wounded and dying.'

'But they are the enemy! We are winning! I wonder where Thomas and the cavalry are?' Simon leaned closer to the window in an effort to see into the orchard. 'Oh, I cannot see from here!' His voice was filled with frustration. 'I am going up onto the roof!'

'Simon! No! Father said...'

But it was too late; the boy was already running from the room and towards the narrow stairway which led to the roof. The frightened girl had no choice but to follow.

Simon dashed out onto the roof and skidded to a halt. He was not sure what he had expected to see, but it was not this. Each side of the roof not facing the attackers was manned by a soldier who patiently waited to pick off any men who tried to make a flanking movement. From the parapet he could see a number of bodies already lying on the ground, while injured soldiers crawled or dragged themselves back through the flower beds towards the trees, leaving a trail of blood and gore behind them. At the front of the house, which was bearing the brunt of the attack, soldiers methodically re-loaded and fired their flintlocks. To Simon's right part of the parapet had crumbled, smashed apart by a cannonball. One of the soldiers had been close by when it hit for he lay in a pool of blood, his shoulder shattered and his arm lying some feet away. The man's face was white, his eyes staring. Simon did not know if it had been the loss of blood or the shock of the wound that had killed him. Behind the parapet another soldier lay dead, two others were injured but the fighting was so fierce that there was no one to tend their wounds. Simon felt a wave of dizziness overcome him and he felt sick.

'I told you'! Elizabeth laid a comforting hand on his shoulder. 'We must get back to the nursery where it is safe!'

Simon took a deep breath and shook his head. 'No. We do not have enough men up here. We can help by re-loading for them, there are spare guns now that...' his voice trailed away as he looked at the dead and wounded. Elizabeth's eyes followed his gaze and she felt herself beginning to shake.

'But I promised Father...'

'What good will it be if we stay in the nursery but the Manor falls? Come on!' Steeling himself, Simon crouched low and ran towards the parapet with Elizabeth close behind. Pulling the discarded flintlocks towards themselves the two youngsters began to re-load, passing the readied weapons to the soldiers closest to them and taking their spent ones in exchange. The soldiers smiled at them grimly.

'Thank you.'

The two children said nothing, focussing on the task and trying to block the noise of battle from their minds. After a time the attackers began to fall back and re-group. There was a lull in the musket fire. Suddenly there was a crash and the decorated chimney closest to them fell in a shower of bricks and mortar. Another hit from the cannon. Coughing in the cloud of dust which rose around him Simon peered over the parapet.

'Elizabeth! Look! It is Thomas!'

Elizabeth cautiously lifted her head above the wall. In the fields to their left Thomas was leading a group of men on foot to out-flank the cannon. It was easy to see them from the roof, but their approach was hidden from the enemy by the hedge which bordered the drive. They reached within ten yards of the cannon then stopped.

'What are they waiting for?'

As though in answer to Simons question, the cavalry broke through the trees on the opposite side of the big gun to Thomas's position. The Roundheads turned to meet the onslaught, musket fire raking the attackers whilst pikes pierced some of the horses and brought them down, screaming their agony, legs flailing wildly. With all attention focused the other way, Thomas and his men leapt to their feet and rushed the cannon. Their matchlocks empty the musket-men struggled to re-load as Thomas and his men took careful aim at the gunners, bringing them down in a ragged volley of fire. Thomas led his men on, sabres flashing as they finished their work on the gunners who would never fire a cannon again. Seeing their objective accomplished the cavalry wheeled away and galloped back towards the orchard. The pike-men turned towards Thomas and his men, but too late. They were already running back towards the house.

A small group of the retreating Roundheads had taken shelter amongst some trees on the edge of the courtyard and Elizabeth cried out as she saw them move in Thomas's direction. Simon watched the two groups of soldiers meet in hand-to-hand combat, barley ten yards away, but his sister turned away, unable to watch the cut and thrust of the fight. Around him Simon heard the click of flintlocks being readied but no-one fired, the two groups of protagonists were too close to ensure that they would not hit any of their own men. Thomas's troops had the upper hand and the Roundheads turned to run at the very moment that another group burst from the trees behind the King's men.

'The Lord preserve us! Surely that is John!'

'John?'

'Yes, my old groom. See? There?'

Elizabeth looked at the man Simon indicated. 'So it is! Look! He is attacking Thomas!'

Simon turned to the soldiers. 'We must help them!'

The men were ready and needed no urging as they rested their flintlocks on the parapet and took careful aim at the approaching Roundheads. Thomas and his men had still not noticed their approach and were unaware of their danger. Simon's hands were shaking as he saw their former employee race towards his brother. If he did nothing Thomas could be killed!

Taking a deep breath Simon took the nearest loaded musket and followed the example of the soldier next to him, resting its length and weight on the parapet. The barrel wavered as he tried to hold John in his sights. Could he do it? Could he shoot a man? Could he try to kill a man that he knew and had liked?

First one musket fired from the roof and then the others followed suit. Simon did not remember pulling the trigger but he must have, for the striking flint caused sparks to fall on his cheek and the recoil threw him back so that, for a moment, he was unable to see the skirmish. When the puff of smoke from his firing cleared he leant forward to look again. The firing from the roof had alerted Thomas and his men to their danger and they turned to face their attackers. There was another volley of shots from Sir Thomas and his men. Sir Thomas called out to his son.

'Retreat to the house! We will cover you!'

Thomas and his men turned and ran for the house as the two mortars opened up with a deadly spray of stones and gravel which tore into the Roundheads, leaving many maimed and wounded. Those still on their feet retreated towards their own lines. As the protagonists withdrew, Simon's eyes were drawn to one still form on the field, part of his head blown away. John was dead.

When Thomas and his men reached the house they turned back to see what was happening. The attack was wavering a little under the continued onslaught of the mortars and the musket fire from the roof. Sir Thomas was leading his men back to the house under the cover of the small but effective pieces of artillery which fired again, and the attackers turned and ran.

'They have given up!'

Sir Thomas shook his head. 'I think not, son. They still out-number us and will just re-group before attacking again. Get your horses into the kitchen garden behind the house. Leave a small guard for your mounts and a dozen men out here to protect the mortars. The rest should get inside and take up positions by the windows, some on the ground floor and some on the first. Make sure that all sides of the house are covered.'

'Yes, Father.'

Thomas ran to the orchard where he gave swift orders to his men who made their way behind the house. As the men ran for cover and Thomas set about positioning the defenders, his father strode into the house and up the wide staircase to the first floor, his swift steps taking him into the nursery.

'Elizabeth! Simon!'

His calls were greeted by silence, and his heart sank as his eyes swiftly scanned the room, taking in the paraphernalia of childhood. He let out a sigh of relief as he realised that the room was as he had last seen it; no sign of damage from cannons, no broken glass in the windows from musket fire. But where were the children? Turning on his heel he strode from the room.

'Elizabeth! Simon!'

As he moved down the hallway towards the back of the house he heard a cry from above him.

'Father?'

Elizabeth. But where was she? His eyes were drawn to the narrow stairs leading to the roof and his mouth set in a harsh, angry line. Boots ringing loudly on the wooden floor he ran the few steps to the stairs and began to climb. As he exited onto the roof Elizabeth threw herself at him and Sir Thomas enfolded his daughter in his embrace, the relief at finding her safe washing over him like a flood, and firing his anger.

'What are you doing here, child! I told you to stay in the nursery! If any harm has come to Simon...'

Elizabeth's face was buried in her father's coat but she pulled back enough to look up into his eyes. 'I am sorry, Father. I tried to keep Simon in the nursery, but he would not listen!'

Sir Thomas's features softened as he stroked the fair hair of his only daughter. 'Of course, Elizabeth. It was wrong of me to speak harshly to you like that. I knew in my heart that the fault would lie with your brother.' He looked around himself, seeing for the first time the damage caused by the cannon, the dead and wounded, and his face blanched. 'Where is he?'

Elizabeth took her father's hand and led him across the roof to where Simon sat with his back against the parapet. His slim body was hunched over, curled in on himself as though in pain.

'Simon?' Sir Thomas knelt in front of the boy. 'Are you hurt, son?'

Simon shook his head and looked up. His face was wet with tears. He angrily wiped them away, leaving his cheeks smeared with brick dust and powder.

'I am sorry, Father. It is not manly to cry.'

'But you are not a man. You are a boy, and boys can cry.' Sir Thomas looked around him at the chaos on the roof. 'Even a man seeing this for the first time would have tears in his eyes.' He shook his head sadly. 'I wish you had not had to see this. Nor your sister. You should have stayed in the nursery.'

'Did I kill him?'

Sir Thomas frowned at the sudden change of subject. 'What? Who?'

Simon's voice was little more than a whisper. 'John. Did I kill him?'

Sir Thomas turned to Elizabeth who was standing with her hand on his shoulder, seeking comfort from the touch. 'What is this he says?'

'He saw his old groom, John, with a group of men attacking Thomas. Thomas did not see him coming so Simon...he had a flintlock...'

Sir Thomas nodded, needing no further explanation. He looked across at the soldier who knelt to his right, watching for the next attack. 'Did he?'

The soldier shrugged his shoulders. 'I do not know, sir. We all fired at the attackers. Any one of us could have hit the man.'

Sir Thomas turned his gentle gaze back to the child. 'See? It was probably not your shot that killed him.' He tried to comfort his son. 'Maybe you did not hit anyone at all. It was a long way off.'

Simon sniffed, trying to hold back his tears. 'But you do not understand, Father. It does not matter if I killed him or not. What matters is that I *meant* to kill him. I pointed that musket at someone I knew...'

'You had your reasons, son.'

Simon nodded. 'I know. He was trying to kill Thomas. I was so afraid that he would succeed so...'

'So you did what you had to.'

Simon lifted his tear-stained face to his father. 'I shot at him. And he is dead.' With a sob he threw himself into his father's arms. 'I *liked* John!'

As Sir Thomas cradled his son in his arms he silently cursed the men of Parliament who had brought England to this, forcing a boy to see, and do, that which he was far too young to experience.

Elizabeth and Simon were back in the nursery. This time neither of them had any intention of leaving the room again until the attackers had withdrawn and the Manor was safe. In the half an hour since they had come down from the roof the defenders had been able to distribute powder and shot to everyone so that all were well prepared for the next attack. The servants and farmworkers, too, played their part; the men, armed with whatever could be found, manned the ground floor while the women carried water and bread to the soldiers.

There was the sound of boots in the hallway and the children turned to the door to see Thomas enter the room.

'Are you both alright?' They nodded, but neither spoke. 'Good. I am going up to the roof and will take charge up there while Father conducts the defence downstairs.' His gaze was stern as he met their eyes, first Elizabeth and then Simon. 'This time do as you are told and stay here.'

Simon's gaze was drawn to the blood-stained coat which his brother wore, to the cut on his cheek, to the bloodied sabre in his hand. He nodded, his voice little more than a whisper. 'Yes, Thomas.'

The young man's gaze softened. 'From what I hear you did an excellent job re-loading on the roof, but there are more of us there now. And it cannot be too long before help gets here.' Thomas looked out of the window at the position of the sun as he spoke. 'It must be well past eleven o'clock by now, so Prince Rupert cannot be far away.' He turned back to his siblings, surprised that Simon had said nothing about Rupert coming. The boy was always so excited by stories of the dashing Prince, and here was a chance for him to see him in person. His brother looked stunned, still numbed by his experiences on the roof, and Thomas was not sure that he had even heard him. Elizabeth noticed the young man's look and placed a hand on her brother's arm.

'Do not worry, Thomas, I will look after him. He will be all right once this is all over.'

Thomas smiled at his sister. 'I think you have both grown up this morning, Elizabeth. Thank you.'

Without another word he turned and left the room.

The attack resumed less than ten minutes later. From his position on the roof Thomas could see the approaching pike-men marching forward behind two lines of men with matchlocks. A quick circuit of the roof enabled him to see all other sides of the house and satisfy himself that no other attackers were coming from a different direction. From what he had seen the Roundheads had too few numbers to divide their forces, which was, in a way, a good thing, for it gave the defenders just one front for their own inferior numbers to defend. Leaving a soldier to watch each side of the house Thomas hurried to the front parapet again.

'Father!' He called down to where he saw his father standing by the door. Sir Thomas looked up. 'They are coming again. Musket and pike!'

Sir Thomas nodded and spoke to the soldier beside him. The mortar, already loaded, was aimed and fired swiftly. From the roof Thomas saw the shot take down a pike-man to the left of the line, but the majority of its force was spent in the trees.

'A little to your left!'

The mortar was re-adjusted and fired again. This time the explosive shot and stones from the courtyard cut a swathe through the attackers. A number of men fell, clutching their wounds; others fell and did not move again. The line wavered for a moment then continued for a few more paces before halting. The front line of muskets took aim at the front of the house and fired. Thomas could hear the musket-balls thudding into the wall below him, punctuating the cries of the wounded. The flintlocks on the roof opened fire, and more of the enemy fell. The second row of Roundhead muskets fired, then withdrew behind the pikes.

'Pikes advance!'

Thomas heard his father's call and leaned over the parapet to see the pike-men who had been defending the mortars move forwards towards the parliamentarian forces. Only a matter of yards separated them, then there was the clash of metal on metal and the fierce cry of hand-to-hand fighting. Thomas could see his father in the midst of the action and clenched his fists in frustration. He could not abandon his position on the roof to go to their aid, and the forces were too closely enmeshed to allow musket fire or an attack by the cavalry. All he could do was watch and wait.

For a moment the defenders pushed hard, forcing the attackers back. The razor-sharp blades of the weapons caused dreadful wounds on both sides and, slowly but surely, the out-numbered defenders were forced back.

'Retreat, Father!' Thomas called down. 'We will cover you.'

Sir Thomas raised a hand in acknowledgement, too focused on the fight around him to look away or call up. The defenders continued to form a solid wall as they retreated step by step, the long pikes holding the enemy back and Sir Thomas's sword dealing with any who managed to break through. Finally they reached the door and the defenders no longer obscured the view of the soldiers on the roof.

'Fire!'

The muskets opened up with a fierce volley. Some of the soldiers picked up broken masonry from the cannon attack and hurled it at the attackers below whilst the others re-loaded their weapons. Thomas heard the angry shouts of the attackers as the door was forced closed against them. For a moment they struggled to gain entry, but the rain of missiles from above was too deadly. When the flintlocks on the roof fired again the pike-men retreated.

Thomas looked down at the attackers who had withdrawn into the trees where musket fire against them would be ineffective. They appeared to be re-grouping, and he realised that another assault would begin soon.

'Are all of the muskets loaded?'

'Yes, sir.'

'Then hold them ready. We must repel the next attack in the hope...'

'Sir! Look!'

Thomas turned to the soldier who had called out, then looked in the direction of the pointing finger. Shielding his eyes against the sun he gazed southward and gave an audible sigh of relief. A dust cloud coming from the direction of Oxford. Rupert and his cavalry. The relief force was out of sight of the enemy, and Thomas realised that this was the chance he had been waiting for. He ran to the stairs, taking them two at a time, racing down to the ground floor where he found his father, musket in hand, at one of the windows.

'Father! Prince Rupert is come!'

'Thank God!'

'Can you go up to the roof and take command up there? I shall take my men round to the other side of the enemy. If we catch them in a pincer movement...'

Sir Thomas nodded. 'Good luck, my son.'

'And to you, Father.'

With that Thomas turned and made his way through the house and out into the kitchen garden. His swift commands soon saw the men mounted and moving quietly round into the orchard once more, desperately hoping that the enemy would not see them until too late. They moved at a slow walk quietly weaving their way through the trees until they could see the bright orange of the enemy sashes. Thomas raised his hand and the riders halted.

The horses could smell the powder and blood in the air; trained for battle they were eager to be away. Some stamped and pawed the ground. Then one neighed.

'Damn!'

The defenders turned towards the sound and began to ready their weapons.

'We must attack now!' Thomas drew his sabre. 'For the King!'

'For the King!'

'Charge!'

The horses leapt forward as one, weaving between the trees, their hooves kicking up an early fall of leaves. The Roundheads raised their weapons and fired, most of their shots finding the trees and few finding their mark. The pike-men stepped forward, thrusting the butts of their weapons into the ground and pointing the blades at the attackers, forming a formidable shield. Thomas knew that their losses would be too high if they hit the hedgehog of blades, he signalled his men to wheel to the left.

The men on foot let out a great cry of victory as the horses peeled away but their elation was short-lived for, at that very moment, there was the sound of thundering hooves behind them. Turning towards the new threat the Roundheads saw Prince Rupert, splendidly attired in maroon and gold, racing towards them at the head of his cavalry. They had barely begun to turn before the first horses hit against the defenceless men whose weapons all faced in the wrong direction.

Men fell beneath the flashing blades and the stomping hooves of the war horses whose momentum carried them swiftly through the opposition and out onto the other side. Seeing the attack Thomas wheeled his men once more and rode at the parliamentarians. More men fell beneath the onslaught and, as Thomas's men cleared the other side, Rupert's men rode in again. This time they attacked more slowly, engaging the men, cutting and thrusting into the ever dwindling group. When Thomas made another attack from the other side the Roundheads knew that they did not stand a chance and lowered their weapons.

There was a sudden stillness. The men, exhausted and bloodied, did not move as they awaited their fate. The only movement was from the horses, full of battle lust and now being brought back under control by their riders. Thomas saw Prince Rupert sitting magnificently on his charger, and rode across to greet him.

'You arrival was perfectly timed as always, Your Highness.'

Prince Rupert laughed. 'I am afraid not, Thomas! This time it was just pure luck!'

Thomas smiled wearily. 'Luck or skill, Your Highness, it was a timely arrival, and we are grateful.'

Prince Rupert looked around him. 'It seems to me that you have had a busy morning. Ride with me to the Manor and you can tell me all about it.'

Thomas watched as the last of the attackers were taken prisoner. He smiled grimly as he turned to lead his commanding officer to his home.

Marston Manor was safe at last.

Simon stood between Thomas and Elizabeth, their father on the far side of his sister. It was only two days since Thomas had returned home, yet Simon felt that he had aged many years in that time. As he looked down at the two rows of graves he willed himself to stand tall and straight, to not let his father down; yet all he wanted to do was to curl up in a ball and weep.

Standing at the head of the two lines of graves was the village priest. To one side stood many local people in their homespun clothing. Most of the dead were unknown to them, but they had felt that someone should pay tribute to the fallen parliamentarians, men who had fought far from home and had no family or friends to be there when they were laid to rest. Opposite them stood the Royalists, their brightly coloured clothes, white lace frills and broad-brimmed feather bedecked hats a sharp contrast to the muted colours which faced them. The priest had conducted a mass for the fallen cavaliers who had been laid to rest in nine graves; he now began to say a simple prayer for the Roundheads who had died. Simon looked over at the much longer row of graves, twenty three in number. More than thirty dead, and dozens more wounded all in the space of a single morning. He looked up at Thomas. How he had envied his brother when he went to war, how he had longed to go with him. Now he was glad that he was too young, and prayed silently that the war would be over before he came of age. He did not know how he would be able to face a full scale battle when a small skirmish had left him trembling and in tears.

Sir Thomas stepped forward as the priest finished his prayer. He stood in silence for a moment, his sad tired eyes sweeping over the assembled crowd. Finally he spoke.

'Here on my left stand those who are for King Charles.' He indicated the Royalists with one hand, then swept the other towards the people facing them. 'Here on my right are those who are for Parliament. And here...' he looked down at the graves as he spoke. '...here lie our fallen. Fathers, sons, brothers, friends, strangers. Men who held their beliefs so strongly that they paid the ultimate price.' He looked from one group of mourners to the other. 'Whilst the good father has said mass for those who follow his church, I believe that for him to do the same for these other twenty three brave soldiers would be, for them and their loved ones left behind, an affront to their own strongly held belief in the puritan way.

Prayers have been said for their souls.' He sighed. 'I know that may not seem enough for some of you, but I promise you now that, although these men lie in the hallowed ground of our Church of England, I invite you to bring a puritan priest to say service over them and to bless them. There will be no opposition to this from myself or the King's men.'

There were murmurs from both sides, Sir Thomas waited for them to subside before continuing. 'All of these men were good Christians. We believe that all of them are now seated at Christ's banquet before the throne of God. And I believe that God looks down and weeps to see how his children fight and kill each other. It seems almost impossible at this time to think that there will ever be peace in our land again, yet look at us today. We stand here together, putting our differences aside for a short time to honour the fallen. I pray that it will not be long before we put our differences aside for good and re-unite our country, our friends, and our families once more.'

There was a moment's silence, then Sir Thomas turned towards the men whose duty it was to fill the graves. 'Allow those who mourn a time to grieve before you begin your work.' They nodded respectfully as Sir Thomas took Elizabeth's hand in his. 'Come, children, let us go home.'

'I will stay a moment, Father, if I may.'

Sir Thomas nodded at his eldest son.

'And I also, Father.'

Sir Thomas frowned down at Simon. He knew how badly the conflict had upset the boy and would have thought that he would be eager to get away.

'Simon?'

'I did not know most of these people, Father, but I did know John. Would you be offended if I stayed…to say goodbye?'

Sir Thomas nodded. 'Of course not, my boy.' He laid a gentle hand on his sons head before turning to lead his daughter away.

Thomas stood quietly for moment, gazing down into the open graves. Five of the faces were unfamiliar to him, soldiers who had been stationed at Marston Manor since he went away, but the other four he knew well. Members of his cavalry, his friends who he had brought home to share a few days of peace and relaxation with him. Gone now forever.

Simon moved away from his silent brother, leaving him to his grief. Moving to the other row of graves he walked along slowly, forcing himself to look into each one until he came to the features he recognised. John. The face looked peaceful in death, if it were not for the bloodied cloth which bound his misshapen head Simon could almost have believed that he was sleeping. This was not the first time that he had seen a dead person, but it was the first time that the corpse was that of someone known to him. He had been too young to remember his mother's death, and he wondered what she had looked like as she had been laid in her grave. John had been her groom too. Simon found himself struggling for composure as he looked into the grave. It was a moment before he sensed the presence of someone beside him, and a moment more before he felt that he was enough in control of his feelings to turn to see who it was.

'Rebekah?'

'Simon. I saw you here and wondered...?'

'What?'

'Why you are standing beside this grave? He would have been your enemy.'

'I...I...' Simon knew that to say more would bring forth the tears he had forced himself to hold back all morning, and he could not bear to disgrace himself in front of the other mourners.

'Can we go somewhere quiet to speak'?

Rebekah nodded. 'But we had best not go together. There may be a truce to bury the dead but people will talk if we...'

'You are right. Can we meet on the far side of my father's orchard?'

Rebekah nodded. 'I will be there in ten minutes.'

With that she turned and walked away.

Simon made his way through the trees. It had seemed so exciting as the horses waited here for the attack to commence; now all he could sense was hatred and fear and death. He sighed sadly, hoping that the feelings this place now instilled in him would, with time, dissipate so that he could enjoy the peace of the orchard once more.

Rebekah was already waiting for him when he arrived. For an awkward moment they just stood and looked at each other. Simon noticed that she had grown even thinner since he had last seen her, but it was a slimness of growth rather than hunger. It had been more than a year since they had last seen each other and so much had happened, so much had changed, since then. Simon still felt the same comfort and familiarity with Rebekah as he had during their few brief meetings before the war, but did she still feel the same? He looked into her eyes, eyes which held an uncertainty, a sadness, but no fear or hatred, and Simon began to relax. Perhaps she would understand.

'What was it like? The attack.'

'It was exciting. Invigorating. I had wanted to join the army for so long and here I was, in the middle of a skirmish!' Simon began, then he shuddered. 'That was until I went up onto the roof and saw what was really happening. The fear. The confusion. The noise. And after...'

'After?'

'When we went outside. There is some damage to the house but that can soon be mended. What cannot be fixed is all the wounded men I saw. The dying. The dead. So much blood and pain. I do not know how they can endure it. I do not know why they do not give up and call a halt to this war.'

'Because what they believe in is so important to them. Would Thomas give in?'

Simon shook his head. 'No, of course not. I am just a coward for thinking such things.'

'No Simon, you are just a boy. Age will bring you courage.'

'I hope so with all my heart, for I do not want to let my family down.'

'I am sure that you will never do that.'

Simon closed his eyes and was silent for a moment. Rebekah, sensing his need to collect his thoughts, said nothing.

Simon opened his eyes and looked questioningly at her. 'Do you remember when we first met?'

Rebekah frowned at the change of topic, but then smiled and nodded. 'Of course.'

'And then I came to your home a week later with some food.'

'How can I forget that wonderful white bread!' Rebekah's eyes were bright and shinning, hoping that thoughts of that day would help to disperse his melancholy. 'And to think you can have that instead of our coarse bread every day!'

'Do you remember my groom? John?'

Rebekah's brow furrowed into a frown once more. 'I remember seeing him, but we did not speak, did we?'

Simon shook his head. 'No, but your father may have known him better. He was a puritan.'

'So what happened when the war started?'

'He left us and joined the Roundheads.'

Rebekah continued to frown, then shook her head.

'I do not remember my father mentioning him.'

'I know your father has gone to fight too, so perhaps they are with different commands. Was your father here? Did he...?'

Rebekah understood his question and laid a gentle hand on Simon's arm. 'No, Simon, my father was not amongst those who attacked your home. But does that mean that your groom...'

Simon nodded. 'I saw him in the thick of the fighting.'

'Oh. So it was his grave...?'

Simon nodded, swallowing in an attempt to control his tears.

'You poor thing, to see someone you know...'

'It is worse than that' interrupted Simon, 'he was moving up behind my brother. He could have killed him at any moment!'

Rebekah's eyes widened, but she said nothing as Simon continued, his tears falling un-heeded now.

'I liked John, but I love my brother. I had no time to think, so I took a musket and...'

'Did you kill him Simon?'

Simon shook his head. 'I do not know Rebekah! There were so many muskets, and mine was so heavy that I am not sure I could shoot straight. But it could have been my ball that killed him.'

'Then it is most likely that you did not kill him, Simon.'

'I know, but I cannot be certain.' He covered his face with his hands. 'To take a life, Rebekah! How could I even think of doing such a thing!'

Rebekah reached out and slowly put her arms around him. For a moment Simon stiffened, then began to relax. 'You do not hate me?'

'Of course not. And you must not hate yourself. You did what had to be done. How much more would you hate yourself if you had done nothing and John had killed Thomas?'

Simon nodded, his head against her shoulder. 'I know. I know. But it does not take the pain away.'

So the two children stood together in the orchard. Simon cried out his grief and Rebekah, not knowing what to do, simply held him. And that was all he needed.

Chapter 8

Present day

Rob sat up abruptly, dragged from his sleep by a crash of thunder so loud that the walls seemed to shake. His head still ached, and his eyes were sore. For a moment he felt disorientated, feeling that he should be outside in the sunshine not hiding from a storm in the middle of the night. His heart was beating rapidly and he felt deeply afraid. Rob frowned. He had never been afraid of thunderstorms before, so why now? And why this strange dislocation? He rubbed his forehead and face, trying to wipe away the throbbing pain at his temples. As his hand brushed across his cheeks he was surprised to find that they were wet. Rob looked up to see if the ceiling was leaking, but it was dry. He wiped his face again. Tears? Why would he be crying?

The thunderstorm was moving away rapidly, and Rob thought that the rumbles sounded like distant gunfire. Suddenly his dream came back to him. The attack on the Manor. Simon crying on Rebekah's shoulder. He grinned sheepishly. How the mind played tricks on you. The sound of thunder, coupled with his discussion with Dave about a re-enactment at the Manor had obviously come together in his subconscious, causing him to dream of an attack. It was strange, though, that the dream had been so intense. He rarely remembered his dreams, never felt any real emotional tie to them, yet it felt almost as though he had lived this dream, experienced what Simon had, felt what he had felt. Although he had great academic knowledge of the period Rob had never before felt such an intensity, such a link to the past. He leant back against his pillows, listening to the sound of thunder fading into the distance. He hoped that he would continue to dream about Marston during the war. His subconscious was providing him with so much which could be useful to him in his work.

'So, what did you find out about Marston during the war? Were there any battles here?'

Rob looked up from his laptop as Paul strode across the library floor towards him. 'Sorry, not yet. But I do have someone looking into it. Hopefully he'll get back to me in the next day or two.'

'Let's hope so.' Paul looked over Rob's shoulder at the computer screen as he spoke. 'What are you up to now?'

'Sourcing period furniture to be used in the rooms on public display.'

'Are you serious? You can do that online? I thought you'd have to go out and spend days searching through antique stores.'

'Oh, I'll do that, never fear. In fact, I do that all the time anyway. I can't pass a decent shop without going in to see what I can find. It's a passion with me.'

'God, I can't think of anything more boring!'

Rob laughed. 'Each to his own! Anyway,' he turned back to the screen as he spoke, 'there are a few specialists who should be able to provide us with what we need.'

'All genuine, or will there be any fakes?'

'There will be no 'fakes' as you put it, Paul. To an historian a fake is something made out to be genuine but which is a con. We will have some reproduction pieces if necessary though, either permanently or until we can find the genuine article.'

'How do they compare cost wise?'

'It varies. With the budget we have I will go for the genuine article and top quality reproductions for the display rooms, but some much cheaper copies for the 'hands on' areas.'

'Such as...?'

'The education centre, where people can try things on, or try different activities. Chances are that things may well get damaged, so there's no point going for the real thing.' Rob grinned. 'I've taken the idea of schools work one step further. Why not come with me to the barn and I'll explain.'

Paul grinned. 'Sounds intriguing. Let's go.'

Rob switched off his laptop and led the way outside and across the yard to the old barn. The sound of hammering could be heard as the two men made their way inside. Paul was surprised to see a hive of activity, with carpenters and electricians hard at work.

'What's going on?'

'Well, I thought that rather than schools just having a few hours here we could run overnight sessions for them. The kids could have a study room decked out in period furniture, eat authentic meals in a seventeenth century dining room, sleep in reproduction beds. We're converting the barn into a dormitory and dining room.' He pointed to the far end of the barn. 'The bathrooms will be at that end. They will be as near authentic as possible but we will, of course, have to have modern toilets. Then there will be the bedrooms in the middle, with the dining room at this end. The workers are putting in the wiring and starting work on the interior walls. The barn itself is in great shape and needs very little doing to the exterior.' He turned nervously towards his employer. 'What do you thing?'

Paul's gaze was thoughtful. 'I like it. I think.'

'Is there a problem?

'Well, I'm sure an academic like yourself will enjoy the domestic side of things, but what about others? Philistines like me? Won't they find it...boring?'

Rob laughed. 'Don't worry, I understand where you're coming from. This will just be for the night. During the day they will get a chance to be more hands on. We'll get costumes for both Cavaliers and Roundheads. The school parties can be split into opposing forces. We can have actors with someone playing Prince Rupert leading the King's armies, and someone playing Oliver Cromwell leading the New Model Army. The students will then learn about some of the battles before having a mock battle of their own.'

'Great idea! I love it!' Paul turned to Rob. 'That way they won't be as ignorant as I am about this whole period of history. I haven't a clue what you mean when you talk about the New Model Army. Sound like some kind of toy!'

Rob laughed. 'I think I'm going to have to educate you, Paul. You need to at least look knowledgeable when presenting your project to other people; giving interviews; working on marketing.'

'I know.' Paul sighed. 'I suppose there's no time like the present. So, tell me about the New Model Army.'

'Well, the Roundheads relied on local militias to fight the King, but these men stayed close to home and rarely travelled to other parts of the country.'

'Not very effective.'

'Exactly. So Cromwell set up a new model for the army...'

'The New Model Army?'

'Right again. The soldiers were full time professionals instead of militia. And to keep it neutral the officers were no longer allowed to sit in Parliament.'

'Makes sense. Fight for the country, not cronies.'

'The only two that didn't apply to were Cromwell and his son-in-law. They were too valuable to loose. The New Model was the best way forward for Cromwell. The Roundheads had an advantage in manpower and finances but hadn't been able to use them. Now they could rely on troops being available when, and where, they were needed.'

'It was a large army, then?'

'Around twenty two thousand soldiers, including infantry and cavalry. Not everyone in the militia wanted to be part of a regular army, some even had to be press-ganged.' Rob smiled. 'So much for democracy!'

'Apart from making it a regular army, was it so different from what went before?'

'Well, it was more centralised. There were new drills and regulations which meant that everyone was working in the same way. A huge step forward for a commander wanting to bring large numbers of troops together for a pitched battle. It also paid well, eight pence for the infantry and two shillings for the cavalry per day was not too bad. Though the cavalry had to supply their own horses. Not so good if your mount got killed and it was the only one you had! Religion played a part, too. You had to be a protestant to be in the New Model.'

'That would rule out an atheist like me then!'

Rob laughed at Paul's comment. 'I suppose so. Though back then you wouldn't admit to being an atheist. Catholic or protestant. That was it.'

Paul frowned. 'Catholic or protestant? You mean Church of England?'

'Well, yes.' Rob paused for a moment before continuing. 'It was a bit confusing at times. Catholics sided with the King. So did most of the Church of England. The other protestant groups were less formal. They were the ones which made up most of Cromwell's army.'

'Still confusing. I hope you're going to make it easy to understand for my customers.'

'Of course. I…'

There was sudden burst of music. Paul reached into his pocket and retrieved his mobile phone. After a quick look at the screen he turned to Rob.

'My accountant. I really need to take this.'

Rob waved a dismissive hand. 'Of course. I'll see you later.'

Without reply Paul turned and made his way from the barn, already speaking rapidly into his phone.

Rob smiled as he watched the builders at work. Such a reliance on the mobile. How had people survived without them in the past? He was sure that he would never let technology take over his life. As though to prove him wrong Rob's phone rang. He immediately pulled it from his pocket and connected the call.

'Rob here.'

'Hi Rob, it's Dave.'

'Dave? I wasn't expecting to hear back from you so soon! Have you got my actors already?'

There was the sound of a chuckle on the other end of the phone. 'I'm good, but not that good! I should have all that sorted for you in a couple of weeks though.'

'So, to what do I owe this pleasure?'

'I just wanted to let you know that a mate of mine in the Sealed Knot has some information on Marston. The Roundhead regiment he's in bases itself on western Oxfordshire and he's found a document that says part of the regiment was involved in an attack on Marston Manor.'

'No way! Are you serious?'

'Never more so. It seems they thought Prince Rupert was there. They were wrong as he had gone on to Oxford to meet the King, but they attacked anyway.'

Rob felt the hairs stand up on the back of his neck. He licked his lips. 'Did they take the Manor?'

'No. Somehow news of the attack got to Rupert and he went himself to its relief. The skirmish lasted little more than a morning. We can use some of the details for your re-enactment if you like.' Dave waited for a reply, but none came. Eventually he spoke again. 'Rob? Are you still there?'

'Um...yes...I'm still here.' Rob found himself shaking and sat down on a pile of timber. How could Dave have known the details of his dream? Surely this was too much of a coincidence? Taking a deep breath he closed his eyes. 'Was the attack in October 1643?'

'Yes. But how did you know? Has someone else got back to you? Rob?...Rob?'

Without thinking Rob disconnected the call. His hand was shaking as he carefully laid the phone on the wood beside him. What was happening? He had had no knowledge of the attack yet had dreamt it in detail. How could a dream be so accurate? And feel so real? Rob leant forward and rested his head in his hands. For a moment he felt again Simon's excitement before the skirmish then, suddenly and overwhelmingly, a feeling of nausea as he thought of John. Rob retched dryly. Had he shot John? Had he killed him? For a moment Rob could hear the sound of musket fire, the cries of the wounded and dying. Then the terror of the fighting was washed away. He could feel two gentle arms enfolding him. Soft breath on his cheek. Tears fell from his closed eyes as he heard a young girl's voice whisper his name.

'Simon...Simon...I am here for you now, just as I was then. Have no fear, Robert. I will let no harm come to thee.'

The voice stopped as Rob leapt to his feet, looking wildly around him for the girl. But no one was there. He was sure he was not imagining it. He had heard a voice. Calling him Simon. And Robert. Why would someone use those two names for him?

A sharp knot of fear began to settle in Rob's stomach as he turned and left the barn.

Chapter 9

18th June 1645

Simon sat on the window seat, gazing out of the nursery window. He sighed heavily. It was still raining, and seemed as though it would never stop. The sky was grey, the clouds black and heavy with rain; those moving about outside ran as fast as they were able through the slippery mud. The boy sighed again as he turned back to his book. How he hoped it would soon clear up so that he could go outside.

Simon turned the pages of his notebook. It was eighteen months since the attack on the Manor and he had not seen Thomas in all that time, their only contact had been through his letters which Simon had lovingly placed in his book. Most of Thomas's letters told of life as a member of the King's cavalry, traveling the country, protecting King Charles, taking part in a few skirmishes. The times when Thomas had seen action were few but, as the months and years progressed since the battle of Edgehill, things had not gone according to the King's plans. His wish for a swift resolution to the conflict had died, and hopes of victory were often tinged with fear of defeat. Simon began to read his brothers letters once more to help pass the dreary day.

'November 1643, somewhere in the North

Well little brother, how is your new horse? With Oxford being the King's Headquarters most of the animals I could find were too big, too strong for you. Even if they had not been they were all trained for battle and needed by Prince Rupert. Eventually I found what I was looking for.

He is the right size for you but is young, so he will grow with you and you should both reach your full height in a few years. He is well broken and a safe ride. But not safe in the way that our sister Elizabeth would want, shall I say more that he has a good temperament and is trustworthy. Do not try to train him for battle too soon. Take a year for you to get to know each other. Ride him out, learn to trust him, and in turn give him reason to trust you. Spend time with him in the stable and fields so that he becomes your friend, he will then be much more reliable if you should ever need to take him into battle.'

Simon looked up from the letter and smiled. He could still recall his excitement when the horse was delivered from Oxford, little more than a week after the attack. It had been led into the courtyard tossing its head nervously in the new surroundings, its fine boned legs dancing on the gravel. The horse had been groomed until his chestnut coat shone in the autumnal sunshine, the saddle and bridle polished so that they gleamed. Simon thought that he had never seen such a beautiful creature before and had promptly decided to name him Rupert, after the leader of the cavalry who was always so beautifully and elegantly dressed. He smiled now at the childishness of such a thought – it could have been seen as an insult! – he was so glad that Elizabeth had persuaded him to call his new mount Prince instead.

Simon turned back to his book and read another of the letters.

January 1644 – somewhere in the north
My dear brother, I hope that you and father and Elizabeth are well. How I envy you the thick walls of our house which keep the warmth in and the cold out! Here we are billeted at an inn of poor build which allows all the winds of winter to enter and howl around us day and night!

I do not think that I have ever felt so cold! The water for our horses freezes overnight and we have to break it afresh each morning. The water in my room is also frozen every morning so that I cannot wash (which I am sure is something you wish for – an excuse not to wash!)

This awful weather does have its advantages though, for it is far too cold for armies to be on the move. We stay in our camps and the enemy in theirs. A goodly portion of each army has gone home to spend the winter with their families, which saves both King and Parliament a great deal of money trying to keep them warm. So we sit here with little to do to pass the time save wish ourselves home. But here we must stay, for if the army were totally disbanded our regiments would give up their strategic positions and then, when spring finally comes – which I hope and pray will be soon! – we will find that we have lost ground to the enemy, and that would most certainly never do!

Keep yourself safe and well, and when you sit in front of a roaring fire with a hearty meal think of me!'

Simon was sure that things could not have been quite as bad as Thomas painted them, he had always had a sense of fun and good humour. But nevertheless, Simon was glad that he was able to spend the winter at home, he just wished that Thomas could be with them. He had especially missed him at Christmas. With a sigh Simon turned back to the letters, for him there was no real joy in any of the letters which Thomas had written during 1644 and 1645.

2nd April 1644
We are back in the south now Simon, yet I am wishing for the north! Father would laugh and say that I am never satisfied! I am sure that you must know that our forces are besieging the Earl of Leven in York. It has meant a division of our forces, some to watch Lord Fairfax in Hull and the remainder to contend with Leven. We who are not allowed to move north are champing at the bit even more than your new horse!

20th April 1644

What terrible news Simon! Sir John Belasyse was trying to prevent Sir Thomas Fairfax going to the aid of his father in Hull and he has been taken with most of his force. That happened on the 11th and must leave York threatened. How I wish we could be there to help, or at least to be closer so that we can hear the news so much sooner.

God protect our forces in the north. To lose York would be a terrible blow to our cause. We must hope that the Marquis of Newcastle can hold out.

4th May 1644

York is besieged. The enemy would not be able to do so if not for the Scots. Why do the parliamentarians not realise that to work with the Scots will just store up trouble for England in the future?

I am so glad that our home is in the south, Simon, and that you, father and Elizabeth are safe there.

We are stationed in Shrewsbury whilst Prince Rupert attends a council of war with the King in Oxford. How I wish to go north!

16th May 1644

We march north!

The King is remaining in Oxford whilst we march. We plan to join with other Royalist forces on the way.

York will soon be relieved!

6th June 1644

Dearest brother, I do not know how or when I shall be able to send this letter to you as things are moving swiftly, so I shall add a little at a time and send it as a much longer letter when I am able.

We have increased our numbers as we marched and have taken Liverpool from the enemy after a siege of just five days! Glorious victory!

16th June

Prince Rupert left the south in a defensive position when we marched, but we have now received news that the garrisons of Reading and Abingdon have been sent west leaving the King exposed so that he is moving to Worcester for safety.

I pray that those troubles will not touch you so close to Oxford. I have wished for so long to march north, but now I just wish to be back home at Marston to protect you. I cannot come, so I place you all in God's hands...

Prince Rupert spoke to a small number of us who are close to him. It seems that the King's letter has left some confusion as to what we are to do, but having read it a number of times the plan seems to be for us to relieve York before marching to the aid of the King...

30th June

The besiegers are divided by the landscape around York, where rivers come between them. So today they abandoned the siege at our approach! A glorious victory without a shot being fired! The enemy have moved up onto Marston Moor, between ourselves and the city, so although York is relieved we still have trouble ahead of us before we reach its gates. The prince has asked Newcastle to bring his relieved forces to our aid...

2nd July

The Marquis of Newcastle wishes us to wait for reinforcements but Prince Rupert believes that the King wishes us to engage the enemy immediately, even though they outnumber us. He knows that His Majesty wants us to go to his aid as swiftly as possible. The enemy set out their position and have the advantage of elevation as they are sited on a small hill. We tried to take a warren on their left but were forced back by the parliamentary cavalry under Lieutenant General Oliver Cromwell, who now holds that position. Their cavalry is huge, numbering around 3,000 I would say. Their centre must consist of at least 14,000 men and I count more than thirty artillery pieces. Their right is held by Fairfax, who has at least 2,000 horse as well as those of the Scots. We believe he has nine divisions and 600 musketeers. A huge army!

We are positioned on the low-lying moor, but there is a drainage ditch in front of us which will disrupt any cavalry attack. We have 2,100 horse and 500 muskets on our left. We have about 10,000 men in the centre, some 600 horse and 14 guns. On the right we have some 2,600 horse and some fairly inexperienced regiments. I am with the prince with the 600 reserve cavalry.

We can hear the enemy singing psalms at their evening prayers, and it is starting to rain. The plan is to attack in the morning when we are rested from our forced march...

The Lord Preserve us! The enemy have attacked as a storm is breaking and night falls...

3rd July York

Disaster! I do not know how to tell this Simon, but we have been defeated! No doubt the news will have reached you before this letter and you must all worry about me, but as you can see I am safe. Though the Lord knows how safe we will all remain in the future, for I believe that it will be impossible for us to hold the north after this.

I wish to think no more of what happened on Marston Moor, but the thoughts and images will not leave my mind and I know that you will want to know all about it. Perhaps my telling will help to lay some of the ghosts.

A storm broke at around 7.30 yesterday evening just as the enemy attacked, making it difficult for us to see, and dangerous under foot for our horses. The first attack came on our right, defeating the cavalry and pushing back Byron's regiments. The prince, as always, seemed to be aware of everything and he led us out in a counter-attack. So early in a battle for the reserve! I should have known that it boded ill as we rode. We faced Cromwell and fought hard and long. I will not give you the details of the cut and thrust, you have seen action at home and suffice to say that it was not a pretty sight. But, heaven help us, Cromwell pushed us back! The prince narrowly missed capture by hiding in a bean field. A bean field, Simon! That proud man in his *beautiful clothes lying in a bean field! Thank God that the enemy did not find him there!*

We fared badly in the centre in that first onslaught, losing three pieces of artillery, which we could ill afford. We were cheered to see that it went better on our other wing, where our muskets faced Fairfax' cavalry. They did a great deal of damage before the enemy broke through and took part of that wing. Some of the enemy came at us along a ditch so narrow that they could only move four abreast and we were able to inflict a great deal of injury to them before Goring attacked and they were routed. Amidst the rain and in the dark it was hard to see what was happening and some of the enemy fled, fearing that they had lost the day. It was nigh on full dark with a harvest moon on the rise, and the fields were full of men, from both sides, fleeing.

It was the Scots who stood firm against us in the centre, fighting off our charges. But still it could have been a drawn battle with generals on both sides captured or fled, if not for Cromwell. He held his men with such discipline, and he drove us back. Many a coward refused to fight further and was ordered back to York. Newcastle's infantry, the Whitecoats, held their ground to give others a chance to retreat. Time and again they repulsed Roundhead attacks until there were but 30 remaining and they were forced to surrender. Such bravery!

But no matter what the bravery dear brother, we lost. Some 4,000 of our men are dead, many fallen in that last heroic stand. There must have been at least 1,500 taken prisoner, though it is hard to say when others have fled and cannot be counted. All of our artillery, Simon! All of it gone! And so many muskets and pikes too. All now to be used by the enemy. What a blow to the north!

We reached York late last night, and I have not slept since the battle. So many wounded lying in the streets, so many dead left on the field. I do not know what will become of us, Simon. I have survived the battle, but will I retain my freedom when Cromwell and his men come?

5th July

We have left the city.

The King ordered that Prince Rupert go to his aid in Worcester once York was relieved or had fallen, and so we march. The prince has managed to get together 5,000 cavalry and a few hundred infantry and we are on our way. We will move swiftly, so many of our cavaliers are dead that we have been able to mount the infantry on spare horses. We left York before the enemy were fully re-grouped, but now they march to besiege the city again. I do not believe that it will be able to hold out.

Simon still found it hard to believe the words of that last long letter. To be defeated in such a manner! He closed his eyes as he imagined the battlefield – the noise, the blood, the cries, rider-less horses running amok, the crash and boom of artillery. And all in the dark, in the midst of a thunderstorm. He could barely comprehend what it must have been like. With a shudder he turned back to the letters, searching for one which instilled less fear and hopelessness in him.

Christmas 1644

My Dear Simon, I cannot believe that it has been more than a year since I last saw you all. No doubt you are now grown into quite the young man.

I miss you all, all of the time. But I miss you today most of all. I know that you will have been to church last night to celebrate the birth of Christ, and that today you will be celebrating at home. I have friends here with me, but it is not the same, and I pray that next year this war will be over and I can spend Christmas with you all. At home. In peace...

Simon continued to read the letters which Thomas had sent throughout 1645, the skirmishes and battles which now seemed to go more often in favour of the enemy; life on the move, or in camp. Three times Thomas had been in Oxford but the family had not known about it until after he left and had had no opportunity to see him, even for a moment. So the war dragged on and Simon wondered if it would still be going on when he was old enough to fight after all. At the outbreak it had seemed so unlikely that the war would last more than a few months, it had seemed so obvious that the King would be victorious. Now nothing seemed certain, and the war dragged on and on. How he longed to see Thomas once again.

Simon looked out of the window. It had stopped raining at last. Perhaps he could soon go out to exercise Prince. As he looked a lone horseman cantered into the courtyard and drew to a halt in front of the steps. The horse's flanks heaved as though it had been ridden hard and it hung its head wearily. The rider dismounted, as tired looking and as covered in mud as his mount. He carried a leather satchel over his shoulder and fingered it nervously as he handed the reins of his horse to a gardener, then strode towards the door.

Simon leapt to his feet. News at last! There had been rumours of a battle three or four days ago and the family had waited impatiently for news. Now it would seem to be here! Simon put down the letters and his book and, within seconds, was out of the door and on the way down the stairs. The messenger had just entered the hall and was being led towards the library.

'Master Simon.'

Simon turned on hearing his name. His tutor stood on the stairs behind him.

'Mister Ely?'

'I would gather that there is news?'

'I believe so! A messenger has come!'

'And you are going down to find out what news he brings?'

'Yes!'

'You think your father will ask you to sit with him whilst he reads a letter from the King?'

'Well…no…but…'

'Do you think he may have to take time to reply?'

'Well…maybe…but…'

'And do you think he will ask for your advice?'

'Well…no…but…'

'Do you think he will ask you into the library with him?'

'Well…no…but…'

'Then where do you think you are going?'

'I…' Simon was silent, then sighed in exasperation. 'All right, Mister Ely. You win. I will wait for father to call me.'

James Ely smiled. 'I win? I did not think we were in competition!'

Simon looked up at his tutor and smiled, then he laughed outright. 'It seems that I shall never learn not to bandy words with you!'

James smiled in return. 'Oh, but you must. It is part of my job to train you so that, when you are grown, you will be able to win such contests!'

The tutor and boy turned and made their way back up the stairs and into the nursery together as the messenger came to a halt in front of the library door. He took a deep breath whilst he waited for the servant to go in and announce his presence.

'This way. Sir Thomas will see you now.' The servant led the tired man into the library as he spoke, then silently exited and closed the door behind him.

Sir Thomas had risen from his desk and stood before the messenger. 'How can I help you young man?'

'I have a letter from Prince Rupert, sir.'

Sir Thomas felt a knot forming in his stomach and a feeling of deep foreboding almost overwhelmed him as the young man withdrew the letter from his pouch and handed it to him. Sir Thomas looked at the wax seal for a moment before lifting his eyes to those of the soldier. The young man looked uncomfortable and soon looked away. Sir Thomas took a deep breath. 'Thank you. You look tired, and no doubt you are hungry. If you go to my servant outside the door he will take you to the kitchen and get you something.'

'Thank you, sir. I have been delivering letters for three days now and must own to some fatigue.'

'Be on your way then. I will call you if there is any reply.'

As the young man left the library Sir Thomas felt some of his agitation subsiding. When first he heard that it was a letter from the prince he had feared the worst. Thomas. But if the young man had been delivering many letters over the last few days then that could not be, it was something to do with the war. He did not doubt it was bad news to be brought to him in such a way, but he feared no longer for the safety of Thomas. At least, no more so than usual.

Sir Thomas took the letter to his desk where he sat down, broke the seal and began to read.

Sir Thomas,

Please forgive me for the brevity of this letter for I am short of time, but the King wishes me to inform you of our current position. I also have a personal message from myself.

You were in Oxford at the beginning of this year in council with His Majesty, my uncle, when I urged that we attack this New Model Army whilst it was still being formed. You know that my advice was not taken and instead we marched north whilst the enemy consolidated. We may find that to be the most disastrous decision of this war.

It is likely that you know by now of the battle that we fought at Naseby yesterday, the 14th day of this month of July. We held a strong position on a ridge, our front occupying some one and a half miles facing the enemy, although some of his number was hidden from us behind a ridge. They outflanked our left, but our right was secure on the Sulby Hedges. The enemy had a strength of some 6,000 horse, 7,000 foot and mayhap 500 dragoons, which outnumbered us greatly, I having only 4,100 horse and 3,300 foot.

We attacked first, though the armies were so close that we could get off but one volley of musketry before it was hand to hand. My cavalry fought bravely with sword and even the butt end of their muskets, and we forced the enemy centre back. My cavalry pursued the fleeing enemy, though it would have been better for us had they wheeled and re-joined myself and the King sooner. On our other flank our cavalry was routed, and we were so heavily outnumbered that Cromwell was able to continue to throw more men at us. My Bluecoats stood their ground valiantly, but were eventually broken by Fairfax. We were hard pressed at that time to refrain His Majesty from riding forth himself to bolster the centre. Such bravery; yet we could not allow him to endanger his life so.

We lost so many good men on that field Sir, all who fought bravely against overwhelming odds. I fear it is my duty to inform you that your son Thomas still lies there on the field, cut down by Dragoons hidden in the Sulby Hedges. I have known your son for all my time fighting here for His Majesty. He was a brave soldier, an honest man, and I counted him to be one I could trust to give me the truth, be it good or ill. I shall sorely miss your son, Sir Thomas, and not only on the field of battle. Yet my grief at his passing can in no way measure against that which you and your remaining children now feel. You have my deepest and sincerest condolences.

The King wishes me to inform you that Fairfax now marches to relieve Leicester, and we can do nothing to gainsay him, for our forces have been shattered. We lost more than 1,000 killed and 5,000 captured. We have lost 500 officers, sir, if you can believe that. 500! Yet I do not believe the enemy lost more than 400 killed and wounded combined. The enemy also took the King's baggage train, and may well have some of his correspondence which could prove ill for us. His Majesty's orders are for you to do nothing; to hold Marston as you have done so ably for him throughout this war whilst we try to consolidate, to re-group and to plan for the future. I know that you will do this for the King, for you are one of his most able supporters.

Remember Sir Thomas, hold Marston and protect the western approaches to Oxford, for if that city falls then I fear that the war is lost.

I am your most humble servant,

Rupert

Sir Thomas sat as though made of stone, stunned to the very core. Thomas was dead. Had been dead for four days. How could he have not known? How can a father not feel when his own flesh and blood is taken from this world so soon? The boy was barely twenty years old, with so much to live for. He had been at war since he was seventeen, no time for the friendships that young men of that age should pursue, no time to fall in love, to marry and raise a family. Tears marked Sir Thomas's face as he thought of all that he had lost, and he felt that his heart would break with grief. And with guilt. He should have gone to battle and left Thomas at home to defend the Manor. No matter that he had stayed because it was the King's wish, Sir Thomas knew that he would never forgive himself the life he now lived whilst his son lay dead on the bloody battlefield of Naseby.

Simon made his way down the narrow pathway through the trees and into the clearing. It was three years since he had been here and the house was showing the effects of that time in its weathered wood and crumbling wattle and daub. Clearly some repairs would be needed soon. He supposed that Henry Sawyer would do that when he returned from the war. Simon paused for a moment, still wondering why he had decided to come here. What was it about Rebekah and her family that drew him, that made him feel that this was his second home? Perhaps it was Ann Sawyer's kindness and gentleness towards him, something that he could not remember receiving from his own mother, although his siblings assured him that she had been the most loving of women. Could it be that Ann had somehow become a substitute mother figure for him, despite their short acquaintance? Or was it Rebekah? He had not seen her since the funeral following the attack on the Manor, but he knew in some mystical way that when he did see her again it would be as though they had never been apart.

He was still standing looking at the house when Ann Sawyer appeared carrying a heavy bucket. Simon went across to help her with it.

'Master Simon!' She put down the bucket as he approached. 'It is good to see you after so long! But what are you doing here?'

'Yes! What a surprise!' Rebekah appeared, also carrying a bucket, which was placed next to her mother's as she smiled happily up into Simon's eyes.

'Does your father know that you are here?'

Simon shook his head at Ann's question.

'No. I do not think that he would approve.'

'Then why are you here?'

Why indeed. Suddenly tears came unbidden to his eyes and his breath caught in his throat.

'My word! What on earth can be the matter?'

'It is Thomas.'

'Your brother?' Rebekah frowned, but Ann needed no further explanation. Her eyes filled with tears as she stepped forward and enfolded Simon into her embrace.

'Oh, you poor boy.' She held him while he cried out his grief, great racking sobs shaking him as the tears wet her shoulder. All was quiet for a time, save for his sobs and they, too, eventually ceased. Simon took a moment to control his breathing then pulled himself gently from the comforting arms.

'I am sorry. I do not know why I came here; and I never intended to behave in such a manner.'

'Is Thomas dead?'

Simon closed his eyes and swallowed hard before turning to face Rebekah. 'Yes.'

There was a world of misery and loss in that one word and the girl reached out to take his hand in hers. 'I am so sorry, Simon. Was it the war?'

He nodded. 'Have you heard about the battle four days ago? At Naseby?'

Ann shrugged. 'Rumours. Nothing more.'

'What happened?'

'I do not really know what happened to Thomas, only that…that he will not be coming back.' Simon took another deep breath. 'It was a terrible battle, by all accounts. Perhaps the largest of the war so far.' He looked at their expectant faces and found it strange to think that they were 'the enemy', that they would rejoice in the defeat of the King's army whilst for him it was a disaster. Steeling himself he said the words that he had hope never to say. 'It was a terrible defeat for the King.'

Rebekah clapped her hands and her eyes shone as she turned to her mother. 'Does that mean that father will soon be home? Oh I do hope so!'

'Rebekah!'

The girl frowned at her mother's rebuke, then her eyes opened wide and she put a hand to her mouth in shame. 'Oh! I am so sorry, Simon. I did not think!'

'And why should you?' The boy sniffed. 'You should be glad that your father may soon be home. I only wish...'

Ann nodded wisely. 'I know.' She smiled gently. 'I think I understand why you came here. There is no other woman at the Manor who could comfort you like a mother is there?' Simon shook his head sadly and Ann knelt down in front of him, taking his shoulders in her gentle hands. 'Never forget, Simon; our family are your friends, and always will be so. You will always be welcome here.'

Simon nodded. 'Thank you, Mistress Sawyer.'

Ann Sawyer stood and moved briskly towards the cottage. 'I have treated many who suffer grief and know that your sleep will be broken for many nights to come. Now, you wait here for just a moment and I will fetch you some herbs which will help.'

As Ann disappeared Simon realised that he was still holding Rebekah's slim hand in his. He looked at their entwined fingers and then into her eyes, eyes which showed her sorrow at his loss, and the strength that would always be there to support him. Rebekah gently squeezed his fingers.

'I am so sorry, Simon. Although I never met your brother I know that he was a good man, and that you loved him dearly.' She sighed. 'How I hate this war! So many families torn apart. So much death. Why do people do it Simon? Why must men always fight?'

Simon shrugged his shoulders. 'I suppose it is that they feel they must protect their beliefs, no matter what the cost.'

'But surely the cost is too great? You are not the only one to have lost a loved one. And it matters not which side they fought for. The loss is equally great.' She looked towards the hut as she spoke. 'And it is not only death which divides us in such times. I know that mother misses father. I hear her crying in the night.' Rebekah sighed. 'I miss him, too.'

'I am sorry Rebekah. I have come here to seek sympathy for the loss of my brother, yet you have your own pain to deal with. Your own fears for the future. I should not have come.'

'Never say that, Simon! We are friends, and friends are always there for each other. I would be a poor friend indeed if I were not able to comfort you.'

'And you do comfort me.' Simon smiled sadly.

'It all makes me so angry!' Rebekah sounded fierce, and Simon turned to face her.

'What does?'

'The way that men rule over us. Do not read me wrong. My father is right when he says that all men should have freedom to worship and that they should have a say in how their lives are lived. But this cost is too high!'

'Then what do you suggest?'

'Compromise, Simon. As we spoke of it when we first met.'

'But strong men often find it hard to compromise. I wish it were not so, but...'

'Men! That is the root of our trouble! We could have the same arguments, but if it were women who made the decisions then I believe there would be more compromise and less suffering!'

'What about Queen Elizabeth?'

Rebekah frowned. 'What do you mean?'

'A great and powerful queen. A great ruler. Yet she led our nation in war against the Spanish.'

'Only because it was a Spanish king, *a man*, who opposed her. If only it had been a woman, I am sure they would have compromised!

'Do you really think so?'

Rebekah looked sheepish, then grinned. 'Perhaps not. I know that father stood against the order of things, but wishing women into power might be a step too far, even for him!'

Simon laughed. He was glad that Rebekah was his friend.

Chapter 10

November 1645

Simon sat on a log and watched his breath as it rose in white clouds when he breathed out. The November air was cold at this early hour, the grass damp, and the dew on the spiders webs made them glisten like crystal, sparkling in the watery sunlight which gave no warmth. Simon shivered and pulled his cloak closer about himself as he took another look around the clearing. There was no one in sight, but smoke was rising from a fire in front of the cottage where a cooking pot hung suspended, no doubt heating the thin gruel for breakfast.

It was almost five months since he had heard of the death of Thomas, and the hurt and loss still cut deep. Things at home had been difficult; his father had blamed himself for Thomas's death and no one had been able to convince him otherwise. Yet Simon had noticed a subtle shift in his father's attitude of late, an acceptance of the loss of his first-born son, an acknowledgement that it was not his fault after all, and that life must move on. Elizabeth seemed to have accepted Thomas's death more quickly, although Simon knew that she still cried when she thought herself alone. Perhaps the knowledge that their father was making plans for her marriage had given her something positive to focus on, whereas Simon felt he had nothing. He had idolised his brother, had thought him invulnerable, had looked forward to sharing so much with him once he himself had grown up; but that would never happen now. It would not be many years before he reached Thomas's age and then passed it, living years and experiencing things that his brother would now never know.

Simon's reverie was broken by the sound of footsteps on the narrow path and he smiled wistfully. Rebekah and her mother would be coming back from the stream and would no doubt ask him to join their meagre breakfast, as they had done so many times in the last few months. He did not know what he would have done without their constant kind support, allowing him to talk or to cry as the mood took him, and he knew that his slow coming to terms with his brother's death had been helped on its way in no small measure by their constant friendship. He rose to greet mother and daughter as they entered the clearing, words of welcome at the ready.

'What are you doing here? Begone and do not come back again!'

Simon's words of greeting froze on his lips. Ann Sawyer stood at the entrance to the pathway, but a very different Ann Sawyer from the one he had always known. She looked thinner, her clothes hanging more loosely than before, her hair was matted and unkempt and there were dark rings around her eyes. Her eyes. He had been used to gentle eyes, alight with laughter or soft with concern, but the eyes which now held his were hard, frightening, full of hatred.

'Mistress Sawyer?'

'Did you not here me, boy? We may not be as wealthy as your family but this is our home and we choose whom to welcome here. You are not welcome.'

Boy? Ann Sawyer had always spoken to him with the utmost courtesy, calling him 'young Master' or 'Master Simon'; never, in all the years he had known her had she called him 'boy'. That, even more than her appearance, disturbed Simon most.

'Mother.' Simon was relieved to see Rebekah behind her mother. He looked enquiringly in her direction, but she shook her head slightly as she laid a gentle hand on Ann's sleeve. 'Please, Mother, we discussed this. You know that it is not Simon's fault.'

'It is the fault of his family, and all of the rich who lord it above us and support the King. None of their kind shall be welcome here again.'

Ann's face was red with emotion and her eyes flashed angrily. She spat in Simon's direction before turning her back on him. 'Get out of here, boy, before I take my Henry's axe to you.'

At thirteen Simon considered himself to be a young man, but at this moment he felt like a small boy rejected by someone he loved, punished for some unknown misdemeanour, and he felt the tears welling in his eyes.

'Rebekah?'

She shook her head sadly. 'You must leave us now, Simon. I have to attend to my mother.'

'What have I done?'

'Speak no more to him, child!'

Rebekah looked at her mother's bowed back, then back towards Simon. He stood slumped, his whole body portraying the hurt and rejection that he felt, and Rebekah's heart went out to her friend. Obeying her mother's command she did not speak, but she did mouth something which Simon could not quite make out through his tears. He roughly wiped his eyes with the back of his hand as Rebekah's mouth formed the words once more.

The orchard. Later.

Simon slowly nodded his understanding then, with heavy heart, turned and walked away.

Simon picked a wizened apple from the tree and took a bite yet, somehow, he found it tasteless and difficult to swallow and he threw the rest of the fruit away uneaten. He had been waiting for three hours now;

three hours of trying to think of what he or his father may have done wrong. But he could think of nothing. How he wished that Rebekah would come soon. Unable to sit any longer he stood and began to walk through the orchard once more. It was then that he saw the slim, waif like figure of the girl through the trees.

'Rebekah!'

She turned at his call and hurried towards him, finally coming to a halt a few paces from away.

'Simon. I am sorry for the way my mother spoke to you. Can you forgive her?'

Simon frowned. 'I do not know, Rebekah. I have always felt that your mother cared for me, but today I felt nothing but hatred. How can I forgive her for that when I do not know what I have done?'

'It is not your fault, Simon. It is father.' Tears welled in Rebekah's eyes and spilled over onto her cheeks. Simon reached out and gently took her hand in his.

'Is he...?'

Rebekah nodded. 'He was killed at Naseby.'

'But that was months ago!'

'Ordinary people do not have messages from a Prince to tell them of such things. We did not hear until five days ago.'

Simon heard the bitterness in her voice and felt he could understand. How would it have been if Thomas had been dead for all this time and he had only just found out?

'I am so sorry, Rebekah. I know how you feel because I still mourn Thomas.'

'That is not the same.' Rebekah shook her head sadly. 'I know you are hurt by the loss of your brother, but this is my father, the man who should be here to support my mother and me, to care for and protect us. And now he is gone.'

'I still do not understand...'

'Mother?' Simon nodded. 'We were told that father was cut down by the cavalry. Mother has got it into her head that it could have been your brother who killed him.'

Simon was shocked. His mouth was dry and his hand tightened around Rebekah's.

'Do you believe that?'

She looked at him sadly. 'It is possible, although with so many cavalry there, it is more likely that it was someone else. But mother needs someone to blame, someone to focus her anger on, and she has chosen your family because you are the only cavaliers that we know.'

'Perhaps if I were to talk to her? I want to see her anyway, Rebekah, to tell her how sorry I am about your father.'

Rebekah shook her head. 'She would not listen to you, Simon. You remember all the times we talked with father and mother about why the war happened?' Simon nodded but said nothing. 'You know then that she, and father, believed that this war would never have happened if the King had been willing to listen to ordinary people like us, to rule us justly and wisely. Even if he had not ruled in such a manner but the wealthy and powerful in the land had been willing to stand against him, people like your father, then this war would never have happened, and my father would still be alive.'

'And my brother.'

Rebekah lifted her tear-stained face towards his and nodded. As their eyes met they recognised in each other understanding, sympathy and support. Without another word the two children embraced and cried out their grief together.

Chapter 11

Present day

Rob blinked rapidly, feeling a strange dislocation. After leaving the barn he had taken his lunch to the library and must have fallen asleep after eating. Now there were tears on his face, and he felt a deep sense of loss the like of which he had never experienced before. His one abiding thought – Rebekah. As he remembered her pain at the loss of her father, he wanted to take her in his arms again and comfort her. It was some moments before he remembered that she did not really exist, that she was just a part of his dream. Yet it had all felt incredibly real, so real that he wanted to prove that his dream was somehow showing him things that had happened in the past. The only tangible evidence he could think of was Simon's diary and letters. He let his eyes rove over the shelves once more. Could the diary actually be real? Could it be here?

Rob stood and made his way over to the shelves where he began to run his hands over the spines of the books. He had not intended to clear the library so soon but, after his dream, he felt he could wait no longer. Something strange, almost sinister seemed to be happening to him and he needed to find the answer. With a deep breath he began to take the books from the shelves, one by one.

An hour later, Rob found himself standing before two sets of boxes. In one group, the smaller in number, were the books that he would keep to display in the library when it had been refurbished. In the other, far bigger, group were the books which would be stored elsewhere, or sold on. Nowhere was there a handwritten book like Simon's diary. No hand drawn maps or collection of letters written by Thomas during the war. Rob felt a strange mixture of emotions. Sad that he had not found any real link with the history of the house during the war, yet relieved that the diary was not there, for if it did exist, then what did that say about his dreams? Dreams which at times felt more real to him than his own past.

Confused, unsure of what to think, or what to do about his dreams, Rob picked up the first of the boxes and left the room.

Rob put down his glass of beer as he heard the key turn in the lock. In one swift movement he rose to his feet and made his way out into the hall.

'Caroline!'

There was the sound of a bunch of keys hitting the floor as the young woman swung round to face him.

'Rob! You scared me half to death! What are you doing here?'

Rob had the grace to look sheepish.

'Sorry. I wanted to see you and so drove straight up. I suppose I should have phoned.'

'Yes, you should! Don't you ever think before doing something? I thought you were an intruder. At best a burglar, worse still a potential rapist.' Caroline began to relax and smiled at him. 'Or you might have walked in on me with my secret lover.'

Rob blanched. 'You don't mean…?'

Caroline laughed. 'You never learn do you? Don't annoy a psychologist, she knows only too well how to manipulate you to get her own back!'

Rob joined in the laughter. 'Touché!' Bending down he picked up the keys which Caroline had dropped. Placing them on the hall table he took a moment to look at her. Shoulder-length ash blond hair framed her face, drawing attention to the sparkling blue eyes, refined nose and laughing mouth. 'It's good to see you.' Caroline closed the door as Rob stepped forward and slipped his arms around her waist. 'I've missed you.'

'And I've missed you.'

The couple kissed, slowly and sensuously, before Rob took Caroline's hand and led her into the lounge. She frowned slightly at the sight of the beer on the table.

'Drinking already? It's only four o'clock. It's not like you to be drinking this early. Is something wrong?'

'Yes…no…oh, I don't know!' Rob sounded exasperated. 'Why don't you kick of your shoes and sit down. I'll open a bottle of wine; then I'll tell you everything.'

'It's too early for me. I'll have a cup of tea.'

'OK.'

As Rob disappeared into the kitchen Caroline wondered what had brought him back to Durham in the middle of the week. She didn't have long to wait to find out. Rob soon returned with a mug of tea which he placed on the side table next to an armchair. Caroline sat down and stretched out her legs in front of her.

'I'm so tired,' she sighed. 'It's been a busy few days.'

'And for me, too.'

'So, what have you been up to?'

Rob sat down on the sofa and began to explain how the work was going at Marston Manor, the plans for the re-enactment, the sourcing of furniture, the education centre. Caroline listened attentively. When he had finished she smiled.

'Well, you have been busy. Which makes it even more surprising that you've taken a day off to drive up here. Is there some research that you need to do at the university?'

Rob shook his head. 'No, I pretty much know what's in the university library after studying the civil war here for so many years. It's you I wanted to see.'

'Why?'

Rob sighed. 'It sounds silly, now that I'm here, but I wanted you to tell me that I'm not going mad.'

Caroline sat up at his words. 'Mad? What on earth makes you say that?'

Rob shrugged slightly. 'I guess it's just the strange dreams I've been having.'

'Dreams?'

Rob nodded. 'It all started on my first night at Marston. I thought I saw a ghost.'

'Dreams? A ghost? Which is it?'

'I thought the ghost was real; but it can't have been, can it. It must have been a dream.'

'And what did this ghost do, or say, in your dream?'

'She said she remembered me from long ago, and that my family had done hers some harm. Something about them being innocent but we caused them to be punished. She seemed to think it was all my fault. She said that I would pay for the sins of my family.'

A smile began to play at the corners of Caroline's mouth, but she held it in check when she saw how serious Rob was, how worried he looked.

'Where you frightened?'

'Yes, but I convinced myself that it was a dream, even though Paul said that he had also seen some sort of crazy old woman as well.'

'It was your first day, Rob. Strange dreams are not uncommon when people are excited by a new job, a new venture. You were probably feeling a little nervous. The dream could well be a way of your subconscious worrying about failure.'

'I suppose so. But then there are the other dreams.'

'Tell me about them.'

Rob sat quietly for a moment, ordering his thoughts; then he began.

'I've been dreaming about the Hardwycke family during the civil war. It's strange, but I'm dreaming from the perspective of a boy, the young son of the household. When I've seen his reflection in a mirror he even looks like I did at his age. I seem to be dreaming about his life in chronological order. What's more, in my dreams he is the same age that the real boy, Simon, would have been at the time.'

'And why not? You said yourself that you believe you are descended from that family. You're steeping yourself in the period. It's not surprising that your brain needs to process all of this. And what better time to do it than when you are sleeping?'

'I suppose so.' Rob frowned. 'The problem is that I dream things, and then later on find out that those things really happened.'

'Such as?'

'Such as Charles I visiting Marston. Or an attack on the Manor.' He looked across at Caroline who was surprised by the shadowy fear in his eyes. 'I dreamt about an attack which really happened. But I didn't find out the details until *after* the dream. How is that possible?'

Caroline frowned. 'I don't know. The mind can play some pretty strange tricks on us. Take déjà vu, for example. People see, or experience something which they believe they have dreamt about before. A sort of pre-cognition. It sounds to me as though you are experiencing something similar, only in reverse.'

'How do you mean?'

'Well, you're dreaming something you shouldn't know, but yet you do.' She chewed her lip thoughtfully for a moment. 'It's not really in reverse though, is it? I only said that because you are dreaming about something which you say happened in the past, not about something in the future. But, in a way, it is in the future because you say you haven't got all of the facts when you dream.'

'I say I don't have the facts? There's no question of it, Caroline. I'm dreaming stuff that I really have never heard of before. Then there was the last dream.'

Rob was silent for a moment, lost in thought. Caroline knew better than to interrupt, and waited patiently until he spoke again.

'My last dream happened in the library. And I'm not sure I was asleep.'

Caroline got up from her chair and joined Rob on the sofa, taking his hand in hers. 'What do you mean? You weren't asleep? Are you sure?'

'Of course I am! I'd know if I was falling asleep, wouldn't I?

'Do drivers realise that they're falling asleep and stop themselves? If so, then why do we have accidents caused by people who fall asleep at the wheel?'

Rob frowned. 'I see what you're getting at. But it was in the middle of the afternoon and...'

'And you've been working hard. And you're under pressure. And you admit that you haven't been sleeping well. I see this sort of thing all the time, Rob.'

'What? People who see ghosts and dream about real historical events they've never heard of before?'

For a moment Caroline thought that Rob was withdrawing from her, but then she felt him relax as a slow smile spread across his face. 'Now you can see why I drove up here. I needed to see my own personal psychologist so that she could tell me everything is alright.'

Caroline smiled in return. 'Of course everything is alright. You have the excitement of a new job. On top of that you find the family link you've been searching for for years. You've been meeting new people, and trying to imagine what life would have been like in the civil war so that you can make the Manor authentic. Dreams like yours would be a perfectly normal reaction to something like that.'

'You're right!' Rob's voice was positive, filled with confidence once again. 'And on top of that, I've been missing you. This was the perfect excuse for me to come and see you. Now, let me go and run you a bath, then I'll take you out for dinner.'

Chapter 12

January 1646

'Are you excited?'

Elizabeth looked at her brother and smiled, though he noticed that her eyes betrayed a nervousness that she did not voice. 'Of course I am excited! Just think, this time tomorrow I shall be an old married woman!'

'Better that than an old maid!'

Elizabeth joined with Simon in his laughter. He would be fourteen in a few months and was growing up fast. Not long ago he would not have understood what an 'old maid' was, now he was showing a more mature humour. His body had decided that it was time for him to mature, too. He had suddenly begun to grow upwards so fast that she almost believed that she could see the difference in him from week to week. Elizabeth remembered how awkward Thomas had been at that age as he struggled to adapt to his changing body, and she noticed the same awkwardness in Simon at times. She sighed wistfully, how she wished that Thomas could be at her wedding. He would have looked so handsome in his colourful velvets and silks with their fine white frills.

'What is wrong?'

'I was thinking of Thomas.'

Simon understood. He, too, wished that his brother could be here. He was finding it hard to adjust to his new role in the family. As the only surviving son he had more responsibilities and was having to grow up fast. The war was going badly. Indeed nothing seemed to have gone the way of the Royalists since Naseby, and their father was spending ever longer periods in Oxford, often away for the whole day and sometimes the nights as well. It was traditional for the son to take charge of the Manor when the father was away, and Simon was doing his best to oversee things, to make sure that Sir Thomas's wishes were carried out. It was difficult, and he relied on Elizabeth to help and guide him, indeed it was she, in effect, who ran things when their father was away.

Elizabeth stamped her feet to warm them. The snow had wet her shoes and stockings so that her toes were already feeling numb, and they had not even started their journey. She wished that the coach would hurry up. As though in answer to her thoughts the horses were led around the house from the stable, pulling the light travelling coach behind them. When it drew to a halt Simon handed his sister up then took the reins of his horse from the groom who led the prancing animal forward.

'Have all the bags been loaded?'

The groom nodded. 'Yes, sir.'

'Good.' Simon turned to the officer commanding the enlarged garrison at the Manor. 'I leave you with thirty men and take ten with us for protection. We should be back by tomorrow evening, the next day at the latest. You know where to find us if there is trouble?'

'Yes, sir.'

As Simon mounted his horse Elizabeth turned away in order to hide a smile. He sounded so confident in giving his orders. Who would have known that he had practised these few words time and time again to make sure that he had them correct and was able to say them with authority!

'Sergeant, position your men for the journey and we will away!' Simon took his position in front of the coach with four of the escort, whilst the remainder mounted and took their places to the rear.

With a clatter of hooves the wedding party began its journey to Oxford.

Simon gazed around him in wonder. He had attended some celebrations in the past, but never one where the king and his entourage were invited. The whole room was a swirling mass of bright colours, and the candlelight was reflected back from thousands of precious stones and pieces of golden jewelry. The marriage service had gone well, though only attended by a few as the king was in conference for most of the day. But now the conference was over and the Royalists had enjoyed the lavish wedding breakfast provided by Sir Thomas. The meal over, the courtiers were talking, laughing, dancing as though the country were not at war and they had not a care in the world.

Simon watched as Elizabeth and her new husband danced gracefully together. The groom was tall and slim, with a physique which spoke of the hours of training and warfare he had experienced during his twenty two years. There was a scar running from the corner of his right eye up into his hairline where his hair grew in an unruly manner from the damage caused by the sabre cut. Simon wondered what Elizabeth thought of the scar. Surely it was not something she had ever expected in a husband. His eyes continued to scan the room. On the far side he could see the king in conversation with Prince Rupert and a number of advisers, including Sir Thomas. Simon still had to pinch himself at times to make sure that it was not a dream and that he was truly moving in such exalted company. He saw his father leave the kings group and make his way to the newly-weds. After a quick word the groom nodded and led Elizabeth towards Simon.

'Your father says that the King wishes to speak with me. Will you look after my new wife, brother?'

Simons jaw clenched as he nodded. What right had he to call him brother? Thomas was his only brother, and he was dead. Elizabeth noticed the flash of anger in his eyes and laid a quietening hand on his arm as she turned back towards her husband.

'We shall be fine, Benjamin. Please go and do your duty.'

As Benjamin left to re-join Sir Thomas and present himself to the king, Elizabeth turned to her brother.

'Say nothing, Simon.'

'But how dare he call me brother! Thomas...'

'Thomas is not here, Simon. But even if he were, then Benjamin would still call you brother. He is my husband now.'

Simon sighed and lowered his head. 'I know. It's just that...'

Elizabeth squeezed his arm gently. 'I know. Now get rid of that long face! I decree that there shall be nothing but smiles and laughter on my wedding day.' She looked towards the king's group. 'We had best make as merry as we can, for I doubt it will last.'

Simon felt guilty and turned the conversation away from thoughts of Thomas.

'So how does it feel to be Mistress Benjamin de Vere, wife of the heir to the de Vere estates?'

Elizabeth frowned slightly. 'I do not really know. To tell the truth, Simon, I feel no different to how I felt when we left home yesterday.' She looked towards her husband. 'I hardly know Benjamin, since he was Father's choice for me. We have spoken a number of times, as you know, and I believe him to be a good and honest man.' She smiled. 'I am also lucky that Father chose such a handsome man for me.'

Simon looked at Benjamin on the far side of the room. 'Handsome? You think so?' Elizabeth nodded. 'What of the scar on his face?' Simon continued.

Elizabeth's smile deepened. 'A scar that shows his courage in battle and that draws attention to his fine eyes. You have a lot to learn about what attracts a woman, Simon!'

Simon had a typical thirteen-year-old boy's aversion to the opposite sex and gave a little shudder. 'I hope I do not have to find out too soon!'

Elizabeth's laughter rang out, causing her husband to look across the room towards her. Their eyes met and they smiled. Sir Thomas noticed and nodded approvingly, a smile lighting his own eyes.

'How can you seem so close when you hardly know each other?'

Elizabeth sighed. 'Because this is the way it must be. I know that father would not choose an unsuitable husband for me. He has known Benjamin and his father for many years. They are good loyal subjects of the King, both of them have served him well during this war and our marriage will cement the two families as allies to the Crown.'

Simon raised a quizzical eyebrow. 'It sounds to me as though you are repeating what you have heard.'

'Oh, Simon!' Elizabeth was exasperated. 'You see and understand far too much for a boy of your age! Yes, my marriage is one of convenience, an alliance for our family. Yes, I hardly know my husband and am afraid of what lies ahead for me. Yes, I am nervous about my new position in life and in society. But I can do nothing but smile and hope that it all turns out well for me.'

'When I marry, it will be to someone of my own choosing.'

'I do hope so, Simon. But if it is not, and remember that father must have the final say in it, then I hope and pray that it will be someone you can like as much as I like Benjamin.' She cast another glance at her husband. 'I believe that I will grow to love him over time.'

'If the war allows.'

'Thank you, Simon, for that! I was trying not to think that my husband will be leaving me in just a few short days to go to war!'

Simon was contrite. 'Please forgive me, Elizabeth. That was thoughtless of me.'

'Yes, it was.' Elizabeth's stern gaze softened. 'But I can hardly blame you for that. You are still a boy. Whereas I...' she bit her lip nervously, 'I am now fully grown, a married woman with all that entails...'

'Look. Father and Benjamin are coming!' The two men had bowed low to the King and were now making their way towards the young people. 'Whatever it is that the King had to say to them they seem very happy; see how they are both smiling?'

Elizabeth did not have time to answer Simon as the two men approached them.

'Good news!' Sir Thomas took Elizabeth's hand in his as he spoke. 'The King and Prince Rupert have magnanimously decided that Benjamin is to be re-assigned!'

'Away from the Prince's cavalry? How is that good news?' asked Simon. 'Surely any cavalier would want to serve with Prince Rupert?'

'Any cavalier, save one who has recently married.' Benjamin said with a smile.

'And what has that to do with matters?'

Sir Thomas squeezed his daughter's hand. 'Benjamin has been assigned to the King's cavalry here in Oxford. He has been given two days leave to return to Marston with us, then he will return here to serve the King. He will not be able to come to Marston every week, but he will be able to visit from time to time. And he would not have been able to come at all if he were with the Prince.'

Benjamin smiled as he took Elizabeth's other hand. 'It is more than we could have hoped for while the country is at war. Giving us time to get to know each other is the best wedding present we could have received!'

Sir Thomas released his daughter's hand and placed an arm around his son's shoulders.

'Come along then, Simon. Let me introduce you to a few people before we return to Marston. We must leave in time to be there before it gets dark!'

Chapter 13

May 1646

Simon and his father watched as the young lambs gambolled in the field.

'A good season's young there. We should make a fair profit by the end of the year.'

'Will we sell to the army again?'

Sir Thomas nodded at his son's question. 'Yes. The King will have need of all the mutton he can get if he overwinters again in Oxford. And we are perfectly placed to provide it.'

'Do you think we shall still be at war when the winter comes?'

'I do not know, son.' Sir Thomas shook his head sadly. 'My heart tells me that we shall still be opposing Parliament and its forces, but my head tells me otherwise. Things are going from bad to worse. In my mind I just cannot see that we will win. And I cannot imagine what will happen if the King loses this war.'

'There have been civil wars before, and the country has continued.'

'Yes. But then it was a claimant to the throne fighting against the king, and if he succeeded then he became the next king. I cannot see how England can survive if the King is defeated and Parliament sets out to rule us alone.'

'Do you really think they would try to do that?'

'It is what they have been aiming for all of these years. They have no claimant to the throne and have put no-one forward to replace His Majesty.'

'But if, hypothetically, the King were to lose the war,' Simon frowned in concentration, 'is it not possible that Parliament would allow him to keep his crown and rule, but perhaps give him less power?'

Sir Thomas smiled warmly at his son. 'That is possible. Indeed that is what I, and many others, think would happen if we lost. You are developing a wise head on your young shoulders.'

Simon had thought long and hard about the situation and was pleased that his father agreed, and that his father recognised his worth. 'But,' he continued slowly, 'what if His Majesty disagreed? If Parliament said that they were to have all of the true power and the King was to be just a figurehead, surely he would not accept that? That is what we have been fighting about. What if the King were to say no to such a proposal?'

'Then it would be exile for him.'

Simon shivered. What would happen to him and his family if the King was defeated and went into exile? Would they be able to survive in a country ruled by Parliament? Afraid of where his thoughts were leading him, Simon tried to imagine what other options lay before them.

'Of course, we could win. Then the King will force Parliament to obey him.'

Sir Thomas shook his head sadly. 'That is what I hope and dream of, son. But if we are realistic we both know that that cannot happen. The war goes worse for us each day. Oxford is now almost entirely encircled by the enemy, and I find it more and more difficult to get away for a day like this. You know also that the King has escaped the city and made for the north, and I have heard nothing from him since. I do not know if he has met the Roundheads in battle or if he avoids them. But I fear that if there is a battle our army is too weak and is sure to be defeated.'

'Surely that is treasonous.'

Sir Thomas turned angrily on his son. 'Do not ever accuse me of treason! I have served my King all the days of my life, and will continue to do so while there is breath in my body! I am willing to sacrifice all for him. I have sacrificed my son for him. How can you say such a thing to me, Simon? To your own father?'

Simon's face was white with shock. Never before had Sir Thomas spoken so harshly, and it brought home to him just how deeply he had wounded him. His voice was shaky as he tried to explain. 'I did not mean to say *you* are a traitor, Father! Please forgive me! It is just that … well … to talk of the King's defeat as though it might happen, not as just a theory…' he ran out of words, unsure of how to explain himself, and was relieved to see his father relax a little as he sighed heavily.

'I am sorry, Simon. I know that you were not calling me a traitor, it is the idea of defeat that you see as treacherous. But I am afraid that I and many others, aye perhaps even the King himself, now see defeat as inevitable. What I say is realism, son, and I would say it to no-one who is not of our family. I value my head too much. Do you understand?'

Simon nodded. 'Yes, Father. I think so.'

'All we can do is pray that God will continue to protect his chosen King, and lead us to final victory.'

'Amen to that.'

Sir Thomas turned to make his way back to the house. Watching the lambs at play in the field was something he usually enjoyed, and which had always engendered a feeling of hope in his heart. But not today. Talk of the war now only brought with it fear for his family as he recognised the desperateness of their situation. Their only hope now lay with…

'Father! Father!'

Sir Thomas and Simon turned as one to see Elizabeth waving at them from the far side of the field.

'What is it daughter?'

'A message! From the King!'

The blood drained from Sir Thomas's face, leaving him white with fear. He could only think that a message from the King was bad news. Something else had gone wrong, weakening the Royalist cause once more. As though he could read his father's thoughts, Simon forced a smile and turned to Sir Thomas.

'It could be good news, Father. Perhaps there has been a battle and His Majesty and Prince Rupert have been victorious.'

'Perhaps so.' Sir Thomas clung on to the slender hope offered by his son, although deep in his heart he feared the worst. 'Come on then, let us go and see what this is all about.'

With that they turned and made their way back towards the house. Barely five minutes later the whole family were gathered together in the library. Elizabeth sat on a chair whilst Benjamin stood behind her, a gentle hand on her shoulder. The two had grown close in the four months since their marriage and needed no words to express their fears, or to offer comfort to each other. Simon stood beside the table which held the family Bible, unconsciously stroking the soft leather binding, as though silently seeking strength from God to be able to face whatever news had come. Sir Thomas sat at his desk, the letter from the King in his hand. He stared for a moment at the wax seal on the reverse, turned the letter to look at the neat flowing script of his name. He did not want to open it, feared what it might say, yet clung to hope for it was written in the King's hand, and if it came from the King then all could not be lost.

'Are you not going to open it?'

Sir Thomas looked across at his son-in-law, who had spoken the words that no one else dared to. With a sigh Sir Thomas picked up his knife, broke the seal and opened the letter.

He read in silence, his hands beginning to shake, and all colour leaving his cheeks. When he finished reading he laid the letter carefully on the desk, then lowered his head into his hands. The silence dragged on, no one daring to speak. Finally Sir Thomas looked up. He looked first at his son, then his daughter. His eyes held those of his son-in-law for a moment before he looked away, his eyes drawn to the portrait of Thomas which hung above the fireplace. Perhaps it would be easier if he spoke the words to his dead son.

'The King wrote this letter the night before he surrendered to the Scots at Newark.'

'What? Surely that cannot be true!'

Sir Thomas turned back to the horrified group. 'I am afraid it is so, Benjamin.'

'What will happen now? Is the war over?'

Sir Thomas shook his head sadly. 'No, Elizabeth; but things are desperate.'

'Why did he do it?' Simon asked the question which they had all been thinking, and Sir Thomas picked up the letter once more.

'His Majesty says here what we all know, that the alliance between Parliament and the Scots is fragile. It is barely forty years since England and Scotland were united under the King's father and there is still bitter history between our two countries. His Majesty is counting on the fact that he is a Stuart, and that in the past it has always been Parliament which has voted for the money to wage war against Scotland. He believes that things have reached such grave difficulties that only a bold move such as this has any chance of saving the monarchy.'

'Do you think his plan will work?'

Sir Thomas shrugged. 'I do not know, Simon. The Scots have been opposed to the King because of his religious beliefs, fearing closer links with Rome, but there is probably more that they have in common with him than they do with Parliament. I believe that the Scots will show more respect for the King if he is there before their eyes every day than they would if he were here in the south. And the King is right when he says that there is little love lost between Parliament and the Scots. There have already been bickerings and fallings out, and their alliance is shaky. Perhaps the King's presence is the catalyst that is needed to bring the Scots to our cause. If they do break the alliance with Parliament, we may have a chance of winning this war after all.'

'It is a risky move.'

'Indeed, Benjamin, but a bold one. Let us pray that the Lord protects His Majesty and gives him the wisdom to tread carefully the treacherous shoals in which he now finds himself.'

'But what does this mean for us, Father?'

Sir Thomas closed his eyes, as though to marshal his strength before answering his son. 'We all know that the enemy all but surround Oxford. We have been safe so far on this side of the city, but if the city falls, then it is likely that we fall too.'

Benjamin's grip tightened on Elizabeth's shoulder as though to comfort her as she raised a hand to her mouth, smothering the cry which fought to escape her lips.

'You mean that we will be taken prisoner?'

Sir Thomas looked long and hard at his son. He had hoped and prayed that the war would be over before it endangered Simon, but now that hope was gone. Worse still, he knew that he would not be here to protect his children. His voice shaking, Sir Thomas gave them the rest of the news.

'His Majesty orders that we hold out in Oxford for as long as possible. It is his hope that he will lead a Scottish army south before the city falls. I must return to Oxford to help in the defence.'

'And Benjamin?' Elizabeth's voice was soft, fearful for her new husband.

Sir Thomas hated to say the words, but knew that he must. 'Benjamin must come with me. You and Simon will have the care of the Manor until further notice. The garrison will remain here to protect you.'

'And if Oxford falls…?'

Sir Thomas shook his head. 'If Oxford falls then you will be safe enough here if I am not with you. In the past the Roundheads have left the families of Royalists untouched, their focus being on our fighting men. It is to the credit of Cromwell that he has never targeted the women and children, although that may be pure politics as this country will have to heal its wounds one day and both sides live together as one.'

'But what if we are finally defeated? What will happen to you if Parliament wins the war?'

'I cannot say, Simon. But if Oxford falls I will come home to you before anything else. This I promise before God. I will not leave you in danger.'

'But if the King orders you to…'

'If the King orders me to be elsewhere, Elizabeth, I shall go, but not until I have seen to the safety of my family. Do you believe this?' Elizabeth nodded at her father who turned towards his son. 'Simon?'

'Yes, Father. Whatever happens, we will wait for you here.'

Sir Thomas rose from behind his desk, a new weariness in his movements. 'Then Benjamin and I must leave. There is no more time to waste.' He looked at his small family with fear and longing. 'May God protect us all in the dreadful months that lie ahead of us.'

Chapter 14

June 25th 1646

Someone was shaking him roughly by the shoulder and whispering his name.

'Simon! Simon! Wake up!'

He groaned and rolled over. Stretching and rubbing the sleep from his eyes, he struggled to focus.

'Elizabeth?' He yawned. 'Is anything wrong? It is not yet light.'

'It is two thirty in the morning, Simon. Now wake up!'

Two thirty? Simon struggled to full wakefulness and sat up.

'What is wrong?'

'Just put on some clothes and come downstairs quickly. Father and Benjamin are here, and they would not tell me what it is about until we are all assembled.'

Simon dragged himself from his bed, swiftly pulling on shirt and breeches as Elizabeth left the room and made her way downstairs. He was not far behind her. Sir Thomas and Benjamin were in the kitchen, hastily filling bags with food and clothing. Simon's mouth went dry with fear as he struggled to find words.

'Benjamin?'

The young man stopped what he was doing and turned to his wife. She could see tiredness and despair etched on his features, and knew then to fear the worst.

'Oxford has fallen.'

Elizabeth stumbled, placing one hand on the wall to support herself and one on her belly as though she were about to vomit. 'Dear Lord God! Please let it not be true!'

'I am afraid that it is, child.'

Tears began to fall from Elizabeth's eyes at her father's words. Benjamin stepped forward and took her into his arms, wiping her tears with gentle fingers and speaking in a soothing whisper so low that Simon could not make out the words. The boy turned his fearful gaze towards Sir Thomas.

'What happens now, Father?'

Sir Thomas was silent, struggling with the words he knew he must say, yet all the time feeling a traitor to his children. 'Benjamin and I will be joining others of the King's supporters who are still free. We shall be going to the west, but shall not tell you where for fear of your safety.'

'You mean that you will be leaving us here?'

Sir Thomas turned sadly towards his son. 'I am afraid so.'

'But when the King surrendered, you promised that you would see to our safety!' Simon felt betrayed. 'You are abandoning us to the enemy!'

Sir Thomas shook his head sadly. 'That is not true, my son, though it may feel as such to you now. Benjamin and I have discussed this much over the last few days and are both in agreement. It is as I told you before, Parliament has never targeted Royalist families, so if you stay here and continue life quietly, without drawing attention to yourselves, you should be safe.'

'Should be?'

'Yes, son. I cannot guarantee it. But I guarantee that you will be safer here than if you come with us.'

'Who will protect us if the Roundheads come?'

'I do not believe they will attack the Manor if it appears peaceful and undefended so...'

'Undefended?' Elizabeth pulled herself from Benjamin's arms on hearing her father's words. 'You mean to take the soldiers with you?'

Sir Thomas swallowed hard as he turned towards his daughter. 'Yes, Elizabeth. We spoke to them as we arrived, and they already await us outside.'

Her eyes flashed angrily as she turned back towards her husband. 'And you agreed to this? To leave your wife and...' she hesitated, '...and young brother-in-law at the mercy of the enemy?'

Benjamin nodded. 'Your father is right. If there are no soldiers here then there is no reason for Parliament to attack. They will focus on trying to find the King's supporters. People like us.'

'I had not expected this of you, Father! I pray to God that you are right!'

Simon had never seen his sister so furious, and wondered at the change in her. To stand up to their father in such a manner! He felt his heart swell in love and pride.

'Do not worry, Elizabeth. If Father and Benjamin feel that they must desert us here, then I will ensure that you are safe. With the soldiers gone we shall call upon our loyal workers to support us. They know where their duty lies.'

Sir Thomas bowed his head sadly. 'You do not know how deeply those words wound me, my son. I know that my duty is to ensure the safety of my family before serving my King. Did I not promise that to you? But I truly believe that you will be in more danger if I remain here. His Majesty is a prisoner of the Scots and Oxford has fallen, but the war is not over. Cromwell has always shown justice and mercy to our supporters' families, and I do not believe that he will change now. Indeed he has less reason to do so for, whether we like it or not, the chances of our winning this war are now impossibly remote.'

Simon closed his eyes for a moment, thinking deeply, a frown furrowing his brow. He felt wounded, betrayed by his father. It appeared that he was breaking his promise and putting the King first. Yet, if he thought about it dispassionately, putting all emotion aside, then perhaps his father was right. How could he expect Elizabeth to live as a fugitive? Where could they go? What manner of place could they find to hide? Would they be on the move for months, maybe even years? It made some sense to remain at Marston, offering no resistance and trusting in the Lord to protect them. Finally, he nodded.

'I will do as you ask, Father, and keep the Manor safe for your return. I will protect Elizabeth for you both, with my life.'

Sir Thomas felt the relief wash over him like a flood. He could live with the fact that the King was a prisoner and that Oxford was in the hands of the enemy, but what he could never live with was the knowledge that he had driven his children to lose their respect for him, maybe even to hate him.

'Thank you, Simon.'

'And what of your father?' Elizabeth turned to her husband as she spoke. 'Will he be joining you?'

'Father is dead.'

'Oh, my poor Benjamin!'

This time it was Elizabeth's turn to offer comfort, embracing her husband as Sir Thomas spoke.

'He was wounded two days ago by a musket ball to the chest. He died a few hours later.' He turned to his son. 'Simon, please help me finish packing. We have to leave in a few minutes and I think Benjamin…'

Simon nodded. Benjamin needed time with Elizabeth. The young couple smiled gratefully and left the kitchen to stand in the hall, talking quietly as Simon and Sir Thomas finished putting together everything that they could find which would be useful in the days, and months, ahead. When they had finished, Sir Thomas held his son's gaze for a long silent minute. Neither needed to say anything for they both understood the others feelings. With a slight nod, Sir Thomas eventually reached out and embraced his son.

'I love you, Simon. Never forget that.'

'I love you too, Father.'

With that they picked up the packs and entered the hall.

'Elizabeth?'

The young woman turned to meet her father's gaze, then embraced him. 'God go with you and keep you safe. And please look after Benjamin for me.'

Sir Thomas kissed her gently on the forehead. 'I will look after him for you. Now come along, Benjamin. We must be away.'

Benjamin took his wife in his arms one more time and held her tightly, fearing to leave her but knowing that he must. At last he broke away and the two men left as swiftly as they had arrived. A moment later, Simon and Elizabeth heard the sound of hooves as they rode away with the last of the defending soldiers. Then that sound diminished and was gone. Simon turned to his sister and saw the tears falling on her cheeks.

'Do not worry, Elizabeth. I will make sure that the two of us remain safe, just as I promised father.'

She smiled sadly. 'Three.'

'Three?'

'I could not tell Benjamin because I knew that he had to go, and that leaving me here was distraction enough.'

'Elizabeth?'

She took her brother's hand in hers as the tears continued to fall.

'I am with child, Simon. And its father may die without ever knowing.'

Chapter 15

Present day

'What's wrong?'

'Sorry. Did I wake you?'

Caroline stretched as she sat up in bed. 'I suppose so. But it doesn't matter, I would have had to get up soon anyway. So, why are you up so early?"

Rob turned from the window. 'Just watching the sunrise. It's peaceful. Calming.'

'Why would you need calming at this time in the morning?'

Rob sighed. 'Trust you to pick up on the key word!'

'Well? Have you had another dream?'

Rob nodded. 'A continuation of Simon's story.' He ran his fingers through his hair as if to straighten his tangled thoughts. 'I didn't think I'd have one of my dreams away from the Manor.'

'And why not? The dreams are your mind processing your thoughts and feelings. They're not confined to a single place. You carry them with you.'

'I guess so. It's just that I've never had dreams like this before.'

'We don't know that for sure, Rob. Everyone dreams. Even you. The fact that you don't usually remember your dreams is irrelevant. This is new, yes; but not something to worry about.'

'You're right. I suppose I'll get used to it. It's just that they are so real. As though I'm actually experiencing what I'm dreaming about. Feeling all Simon's emotions...'

'Everyone experiences emotions in their dreams, Rob. I've dealt with people who have had the extremes of emotions, from fear to love and everything in between. Just relax and enjoy the dreams. There's nothing in them that can harm you. And they may even help you with your work!'

Rob smiled. 'I know. Thanks for getting everything into perspective for me.'

Caroline sighed. 'I wish you didn't have to go back today.'

'Sorry, love, but I shouldn't really have come in the first place. Paul will be annoyed at me, wasting time like this.'

'Then don't let him know. Tell him you had to come up here to do some research. Or something else to do with the job.'

'I suppose so. After all, putting my mind at rest will mean that I can work better anyway.' He stretched tiredly. 'I'll go and have a shower, then get out on the road.'

'When will you be coming up again?'

'I don't know. It all depends on how things go. Paul's pretty keen to keep things moving at a fast pace. I hope I can come back in a couple of weeks, but if not then why don't you come down for the weekend?'

Caroline smiled as she climbed out of bed.

'It's a deal. Now come on, I'll help you take that shower.'

***

Rob sat underneath the old apple trees on the boundary of the orchard. The dappled shade held back the heat of the day as he relaxed, taking in the vista before him. From where he sat he could see the old Manor house nestled in its fold in the hills. To the left were the barn and stables whilst to the right he could see where work had already begun on the formal gardens. It was a beautiful place. Warm and welcoming. He could hardly wait for the project to be completed. Rob smiled as he imagined the buildings which were spread out before him, thronged with people dressed in seventeenth century costumes. How amazing that he would be able to see how his ancestors had lived, what their house had been like, even taste some of the food they had eaten. When he had accepted the job of setting up the period Manor he had been excited; but knowing that this was where he came from, his roots, gave him a sense of ownership the like of which he had never felt before.

'Well met, Robert.'

Rob started at the sound of the voice, jumping to his feet. As he swung round his eyes met those of the young woman, and he smiled.

'Rebekah. It's good to see you.'

'I, also, am pleased to see you.' She smiled. 'I have seen you moving around the Manor but you always seem so busy and I feared to intrude. But today…'

'Today I am relaxing. Thinking of how this place must have looked in the past.' Rob returned her smile. 'But you shouldn't worry about disturbing me. My time is my own, and I will always be glad to talk with you.'

'I am glad that that is so, Robert.'

Rob felt the hairs on his neck stand up as she spoke his name, and wondered why that was so. Her voice, her way with words, her accent, all were totally outside his experience, so why did they seem so familiar? And why was he so happy to see her again? After all, he had only met her once before, and then for the briefest of times, yet he felt that, somehow, he belonged here with her.

'Why do you frown so?'

'Was I frowning?'

'Yes, it is as though some thought came to trouble your mind. May I help?'

It seemed as though she had read his mind and that she knew exactly what he was thinking. Far from feeling uncomfortable at this, Rob felt that it was the most natural thing in the world. He smiled.

'Just a stray thought, Rebekah, but nothing to concern you.'

'I am glad. I would not like to see you troubled, Robert.' She turned to look towards the Manor where a lorry had just arrived, laden with wood. 'What is it that you do at the big house?'

'We are trying to turn it into a tourist attraction. The idea is to re-create what it was like in the seventeenth century, at the time of the Civil War.'

Rebekah frowned. 'I do not understand. How can you create again that which is long past?'

'We will furnish it with items from the period. And get people to dress up in costume?'

'Why?'

Rob smiled. 'A tourist attraction. You know? Something for people to visit so that they can experience what life used to be like?'

'Why would they wish to do that? I am not educated, but I do know that life in the years of the war was hard. People suffered. Why would anyone wish to experience that?'

'You do ask the strangest, yet most pertinent questions! I suppose that, in one way, it is odd that we try to experience the past like this. But we do it in a sanitised way, of course.'

'What do you mean?'

'Well, we won't actually be hungry, or afraid of attack, or suffer illness or wounds. It is simply a way of trying to understand our history.'

'So you do not remember what it was like?'

It was Rob's turn to frown. 'How could I possibly remember what it was like? I'm only thirty, not over three hundred! There's no one alive today who can remember what happened.'

Rebekah was silent. Rob noticed a deep sadness in her eyes as she looked at the Manor. It was as though she could see something that his eyes could not; hear sounds that his ears could not. He had the strangest feeling that she could feel what life had been like when the Rebekah in his dreams had been alive. He felt his heart suddenly beat wildly, the sound of his pulse drumming in his ears. Why had he thought that the Rebekah in his dreams had been alive? After all, she was just a figment of his imagination. Yet when he looked at the young woman by his side, he could see in her the more mature features of the young girl of his dreams.

'You look at me strangely, Robert. Why is that?'

Rob turned away, flustered and uncomfortable with his thoughts, unable to explain how he felt. 'Perhaps you remind me of someone', he finally said. 'Someone I may have known before.'

Rebekah nodded. 'It is the same for me.'

Rob turned back to his companion. 'Good. Although I don't know where I know you from, I would like to get to know you better. Perhaps you would like to work at the Manor when Paul starts hiring?'

'Who is Paul?'

'He owns Marston Manor.'

Rebekah looked shocked. 'It does not belong to you?'

'No. I believe it belonged to my family in the past, but now it belongs to Paul Hetherington. He's employed me to run the project.' He threw a puzzled look at Rebekah. 'Why did you think I owned the Manor?'

She was silent for a moment. It was as though she wished to say something but was afraid to do so. Finally she spoke. 'It was an assumption on my part. One which I should not have made. I apologise, Robert, and ask your forgiveness.'

Rob reached out and took her hand in his. 'There's no need to apologise, Rebekah. It doesn't matter one way or the other. I'm just surprised you thought I was the owner.'

'It is merely that you seem to belong here.'

'And so do you.'

Rob was suddenly aware that he was holding her hand. It felt so natural, as though they belonged together in a way he had never felt with anyone else before. For a brief second he thought of Caroline, but drove the image of her from his mind. He almost felt guilty, as though thinking of her was a betrayal of Rebekah. But how could that be? She was little more than a child and he barely knew her, yet somehow she touched him in a way that no one had done before. It was as though the most natural thing in the world would be to take her in his arms and kiss her. He looked into her eyes and saw there the mirror of his own feelings. Her gaze seemed to stir emotions deep in his heart which had laid long buried but which were now coming back to life.

Without further thought, Rob leant down and touched his lips to hers.

Chapter 16

June 1646

Three days had passed since the midnight visit. Three days filled with fear and dread. But nothing happened. It seemed that Sir Thomas had been right after all, and his two children were safe. They were just beginning to relax when there was the sound of hooves in the courtyard. A maid ran into the breakfast room, her face white. She was wringing her hands in agitation.

'Master! Mistress! What shall we do?'

Elizabeth looked up from her breakfast. 'What is wrong, Mary?'

'Roundheads!'

The siblings looked at each other. The moment they had dreaded had arrived.

'Remember, Simon, speak truthfully to them. We do not know where father and Benjamin are so we cannot betray them. And lies will only antagonise the enemy.' Elizabeth rose from the table as she spoke. 'Show them to the library, Mary. We will speak to them there.' The maid nodded and left. There was the sound of heavy footfalls in the hall, then silence.

'I do not think I can do this, Elizabeth.'

'Yes you can. You are the head of the household now, so be brave.'

Simon nodded as he rose to his feet. Taking Elizabeth's hand in his, they made their hesitant way to the library. As they entered, their eyes were drawn to a half dozen soldiers standing to attention behind their father's desk, muskets in hand. Simon wondered if the weapons were charged or just for show. There was an officer seated at the desk and as Simon turned towards him his heart began to thump wildly.

'Sir Francis!'

'Good morning, Simon. Elizabeth.'

'I am not sure how you can describe it as a "good" morning, Sir Francis, with you seated in my father's chair backed by soldiers.'

Elizabeth had recovered first and her words were scathing. Simon cast her a worried glance, fearful that she had gone too far, but Sir Francis nodded in acknowledgement.

'My apologies, Mistress Elizabeth. I am aware that this situation does not appear good to you. It was a turn of phrase, nothing more.'

Elizabeth gave a small inclination of her head in acknowledgement. The exchange had given Simon a chance to recover himself. He drew himself up to his full height and took a deep breath. No matter what his feelings he must play the role of the Lord of the Manor.

'To what do we owe this pleasure, Sir Francis?'

'I am sure that you know the answer to that, Master Simon.' Sir Francis leant forward, placing his elbows on the desk and forming a steeple with his hands as he paused for a moment. Then the questions began.

'Where is your father?'

'We do not know.'

'Who is he with?'

'We do not know.'

Sir Francis cast a quizzical glance at Elizabeth.

'Is that true?'

Elizabeth placed a hand on her brother's arm. 'The truth, Simon. Remember, that is our best protection.'

'But...'

'Father is with my husband and the soldiers who were protecting this Manor. We do not know if they have met with anyone else.'

Sir Francis nodded in acknowledgement. 'Thank you, Mistress Elizabeth. So, when did you last see your father?'

'In the early hours of the morning of the 25th.'

'Did they say where they were going?'

'West,' Simon answered. 'But they refused to tell us more, for our own protection.'

'I see.' Sir Francis turned to his soldiers. 'Go and gather together all the estate workers. Meet me in the courtyard with them.' Five of the soldiers began to leave. 'You go with them,' Sir Francis ordered the last remaining soldier.

'But sir...'

Sir Francis smiled. 'I am in no danger here.'

The soldier saluted and left. When the three were alone, Sir Francis rose from behind the desk.

'Well, here we are again.'

'I have to thank you, sir, for your warning of the attack on the Manor. I believe you may have saved our lives.'

'It was as I promised you at the start of all this madness, Simon. Did I not say that I would do nothing to endanger you or your family?'

'Yes, but here you are...'

'Yes. Here I am. Three days after I should have been if I had visited the most important Royalist home in my area first. It was a risk for me not to do so.'

'Then why did you wait?'

'He waited to allow father to escape. Is that not so?'

There were footsteps in the hall and Sir Francis cast a fearful glance at the door. Thankfully, whoever it was continued on.

'Perhaps we should be a little more circumspect with our words?' he said softly. The other two nodded. 'I was ... er ... held up,' continued Sir Francis with a wry smile. 'I shall always very much regret it if that allowed any Royalists to escape my net. But now all Royalist sympathisers must be questioned.'

'Why you and not someone else?'

'Would you prefer someone else, Simon? Someone less sympathetic?'

Simon shook his head, realising that Sir Francis was using his position to protect them. He smiled gratefully. 'We have told you everything we know, Sir Francis.'

'I do not doubt that. Your father would not be foolish enough to endanger you by telling you of his plans, if indeed he had any so soon after the surrender of Oxford. I will fulfil my duty and question your workers, but I acknowledge that I shall learn little, if anything at all, from them.'

'Then what happens?'

'Marston Manor falls under my jurisdiction and I promise that, as long as you take care of the Manor and do nothing more, then you shall not be bothered.'

'Thank you, Sir Francis.'

'You are welcome, Mistress Elizabeth. I will, perhaps, need to make further reports. It would not disturb you if I were to come and see how you are progressing?'

Elizabeth smiled, though a parliamentarian Sir Francis was obviously doing his best to protect them as the family of his friend.

'You will be welcome here as always, Sir Francis.'

'Thank you. Now,' he made his way to the door as he spoke, 'if you will excuse me I must go and question everyone else.'

***

Sir Francis returned two weeks later, this time with just two soldiers accompanying him. As Simon watched the men approach, his heart was in his mouth. Was there news of his father and Benjamin? Were they safe? With a deep breath he controlled his nerves, his face impassive as the three men drew to a halt in front of the house.

'Good day to you, sirs.' He nodded towards the soldiers. 'If you would like to take the horses round to the back, I am sure something can be found for you to eat. Sir Francis,' he turned to his guest as he spoke, 'please do me the honour of joining me inside.' With that he turned and led the way into the house.

Sir Francis followed the youngster into the study, a smile on his face. 'You play the host well, Simon.'

Simon nodded. 'I do my best, in the absence of Father.' He indicated a chair. 'Please, be seated.'

A deep sigh escaped the man as he sat down. 'I miss my old friend, so can only imagine how much more you must miss him, my boy.'

'With the King in the hands of the Scots, it would seem that the war is all but over, although I hate to say it. Perhaps it will soon be possible for him to come home.'

'I certainly hope so. It is strange that, in the last weeks, many of those who have fought against the King now show a measure of sympathy for him. It is that Divine Right to rule that your father deems so important. There seems to be a feeling that the King has some sort of aura of divinity, that he has suffered in his role as God's anointed. This change in the opinions of the public is most puzzling.'

'Do you think that there will be a settlement with His Majesty?'

'I certainly hope so, Simon. After so many years of war we need to settle the peace swiftly.'

'But can Parliament come to terms acceptable to the King?'

'If they are wise they will do so. You know how I have fought for their cause. I still believe that the King was wrong in the way he treated his people. But the war has changed things. It saddens me to acknowledge that Parliament has been as bad, if not worse, than the King.'

'In what way? We are confined here, Sir Francis, and unable to hear the talk of ordinary folk.'

'As you know, this whole sorry conflict was started, in part, in protest against the taxes which the king demanded from the people. Yet, to wage the war, Parliament has raised even more taxes and people are much the poorer. They do not feel that they have achieved greater freedom, and with the soldiers billeted on them they feel that there is no respect for their property.'

Simon looked puzzled. 'It sounds to me that you have sympathy now with the Royalist cause?'

Sir Francis held up a hand. 'No, Simon, do not get me wrong. I still believe that it was right to go to war with the King to prevent his excesses. I am just a little disillusioned with Parliament for not fulfilling what the people wanted from them.'

'So what happens now?'

'No man is sure. The Royalist armies are disbanded, but much of the Parliamentarian army is still in arms. The soldiers are not happy. They have not been paid for some time, and will not be paid if Parliament cannot raise the money.'

'Surely the taxes will cover that?'

'That should be the case, but many people are now refusing to pay. They begrudgingly paid the tax on meat, beer and salt to be able to defeat the King. Now that he is no longer at liberty, they do not want to pay. They say that the money is needed to repair and replace what they have lost during the war.'

Simon gave a bitter laugh. 'Is this not the reverse of the situation when I first overheard you and Father arguing the matter?'

Sir Francis nodded. 'The irony is not lost on me, my boy. It seems that both my friend and I were right. What is needed now is the curbing of the power of both King *and* Parliament!'

'And how can that be achieved?'

'There are proposals that the King should share his power to choose his advisors and command the army.'

'He would never agree to that.'

'Perhaps if it was for a limited time until he showed good faith? Or maybe for his lifetime, with the full powers reverting to the Prince of Wales when he ascends the throne? Surely he could agree to that?'

'I am not sure that he would give up those rights. And what about the church?'

'The church.' Sir Francis shook his head. 'Parliament itself is divided on the matter of the church. Some want to retain the bishops, some want to keep the Prayer Book, some want total freedom from Rome.'

'Do they have nothing in common?'

'To move the church further from Rome is the only unifying factor.'

'How could that be achieved?'

'Parliamentary leaders could compromise and settle for the abolition of bishops.'

'The King would never accept that.'

Sir Francis threw up his hands in frustration. 'The King will have to accept the fact that he is in no position to quibble! Those who are defeated in war have to make concessions. It is the way of the world. If he is allowed to keep everything, then what have we been fighting for?'

'If I understand correctly what Father has told me, then I would say that the King does not believe the powers we have been discussing belong to him personally, but to be privileges and rights of the monarchy. What he could give up for himself, he will not give up for the Crown.'

'You may well be right. But where, then, does that leave us? There can be no settlement without the King, but Parliament is not willing to concede much. After all, they were the victors in this war.'

'Then let us pray that they all see reason, Sir Francis. Then Father can come home.'

The older man smiled sadly at Simon. 'That is the main reason for my coming today.'

'Is Father coming home?!' Simon felt his heart beat faster with excitement.

'I wanted you to hear from me that Parliament has granted parole to those Royalists who renounce the fight and give up their arms. They can then return home in peace.'

Simon was thoughtful. He knew his father. He would not consider the war won or lost until an agreement was reached and the King was free. Whether free to rule or in exile would not matter. He looked out of the window but did not see the familiar landscape; his thoughts were directed inwards. Sir Thomas would not leave the King. And that meant that he would not be coming home. The young man turned towards his companion.

Sir Francis nodded. 'I see by your face that you have come to the same conclusion as I have. Your father is honest and true. I do not believe that he will leave the King. I have come, therefore, to offer my promise once again. I will continue to watch over you in your father's stead. If you need me, do not hesitate to call.'

Simon turned back to the window so that Sir Francis would not see the childish tears that threatened in his eyes.

'Thank you, sir. We are in your debt.'

Chapter 17

End of January 1647

Simon heard another heart-rending cry from Elizabeth's room and shuddered. At fourteen years of age he had no experience of pregnancy and birth, and the thought of the coming hours filled him with dread. Sir Francis had been as good as his word and called in at Marston Manor every few weeks to ensure that they were doing well. His concern for their protection from other parliamentarians, as well as ensuring that they had enough workers to keep the estate running, touched Simon deeply. He was thankful that his father had such a good friend.

Simon had noticed that Sir Francis was beginning to look at Elizabeth speculatively, but it was not until late September that he had been bold enough to ask her about her condition. With a mixture of shyness and pride she had confirmed his suspicions, and Sir Francis had immediately arranged for a physician to visit her on a regular basis to ensure that her pregnancy progressed well. Simon knew that she had initially found it difficult to consult with a man, as Benjamin was the only person with whom she had ever been intimate in such a manner, but her concern for her child had won out in the end. It was not long before she was confident in placing her trust in Doctor Morton, and even looked forward to his visits.

Simon had been glad of the support of such a professional, knowing as he did how vital it would be to have someone at Elizabeth's side when her time came. Now the time had come and she was alone. He paced his room in frustration. The first early pains had come two nights ago and Elizabeth had endured them, saying nothing for fear that it might be a false alarm. But as she lay in bed the snow had begun to fall, gently at first and then harder, until a full blizzard was blowing. By the time morning came, Elizabeth knew that she really was in labour and asked Simon to send for the doctor. Simon had looked out into the raging storm and refused, knowing that to send a man out into such weather would be to send him to his death. He had hoped and prayed that the snow would stop falling and the wind would drop, but his prayers had not been answered. Instead he found himself pacing the length of his room uncounted times as he listened to his sister's cries and the whispered words of support from her maid. Simon knew that it was not uncommon for a woman to die in childbirth, which compounded his fear and feeling of complete helplessness.

At last the snow ceased to fall, and a weak sun broke through the grey clouds which hurried away southwards on the wings of the wind. With a quickening heart, Simon left his room and made his way swiftly to where his sister was lying in. He opened the door and slipped inside.

The air in the room was hot and stuffy. A fire had been lit to keep Elizabeth warm and to boil water for when it was needed. Herbs had been thrown onto the fire to sweeten the room, but Simon thought that what it really needed was a blast of fresh air. He took all of this in as he steeled himself to look towards the bed; when he found the courage to do so he was horrified. Elizabeth looked shrunken. Black circles ringed her eyes and stood out stark against her pale, almost white face, which was beaded with sweat. Her breath was coming in short gasps and her hands clenched the sheets as another cry escaped her. Simon felt sick. Never had he heard such agony in a voice before, save in those injured after the battle for the Manor, and he dared not think of how much pain his sister must be in. She turned onto her side and curled herself into a ball as she tried to control the pain whilst all the time the maid gently mopped her brow and whispered encouragingly. When she heard the door close, the maid looked up. Simon could see from her face that she was deeply worried. At last Elizabeth slowly relaxed as the wave of pain brought on by the contraction subsided.

'Elizabeth?' She did not respond to her name and Simon stepped closer to the bed. 'Elizabeth?'

Her eyes fluttered open. 'Simon? Where is Benjamin?'

'He is still with Father; you know that.'

Elizabeth frowned, then nodded. 'I wish he was here. This is taking so long that I fear for the baby. I wish he was here to see it in case...'

Her voice trailed off, and Simon reached down to gently take her hand. 'Do not think like that, Elizabeth. You and your child will both be well. The storm has almost stopped and I can send someone for the doctor. He will be here soon.'

Elizabeth relaxed visibly. 'Thank you, Simon. I am so afraid.'

'You do not need to be afraid. I will look after you, as I promised.'

Elizabeth smiled weakly then closed her eyes to rest before the next wave of pain should engulf her. Simon made his way over to the door, closely followed by the maid.

'How long do you think it will be before the doctor gets here, sir?'

Simon shrugged. 'The snow is deep and drifted. It will take someone at least four hours I would guess, to get to Doctor Morton and bring him here.'

The maid looked across at the bed then lowered her voice even further. 'I fear that may be too late, sir. Perhaps a local midwife...?'

Simon felt faint. Too late? Could he really lose Elizabeth and her child? He nodded numbly.

'Continue doing what you can for her. I will send for the doctor, but I also know of a healer close by. I will go and bring her.'

The maid nodded. 'I think that would be best, sir.'

Simon crossed to the bed once more and gently stroked his sister's brow.

'Elizabeth? I will send for the doctor now, and I am going to find someone else who will be able to help you. Hold on. It will not be much longer now.'

Elizabeth's eyes flickered open. 'Do not leave me, Simon.'

There were tears in Simon's eyes as he spoke. 'I must go, Elizabeth. But I will hurry back, I promise. Then all will be well.'

With that he turned and left the room, afraid to go yet afraid to stay. As he raced down the stairs, Elizabeth's screams pierced the winter air once more.

***

Simon had sent a man for Morton, but after having seen Elizabeth's condition for himself he knew that the maid was right to fear that his help would come too late. Now, as he rode into the clearing where Rebekah and her mother lived, he was shaking with a mixture of fear and cold. The house looked warm and cozy beneath its mantle of snow, but he knew that this was deceptive and it would be damp and uncomfortable inside. He sat for a moment, looking at the house, building up the courage to ask for help. He had not spoken with Rebekah and her mother since that awful day when he had learned of Henry Sawyer's death. He wondered if Ann's heart was still as full of hatred for him. He took a deep breath and straightened his spine. He would never know how she felt if he did not ask. Dismounting, he tethered his horse to a tree, along with the mare he had brought with him in the hope that Ann and Rebekah would accompany him back to the Manor. Then, taking a deep breath, he called out.

'Mistress Sawyer? Are you there?' Silence. 'Is anyone at home?' Although there was no answer, Simon knew there was someone there, as a patch of snow on the roof had melted and a thin whisp of smoke found its way out through the thatch.

'Please! I need your help! I am afraid that my sister might die!' As he called out the words, Simon knew that they were true and he did not lie. Fear knotted his stomach and dried his mouth, yet left his hands wet with sweat, and his cheeks wet with tears. 'Please?'

Finally the door was opened a crack. Simon made his way to the house and began to push the snow from the door with his feet until it could be opened further; then he stepped back. A moment later Ann Sawyer came out bundled in shawls against the bitter January cold. She looked older than Simon remembered, thin and tired, but her eyes were the same. They gazed at him in unconcealed animosity as she pushed a stray strand of hair from her face.

'What do you want?'

'It is my sister. She is in childbirth, has been for nigh on two days now. We could not send for a doctor because of the storm, and although I have sent for him now, I fear that it may be too late if we wait for him.'

'Women die in childbirth all the time. Why should it be different for your sister?'

'Surely you do all you can to help the village women when their time comes? It is said that you have saved many a life with your skill. All I ask is that you treat my sister in the same way.' As he was speaking Rebekah came out of the hut and stood beside her mother. Simon turned his tear-stained face towards her. 'Rebekah?'

'Mother.' Rebekah laid a gentle hand on Ann's arm as she spoke. 'Would you let a woman and child die because of Father's death?'

'The Bible says an "eye for an eye"; to me that says a life for a life,' Ann muttered, but Rebekah shook her head.

'You know that Father would not want an innocent woman and child to die in his name. And even if you are right, Simon lost his brother in the same battle. A life for a life. Surely the debt has been paid? Can we not put it behind us?' Ann said nothing. 'Look at him, Mother. This is the same Simon who you cared for as a boy when he fell from his horse. The same boy whom Father liked so much. The same boy who you said should not be involved in the war until he was a grown man. Will you drag him into it now while he is still just a boy?'

Ann turned and looked at Rebekah. 'You think I should help?'

'Oh, Mother! Do you think you could live with yourself if you did not, and she were to die? Maybe the child as well?'

Ann was silent for a moment, then nodded slowly. 'I do not know where such wisdom comes from in one your age, child. Maybe it is from the Lord.' She looked at Simon once more, and this time her eyes held a hint of compassion. 'The Bible also says "love your neighbour as yourself". Perhaps that is God's message which I must cling to.'

Simon's tears were flowing freely now. 'You will help?'

She nodded. 'I will come with you and see what can be done.'

***

When they entered Elizabeth's room, she lay so still and quiet that Simon feared for a moment that she was already dead. Then she opened her eyes and tried to focus on who had just come in.

'Benjamin?'

'No, sister, it is Simon. I have come back as I promised and look...' he moved as he spoke so that Elizabeth could see who accompanied him, '...I have brought someone to help. This is Mistress Sawyer, who is well experienced in childbirth. She will help you.'

'Doctor Morton?'

Ann Sawyer had taken in the scene while the two were talking, and was glad that she had come. How could she have thought, even for one minute, that a woman in childbirth should suffer because of the death of her husband? Woman? As she looked at the bed she realised that Elizabeth was not much more than a child herself. Throwing off her cloak, she went over to the fire and poured some hot water into a bowl; she used it to wash and warm her hands as she spoke. 'Do not worry about the doctor, child. By the time he gets here you will have your baby at the breast and he will have nothing to do. Now, let me look at you.' She moved over to the bed as she spoke. 'I am afraid that you will have to forgive my cold hands, my dear!'

Ann felt Elizabeth's swollen belly through her nightgown, which was wet with sweat. She spoke quietly to the maid as she worked. 'Are the contractions still strong?'

The maid shook her head. 'They are not as strong as they were. I have never been at a birth before, but I think she is too weak now.'

'No, she has strength enough, do you not my dear?' Ann spoke comfortingly. 'I believe that your child wants to come into this world feet first and has got himself stuck. Together we should be able to end this all in a matter of minutes.' She turned to her daughter. 'Rebekah, get out my linen thread, and place my small knife into the fire to clean it.'

Simon swallowed hard. 'Knife?'

Rebekah smiled at him shyly. 'Surely you have seen plenty of sheep give birth? You have seen how the mother breaks the cord which binds the two together? It is easier and safer if Mother cuts that cord for your sister. But do not worry, the mother and baby do not feel a thing.'

Simon turned to leave the room as the women got to work.

'Where do you think you are going?'

'I...'

'I will need Rebekah and your maid to help me. You will have to hold Elizabeth's hand, encourage her. Things will go more smoothly if someone she loves is with her.'

'But...'

Ann Sawyer smiled. 'Always "but" from you! This time though, you must listen and do as I say. Now go to the head of the bed and stand there.'

Simon nodded silently, afraid to speak as he took up his place and held Elizabeth's hand. After a moment he knelt facing his sister so that he could not see what the women were doing, but every word spoken was forever imprinted in his memory.

'Rebekah, and you my dear; what is your name?'

'Mary,' answered the maid.

'Well Mary, you two must hold her legs whilst I feel for the child. Can you do that? Good... Yes, I was right... I can feel the feet... Elizabeth my dear, I will guide his feet but you must try not to push until I tell you to. Do you understand? I want to have my hand on his head to help him through.'

Elizabeth nodded through gritted teeth. Simon squeezed her hand, whether to support her or through his own fear he did not know.

'Good ... now I have the feet...' Ann's voice was softly encouraging. 'It will not be long now, my dear... I feel the head ... the chord is around your baby's throat so we must go gently. Now ... push, my dear.'

Elizabeth groaned and bore down hard.

'Well done... And again... Good... Here it comes!'

Elizabeth relaxed visibly, and Simon turned round to see what was happening. Ann was holding a child, its skin blue beneath the blood, the thick rope from its birth was entangled around the baby's neck and it did not move. A wave of dizziness washed over Simon, but he forced himself to continue looking. As he watched, Rebekah passed a small knife to her mother, who cut the cord and gently removed it from around the baby's neck. She laid the child across her knee, and for long moments gently rubbed then slapped its back. There was no movement.

'My baby?'

No one spoke as Ann continued to work on the child, Simon could see the worry on her features and feared the worst. Then, suddenly, the baby convulsed and a harsh cry escaped its lips. Ann sighed and relaxed. 'Your baby is fine, my dear.' She gently wiped the child with a warm damp cloth, then wrapped it in a little woollen blanket before moving to the head of the bed and placing it in Elizabeth's arms. 'Say hello to your daughter.'

Elizabeth looked down at the child, and Simon's gaze followed hers. The blue colour had left the baby's face as the life-giving air filled her lungs. She seemed so tiny to Simon that he wondered how she could have survived such a birth unbroken.

'She is beautiful, Elizabeth.'

Elizabeth smiled but said nothing.

'Thank you for your help, Simon.' He turned to Ann as she spoke. 'The child will be exhausted after its long ordeal and will need to feed. And I need to deliver the afterbirth and make sure that your sister is comfortable. Perhaps you could wait downstairs for the doctor?'

Simon nodded and gladly left the room to the women, the relief that both Elizabeth and the child were alive washing over him like a flood.

***

Doctor Morton did not arrive for another two hours. Ann had completed her work and was sitting quietly by the fire when Simon and the doctor entered the room. Simon looked quickly around, then let out a gentle sigh of relief. The room was back to normal, the bed tidily made, the bowls of water and bloodied cloths gone. Rebekah was seated beside her mother, gently rocking the child in her arms whilst Elizabeth, looking exhausted but happy, lay on her bed and watched.

'Hello, Mistress Elizabeth. How are you feeling?' Morton made his way over to the bed as he spoke. Placing his hand on the young woman's brow he was pleased to note that she did not seem to have a fever.

'I am tired, sir, but I think that other than that things are well with me.'

The doctor turned to Ann. 'You delivered the child?'

She nodded. 'She came into the world feet first. The cord was around her neck and she took a moment to take her first breath.' Ann took the child from Rebekah and held it out towards the doctor. 'She is fine now, I believe.'

Morton took the child and laid her on the table before opening her blanket. As the cool air reached her skin, the baby cried. Everyone in the room smiled.

'There appears to be nothing wrong with her lungs!' The doctor swiftly but expertly examined the baby as he spoke. With a satisfied nod he wrapped her in her blankets once more, and handed her back to Rebekah. 'You have done a fine job. She seems perfect.'

'She is perfect.' Elizabeth's voice was soft and tired but filled with pride, and Morton smiled.

'She is indeed. Now, let us see how you have fared.' He turned to Simon. 'Perhaps you would like to wait for me in the study?'

Simon needed no further bidding and swiftly left the room, making his way downstairs where he waited anxiously for the doctor to finish his examination. It was not long before Morton joined him.

'How is she?' asked Simon anxiously.

The doctor smiled. 'She is fine, young man.'

'I am sorry that you had a wasted journey.'

The doctor shook his head. 'It was not wasted; I needed to see that she is well. Who sent for the midwife?'

'I did. Did I do right?'

'You most certainly did. I do not think that either the mother or child would have been alive when I arrived if not for her. She is a very skilled healer.'

'What happens now?'

'Your sister is exhausted after her ordeal so she will need to rest. Your maid will help to care for her and the child until Elizabeth feels well enough to rise.'

'Can I do anything to help? I promised Father and her husband that I would care for her.'

'Which you have nobly done. Your one concern now is to ensure that they are kept warm and well fed.'

Simon smiled. 'I think I can manage that.'

'Good. I shall return tomorrow just to make sure that all is well. Now,' Morton reached for his coat as he spoke, 'I had best be on my way so that I can reach home before dark.'

Simon showed the doctor to the door. 'Thank you, sir. I look forward to seeing you on the morrow.'

As Morton left and the door closed behind him Simon leant against the wall, his reaction to the last few hours causing him to shake with relief. After a moment he straightened and, with a broad smile began to make his way upstairs. He knew, deep down, that his father would be so proud of him, and that gave him almost as much joy as the birth of his niece.

Chapter 18

February 1647

A cold wind howled around the house. Simon was glad that he was inside and did not have to face such inclement weather. It had stopped raining two hours previously, just as the winter sun dipped below the horizon and the long dark night set in. He glanced across at Elizabeth who was seated on the other side of the fire, her face lit by its gentle yellow glow. He smiled. She was fully recovered now from the birth of her daughter, her skin no longer pale, no more dark rings beneath her eyes, which met his with an answering smile.

'Hark how the wind does moan, Simon. One could almost imagine fell beasts flying on its wings!'

Simon laughed. Her tales of ghosts and dragons no longer frightened him as they had done when he was a child. 'Yes, and if you listen carefully sister, you will hear the hooves of those whose business can only be conducted in the dark, too sinister for the light of day!'

Elizabeth cocked her head to one side as though listening, a small frown furrowing her brow. 'I think I hear them, Simon!'

Simon laughed. 'I am not a child any more, Elizabeth! You shall not be able to trick me like that!'

Elizabeth shook her head, no smile lighting her lips. 'Truly, Simon, I do believe I can hear horses! Listen!'

Simon was silent for a moment, straining to hear, then his eyes widened. 'You are right! Stay here and I will see who it is that ventures out in such weather and at such a time of day.' He went over to the desk and opened a drawer to reveal two pistols. He quickly charged them and moved towards the door as Elizabeth rose from her seat. 'Stay here I said!'

'But...'

'The baby is in the nursery and will be fine. Whoever it is will not be seeking a child. She will probably be safer there with Mary than with us, until we know who it is.'

Elizabeth nodded reluctantly, but said nothing as Simon opened the door and made his way into the hall. He stood for a moment, hidden by the curtains but able to look out through the window. He saw two horses being drawn to a halt in the courtyard, their riders tying them to a nearby post. He frowned. Only someone who had knowledge of Marston would have known that the post was there, it would have been impossible for a stranger to see it in the dark. He tightened his grip on the pistols, hoping it would help to still the trembling of his hands as the two riders made their way towards the house. They were well wrapped against the cold, their cloaks muffling the shape of their bodies, scarves covering most of their faces and hats pulled low. Chewing on his lower lip, Simon wondered what he should do. If he went outside to confront them, he would be at a disadvantage moving from the hall out into the deep darkness, and the opening of the door would alert them to his presence. Much as he disliked the thought, he believed that his best course of action would be to surprise them as they entered. He moved quickly across the hall to stand behind a pillar, which would hide him from view but give him a clear field of fire if he so chose. He cocked the pistols just as the handle on the door began to turn. The door opened swiftly and the two men entered, one turning to close the door behind him and so offering his back to Simon. He could see that both men wore swords, but neither carried a weapon in his hand.

'I would advise you to make no further move, sirs.'

The two men whirled towards the voice, unable to see who had spoken. The one in the lead lifted a hand.

'Please do not move, sir. I do not want to shoot you.' Simon was surprised at how calm and level his voice was, for it did not echo his feelings. He had not felt this afraid since the battle for the Manor. 'Now, tell me your names, and what your business is here.'

'Is that you, Simon? For the Lord's sake let us close the door and come in! Or do you intend to shoot your own father?'

Simon stood rooted to the spot. Although the voice was muffled by the scarf, it was unmistakable. His father was back! Stepping out from behind the pillar he carefully un-cocked the matchlock pistols before placing them on a small table.

'Father! And Benjamin?'

'Yes indeed, it is I,' said the second man as he closed the door.

'I am so sorry! I did not know that it was you! I would never have threatened to use the pistols if I had!'

The two men unwound their scarves and Simon could see that they were smiling.

'Never apologise for protecting your home and family, my son. The way you greeted us this evening makes me proud, and puts at rest any fears I may have had for the safety of yourself and your sister!'

Simon covered the ground between them in swift strides and embraced his father.

'It is so good to see you after all these months! Here...' he took their hats and scarves as he spoke, '...leave your wet things here and come into the study. Elizabeth and I spend most evenings there as it is so easy to keep the room warm.'

'Warm!' murmured his father.

'Elizabeth!' murmured Benjamin.

Simon opened the door to the study to find Elizabeth standing beside the fire, her knuckles white where they gripped the back of the chair.

'Who was it?'

Simon laughed. 'Two bedraggled rats that the cat dragged in!'

Elizabeth frowned, glad to see that there was no danger but wondering who could be calling at such a time, then her brother stepped aside and she saw who it was. Tears sprang to her eyes. 'Father! Benjamin!' Not knowing who to embrace first she placed an arm around the shoulders of each and drew them close. 'You do not know how much I have longed for this moment over the last eight months!'

'Is it only eight months?' Benjamin smiled down at his wife. 'It seems a lifetime since I last held you!'

'Much has happened to us in the months we have been away.' Sir Thomas moved over to the fire where he held out his hands to its warmth as he spoke.

'And much has happened here whilst you have been away. Elizabeth...' Simon caught his sister's imperceptible shake of the head and was flustered for a moment, obviously she did not want him to tell the news of her child. '...Elizabeth and I' he continued 'have fared well, in great part thanks to Sir Francis.'

'Sir Francis? What had he to do with matters?'

Simon smiled. 'Do not worry, Father. Marston still holds for the King, and would be seen as a threat if you were here. Parliament placed us in the charge of one of its own, and Sir Francis ensured that it would be he who questioned us and made sure that we did not aid the King.'

'Questioned?'

'Yes. But do not worry, Father,' Elizabeth smiled. 'Sir Francis remains true in his friendship to you, and has made sure that all is well with us to the best of his ability. We have been lucky.'

Benjamin entwined her warm fingers with his own cold digits. 'I shall welcome the opportunity to thank him, my dear, though who knows when that might be.' The young man smiled at his wife. 'You look well, my dear.' And indeed she did; she was as beautiful as he remembered, but more feminine in a way. She had been little more than a girl when they married, but the last year had seen her develop more womanly curves. There was also a light and beauty about her which was different, and something he could not quite define.

'Enough of me!' Elizabeth led her husband to a chair as she spoke. 'What news do you bring? How is the King?'

The two men looked at each other, their faces solemn, and Simon realised that it would not be good news. He went over to the desk and poured two brandies, which he handed to the men.

'Drink this, it will warm you. Then tell us your news, for I cannot wait until you have dried yourselves and eaten!'

Sir Thomas took the glass gratefully as Simon brought two more chairs to the fire and the family sat, together again for the first time in eight long months.

'You do not know how wonderful it feels to sit here in my own home again.' Sir Thomas sighed. 'We have spent most of the time since we last saw you at the King's side. In Scotland.' He smiled sadly. 'What an awful place! It has a strange rugged beauty in places, but not a place I could love like Oxfordshire. And the people! So dour. So uncommunicative.'

'But the King?'

Sir Thomas shook his head sadly. 'Throughout last year, His Majesty was constantly in touch with Parliament through his envoys.'

Simon nodded. 'Sir Francis has kept us informed, as much as possible, regarding the hopes of a settlement.'

'We all knew when Oxford fell that there was little hope of victory for us unless something changed dramatically,' his father continued. 'His Majesty was trying to convince Cromwell to reduce his demands. A face saving could then have resulted, the war ended and the King resumed his rightful place on the throne.'

'But that has not happened.'

'No, my dear.' Sir Thomas turned towards his daughter as he spoke. 'The King felt, and most rightly so, that Parliament could not be trusted. They would not allow him to keep his powers, and he could not act as a puppet for them. His pride would not allow it. So, also during the year, he was negotiating with the Scots.'

'At the same time?' Simon frowned. 'But I thought that he was trying to negotiate a peace with Parliament? I had assumed that Scotland was a refuge to him, nothing more.'

'That was a ruse, brother.'

Sir Thomas frowned at Benjamin. 'You know I do not like that word. It dishonours the King's actions. He had to negotiate for what is best for his kingdom, with whoever could help. To be in discussion with both Parliament and the Scots was a wise tactical move.'

'But one which made Parliament feel that they could not trust him.' Benjamin held up a hand to silence Sir Thomas's protest. 'I say that is what Parliament thought. It is not my belief and you know it, Sir Thomas. But we have to accept that talking to both at the same time is what has led to the sad situation which we face now.'

'But what is the situation?' Simon was on edge, sensing that something momentous had happened and fearing the worst. 'You tell us everything and nothing!'

'I am sorry, Simon. This is a continuation of a conversation which Benjamin and I have long been conducting, as you may well gather. The truth is though, that the King negotiated with Cromwell whilst at the same time trying to persuade the Scots to his cause so that they would invade England...'

'Invade! Have they done so?'

Simon took his sister's hand in his. 'Fear not, Elizabeth. If the Scots had invaded we would have heard of it by now.'

'Simon is right, my dear.' Benjamin held Elizabeth's other hand as he spoke. 'But I am afraid that it is far worse than that.'

'Worse? How could it be worse?'

'Unbeknown to His Majesty, the Scots were also playing a double game and were in negotiations with Parliament. Just days ago they sold the King to the enemy. For four hundred thousand pounds.'

'No! It cannot be true!'

'I am afraid it is, son.'

'Then we must rescue him!'

'I am afraid that that is not possible at the moment, Simon. And it is why we have ridden hard to be here ahead of the news. There may well be those who try to lead an army to free him, but they will not succeed. I could not let you join such a group and lose your life for nothing.'

'For nothing? What of the King?'

'It would be for nothing if he were not rescued. But do not think that we have abandoned him.' Sir Thomas smiled reassuringly at his son. 'His Majesty is being held at Holdenby Hall in Northamptonshire. When we have rested we shall resume our disguise and make our way there to see what can be done. We must show patience, my son, if we are to win our King back.'

Elizabeth's face fell. 'How long can you stay?'

'A night; two at most.' Benjamin's eyes held a deep sadness as he spoke. 'I wish I could stay longer, but it is impossible.'

Elizabeth nodded. 'I know. But I am so anxious for this war to be over so that we can be together in our own home. I hardly feel like I am married, living here with my brother.' She smiled at Simon. 'Please do not take offence at that, for you know how dearly I love you. And how much I owe you.'

Sir Thomas and Benjamin frowned.

'What is it that you owe your brother?'

Elizabeth and Simon smiled at each other before she turned to her father. 'I believe it will be easier for me to show you than to tell you. Please wait here.' With that she rose and left the room.

'Simon?'

The young man smiled at their puzzled expressions. 'Obviously she wishes to tell you herself, so please be patient. After all, you will only have to wait a few minutes whilst we have had to wait months for your news!'

Sir Thomas laughed. 'Touché, my son!'

Five minutes passed, a long five minutes for the three waiting in the study. Sir Thomas and Benjamin could not hide their curiosity, whilst Simon found it almost impossible not to blurt out Elizabeth's news. Only the anticipation of seeing the expressions on their faces when she came back held him silent. At last the door opened and Elizabeth entered, a bundle cradled in her arms.

'My dear Benjamin, you cannot believe how much I have prayed for this day.' She smiled across at the young man. 'Come. Let me introduce you to your daughter.'

Benjamin was thunderstruck. 'My ... daughter?'

As Benjamin rose and made his way with hesitant steps towards his wife, Simon turned towards Sir Thomas, laughing at the expression of surprised disbelief on his face.

'Yes. Welcome home, Grandfather!'

Benjamin reached out a tentative hand towards the bundle, then drew it back. Elizabeth smiled shyly as she held out the child.

'Take her, my dear. I have told her all about her father, and I am sure that she is longing to meet you.'

Benjamin took the child, holding her awkwardly. He studied the tiny face, relaxed in sleep, then looked up at his wife.

'She is beautiful. Is everything all right with her?'

Elizabeth nodded. 'She is perfect. Ten fingers. Ten toes.'

'Let me see.' Sir Thomas peered over the shoulder of his son-in-law, silent for a moment before turning to his daughter. 'She has the look of you as a baby.'

'She is so small. How old...?'

'Just weeks, my dear.'

'If I had only known I would have been here for you. I would never have left you.'

Elizabeth smiled sadly. 'Yes you would, Benjamin. Your loyalty to the King would demand that you leave. Had you know you would have spent far too much time worrying about me, and not focussing on what you had to do.'

'You knew then? When last I was here?'

Elizabeth nodded.

'My poor dear. You should have told me. To face this alone...'

'Not alone. I had Simon.'

Sir Thomas turned a questioning look towards his son. 'Simon?'

'Yes, Father. Although I had help. When Sir Francis realised Elizabeth's condition he made sure that she was attended regularly by a doctor to ensure that all progressed well.'

'Then I am doubly indebted to my old friend. And the birth?'

'It was ... difficult.'

Benjamin turned a worried gaze to his brother-in-law. 'Difficult? How so?'

'Her time came during the worst storm of the winter, and the child was ill-presented. But the doctor eventually came...'

'You do yourself a disservice, Simon.' Elizabeth turned to her father. 'You should be so proud of him, Father. He sent for the doctor, then went out himself to bring back a local woman who is experienced in these matters. If he had not done so, then you would likely have found me, and my child, lying together beneath the snow.'

'I just did what was needed.' Simon was embarrassed by the praise. 'I had promised father and Benjamin...'

'Simon, you can never know how much this means to me. I will be forever in your debt.'

'Not so, Benjamin. Do not forget that she is my sister. I would do anything for her!'

'I am so proud of you, son.' There were tears in Sir Thomas's eyes as he spoke. 'I did not say when we last left home, but I was worried about how you might cope with us gone. Yet here you are, still looking little more than a boy yet playing the role of a man! Your defence of your family tonight was admirable. And I, like Benjamin, will never be able to thank you enough for the life of my daughter. And...' he reached out a finger to gently stroke the cheek of the baby '...and the life of my little granddaughter.' He smiled at his son, before turning to Elizabeth. 'What do you call her?'

'Yes. Have you named her?'

Elizabeth frowned slightly at her husband's question. 'We did not know when you would return, and I could not just call her 'the baby,' so I have named her. But it is only a name we have used for a few weeks,' she added swiftly, 'it would be an easy matter to change it if you so wish?'

Benjamin smiled. 'Let me hear it first.'

'Ann.'

Benjamin's brow furrowed into a frown. 'Ann? I had thought maybe she would be named for your mother? Or mine?'

'I thought that, but did not know which of the two names you would prefer, so...'

'Why Ann?'

'For the woman who delivered her. It seemed fitting that she should be named for the woman who saved her life.'

'Indeed so!' Benjamin smiled indulgently at the small bundle in his arms. 'Hello, little Ann. And, with the permission of your mother and grandfather...' he looked at them both before gazing down at his daughter once more. He smiled. '...Mary for your mother's mother, and Henrietta for my own.'

Sir Thomas smiled. 'Ann Mary Henrietta de Vere. What a fine name.' He turned towards his son. 'Come, Simon, let us away to the kitchen to see what can be found to eat, while Benjamin gets to know his daughter!'

***

Sir Thomas saw much more of his son in the next two days than he did of his daughter. Benjamin and Elizabeth spent almost every hour of the day together with their child, storing up memories to last for the next period of separation, however long that might prove to be. Simon was sitting opposite his father in the study, puzzled by the slight frown which furrowed the older man's brow.

'What is wrong, Father?'

Sir Thomas laughed. 'I owe you an apology son! Last night I said that you were little more than a boy still. Yet when I look at you now I see the maturing of your features keeping apace with the maturity of your actions over the last few months. Technically, I suppose that you are still a boy...'

'I will be fifteen in a matter of months! Only two years younger than Thomas when he went to war!'

Sir Thomas smiled, a sad smile. 'I know, my son. Your look and your actions show that you are a young man.' He sighed. 'Seventeen. Such a young age for Thomas to go to war. And we all believed it would be long over before you had to face this conflict which tears our country apart. Yet, here we are, five years later and still at war.' He shook his head sadly. 'I pray that we shall free His Majesty and fight on to win this war and place him back on his throne. Yet time speeds on its way, and the longer that takes the more likely it is that you will be dragged into this. I could not bear to lose you too.'

'I am dragged into it already, Father. I may not hold a musket or sword and fight for the King, but I hold Marston for him in your absence.' He shook his head. 'Do you remember how I pleaded with you to allow me to go to war?' Sir Thomas nodded, but said nothing. 'How naïve I was,' Simon continued. 'All I want now is for the war to be over and for us to live in peace. Do not misunderstand me!' he continued hurriedly. 'I hope and pray that we will be the victors in this conflict, and I am prepared to fight to achieve that. But…'

'Be not ashamed of your "but" in this instance, my son. God grant that, no matter how bad matters appear now that the King is in the hands of Cromwell, this may be the catalyst needed for people to make the necessary compromises for peace.'

'Compromise. We really are no further forward than when I walked into your discussion with Sir Francis five years ago, are we? Save that so many good men, on both sides, lie dead.'

'And, though I hate to say the words, our King is in a vulnerable position we could not have dreamt of on that day.'

'What will happen now?'

Sir Thomas shook his head sadly. 'I do not know. But I guess that Cromwell will try to bring the king to his way of thinking. His Majesty may make some concessions. And they may be enough for him to keep his throne. But if not, then I fear that we will have to free him and fight on.'

'Will that be possible?'

'I cannot say, son. That is what we go to Holdenby to find out!'

Chapter 19

Present day

Rob urged Tully into a gallop and sped across the open pastureland. The thundering of hooves and the wind in his face took his breath away. The bunching of the horse's muscles beneath him, the sheer power of it, was exhilarating. As he rode, he concentrated hard on the ground in front of him to avoid rabbit holes which could cause the horse to fall. There was no room for thoughts of the dreams that were becoming increasingly real to him. There was no time to think of the family who had invaded his sleep yet again, drawing him into their reality so that he felt at one with Simon, experiencing his fear during his sister's labour, his excitement at the return of his father, his hopelessness at the news of the king. Feeling at one with horse and nature, a sense of freedom overwhelmed Rob and he laughed out loud. Reaching the end of the pastureland he gradually reined in the stallion until he was moving at a gentle trot. Rob reached down and patted the horse on the neck.

'Well done old boy! That certainly helped to blow the cobwebs away!' The horse tossed his head, as though in agreement, and Rob laughed again as he slowed the creature to a walk. 'Time to cool off before we head back home.'

Home. Rob frowned. Why was it that he was beginning to think of the Manor as his home? Surely he wasn't being influenced by the fact that his distant ancestors had once lived there? Or by his dreams? That would be absurd. When he thought of home he should be thinking of Durham, or maybe his childhood home in Faringdon. Yet, somehow, Marston Manor seemed to have displaced those places from his heart. Thoughts of Durham naturally led to thoughts of Caroline, and a wave of guilt washed over Rob. Unconsciously loosening the reins he gave Tully his head, letting him pick his own way home as Rob, frowning now, focused his thoughts inwards.

He had met Caroline during their first year at Durham University. The attraction was immediate and, apart from the year that Rob was studying for his post graduate teaching certificate, they had rarely been apart for any length of time. After gaining his PGCE he returned to Durham to take up his first teaching post, and it seemed the most natural thing in the world for him and Caroline to move in together. Their life had settled into a comfortable routine, with Caroline working as a psychologist for the health service and him immersing himself in school life. The disillusionment which had eventually engulfed him was with the teaching profession, not his personal relationship. Caroline had been with him, supporting him through his deepening dislike of the target-focused education system until he feared losing his love of history, seeing it overwhelmed by league tables and statistics. It was at that point that he decided to leave teaching and work in the archives of the university. He understood Caroline's fear that he might be burying himself there, but there seemed little else he could do if he wanted work with a focus on the English Civil War. It was at that point that Paul Hetherington had approached him to oversee the project at Marston. As usual, Caroline had been by his side, supporting, encouraging. Not once had he thought of living a life without her. Not once had he felt an attraction to another woman.

But now there was Rebekah. As he thought about the kiss they had shared, he closed his eyes and felt again the emotions she seemed to draw from him. Being with her seemed right and natural in a way that he had never thought possible. It was as though she were a part of him which had always been missing; which, perhaps, he had been searching for without even knowing it. Yet to kiss her was a betrayal of all that he and Caroline shared. He frowned as he tried to analyse his feelings. The way he felt about Caroline had not changed. He loved her and, if he had not met Rebekah, would have been content to spend the rest of his life with her. Yet Rebekah touched him deeper, more profoundly than he had ever thought possible. With a jolt he realised that he loved the young woman.

But how was that possible? How could he love a woman whom he had known for most of his adult life, someone who understood him completely and who he felt totally at ease with, yet also love another woman whom he had barely met? Did he really love Rebekah? As he probed his thoughts Rob was aware that his attraction to her, while stirring a need in him, was not purely physical. It was much more than that, although he struggled to define it. All he knew was that he felt totally alive when in her presence, as though he could do anything he wanted to do, be anyone he wanted to be, as long as she was by his side.

Feeling more confused than when he had set out on his early morning ride, Rob turned Tully back towards the Manor.

***

Rob looked at the sheets of paper spread across the desk in front of him; a mixture of handwritten notes, photocopied sheets and computer printouts. So much information on the Manor. A gold mine for the historian.

'What have you got there? Anything interesting?'

Rob turned at the sound of Paul's voice. 'It's all interesting, but I'm afraid there's not much relating to the period we're focusing on.'

'Where did it all come from?'

'I spent the day at the Oxfordshire History Centre. They have a lot of information on the Manor, most of it deposited there after the war.'

'Which war?'

Rob grinned. 'Sorry. As a historian I should be more specific. Second World War.'

'So why is it all spread out on the desk in my seventeenth century library?'

'Sorry. I suppose I should take one of the rooms upstairs as my office. It's just that this room has such a great atmosphere. A calming place to work.'

'Okay. For now. But get yourself an office sorted next week.'

'Yes, Paul.' Rob felt annoyed that he would not be able to work in the library, yet realised that his frustration was unreasonable. After all, it was Paul's Manor, his project. Rob would have to make sure that he did not make himself too comfortable while working there.

'So, how much of this relates to the Civil War?'

'Virtually nothing.'

'Then why make all these copies?'

'Just because I'm focusing on the seventeenth century doesn't mean I'm going to ignore the rest of the history of the Manor. It's all important.'

'But not likely to bring in money, so you can ignore it for now. Unless you're trying to research your own family history on my time?' Paul's voice was harsh, and Rob swiftly shook his head.

'No. Not at all. I was hoping for much more information from earlier times, but I may have to look elsewhere for it. Anyway, we can still use some of this. Maybe write a history of the Manor from its building to present day? Including your work in creating a period attraction? It's bound to sell.'

Paul was thoughtful, then nodded. 'Okay. I get where you're going with this one. But put it on hold for now. Concentrate on the renovations and setting up the Manor. If you want to write a book to go along with it, make it something to do with the Manor's role in the civil war. If we want to go ahead with the other book, that can come later.' Rob nodded. 'Good. Now I'm off to take a shower. It's been a hard day at the office, and I fancy putting my feet up with a nice bottle of scotch.'

Paul turned and left the room, but a distracted Rob barely saw him go. Was Paul right? Was he actually focusing his search of the records to try to find out more about his ancestors? If he was honest with himself, Rob thought that the accusation might be true, in part. But it didn't interfere with his work, so he would continue to find out as much about his family as he could.

Rob shivered. The room seemed suddenly cold and claustrophobic. He looked towards the window, but the scene outside was still lit by sunshine which bathed the courtyard in a warm glow. He wondered what it could be that had caused him to feel so cold, caused the hairs to stand up on the back of his neck.

'So, I find thee once again, Hardwycke? What is it that thou doest here?'

At the sound of the voice, Rob spun round. Standing beside the door was the same old woman he had seen in his dream when he first arrived at Marston. With a startled cry he leapt to his feet, knocking his chair to the floor.

'Who are you? What do you want?'

'Do not toy with me. I know that thou knowest who I am.'

'No, I don't!' But as he looked at the creased face he realised that she was not as old as he had first thought, maybe only in her forties. Beneath the strange purple hue of her skin there was something in her features that he recognised. He frowned, trying to place it. Then a cold fear spread in the pit of his stomach. The woman looked like Ann Sawyer, the peasant woman in his dreams. He knew that was impossible. Maybe this woman was her descendent. But where had she come from? What did she want? Rob took a step backwards, further away from the apparition, his voice tight with fear as he spoke. 'I don't understand who you are. Tell me what you want.'

'Thou knowest me well. I see it in thine eyes though thy words deny me. Again.' The woman's eyes blazed like fire, her voice filled with hatred. 'It is ever the way with thy kind, to treat us so. But be warned, thou wilt not succeed in what thou doest. I was weak before, unable to defend myself. But now the weakness is thine. Victory shall be mine this time and thou wilt pay for thy sins.'

'But...'

The old woman laughed, a cruel sound which silenced Rob's words on his lips. 'But? But! Always the same words from thee. Time has changed thee not. Yet its slow passage has changed me. Where once there was weakness there is now strength, and I promise thee that nothing of thy family wilt remain here when I am gone. Thou shalt lose all. Just as did I.'

Rob shook his head and closed his eyes. 'No. I don't understand you, and I deny you. You are nothing more than a figment of my imagination. This is nothing more than a dream.'

Silence was all that greeted his words. The room regained its former warmth. Cautiously, he reopened his eyes. There was no sign of the woman. The room was as it had been before, save for his chair lying on its side. Rob let out a breath he had not realised he had been holding. He felt himself beginning to relax. It was another dream, after all. He must have fallen asleep at the desk and begun to dream, only to be rudely awoken when he fell off his chair. No wonder he had felt disorientated! He picked up the chair and set it back beside the desk before heading towards the kitchen. What he needed now was a strong cup of coffee.

As he opened the door his phone rang. There was a rueful smile on his face as he took the phone from his pocket and answered it, but the smile was wiped away by the panicked voice on the line.

'Rob? It's Jim. Get over here. Now. The barn's on fire!'

***

Paul stood with Rob and Jim in the smoky barn. Firemen were raking through a pile of charred timbers where the builder's store of wood had so recently stood. To one side a new stud wall was badly burned, but there was little other damage.

'Thank God you caught it quickly.'

Jim nodded at Paul's words. 'Yes. It would have been a disaster if the fire had broken out during the night. The whole barn could have gone up. As it is, we'll need to replace the wood and get rid of anything that has been damaged by smoke. It'll only take a couple of days.'

'Good.' Rob let his eyes rove over the scene as he spoke. 'So it won't put back the finish date?'

'No. We built in some time for unforeseen events.'

'This certainly falls into that category.' Paul's face looked like thunder. 'I assume we're covered by insurance?' Jim nodded. 'Good.'

'Excuse me.' The three men turned at the sound of the voice. The fire officer who approached them removed his helmet and wiped the sweat from his face. 'Who's in charge here?'

'Well, I'm the manager,' Jim began, 'but this is Mr. Hetherington. He's the owner.'

'Good evening, sir. You've been lucky here.'

'Lucky?' Paul seemed outraged. 'How can you say that?'

'Sorry, sir. I only mean that your staff did well to contain things until we got here. Things could have been far worse.'

'Do you know how it started?'

'Well, I can't commit myself until we've finished our investigations, but it seems to have started in the wood pile. There's no smell of petrol or other accelerant so, for now, I'm working on the theory that it was an accident.'

'But it could have been arson?'

'As I said, I can't commit myself on that. Now, if you'll excuse me,' the officer turned as he spoke, 'I'll make sure that things are being damped down properly.'

Hetherington was frowning as he watched the retreating back. 'Can't commit himself? It's bloody obvious that those travellers did it. They'd do anything to annoy me.'

'We can't be sure of that, Paul.'

'You can't. But I can.' Paul glared at Jim. 'I'm going to the camp. It's time they were moved on.'

Rob laid a restraining hand on his employers arm. 'Don't do anything hasty, Paul. Let's wait for the fire officer's report.'

Paul glared at him. 'Remove your hand.' His voice was ice.

Rob quickly withdrew. 'I'm sorry. I was just thinking...'

'Well don't. I'm going there now, and you can't stop me.' Paul turned and strode towards the barn door.

'Jim?'

The estate manager looked equally exasperated. 'I'll go with him, Rob. You stay here and keep an eye on things.' With that he turned and hurried after his boss. Rob followed more slowly, exiting the barn in time to see Paul climb into the driver's side of Jim's land rover. Jim joined him in the passenger seat, and the vehicle sped away.

'Damn!' Rob didn't know Paul Hetherington well, but it was obvious that he was a harsh man. And he could have a temper. Rob worried about what would happen if the travellers were accused of starting the fire. Cowan wouldn't take it lying down. There was bound to be trouble. 'Shit!' Rob reached into his pocket for his phone, dialling for the police as he made his way swiftly towards his own car.

***

The land rover pulled into the campsite, throwing up a cloud of dust as it screeched to a halt. Paul jumped out, closely followed by Jim who stood by the vehicle, one eye on the shotgun in the footwell, the other on his boss.

'Where's Cowan?'

The small crowd of people who had gathered at the sound of the approaching car stood in silence. Watching. Hostile.

'Well? Where is he?'

Nothing.

There was the sound of another vehicle approaching, this time from the main road. It pulled in to park next to the landrover. Cowan climbed out.

'What are you doing here?'

'It's my land. Remember?' Paul stepped aggressively towards the other man. 'Where have you just come from?'

'That's none of your business. Now push off.'

'You started the fire, didn't you?'

'What fire? I've no idea what you're talking about.'

'Liar!' Hetherington stepped threateningly forward.

'Paul.'

'What?'

'I don't think this will get us far.' Jim stepped forward, reluctantly moving away from the gun. 'Let's wait for the report.'

Paul turned angrily towards his manager. 'Whose bloody side are you on?'

'Yours. But starting something here won't do us any good.'

Cowan laughed. 'That's right. Don't start nothing with me. You won't win. So bugger off!'

Jim stepped closer. 'You're wrong there, Cowan. It's just that you're not worth it. I wouldn't waste my time on a slug, so why would I waste it on you?'

'Why you arrogant bastard!' Cowan turned towards Jim, who nervously stood his ground. He didn't want to start a fight, but at least he had diverted attention from Paul. Maybe he could now calm it all down.

Cowan reached into his vehicle. Moments later he had a large cudgel in his hand as he stepped towards the two men from the Manor. 'Who do you think you are? Coming here, accusing me of starting some fire? Threatening me? I think you'd better leave.'

Jim looked around at the small crowd which was slowly moving closer. One or two of the men had drawn knives. He took a step towards Paul, laying a hand on his arm. 'Come on. We can deal with this later.'

Cowan laughed. 'That's right, you pussies. Piss off and leave us alone or…'

Cowan's rant was interrupted by the sound of sirens as a police car pulled off the main road and into the campsite, closely followed by Rob in his car, coming down the driveway from the opposite direction. Jim noticed that the knives which had been so much in evidence a few moments earlier had now disappeared.

'What the…?'

'What's wrong, Cowan? Scared?'

Cowan stepped forward, tightening his grip on the cudgel. 'I'm not frightened of you, you toffee-nosed git!'

The patrol car halted and two officers got out. They took in the state of things at a glance, moving to stand between Cowan and Hetherington. One officer placed his hand on his truncheon as a warning. The other looked at Paul.

'Was it you who called us?'

'Me? No.'

'That would be me.' Rob climbed out of his car as he spoke. 'I didn't expect you to be here this quickly.'

'The caller said that there was trouble here. The implication was that there was a fight.'

'I think there would have been, if you hadn't got here so quickly.' Rob turned to Jim as he spoke. 'Everything okay?'

'Yes. It is now.'

'No it isn't.' Cowan spat on the ground in front of Paul. 'This shit accuses me of starting a fire. Now you say I was going to start a fight. You weren't even here, so don't go accusing me!'

'Now then, sir.' The policeman's voice was placatory. 'This gentleman didn't say who was starting a fight, so no one's accusing you. Now, what's all this about a fire?'

'I've no bloody idea.'

'Yes, you do.' Paul took a step towards Cowan. 'Someone started a fire in my barn and...'

'And I wasn't here! I've been out all afternoon. On business.'

Paul laughed maliciously. 'So, who've you been cheating today, if you haven't been setting fire to my barn?'

'Now then, sir. I'm not sure that's necessary.'

Cowan laughed as Paul turned to the officer. 'God! Why is it that the authorities always take the side of these gyp ... travellers? My barn has been set on fire. It could have cost me thousands of pounds. Never mind endangering lives. And you don't think my being here talking to this ... man ... is necessary?'

'Do you have proof that this man started the fire?'

'Proof? He's been nothing but trouble since he arrived here with his gang of layabouts. Now there's a fire. What more proof do you need?'

'We need more than conjecture, sir.'

Cowan laughed at Paul's thunderous expression. 'That's right. Just piss off. I know my rights!'

Jim laid a hand on Paul's arm. 'Come on. Let's go and talk to the fire officer. Perhaps he can give us the evidence we need?'

Cowan stepped forward, raising his cudgel as he did so. 'Just what I'd expect! So you'll go up there and concoct some evidence to fit me up and...'

'That's not what he meant, and you know it!' Rob stepped forward. 'All he's saying is that we should go and see what evidence, if any, the fire officer has found. When we've seen that we can decide what to do next.'

'That's right.' The police officer moved forward in such a way that Paul was forced to take a step back towards the car, then another. 'We'll come up to the big house with you, sir. We'll soon get this sorted out.'

'But this is my land! You can't move me on and let him stay here!'

'Until I have evidence that he's done something wrong, I'm afraid that he has every right to stay here, sir.'

Cowan laughed. 'I told you you wouldn't be able to get rid of me that easily!'

'Why you...!'

The officer ignored Paul's outburst as he squared up to Cowan. 'I said I need evidence that you've done something wrong before I can move you on. And you've come close to giving me all I need by waving that about.' He indicated the cudgel as he spoke. 'Now, get rid of it. If I see it again, or hear that you've been threatening anyone with it, I'll get you moved on so fast your feet won't touch the ground.'

Cowan glared, then threw the club back into his car. 'Satisfied?'

'Yes, thank you, sir.' With that the officer turned to the three men from the Manor. 'Right, gentlemen. Please go back up to the big house. I'll join you in a moment and we'll see if there's any news about how this fire started.'

Jim urged Paul into the jeep, then drove away. Rob climbed into his car and followed them. Looking in his mirror, the last thing he saw was the police officer talking quietly with Cowan.

***

'Bloody gypos!'

'Look, Paul, the fire officer said it was an accident. You can't blame Cowan.'

'Yes I can.' Paul glared at Rob. 'It was them, or spontaneous combustion!'

'Now, come on...'

'No, Rob. Just because they can't find evidence of an accelerant doesn't mean that it wasn't started deliberately. Just setting a small fire of paper and wood shavings in the middle of the wood pile would have set it off.'

Rob sighed. Regardless of the evidence, Paul was going to blame the travellers. It was therefore in his own best interest not to disagree. 'I suppose you could be right. But there's nothing we can do about it.'

Muttering to himself, Paul kicked a pile of charred wood. Dust and ashes rose up in a grey cloud.

'The damage was small, so we can still open on schedule. At least we can be thankful for that. Come on,' Rob led the way out of the barn and towards the main house, 'I think we could both do with a drink.'

Once inside the library Rob poured them each a whisky. As he handed a heavy cut glass to Paul his eyes fell on his research papers on the desk. A sudden chill ran down his spine as he thought of his experience just before the fire. Just before the fire. Was that significant? Could the fire have had something to do with the old woman? Was she a ghost or just a dream? He shuddered.

'What's wrong?' Paul threw himself into a leather armchair.

Rob forced a smile. 'Oh, just thinking.' He paused for a moment, then 'Do you remember your dream about the old woman?'

Paul laughed. 'Of course! I really thought she was a ghost at the time. But it was just a dream.'

'Yes, but what about the stories that the Manor is haunted? And don't forget, I dreamt about her too.'

Paul threw a quizzical gaze at the historian. 'Where's this going?'

'Well,' Rob was hesitant, 'I dreamt about her again. At least I think it was a dream. I was in here and must have fallen asleep.' He frowned. 'She threatened me again. Said she's stronger than me. And I won't succeed in what I'm doing.'

'When was this?'

'Just before the fire started.'

'Hell's teeth, you're not suggesting that she started the fire?' Paul put his glass on the small table beside him as he spoke. 'Are you telling me that you believe in ghosts?'

Rob grinned ruefully. 'No, I guess not. It's just a coincidence.'

'Too right!'

Rob said nothing. Maybe it was a coincidence. But she had seemed so real. And why had he felt so cold and afraid? Yet, why would a ghost want to hurt him? What could he have done to inspire such hatred? Not liking where his thoughts were taking him he tried to focus on the work in hand.

'What have you been doing today?'

'You'll like this.' Paul smiled as he leant back in his chair. 'In one of my meetings at work they were discussing the Christmas do.'

'What, already? It's still only summer!'

'Forward planning, Rob. But it got me thinking. We should get a lot of people visiting here in the summer, but the winter will be quieter. Perhaps we can do some themed Christmas parties? Not just works dos. Maybe we could do some sort of Christmas market as well? What do you think?'

Rob grinned. 'A great idea! I'll do more research into Christmas celebrations on the Royalist side, before or during the first years of the war. After all, Cromwell banned all Christmas celebrations, so setting such parties in the years after the war would be a waste of time!' He was thoughtful for a moment, then, 'You've mentioned themed parties before, but this takes it one step further. And we could do wedding receptions.'

'Maybe have the weddings here as well?'

Rob nodded. 'I'm sure there's a market for that. Can you get some of your legal boys onto it? You'll need a license of some sort for marriages, and to serve alcohol.'

'I'll get onto it tomorrow. Right now, I need to relax.'

Taking the hint, Rob gathered up a sheaf of papers from the desk and left the room.

Chapter 20

November 1647

Simon ran his hand over the smooth leather of his notebook. He had never dreamt, when he first started keeping his own personal record of the war, that he would still be making entries so many years later. He was afraid that, if things did not improve, he would need another book before the war was finally over. Admittedly, the entries were fewer this year than they had been in the past. No battles, the King a prisoner. The land was not settled, yet there was little action, and little news. He glanced down at the last entries.

April 1647

It is two months now since we saw Father and Benjamin. As always they must keep secret to protect themselves, and us, so we have no idea where they might be. We had hoped against hope in February that they would be able to free the King. But nothing happened. Sir Francis told us that while His Majesty was being held in Northamptonshire, Cromwell and Parliament drew up proposals to put before him, describing the conditions under which he might govern in the future. I do not know what those conditions were, and Sir Francis was vague, but I can guess. They would have proposed limits to the King's powers to raise taxes; they would have insisted that they had the right to dictate the King's actions to a greater degree. No doubt they would have had conditions pertaining to how the King, and this country, should worship. I doubt there was anything new to their demands, only the fact that they held His Majesty changed the balance of things.

From what Sir Francis tells us, Parliament is treating His Majesty discourteously. Sir Francis himself seems to dislike this, although he is at pains not to say as much. To withhold the King's chaplains and household servants seems so petty. Do they think that His Majesty will bow to their demands in the hope that they will treat him with the respect he deserves? I believe he is a better man than that.

May 1647

It all seems so strange. While our army fought them the enemy were strong, but now that they hold the King, it appears to me that they weaken. The western and northern armies have been disbanded, but Parliament has not paid their arrears. It is said they argue that the soldiers have stolen so much from the population that the government owes them nothing. The Lord knows I hate the Roundheads, but I do feel for them in the way they are being treated. To have fought and not been paid their due seems a gross unfairness by Parliament.

Trouble continues in Ireland and it is said that Parliament wishes to send a part of the New Model Army to fight there. It seems that the men are not happy. They volunteered to fight for their beliefs, to fight the King. They take it badly that Parliament now intends to send them to a foreign land, perchance to die in a fight which they do not believe to be their own. It is said that Sir Thomas Fairfax has organised a petition to place before Parliament with their demands. From what Sir Francis has told me, these demands are little enough. The soldiers say that they fought for Parliament. All that they now want is freedom from prosecution for any of their actions during the war, their arrears of pay to be honoured, provision made for maimed soldiers and the widows and orphans of soldiers who died in battle. It would seem to me to be a fair asking. They also ask that those who volunteered to fight for Parliament should not be sent abroad to fight against their wishes. Parliament is taking this as mutiny, and orders Fairfax to desist. Are Parliament fools to now call these men who fought for them against the King, traitors? These actions do nothing more than enforce in me a belief that the King should rule alone, for these men appear to be nothing more than squabbling children!

It seems that Parliament have seen the error of their ways, or are afraid of the monster they have created in the New Model. They have agreed to payment of some of the arrears and given the soldiers partial indemnity for their actions during the war.

I hear that Parliament has granted money to London to prepare defences – against the army! It seems that they hope to drive a wedge between the officers and the men, but so far this is unsuccessful. I cannot say that I know all that has been happening, but Sir Francis has told me enough. These men wanted only their due money and rights, yet now Parliament seems to be pushing them to more drastic action. I can only hope, and pray, that these divisions will play into the hands of the King. Handing himself to the Scots may have been the best strategy after all!

June 1647
Oh how I wish I were not confined to the Manor, but could go out about the country and see for myself what is happening! My forced inactivity here chafes. While we were at war and there was ever danger of battle, I knew that to be here was the safest place for me. But now I want to be free to move around, free to find out for myself what now ails the country, instead of relying on Sir Francis. Free to be with Father. I do not know where he is, or what he is doing. Is he with the King? In hiding? If he knows, then Sir Francis is not telling. When will this stalemate be over and life begin again?

I hear from Sir Francis that on the 3rd of this month a junior officer, Coronet Joyce, took the King from his 'house arrest' at Holdenby House! Our benefactor appears to be as frustrated as I. He tells me that the King has spent the first months of this year discussing with different factions amongst Parliament. The Lord alone knows what he hopes to achieve by this. If Parliament is divided there can be no hope of a settlement.

Sir Francis says that His Majesty appears to have gone willingly with his new captor, perhaps seeing it as one more way of playing the rival groups one against the other.

It seems the New Model are treating the King with more courtesy than Parliament did when he was in their hands. He is now allowed his chaplains, I can only guess what comfort it must be to him to be able to worship properly once more. He has been taken to the main body of the army at Newmarket. It would seem that the New Model now believe that they can only get satisfaction for their grievances as part of a wider political settlement – and for that they need the King. It appears that they hold him no personal animosity, nor indeed us Royalists as a whole. It makes my head hurt! I am no closer to understanding the politics of this matter than I was when I first began my records in this book when I was a child!

Strange that all I know of what happens now comes from our enemy. I find it hard to call Sir Francis such, but I must do so, for he still stands with Parliament against our beloved King. But strange enemy is he. Still he cares for us in our father's place. And still he brings us the news which would be so difficult for us to come by as Royalists. There are always rumours admittedly, but nothing can take the place of hard fact.

Today he tells me that the army put together a manifesto placing their grievances in the wider context of the nation. They are claiming the right to propose measures designed to settle the kingdom and to achieve the ends for which the war was fought. One can hardly hold that against them, for it is they who fought the battles. They hold that they are not a mere mercenary army, hired to serve any arbitrary power of state, but called forth and conjured by Parliament to the defence of its own, and the people's, just rights and liberties. They say that they took up arms in judgement and conscience against all arbitrary powers whatsoever. It seems that they now see Parliament in the same light as they once saw the King, as an arbitrary power which does not defend their liberties. Oh, how fickle fate can be! These soldiers who once opposed my King because he wished to rule without a Parliament now call for the removal from that body of those guilty of corruption and unjust proceedings against the army. The wheel is turning, and brings us back round towards where this whole sorry affair began!

The army demands that a date be set for the end of this Parliament and measures taken to ensure regular Parliaments in the future. They even want the electoral system to be made fairer, which would make the Commons more answerable to the people, and biennial elections. A step far beyond what the King ever did! They want the powers of Parliament to be defined and limited. They also address the role of the King, limiting his veto over legislation and the militia. Whatever controls they wish to place on His Majesty would be for a ten year span, after which he could rule again in his divinely appointed way. I know little, but to me this seems a way to peace. I pray to God that all will take it!

I believe that the army thought they might bring the whole matter to a conclusion if they could negotiate a deal with the King. Fairfax has said that he seeks a tender, equitable and moderate dealing both towards His Majesty, his royal family and his late party, and sees this as the most hopeful course to take away the seeds of war. But the King has rejected the proposals. I must own that I become frustrated with him, although I could say that to none other and only admit it here in these pages. Here was a way to end it all, but he refuses! I have only seen His Majesty on two occasions, but he appeared to me to be so certain of his role as God's Divine Ruler that he cannot conceive this country without him in full control. I can no longer conceive of it with him in that position. Can he not see that this compromise is better than exile?

August 1647

The New Model has entered the city of London and dismantled the city defences. They have set up their headquarters near London, in Putney.

The country seems as disheartened by these protracted manoeuvres and negotiations as I. The one positive I see in it all is that many people are becoming disgruntled with Parliament, and turning back towards the King. If only we had had such support last year!

I have talked long with Sir Francis around these matters, and we can see but two choices. Either things are settled on the King's terms, which would mean abandoning all that the war had been fought for, or a settlement must be reached without him. Both are unthinkable. Sir Francis believes that the King is the biggest obstacle to a settlement. I say nothing openly but, if all that he tells me is true, then I have to agree with him.

As Simon read the last entry, he wished it could all be over and things return to how they had been before the war. But it could never be as it was. Thomas was dead. Elizabeth was married. And he was no longer a boy. The sound of approaching hooves broke into his reverie and Simon rose quickly to his feet. They had few visitors so it must be Sir Francis, although why he should be coming at night Simon could not guess. With a furtive glance towards the door, he rose quickly to his feet and hurried to hide his book on the shelves behind the desk. Sir Francis had proved to be a great friend over the last year, but if he were to find and read the book Simon felt that he would have no choice but to denounce the young man.

With a deep breath Simon made his way out into the courtyard, where his face broke into a broad grin when he identified the riders.

'Father! Benjamin!'

The two men dismounted and handed their reins to the young man, who swiftly tied them to a ring in the wall.

'Shall we go inside, son?'

Simon nodded as he led the way, sure that there must be some news for the two men to come again, at night. He fought down his eager questions until they were inside, where his sister waited anxiously in the hallway. Her face broke into a smile to equal Simon's.

'Benjamin! Father! Oh, how I have missed you both!'

'No more than I have missed you. And our daughter. How fares she?'

'She is well, my husband. She has grown so much in the last ten months that you will not know her!'

Simon took the travelling cloaks from the two men as they made their way into the study where they seated themselves comfortably. Simon could hold his impatience no more.

'Do you bring news?'

Sir Thomas smiled. 'Yes, my dear boy.' He paused for effect. 'The King has escaped!'

There was stunned silence for a moment, then Elizabeth spoke. 'How?'

'He was being treated well by his captors,' Sir Thomas began. 'He had his own servants with him and his accommodation was almost palatial. They had even brought some of his paintings from Whitehall for his pleasure. The suite of rooms he was being held in overlooked the Privy Garden, so it cannot be described as a prison, save that he was not at liberty to leave.'

'But leave he did!' Benjamin laughed.

'So what happened?' Simon could hardly wait to hear. 'Was there a great deal of fighting? Loss of life?' He wore a puzzled frown. 'Why are you laughing, Benjamin?'

'Because of the manner of his escape. Each day at five o'clock the King was accompanied to chapel by Colonel Whalley. On this day His Majesty's servants said that the King was writing letters and should not be disturbed, so the Colonel left. The same happened at six o'clock. At seven, Whalley was worried that the King's servants might be hiding the fact that he was, perhaps, ill. So he looked through the keyhole to the King's room but could see nothing so he began to bang on the door, but still could get no entrance. Whalley had to go down to the Privy Gardens and up the Privy stairs to enter the King's bedchamber. What do you think he found?'

Simon leant forward in his eagerness. 'I do not know! What did he find?'

'The King's cloak, but no sign of the King himself!' Benjamin laughed again. 'It seems that His Majesty had been long gone. Maybe as long as five hours! He had locked his bedchamber, crept down the stairs to where a boat was waiting for him at the river's edge, and escaped!'

'How could he have been held so loosely?' Elizabeth was puzzled. 'Surely Cromwell does not want the King to be free again?'

'No. But perhaps he no longer wanted him held by the army, and so helped his escape.'

Sir Thomas turned his puzzled gaze towards his son.

'What makes you say that?'

He shrugged. 'I am not sure. It is just that...' His words petered out.

'Go on, Simon.'

Simon lifted his gaze to his father's and rushed on. 'I have been talking with Sir Francis, and he seems to reflect a growing frustration with the way that negotiations have been going. Or more correctly, have not been going. I think that Cromwell and his Parliamentarians are beginning to fear the power of the New Model Army. With the King in their hands they are strengthened. Maybe Cromwell allowed the escape, to weaken the army? If the King were at loose, even for a short period, would it not re-unite the factions against him, and bring the army back to Parliament's heels?'

Sir Thomas shook his head in amazement. 'I forget sometimes that you are now more man than boy. Your thinking is clear. Save that the King is free and not in Cromwell's grasp.'

'As long as he is able to remain free. Where is he now?'

'We do not know,' said Sir Thomas. 'That is why we have come home, to await news. I believe his plan was to make for the continent to raise troops to fight Parliament once more. We have let it be known to those that matter that we will be waiting here at Marston, in hiding of course, when His Majesty needs us.'

'When did this happen?'

'Yesterday, brother. So we shall probably hear no news for a few days yet.'

'Enough talk.' Elizabeth rose to her feet as she spoke. 'You must both be hungry and tired, so I will get some food, then we will find somewhere for you to rest for the night. Morning will be time enough to plan your hiding.'

'But I have so many questions!' Simon was exasperated. 'I want to know all about Putney and...'

'Putney?' Sir Thomas looked surprised. 'You are becoming quite the politician, my boy. But your sister is right. That can wait until the morrow. Tonight we want to eat and drink, and hear about your life here at Marston for the last months. Tonight is for family. Tomorrow is soon enough for politics!'

***

Simon and his father sat together in a small room beneath the eaves of the house. Benjamin was spending time with Elizabeth and Ann, so the two were alone. Sir Thomas smiled across at his son.

'How you have grown in the months since I last saw you. You are quite the young man!'

'I am fifteen, Father.'

'Fifteen! I look at you and know it to be so, but my heart and memory say otherwise.' He sighed. 'I am sorry that I have been away, and not here to watch you grow. To guide you.'

Simon recognised in his father his own frustrations. He nodded. 'I wish you had been here, too. I have tried so hard to look after the Manor for you, but I am sure that I have failed in many instances.'

Sir Thomas shook his head. 'You are wrong there! The Manor is healthy, thriving as much as any can in such troubled times. You have kept yourself, your sister and your niece safe. You appear to know what is happening politically, yet have not endangered yourself by speaking out. I am proud of you, my son.'

Simon felt his colour rising, although he was more than pleased at the praise. 'Thank you. I have done my best. But could not have done half so well without Elizabeth. Or Sir Francis.'

Sir Thomas's look was thoughtful. 'You mentioned yesterday evening that you had been discussing politics with him. Is that wise?'

'It is safe, Father. Although he has said nothing, I know that he takes his vow to you seriously. He has kept us safe, and I believe that he tries to further my education with these discussions.' He grinned. 'I do not tell him all of my thoughts. At times when there are matters I wish to discuss he allows me to play devil's advocate.'

'I can see that I owe my old friend a great deal. I only hope that I will be in a position to repay him some day. Now,' his manner became more brusque, 'yesterday evening you mentioned Putney. What do you know? And what do you want to know?'

'I know that it was a meeting between the New Model Army and their civilian associates. Mainly the Levellers. Sir Francis said that they began talks towards the end of last month, but I do not know if they have finished yet. Or if so, what was decided.'

'The talks finished on the ninth of this month.'

'Two days before the King's escape? Are the two linked?'

'Maybe. The army were demanding the right to freedom of conscience, freedom from impressment for service in Ireland, and indemnity for soldiers for their actions during the war.'

'Little change from their previous demands.'

'True, although they were also asking that this Parliament should dissolve by the first of September next year, and that there should be provision made for biennial Parliaments which could sit for no more than six months at a time. They also want Parliament to review the franchise and how seats are to be distributed. They argue that the monarchy and the Lords should continue, but with reduced powers. Then there is the whole question of who should control the army.'

'They are trying to dictate to the King *and* Parliament? Do they have the power to do so? Surely Cromwell will not be happy with such a state of affairs? He will never let the New Model Army dictate terms to him!'

'That is so. But both the New Model and Parliament are becoming frustrated with His Majesty's refusal to come to terms.'

'Can you blame them?'

Sir Thomas frowned. 'What do you mean?'

'I mean no disrespect to His Majesty, but surely this could all have been settled months ago if he had been willing to compromise?'

'And give up his royal prerogatives? He could not do that.' His frown deepened. 'Perhaps you have been spending too long with Sir Francis?'

'No, Father! It is just that *someone* has to compromise. Perhaps His Majesty could give up some rights for his lifetime which would be restored to his heir? Or maybe he could abdicate in favour of the Prince of Wales, on the understanding that the new King has all of the powers of the old? It would not be ideal, but perhaps it could bring the war to an end at last.'

Sir Thomas sighed. 'I am afraid we both know that His Majesty is more of an oak than a willow and will not bend with the storm. Sadly, our enemy knows the same. At Putney they also began to discuss what should be done with the King.'

'How do you mean? Done with him?'

'This stalemate cannot go on for ever. Some wish to send him into exile and put his son on the throne. Some wish to exile his whole family and have a country without a king.'

'England without a king? Surely not!'

Sir Thomas smiled. 'I see that you are still as strongly for the monarchy as ever.'

'I cannot imagine that anyone, even the enemy, believes that England can stay strong without a king.'

'I pray that the country agrees with you. Although some, notably that damned Colonel Harrison, believe that the King should be tried and executed.'

'No!'

'Yes, I am afraid so.'

Simon shook his head in disbelief. 'I am sure that will never happen!'

Sir Thomas nodded. 'I do not believe that even Cromwell wishes that. But you may have been right yesterday evening. Cromwell would not have wanted the King to remain in the power of the Army. He may have helped His Majesty's escape, or at least not hindered it.'

'So what happens now?'

'We wait to hear from the King. If all goes well and he is able to secure troops from abroad he may be able to take advantage of the divisions within the enemy and finally win this war.'

'And if not?'

'I do not know, my son. But I fear the answer.'

***

The two fugitives had been at Marston Manor for three days. While daily life continued around them, they hid themselves in the small room where Sir Thomas and Simon had had their conversation. But at night, when all the servants but two had been dismissed, they were free to move around the house at will. These two house servants knew that their master was home, but would have died before giving the men up.

Benjamin and Elizabeth had retired for the night, leaving father and son to go over the estate books. Sir Thomas nodded proudly.

'As I said. You have done well, Simon. I know that I can leave things in your capable hands.'

Simon sighed in frustration. 'Although I do not wish to go to war, I do wish that I could travel with you when you go. I feel like a prisoner here!'

'I am sorry. I know that your youth has not been as it should have been. But for the war we would have travelled together. You would have spent time in London at court, met young men of your own age. I know how galling it must be.'

'I do not think you do!' Simon's voice was harsh, then he smiled sheepishly. 'I am sorry, Father.'

Sir Thomas smiled. 'You are right. It must be...'

There was a hurried knock at the door and a servant entered. Sir Thomas frowned to see the fear in his eyes. He opened his mouth to speak, but the servant shook his head. Never taking his eyes from Sir Thomas, he addressed Simon in a loud voice.

'Master Simon. Sir Francis is here. In the hallway. He wishes to speak with you.'

Father and son looked at each other in fear, before Simon turned and made his way towards the door.

'I am coming.'

As he left the room Sir Thomas made his way over to stand behind the door, where he could hear but not be seen.

Once in the hall, with the door partially closed behind him, Simon waved a dismissive hand to the servant who retreated to the kitchen.

'Good evening, Sir Francis. To what do we owe this pleasure?'

Sir Francis looked pointedly towards the study. 'I cannot stay long, a few moments only, so I will decline the comfort of the study if I may.' He looked back at the young man. 'A rumour reached my ear that two vagabonds passed this way a few nights ago. I assume that they may still be in the area and so wished to give you warning.'

'Vagabonds you say? We saw no one.'

'That is good. You heard that the King escaped?' Simon nodded but said nothing as Sir Francis continued. 'His freedom did not last long. He has been retaken.'

'What? So soon!'

Sir Francis frowned. 'Careful, Simon.'

'I only mean that the army must have acted swiftly.'

Sir Francis nodded. 'It seems to me that this was the last bold attempt of a desperate man, and that the King will now have no choice but to concede.'

'Where is he to be held?'

'At Carisbrooke Castle, on the Isle of Wight. His gaoler is Colonel Hammond.'

'Cromwell's nephew?'

'Yes. By all accounts he is not best pleased to play this role. His brother is one of the King's favourite clergymen, so Hammond finds himself in a cleft stick.'

'But he will hold him?'

'Of course.' He looked towards the study again. 'I would advise any Royalist who has not already given their parole to do so, so that they may return home and live in peace.' He sighed. 'I wish your father would do that. I miss his friendship greatly.'

Simon shook his head. 'He has been with the King from the start. I doubt he will give his parole. He will remain loyal until this whole business is settled.'

Sir Francis nodded as his gaze once more sought out Simon. 'I would assume so.' His features softened. 'I am going to be busy over the next weeks and months, and may not be able to come to visit as often as I have in the past. Indeed, my time will be so short that perhaps it would be better if I were to send a message in advance of my visit, to ensure that you are ready to receive me?'

Simon desperately wanted to look towards the study. Did Sir Francis know that his father and Benjamin were there? Was he saying that he would give warning of his visits so that they could hide? His mouth felt dry and his hands shook. With a great effort at a calmness he did not feel, he spoke.

'Thank you. That would be most agreeable.'

'Good.' Sir Francis turned towards the door, then stopped. 'No doubt with the situation as it is, there will be many vagabonds in the area. I shall not have the time to chase them all down. So, unless they cross my path, I will find a better use for my time. Good evening, Simon.'

'Good evening, sir.'

Simon watched the older man make his way towards his horse. It had been tethered some way from the house, which is why he had not heard its approach. Within moments, Sir Francis had mounted and ridden away. Simon went inside, closing the door behind him and leaning weakly against it, before summoning his strength and hurrying to the study. His father was waiting for him inside.

'He knows that we are here.'

'Then you will have to leave.'

Sir Thomas shook his head. 'I think not. If he had wished to take us, Francis would have arrived at the gallop with a troop of soldiers. Riding so that we could not hear his approach and take fright was a message; as were his words. He knows we are here. And as long as we stay hidden and do nothing he will not betray us.'

'But that means he is betraying Parliament!'

'Perhaps. But he seems to genuinely believe that it is all over now, save for the signing of an agreement, and that we are no longer a threat.' Sir Thomas's features were bitter, angry. 'Maybe he is right. If the King has been taken again, and I have no reason to doubt Francis's word, then I do not know what we can do to end on the winning side.'

'You are giving up?'

Sir Thomas looked down at his son, his eyes steely. 'No, never that. I will wait here, as agreed, until I hear from the King. Then I will serve him. As always.'

Chapter 21

December 1647

Simon found that he was looking forward to Christmas. His father and Benjamin must stay in hiding, of course, but at least they would be together. He smiled happily as he rode into the village. To be able to celebrate Christmas as a family was something that he had missed. Simon tethered his horse and made his way into the church, where he greeted the priest warmly.

'Good morning. And a merry Christmas to you.'

The priest frowned. 'A merry Christmas indeed.' He sounded bitter, angry. Simon was puzzled.

'I have just come to ask what arrangements you are making for the Christmas celebrations tomorrow.'

The priest shook his head sadly. 'Obviously you have not heard the news. There will be no celebrations. Christmas has been banned this year.'

'Banned? But that is impossible! How can we not celebrate the birth of our Lord!'

'Oh, we can hold a church service, as long as it is Puritan. But Cromwell has said that there are to be no celebrations. The birth of our Lord Jesus is too serious a matter for that!' he spluttered.

Simon shook his head in disbelief. 'There has been little enough to celebrate over the last few years. The people will not like this.'

'The Puritans should have no complaints, after all this is how they want to worship. But they should leave us to worship in our own way, too.'

'That is never going to happen.' Simon sighed deeply. 'So we can come to church on the morrow for the midnight service as usual?'

'Yes, sir. If you can call the truncated act that I must perform a service!'

'Just remain strong. We will celebrate joyfully in our hearts, even if we cannot do so in our church!' With that Simon turned and left.

'Master Simon!'

The young man turned at the sound of the voice. He smiled when he saw the woman and girl.

'Mistress Sawyer. Rebekah. I would take the liberty of wishing you a merry Christmas had I not just been informed that there is to be no Christmas this year!'

Rebekah looked unhappy. 'Father would have hated that.'

'But he was a Puritan!'

'Yes,' Ann nodded towards Simon as she spoke. 'He believed in a simple form of worship. But he also believed that there should be joy in worship too.' She sighed. 'I understand the ruling. Christmas is not about the drunkenness and debauchery which we so often see, but surely that could be limited without banning all celebrations?'

'Yes. And Master Sawyer also believed in the freedom to worship as one chooses. Is that not so?' Ann Sawyer nodded as Simon continued. 'He would not agree with Parliament preventing people of my church from celebrating Christmas with our usual rituals.'

'He fought, and died, for freedom of worship. Now we see the people he fought for taking it from us.' Rebekah sounded bitter. 'Did he die for nothing?'

'No, of course not.' Simon spoke comfortingly. 'Neither side will have everything they want when this war is over, but I do believe that you will have the better life that your father dreamed of.'

'And what of you? What...'

Rebekah's voice was drowned out by the sound of chanting from the end of the street and the three people turned to see what was happening. A group of youths ran around the corner, feet slipping in the mud. They waved wreathes of holly above their heads as they came, laughing and slapping each other on the back as they called out.

'Merry Christmas! Merry Christmas! Merry Christmas!'

'What in the Lord's name are they doing?' asked Ann.

'They look to me to have taken a little too much beer.' Simon shepherded Rebekah and her mother to the side of the street as he spoke. 'It seems we are not the only ones who think that there should be Christmas celebrations!'

Rebekah laughed gaily as she waved at the crowd of youths. 'Merry Christmas!'

Ann Sawyer slapped down her daughter's hand. 'Hold your tongue, child!'

Rebekah was shocked. 'What is wrong, mother? It is merely harmless fun.'

'Fun maybe, though anything but harmless.'

Simon nodded. 'Your mother is right. The authorities will not let them get away with this.' He watched the approaching youths intently. 'If I may be so bold as to suggest that we leave here?'

Ann nodded and turned to follow him down the street, away from the crowd. The trio had gone no more than a few steps when hoof-beats were heard ahead of them and a small group of riders came around the corner.

'Sir Francis's men. They should be reasonable.'

As if to prove the lie of his words, Simon watched as the horsemen approached, clubs in hand. The chanting from the other end of the street faltered for a moment as the youths saw the horsemen, then one voice cried out loudly.

'A merry Christmas to you all!'

The leader of the horsemen held up his hand and called a halt before riding a few steps closer to the youths.

'You know that Christmas celebrations are forbidden. Go back to your homes in peace.' Although his words were conciliatory, Simon could see the tension in the young rider's shoulders, and realised with a sickening clarity that they were trapped between the two groups. He gently pushed his companions back against the wall and stood in front of them. The leader of the youths at the end of the street took a couple of hesitant steps forward.

'We will not go home!' he called. 'Why do you not join us?'

'It would make sense,' Rebekah muttered, but Simon shook his head.

'No doubt they have their orders. They will not let this go.'

'But they are just drunken boys making merry!'

'I know, Mistress Sawyer. But a ruling by Parliament must be upheld. Stay quiet and they may leave us alone.'

The chant was taken up again at the end of the street. 'Merry Christmas! Merry Christmas! Merry Christmas!'

Simon watched the group of riders. The officer in charge raised his hand as he urged his horse into a slow trot.

'Stay behind me and stay down!' Simon held out his arms to shield Rebekah and her mother as the horses approached. He watched in horror as the first blow was struck, a club knocking the leading youth to the floor. There was stunned silence for a moment, then the cries of 'merry Christmas' suddenly turned to shouts of anger as the youths ran forwards to meet their attackers. Riders swung left and right into the crowd, drawing blood and breaking bones. After the initial charge the small group of revellers regrouped, dragging one of the men from his horse and raining blows on his head. The clubs swung again as Simon turned to his charges.

'We must get out of here. Come on.'

As he led the way towards the end of the street Simon could still hear the cries of anger and pain behind him. To his dismay, he saw another group of horsemen rounding the corner ahead of them.

'Get down!'

The two women scrambled to do his bidding and Simon crouched above them protectively. He saw the club descend towards his head and raised his arm to deflect the blow. He felt a flash of pain as he fell back, stumbling against Rebekah who fell to the ground. Mercifully the rider continued on his way to join the melee at the other end of the street. The sounds of anger were already dying down, the small group of youths no match for the mounted men. Seconds later Simon saw another rider galloping around the corner, his voice ringing out.

'Withdraw! Halt! Withdraw, damn you!' Simon recognised Sir Francis as he flashed past, urging his horse between his men and those on the ground. 'Enough, do you hear! Halt!'

The riders finally reined in their horses and lowered their weapons.

'What in the Lord's name do you think you are doing?'

The lead rider flinched at the fury in the older man's voice. 'Our duty, sir. You ordered us to stop any celebrations of Christmas.'

'But not by beating up a few drunken boys!' Sir Francis glared around him angrily before turning back to the mounted men. 'Let me make myself perfectly clear now. You will not allow any Christmas celebrations. If any take place you will arrest those responsible. If it looks to come to blows, then you stand back and send for me. Is that clear?' There was a murmur from the horsemen. 'I said is that clear?' There was ice in Sir Francis's voice and the men flinched.

'Yes, sir.'

'Good.' Sir Francis looked around at the angry crowd which was gathering. 'Now get back to camp. I will clean up your mess.' He watched as the horsemen turned and rode away, then turned back to the crowd which was slowly approaching. He took a deep breath and spoke softly. 'Come and tend to your injured. I give you my word that there will be no more violence. But mark my words.' A touch of steel crept into his voice. 'Parliament has ordered that there will be no Christmas celebrations. The day shall be treated as any other Sabbath. It would be wise to abide by that ruling.'

With that he gave a nod of his head and turned to ride back along the street. He had passed the three people crouched on the ground before recognition hit him and he turned.

'Simon?'

The young man grimaced in pain as he rose to his feet. 'Sir Francis.'

'What are you doing here?'

'Visiting the church. Then protecting these innocents from your men.'

Sir Francis looked at Rebekah and her mother cowering behind Simon. His eyes were sad. 'I am sorry for what you have witnessed. Please make your way home in safety.'

Rebekah cast a worried look at Simon as her mother spoke.

'Will you be able to travel home alone, master?'

Simon smiled. 'Yes. Thank you, Mistress Sawyer. Now that the men have gone, you will be safe.'

'But what of you?'

Sir Francis looked at the young girl who had spoken. 'I guarantee that Master Simon will come to no harm.'

Ann Sawyer nodded. 'Come, Rebekah, we must go.' She took her daughter by the hand before casting an angry glare at Sir Francis. Then she turned to Simon. 'Thank you for your help, sir. And a merry Christmas to you.'

With that she turned and walked away. Sir Francis watched her go. 'Who was that?'

'A Puritan whose husband died for your cause. To protect people like these from overbearing lords who treated them badly.'

Sir Francis's eyes were sad when they met Simon's. 'It seems that the peace will be as hard to win as the war.' His eyes dropped to Simon's arm, which hung at an awkward angle. 'Are you hurt?'

Simon nodded, clenching his teeth against the pain. 'I think it is broken.'

Sir Francis hurriedly dismounted as the young man began to sway on his feet. 'Come on lad. Let me get you to a doctor.'

***

Christmas had not been what Simon had hoped for; a short service was held at church with no decorations or festivities. But at least the family had been able to celebrate quietly together at home, although Simon's enjoyment had been spoilt by his anger at what he had seen. He knew that Sir Francis would never have ordered the attack, but that was not the point. He had believed, after all of his talks with his father's friend, that a settlement between King and Parliament was the only way forward. Now he was not so sure. Could they honestly leave the country to a ruling group who would ban all celebrations? Who would perpetrate violence against a group of boys, who simply wanted to enjoy a few mugs of beer and celebrate Christmas? He found himself thinking even more deeply about the war. He knew that the King had often overstepped his rights and that the people had some cause to ask him to moderate his rule, to play the part of a divinely appointed monarch who protected and cared for his people. He had even hoped that a compromise could be negotiated. But would it be possible to negotiate with a parliament which was so entrenched in its thinking? He sighed deeply. It was now New Year's Eve. 1648 was about to begin. What would the new year bring?

There was a knock at the door and a servant entered. Sir Thomas looked up from his book.

'Yes?'

'A messenger has arrived, sir. On foot. He says that he has a letter for the Lord of the Manor.'

There was a palpable tension in the room. Was it a message from the King at last? Or was it a trick?

'Where is he?'

'In the hallway, sir.'

Sir Thomas made his way to the door and peered through the crack at its hinges. After a moment he turned back to those in the room.

'I know this man. Wait here.' With that he turned and left the study. No one spoke, but Simon could see that Benjamin was just as nervous as he. Elizabeth had gone over to where her daughter played on a rug in front of the fire and picked her up protectively. Moments later Sir Thomas again entered the room.

'Is the news good?'

Sir Thomas turned to his son in law. 'I do not know. I do not know what to think!' He instinctively looked up at the empty space where the portrait of King Charles had once hung on the wall, then turned back to face his family. 'The King has made yet another agreement with the Scots. An invasion is coming!'

Chapter 22

Present day

Rob rubbed his left arm to try to ease his discomfort. It had been hurting since he woke up, and he assumed that he must have slept in an unusual position, which had caused the muscles to knot. He refused to let himself think about the fact that his arm ached in exactly the same place as Simon's arm had been broken in his dream. To think that the two were connected was just too much to contemplate. Thankfully, the throbbing which had engulfed his arm when he woke was now little more than a dull ache, and diminishing all the time.

As he looked at the smoke-damaged barn, Rob wondered if they would ever find the cause of the blaze. The investigation showed that a small, fierce fire had started in the wood pile, but there was still no indication of an accelerant. The forensic officer was puzzled. If the wood had been stored outside, the fire could have been caused by sunlight concentrated through a piece of glass. But the interior of the barn had been dim. His official report would say that the fire had been an accident, but Rob knew that he was not happy with the open-ended conclusions.

'I am sorry about the fire. It should not have happened.'

Rob whirled round at the sound of the voice, then smiled. 'Rebekah! You startled me! I didn't hear you coming.'

Rebekah returned his smile. 'That is not unusual. It is well known that I tread lightly.' She turned to gaze once more at the charred heap of timber. 'I wish that this had not happened.'

Rob frowned. 'Do you know something about how the fire started? Was it Cowan?'

Rebekah shook her head. 'The people from the camp have not been here.'

'But you sound as though you think it's deliberate.'

'Perhaps it is that someone else harbours evil thoughts. If so, they may have done this.'

'Who else would feel like that? Can you tell me?'

Rebekah dropped her gaze to the floor. 'I am sorry, Robert. I was not here so I cannot say what happened.'

'But you would tell me if you knew?' There was silence. 'Rebekah?'

The young woman finally raised her eyes to his. 'If I could show to you who had started this fire and why, then I would do so.'

'Promise?'

'Yes. I do so swear.'

'Okay.' Rob felt that there was something Rebekah was not telling him, something hidden that he could not quite put his finger on. He was puzzled, and absent-mindedly rubbed his arm as he pondered her words.

'Are you in pain, Robert?'

'What?'

'You hold your arm as though you are in pain, and your brow is furrowed.'

'Well, yes. My arm aches a little.'

'What injury have you done?'

'Now that's the strange thing.' Rob was silent for a moment, then, 'You promise you won't laugh?'

'Why should an injury to your arm cause me mirth?'

'Because I haven't really injured it.' Rob took a deep breath. 'I've been having the strangest dreams. In the last one I broke my arm. When I woke up my arm was still aching. How weird is that?'

'Weird? I do not know the word.'

'Strange. Unusual. Not normal.'

Rebekah nodded. 'I understand. Yes, it would appear strange for such a thing to happen. But the world is full of strangeness which we are unable to explain. What happened in your dream?'

'Well, the really weird thing is that I've been having dreams ever since I came here. Dreams about someone called Simon, who looks just like me when I was younger. And dreams about a girl called Rebekah, who looks like you.'

'What happens to Simon and Rebekah in your dreams?'

'They are living in a time hundreds of years ago, when the country was at war. I seem to be dreaming about the war through their eyes.'

'What happened to your arm in your dream?'

'It was broken by a soldier during a skirmish. Christmas 1647.'

Rebekah was silent.

'I knew it! You think I'm mad, don't you!'

'No, Robert, I do not think that you have lost your senses.'

'Then how can you explain what I've been experiencing?'

'Maybe the spirits of Simon and Rebekah are speaking to you in your dreams.'

'You mean ghosts?'

'Perhaps.'

'You actually believe in ghosts?'

'There are many things in this world that we are unable to see with our eyes, or hear with our ears. But they still exist.'

'You mean like oxygen? Or electricity?'

'I do not understand those words. I only say that maybe unhappy spirits live on after death. That they may be all around us.'

'Why would Rebekah and Simon be unhappy?'

'You do not know?'

'No.'

'Then perhaps that is why they invade your dreams. To tell you their story.'

Rob laughed. 'I can't believe I'm having this conversation! Ghosts from the past talking to me in my dreams?' He laughed again. 'Well, Rebekah, you have certainly cheered me up!' Rebekah smiled a strange, enigmatic smile, but said nothing as Rob continued. 'I really enjoy your company! Do you fancy going out with me sometime?'

'Going out?'

'Yes, you know. Spending time together? Getting to know each other?'

'Are we not doing that?'

'Yes, I just mean something a little more … intimate.'

Rebekah smiled. 'You mean walking out together?'

Walking out? Rob frowned at the old fashioned expression. Rebekah's strange use of language was one of the things which intrigued him about her. But it also seemed to point to an innocence in her which was unusual. Would he be taking advantage of her if they went out together? And what about Caroline? He had not thought of her when he had made his suggestion. What did that say about their relationship? Why had he suggested taking Rebekah out in the first place? His confusion must have shown on his face, for Rebekah laid a gentle hand on his arm.

'I do not think that I should walk out with you, Robert. At least, not yet. I think that it would be wise for us to know each other better first. And besides, I cannot leave this place.'

'What do you mean? Can't leave here? Does Cowan make sure that everyone stays in or around the camp all the time? Why don't you stand up for yourself?'

'It is my choice to remain here, Robert. When those who camp in the woods move on, I will remain.'

'You're not part of their group?' Rebekah shook her head. 'Then where do you live?'

'My home is close by. One day I shall show it to you.'

Rob shook his head. 'You really puzzle me, Rebekah.' He smiled. 'But that's what I like about you. I tell you what. If you are local and will be living round here for the foreseeable future, why don't you take a job with us? That way you can come and go as you please, and we will have the chance to get to know each other better.'

'A job?'

'Yes. Perhaps as a character inhabiting the Manor?' He looked around thoughtfully. 'How would you like to work in the other barn? Perhaps looking after the cows? You would dress up in costume and learn all about the dairy three hundred years ago, so that you could tell visitors.'

Rebekah let out a peel of laughter. 'A dairy maid?'

'Yes.' Rob looked sheepish. 'Sorry if you don't like the idea. There are lots of other characters you could play. Or you could do some other work if you prefer. Just say that you would like to work here. And spend more time with me.'

'Do not worry. I have experience with cattle. I can even make butter and cheese. I am sure that I would do most well as a dairy maid!'

As Rebekah continued to laugh, Rob wondered what it was about the idea that she found so amusing.

Chapter 23

January 1648

A light winter snow had fallen overnight, leaving the gardens covered with a blanket of white. Sir Thomas breathed in deeply, savouring the fresh, clean air.

'It is good to be home. I have missed Marston.'

'And Marston has missed you.'

Sir Thomas smiled sadly at his son. 'It will be hard to leave again.'

'Will you have to?'

'Yes. As soon as we know what His Majesty expects of us.'

'When will that be?'

'I expect a messenger today. That is why we are taking this stroll to the orchard.' Father and son reached the edge of the trees as he spoke. There was a rustling amongst the trees and a young man stepped out.

'Good morning, Sir Thomas.'

'Good morning.' He indicated Simon, by his side. 'This is my son.'

The messenger nodded towards the young man but said nothing as he retrieved a letter from his leather satchel. 'From the King.'

Sir Thomas took it and slipped it inside his coat. 'Thank you. Can we provide you with some food perhaps?'

The messenger shook his head. 'Thank you, but no. I have other messages to deliver and am on a tight schedule.'

Sir Thomas nodded. 'Good luck.' With that he turned and walked away. A second later Simon turned to follow him, barely controlling his eager excitement.

'Who was that?'

'It is best that you do not know. Let us just say that he is a loyal friend.'

'Did you deliver letters like that when you were away?'

Sir Thomas looked across at the eager face of his son, surprised to find that they were now almost of a height. 'Sometimes. But more often I was the recipient. As today.'

'What does it say?'

Sir Thomas laughed. 'You know that I have not read it, so how can I know what it says!'

'But, are you not going to open it?'

The smile left his father's eyes. 'Of course. But it should not be where prying eyes might see. Our servants who are working close to the house know that I am here, but I do not want to stay outside for too long in case we are seen by someone else. I will read it inside.'

Five minutes later they were seated beside the fire in the study when Benjamin came in to join them.

'You have a letter?'

Sir Thomas nodded as he broke the seal and began to read. There was a moment's silence.

'What does it say?'

Sir Thomas looked at his son, then turned back to the letter and began to read.

Sir Thomas,

You had only the slightest of news telling of my Engagement with the Scots. I can understand that you will have been eager for more news, and I thank you for your patience.'

'Not that we could have done anything about it anyway.'

Sir Thomas smiled at Benjamin's interruption, then continued.

It would be unwise of me to tell how the negotiations were conducted from my prison here, suffice to say that the subjects of my other realm have agreed to bring an army into England. The purpose is to restore me to the throne of England with the full powers and privileges that pertain to such high office.

It was not easy to secure such a promise, but when they were informed that I had been carried away from Holdenby against my will by the army, my loyal subjects north of the border were incensed. They have undertaken to join with me and take me directly to the Commons to negotiate with the men who sit there. In return, I shall establish the Presbyterian Church in England for a period of three years, and promote an Act of Parliament to suppress any sects.

'Replace the Church of England with the Presbyterians? Surely he does not mean to do so?'

Benjamin turned to Simon with a frown. 'I would hope not, brother. To do so is a sign of desperation. Perhaps he only says this to gain the support of the Scots, but does not intend to carry it through.'

'Benjamin! You malign the good name of His Majesty!'

'Come now, Sir Thomas. We both know that this would not be the first time that he has negotiated with no intention of upholding his side of the bargain.'

Sir Thomas sighed. 'I must accept that you are right. Although I feel a traitor to do so.'

'You are no traitor, sir. His Majesty could find no more loyal a follower than you. You have been at his side since this started, and will be there at the end. It is no fault of yours that the king is his own worst enemy!'

Simon frowned. 'You mean that we would have had a settlement by now if he had wished to compromise?'

Benjamin nodded at his young brother-in-law before turning back to Sir Thomas. 'What else does his letter say?'

The older man continued to read.

This last year has shown me that there are many of my subjects in England who support me, but it is the Parliament which forces this conflict to continue. I could not agree to their latest proposals, for if I had done so I would have had to relinquish my control of the army. That is something I cannot do. God has placed into my hands the defence of this realm, and I cannot defend it without an army. I believe that if it becomes known that I am held by the army, not an elected parliament, many of my loyal subjects will rise up and aid the Scots. If they turn against this damnable New Model, then maybe the Commons will be persuaded to my position.

'That is a grave risk to take.' Sir Thomas frowned. 'The people may not be happy with the New Model, but they are not likely to support a foreign invasion against them.'

'Not even for the King?'

'I do not know, Simon. His Majesty is correct to say that the people are turning to him again, as things under Parliament appear to be no better than before the war started. But a foreign army?' He was thoughtful for a moment. 'It may work. For he is King of both realms, so can argue that the army he brings is that of loyal subjects, and ask his loyal subjects in England to support them on the understanding that the Scots will return home once his throne is secured. It would be different if he sought aid from Ireland, but Parliament has defeated the Confederate Catholics, so no help will come from there.'

'So, what does His Majesty want you to do?'

'Ah. There is the question, my boy.' Sir Thomas turned back to the letter.

Our Agreement is that the Scottish army will invade in the month of May. It is our plan that there should be risings throughout England at that time. In that way we shall be able to divide Parliament's forces so that they will not be able to put together an army large enough to defeat the Scots, who will then march south and join with those who have taken part in the uprisings. One group will be assigned by myself to affect my escape from Hammond. Then we march on London. Dismiss Parliament. Take control of the New Model Army. I shall then be restored to my throne.

What I require of you, Sir Thomas, is that you make your way to the south east to help with the risings there. You are to meet with Lord Capel and follow his instructions. I know where you currently reside, and give you two weeks more there before you move. Take your time to join with Capel. I want you to go via London, to see what is happening there and to take your intelligence to Capel in the spring. I ask you to leave Sir Benjamin where you are at present. If there is a rising in the Oxford area he is to join with it and help to bring forces to London from the west.

'What! I am to stay here?' Benjamin appeared confused. 'Surely it would be better if I came with you?'

'If you did, you would be just one more man. But here, you could help to lead a group of loyal locals. They know that you are married to my daughter, and so would follow you. It is a sound plan.'

'I cannot say that I would not be happy to remain longer with my family, although it will be hard for me to continue to conduct my life in secret if the time is prolonged. What else does the King say?'

'Little more,'

You are aware of the trust and honour I place in your hands, Sir Thomas. I know that you will follow my wishes until we meet again.

'That is all.'

There was silence for a moment, broken by Simon. 'You will travel alone, Father?'

'It seems so.'

'Then may I come with you? In Benjamin's place? I would not stay with you until May, as I know that you would not wish me to fight. But while there is relative peace in the land, may I not just travel with you for a week or two?' He frowned thoughtfully. 'If we travelled as father and son to London, maybe as merchants, it would be an admirable disguise.'

'You are right to say that peace is relative. I am still a wanted man and will be hunted down if recognised. It may be too dangerous, although I will admit that there is unlikely to be any fighting before the invasion.'

'No more dangerous than the months and years I have spent here. And I promise that I would return here before the Scots come.'

Sir Thomas was thoughtful for a moment before speaking.

'I know that Marston has become all but a prison for you, but I would not exchange it for a prison in truth. I will have to think about this, Simon.'

'But you are not saying no?'

Sir Thomas shook his head. 'I am not saying anything. Yet. We have two weeks to see what other news may come, then I will decide.'

***

Benjamin paced anxiously in front of the fire. 'Are you sure that he can be trusted?'

Sir Thomas nodded, although there was a tension in his shoulders which told of his own nervousness.

'Sir Francis has been my friend since we were both younger than you. He would not harm me, or my family. Indeed, if he wanted to do so he would have come himself with soldiers rather than sending a message.' He looked again at the note that had been delivered to Simon that afternoon.

Simon. I shall call on you this evening. There is much happening that your family should be made aware of, so please do let your sister know that I am coming. Although the threat of war hangs over us again the land is at peace at present. Let us hope that the current situation lacking threat to the peace of Oxfordshire continues. Sir Francis.

Benjamin turned to Simon. 'But why does he mention Elizabeth?'

'This is not typical of his letters, Benjamin. He would normally send me a short message to say he was coming. He mentions the family, and my sister. He could hardly have mentioned Father or yourself openly, but I do believe that his message of peace in Oxfordshire and wanting to speak with the family mean that he wishes to speak with Father.'

'I agree.' Sir Thomas took a deep breath. 'I hear a horse, so we will soon know for certain.'

Simon made his way to the door. 'You must both wait here. I will go and meet him.' With that he turned and left the room in time to see the servant open the front door and Sir Francis enter.

'Good evening, Simon.'

'Sir Francis.' Simon nodded towards the servant. 'You may leave us.' The old man frowned at his young master, then turned and made his way to the kitchen.

'You received my note?'

'Yes, sir.'

'It may not have been clear as I had to guard my words, but if any vagabonds in the area are available I would like to talk with them. I am alone and they are in no danger.' His eyes held Simon's for a moment. The young man could see nothing but honesty and openness in them. He nodded.

'This way.'

The guest followed Simon into the study. He stopped on the threshold. Benjamin was standing, hand on sword hilt although it had not been drawn. Sir Thomas was also standing now, his face a mask of mixed emotions. At last he broke the silence.

'Francis. After so long. It is so good to see you.'

The two men closed the distance between them and shook hands. Both were smiling, although their eyes glittered with unshed tears.

'Thomas. How I have missed you, my friend.'

There was a moment's silence, then Thomas led his friend towards a chair.

'Come, be seated. I am eager to know what it is you wish to tell me. But first of all, I must offer my thanks for the way in which you have protected my family.'

Sir Francis waved a dismissive hand. 'No thanks are necessary. You would have done the same for me and mine.'

Sir Thomas nodded. 'Indeed. But I was unable to, whereas you have kept my children safe to the best of your ability. I shall forever be in your debt.'

'And I.' Benjamin took his hand from his sword as he spoke. 'Simon has told me how you cared for Elizabeth and our daughter. You are an honourable man.'

Simon brought a tray of wine for the men and they were all seated.

'I do my best to behave honourably, although the situation is so fluid that sometimes it is difficult. But it is my honour that brings me here this evening.' Sir Francis sighed. 'I cannot stay for more than a few minutes, but I come to ask you not to help the King to wage another war against his people.'

Sir Thomas frowned. 'You know that I must stay with the King.'

'I remember our talk here in this room, the last time we met. We both chose our sides because we believed that the people we supported were in the right. Now neither of those forces are as they were then. I freely admit that Parliament has failed to change things for the better for the people. And you must admit that the King has failed to take opportunities to reach compromise and end this war.'

Sir Thomas nodded, but said nothing.

'Towards the end of last year I thought that compromise would come. Then we heard of the King's engagement with the Scots!' Sir Francis's voice was raised in indignation. 'Parliament was outraged, and I have to agree with them. For the King to lead a foreign army into his own country will lose any support that was being built in his name. It is seen as more evidence of his bad faith and...'

'You malign the King's name!' Simon was surprised at Benjamin's words. It was what Benjamin himself had said. Though Simon supposed that he would not care to hear it from an enemy. Sir Francis held up a conciliatory hand.

'There are many things we will not be able to agree on, Sir Benjamin. And it would be a waste of our energy, and my limited time, to debate them. Please let me say what I have come to say. You can agree or disagree as you wish.'

Sir Thomas nodded. 'He is right. Please continue, my friend.'

'Things are happening swiftly in Westminster, and rumours abound. I wanted you to know the true situation before you make any decisions. Only a small faction within Scotland supports this Engagement with the King. Many do not support his idea of imposing Presbyterianism for three years only. It would be impractical, and they would never be able to agree to what would happen *after* the three years.'

'But there should be enough support, I feel.'

'Maybe, Thomas. I still feel that a negotiated peace is the only way forward. However, because of the Engagement, Parliament passed a Vote of No Address on the third of this month.'

Simon was puzzled. 'What does that mean?'

'That Parliament will put no further proposals to the King. He must accept what is on offer now, or nothing. Some are even calling for the country to be settled without the King. There were even calls for him to be impeached. And the army agreed with the vote. Far from dividing the Commons and the army, the King's actions seem to be pushing them closer together.'

'What about the Lords?'

Sir Francis shook his head sadly. 'The Lords are an example of the bitter divisions the Engagement is creating. They delayed approving the Vote for as long as they could. But the army brought two regiments close to Westminster and so they have agreed. No more approaches will be made to the King. As for the people who last year were turning back to the King, they are furious that he threatens England with a Scottish army. And they hardly dare to believe that he is willing to sacrifice the church that he has fought for. Even the English Presbyterians are angry that he has come to agreement with the Scots rather than our own elected Parliament.'

'Understandable. But how is this new?'

'Because, Sir Benjamin, many in Parliament do not trust the King. They are asking for a settlement to secure Parliament and the kingdom without a monarch.'

'Is that possible?'

'Anything is possible, Simon. Which is why I have come this evening.' He turned to his old friend. 'I ask you, Thomas, to consider not fighting for the King, but trying to persuade him to a settlement, or we may lose the monarchy altogether. Neither of us ever set out with that objective in mind. To all intents and purposes, Parliament has lost control of the government to the Army. Their prohibition of Christmas and strict observance of the Sabbath are unpopular. If the King went for a settlement he would not get everything he wants, but he would get more than he deserves. And still get to keep his crown.'

'As you know, I saw the trouble at Christmas. If these new rules are so unpopular, surely that means that we have a strong bargaining position?'

'I am afraid not, Simon. I fear it will lead to anarchy. The trouble you saw here was nothing. In Canterbury the mayor refused even to allow a sermon on Christmas Day and told the shopkeepers that they must stay open. Those who did were attacked and their shops looted.'

'Lord preserve us!' said Sir Thomas.

'It is much worse than that. The men of Canterbury went ahead and played a football match, although it had been banned. Somehow this led to a riot and a general attack on the mayor, the Presbyterian ministers, and the magistrates. The mayor and sheriff were badly beaten. The riots grew in strength the next day. The rioters seized the city magazine and weapons, and controlled all access to the city. They gave up after a few days, of course. But there is now a debate as to whether they should be put on trial or judged by martial law.'

'Surely, if this is the case, then it strengthens His Majesty?' Sir Thomas chose his words carefully. 'If the people stand against Parliament, then we have won.'

'Only if they stand together. These riots are piecemeal and unorganised. They can only lead to harsh retaliation by the army. And no matter how much people support the King, I cannot see them welcoming a foreign army.'

'They can cause no more problems than the New Model, who are still taking free board and lodging.'

'They can kill, Simon.' Benjamin turned towards their visitor. 'I understand what you are saying, Sir Francis. But that merely shows that we need the King to control the army. If this continues, people will be asking for Parliament to settle with the King, and he is likely to be able to dictate the terms. Anything would be better than being pushed around by the army. Perhaps His Majesty's Engagement with the Scots is the best course of action after all.'

Sir Francis rose from his seat. 'Only you can decide that. But I urge you to put pressure on the King to accept a settlement. To honour it. I can see no other way to bring a lasting peace to the land. Any other action can only bring more death and destruction.'

Sir Thomas rose, too. 'I promise you that I will think about what you have said. I cannot betray my King, but I can promise you that, if I decide that the best way is to agree a settlement with Parliament, then I will do my best to persuade His Majesty to that course of action.'

Sir Francis nodded sadly. 'That is all I can hope for.'

Chapter 24

March 1648

The twenty-seventh of March found father and son in Norwich. For eight weeks now they had been on the move, the majority of the time in London where they were heartened to see the dislike in which the House of Commons was held by the general population. The great city had been a stronghold of the King's enemies throughout the war, but things had been handled so badly by the Puritans that many were saying, in quiet unobserved moments, that they would be happy to see the King restored.

From London they had travelled slowly towards the north-east, two merchants looking for business. Bishops Stortford. Saffron Walden. Newmarket. Thetford. At each place they were heartened to see how deeply the local people disliked the current situation. Sir Thomas was delighted to see this. With so much support, he felt that the King hardly needed the Scottish army. If he were to negotiate and reach an agreement with the Commons the people would be on his side, and he would secure his throne with little loss of his powers from before the war. He had said as much in a letter to the King but Charles, as ever, was immoveable. He refused to compromise. No matter how hard Sir Thomas and other Royalists pressured the King, he would not make any peace with Parliament which diminished his powers. Far from seeking peace, the King had tried to escape from the Isle of Wight on a number of occasions, thereby making his intentions clear to the Commanders of the New Model Army. So Simon and his father continued on their slow journey, identifying key points of resistance, key personnel. Once this was all co-ordinated, there would be a considerable force for their cause. Together with the Scots, this provided the most promising possibility for peace in years.

As night fell on the evening of the anniversary of the King's accession, Simon watched torches being thrust into a great bonfire. Within moments the kindling had caught and thick grey smoke began to billow, followed swiftly by flames which licked at the wood. Throughout the city, more and more fires were lit in celebration of the King. Sir Thomas shook his head in amazement.

'Who would have thought this a year ago? There were no fires lit then, yet this year it seems to me that there are more than I have ever seen to celebrate the King's Coronation.'

'It is one way for the people to make their feelings known.' Simon moved away from a billowing cloud of smoke as he spoke. 'Look! They are burning an effigy of Robert Hammond!'

Sir Thomas smiled. 'The poor man. He has made it abundantly clear that he does not wish the position of King's Gaoler, but they burn him nonetheless!'

'I wonder if it is the same throughout the country?'

'I do not know, Simon. No doubt we will receive intelligence as we move, or when we join with the others. But for now, let us enjoy this celebration for our King!'

Simon laughed gaily. 'Indeed!' He raised his hat and began to wave it wildly above his head, joining in the cries and cheers which echoed throughout the centre of the city.

'Long live the King! Long live His Majesty King Charles!'

***

The next morning found them at the City Hall as the Mayor made his way to his office. Sir Thomas stepped forward, offering a brief bow.

'Good morning, sir. I thank you for allowing last night's celebration of His Majesty's reign.'

The Mayor looked at him, a small frown furrowing his brow. 'And who might you be, good sir?'

'One who loves the King, and would speak with others of the same mind.' Sir Thomas's words were cautious. While the Mayor's actions in allowing the celebrations of the night before showed that he had some sympathy for the King, to approach him openly would be dangerous. He recognised that some time would need to be spent in fencing with words before he could speak safely. The Mayor was equally circumspect.

'There are many in this city who side with the King. I merely gave them freedom to express their feelings.'

'Even though such freedom has been forbidden!'

The two men whirled around at the sound of the voice. Simon turned a second later, and his heart sank when he saw the small group of Roundheads, an officer in their lead. Had they heard his father's words? Were their lives in danger? The officer spoke again, his voice aggressive as he addressed the Mayor.

'You are called to appear before the County Committee. You will accompany me now.' He turned toward Simon and his father. 'Did you have any hand in the planning of this?'

'No, sir. We are not from this town but merely here on business. I wished to speak with the Mayor concerning the sale of fleeces from Oxfordshire.'

'So you say.' The officer frowned. 'It would be more than my life is worth to allow any to escape who were part of the organisation of last night's despicable display of loyalty to the tyrant King. I think it would be best if you, too, would accompany me.' He inclined his head towards the three prisoners, and his handful of soldiers encircled them, leading them swiftly across the square and into a building protected by a detachment of soldiers.

'What is this place?'

The Mayor turned towards Simon. 'Head-quarters of the County Committee. And arsenal for the city.' He lowered his voice so that Sir Thomas had to strain to hear. 'I do not know who you are, but if you serve the King it would profit you to make good your release from these people swiftly. They are not renowned for their generosity of thought, or kind treatment of Royalists.'

Sir Thomas nodded slightly, but said nothing as they were marched into the building. The young officer ordered half of his men to wait in the hallway while the remainder accompanied him and his three prisoners into the hall. Three members of the County Committee were seated at a table, flanked by soldiers.

'Good morning, gentlemen.'

The three men glared at the Mayor, but did not return his greeting. The man in the centre, the obvious leader, spoke.

'All celebrations of the traitor king's accession were banned. You knew that. Why then were so many bonfires lit last night, and you did nothing to put them out?'

'I am but one man. I could not put them all out.'

'You have men under your control. You are the Mayor, and as such you are responsible.'

The Mayor inclined his head in a brief nod. 'As you say.'

'You do not deny it?'

'It would little profit me to do so.'

'Then you are to go to London. You will appear before Parliament to answer for your treasonous actions.'

'I see no treason in men celebrating the day that their King, ordained by God, came to the throne of England. I will not go to London.'

'You will have no choice.' He turned towards Sir Thomas and Simon. 'And who are you?'

Simon felt his heart beating rapidly. Sweat beaded his brow and his hands were shaking, although he did his utmost to conceal it. He found that he was holding his breath as his father spoke.

'We are simply traders from Oxfordshire, sir. This morning was the first time that I have ever seen or spoken to the Mayor.'

'Why did you seek him out?'

'In pursuit of a market for our fleeces. But he was obviously the wrong man to approach.' Sir Thomas forced a grim smile. 'I had not perceived that the power of the city lies with you. Perhaps you can advise me on where to seek the people I need to meet with?'

'We have not the time for that,' the man to the right of the chairman growled angrily. 'Find them for yourself.'

'Yes, sir.' Sir Thomas bowed. 'With your permission?'

The Committee member waved a dismissive hand. Sir Thomas took Simon by the sleeve and turned to leave the room. As the door was closing behind them, Simon heard voices again.

'The only way you will get me to London is in chains.'

'Then so be it.'

As they exited into the spring sunshine, Sir Thomas was surprised to see a group of about fifty men gathered in front of the steps. The soldiers on guard duty had angled their muskets towards the angry looking men. Simon hurried down the steps on his father's heels. As they turned to walk away one of the men intercepted them.

'Who are you? I do not think I have seen you in our city before?'

'Indeed not. I am a simple merchant wishing to go about my business.'

'And this one?' he indicated Simon.

'My son.'

'Are you the two who were led away with the Mayor a short time ago?'

Sir Thomas nodded. 'A simple case of mistaken identity. Thankfully this was recognised and we have been released.'

'And what of the Mayor?'

'He is to be sent to London to answer for last night's celebrations for the King. In chains.'

There were angry murmurs amongst the gathering crowd. Their leader thought for a moment, then began to bark out instructions.

'One man from each parish take the news. Tell all those who took advantage of the Mayor's leniency last night that it is he who is to pay the price. Any who wish to help him should hurry here.' Within seconds half a dozen young men had run off in different directions. The man turned towards Sir Thomas. 'What of you, sir? Are you a king's man?'

Simon eyed the angry crowd which was growing rapidly. Anyone who was not for the King was likely to face trouble, yet he knew that his father did not want anyone to know just how close to the King he really was. Simon need not have worried, for his father's words were as diplomatic as ever.

'We are loyal men of England. His Majesty is our rightful king. But I do not feel it is our place to stand with you when we are not men of your city.'

The young man nodded. 'As you say.' He looked around at the angry crowd. Muskets and swords were now in evidence as the people began to move slowly towards the guards in front of the building. 'If you do not wish to engage with us then I advise you to withdraw.'

Sir Thomas nodded and turned away without a word, striding to the other side of the square. A moment later Simon turned and followed him.

'Should we not stand with them, Father?'

Sir Thomas shook his head. 'There are enough of them to free the Mayor should they so choose. But it will not be without injury, and perhaps loss of life. The information which we carry is too important to be risked in such a small skirmish.' He turned a stern gaze towards his son. 'As is your life.'

'Yes, Father.' Simon looked back across the square to where angry cries were now being raised. 'But should we not observe what happens? It would be useful information about the numbers and strength of the King's followers.'

'And how they are met by the enemy.' Sir Thomas led Simon into a side street as he spoke. 'We will watch from here, where we can see but be in no danger.'

Suddenly, the sound of a flintlock rent the air. There was a cry of pain followed by stunned silence. Simon turned to see a young man on his knees, arms folded across his stomach where a deep red stain was beginning to spread. A voice came from the small detachment of soldiers guarding the building.

'Disperse if you do not wish to be met with the same.'

There was a stillness in the square as the soldiers levelled their weapons. Then a cry went up.

'For the King! For His Majesty!'

A shot rang out from the crowd and was met with a volley from the soldiers as the angry mob surged forwards. There was no time for the defenders to reload, and only time enough for two of them to draw their swords. Within moments they had withdrawn into the building, leaving three of their men lying wounded on the ground. A fourth had fled towards the nearest exit from the square. The doors of the building were slammed closed. More shots were fired from the windows above. More men fell wounded and dying as those in the front forced the door open and raced inside. There were more shots. The sound of steel on steel. Then silence.

For a moment Simon was stunned. It was all so unexpected. All over so quickly. He found himself shaking with excitement and fear. For a moment he was back at Marston during the attack there, seeing again the death and destruction, knowing what it must be like inside the building.

'Are you well, son?'

Simon took a deep breath and nodded. 'Yes. Who won?'

Sir Thomas shrugged. 'We must wait and see.'

As if in answer to his question, a number of men exited the building and began tending to the wounded. More people approached and the leader of the attackers called to them to carry the injured and dead away. Many of the new arrivals ran into the building as the sound of approaching horses could be heard. A moment later a troop of soldiers galloped into the square. Simon felt his father's hand on his arm as he pulled him into a doorway, better to conceal themselves from the new arrivals. But the soldiers were unaware of them, their concentration focused on the Headquarters of the County Committee. An officer was shouting orders as a shot rang out from the rooftop. A soldier fell. Then the troops were moving forward.

This time it was the Royalists who defended the building. Simon could hear the sound of fierce hand-to-hand fighting interspersed with the occasional sound of gunfire. He was stunned by the speed of events.

'How did they get here so quickly?'

'The soldier who ran. But you are right, they have moved with remarkable speed.' Sir Thomas's eyes widened, and he nodded his head. 'The magazine!'

'Father?'

'The Mayor said that this building also contains the magazine. The army cannot let that fall to a riotous mob. The damage they could do is unimaginable.'

'But what if they can secure the arms? Would they give them to us to be used for the King?'

Sir Thomas shook his head. 'I doubt it. After today they will need it to defend themselves from…'

The earth beneath their feet shook and heaved, throwing them to the ground as the sound of a tremendous explosion battered their ears. Bricks and dust began to rain down on them and they covered their heads with their arms to protect themselves. The chaos seemed endless but, slowly, the dust began to settle and they raised themselves shakily to their feet. On the far side of the square, nothing remained of the building but a pile of rubble.

Chapter 25

April 1648

Sir Thomas looked across at his son as they rode in silence. Simon had been withdrawn since the incident at Norwich, but his father could understand that. No one knew what had caused the magazine to explode, but the results had been catastrophic. More than one hundred dead! It did not seem possible, yet they had seen it for themselves. And the wounded. They had helped to carry injured people from the vicinity of the building. Men who had lost limbs, who had been badly burned, who were bleeding to death. It had hit Simon hard, but he seemed to be coming to terms with it now. He was no longer as pale as he had been in the first few days, and he had begun to eat properly again. Sir Thomas could understand the impact that the explosion had had on his son. After all, in the past he had taken part in battles himself, yet the extent and horror of what they had seen in Norwich still gnawed at him. They had spent the last month travelling and collecting information. Ipswich. Colchester. Chelmsford. Dartford. Gillingham Reach. At last they were close to their destination and would reach Canterbury within the hour. Then Sir Thomas would have some decisions to make.

***

The two were dirty and dishevelled after their weeks in the countryside, but Sir Thomas was recognised immediately and taken straight to see the Earl of Norwich, who greeted them warmly.

'Thomas! It is good to see you, my friend!'

Sir Thomas smiled. 'And you too, My Lord'.

Simon took a step forward and his father waved a hand in his direction. 'May I present my son, Simon.'

The young man bowed. 'I am pleased to meet you, Your Lordship.'

The Earl looked thoughtful for a moment before acknowledging the greeting. 'Welcome to Canterbury. You have the look of your brother about you.'

'You knew Thomas?'

'Indeed I did. And a fine young man he was.' He turned to Sir Thomas. 'Has young Simon been travelling with you?'

'Yes. And he has been a helpful disguise. We have much to tell you.'

Norwich waved a hand towards a table, set for lunch. 'Come and eat with me while you give me your news.' He smiled at Simon. 'As I recall, a growing lad like this is always hungry!'

They all laughed as they made their way to the table and were seated. As the food was served, Sir Thomas began to give his report. The Earl listened intently.

'It seems that His Majesty's plans were well considered,' he began. 'We spent much time in London, where people are showing a great indignation at how this country is being run, and a longing for things to be as they were. It is quite possible that London will rise, but the army is strong there, and the Commons are more or less under the control of the generals, so nothing can be guaranteed.

'The east holds strongly for the king.' His eyes met those of their host. 'We were at Norwich for the incident surrounding the King's accession day and know how such a loss must sadden you.' A range of emotions played across Norwich's features – anger, sadness, bitter determination - but he said nothing as Sir Thomas continued. 'As I am sure you are aware, this month has seen many petitions to Parliament from ordinary people, asking for the Commons to negotiate with His Majesty and disband the army.' He smiled grimly. 'What was a great weapon in Cromwell's hands is become a millstone around his neck. The New Model may well be the deciding factor in a settlement.'

'Indeed. If we could have the army disbanded I do believe that the King could regain his throne tomorrow. What say you, Simon?'

Simon looked up from his plate, swiftly swallowing a piece of chicken to allow himself to speak. 'I know little of politics, My Lord, but I do believe that could be so. We saw a number of groups marching to London with their petitions. They were peaceful, but there were always two or three hundred people marching together. If there are as many groups in the rest of the country as there are from Essex and Surrey, and if they were all to join together, the army would not be able to stand.'

'Your reckoning is sound, but numbers are not everything, Simon. The New Model is well armed and well trained. They also have experience on their side.'

'Yes, Father. But if the common people here in the south rise up alongside the Scottish army, then the New Model will be hard pushed to defeat them.'

The Earl laughed. 'You know more of politics than you are willing to admit, young man! What else have you learnt on your travels?'

'We heard of the incident in Moorfields, which strengthens our argument about the way people feel against the ministers and army. I am not well travelled, but I know that the men on our estate appreciate a day from work where they can rest or take fun as the mood takes them. If the ministers continue to declare games such as tipcat as ungodly, then the people are going to rebel. To send armed men to disperse a game seems foolhardy, and it is not surprising that they were overwhelmed. It was but a step from there for the aggrieved people to march down Fleet Street calling for the King. Once that had happened, escalation was inevitable. The army was sent in to disperse the crowd, who attacked the Lord Mayor's house in retaliation so that he had to seek refuge in the Tower. The Commons sent in the New Army cavalry to disperse the crowds and several were killed. In my humble opinion, sir, Parliament is making matters worse in this way. And that can only strengthen our cause.'

'Indeed,' agreed Sir Thomas. 'The way that Parliament has been handling these petitions is playing into our hands. Not everyone who signed petitions for change is a Royalist; but the more heavy-handed the Commons are, the more of those people turn towards the King. I have already seen this being channelled in Essex, and believe that you are doing something similar in Kent?' The Earl nodded, but said nothing. Sir Thomas continued. 'A goodly number of men in these counties have always been for the King, but these lands were held by the enemy during the war, and so our supporters remained quiet.'

'It saddens me to agree.'

Sir Thomas hurried to assure the Earl of his support. 'I did not mean to imply that your lands did not play their part. Those who could fight travelled with the king, and fought bravely beside him. It would have been foolish and costly for those who remained at home to defy the Roundheads in such a stronghold as this.'

The Earl nodded and smiled. 'Yes. But they defy them now. We must focus this emotion to keep a portion of the New Model facing this way. That will give more freedom to the Scots in the north. With the Scottish army coming, Parliament has suspended the Vote of No Address. A large majority of them have resolved that they will not alter government by King, Lords and Commons. Maybe there will be a settlement and no need to fight after all.'

Sir Thomas frowned. 'That would be the ideal solution. But I fear for the safety of my son, should it come to war again.'

'Father...'

Sir Thomas held up a hand. 'No, son, let me speak.' He turned back to their host. 'Do you believe that there will be fighting here?'

'Who can say? We will hold for the King, but I feel it likely that the fighting will be more focussed in the middle lands and north. Are you planning to send your son home?'

'That had been my intention. But an unsettled London will make it difficult for him to travel. And I cannot be spared to take him back.'

'I am not a child, Father. I could travel alone.'

'Or you could stay here.' The Earl was thoughtful. 'With an army coming from the north, who can say whether Oxford will be safer than Canterbury? At least we have city walls here strong enough to hold the enemy at bay.' He turned towards Sir Thomas. 'What do you think? It is obviously your decision to make, but if you wish to keep Simon with you here I am sure that I can find work for a fine young mind like his.'

'Work?'

'Yes, my friend. There will be many reports coming in, so another pair of hands to scribe for me will not go amiss.'

Simon was stunned. Work on the staff of the Earl of Norwich? Could he really be that lucky? He turned towards his father, his eyes alight with excitement.

'This is something I can do for the King without placing myself on the front line! What do you say, Father?'

Sir Thomas was thoughtful. 'Seeing the disquiet in the land, I realise that Marston is not as safe as it was when His Majesty held Oxford. It is not a decision I can make lightly, Simon. I will think on it.'

Simon smiled happily as he turned back to his meal. His father would think on it. That was half the battle!

Chapter 26

May 1648

The late afternoon sun slanting through the window lent a yellow glow to the room. Simon put down his pen and rolled his tired shoulders as he watched the Earl of Norwich pace angrily across the floor. He waved the latest dispatch in the direction of Sir Thomas.

'This is a disaster! The risings are happening, but no one seems to be co-ordinating them!' He looked at the message again. 'Our people in south Wales have been defeated at St Fagan's. Though by all accounts they are still holding some of the castles.'

'Those castles are strong, My Lord, and will hold for some time yet.'

'I know, Thomas. But it will take fewer of the enemy to hold the King's men there in a siege than if they were in open opposition. Men who could be fighting for His Majesty are now sitting behind stone walls. They are no good to us there.'

'Can they not break out?'

'I doubt it, Simon. It appears that they lost many of their number in the battle.' The Earl paced across the floor to stand glaring at a map of England affixed to the wall. 'And where is the Scottish army? They were supposed to invade on the first. It is now the twentieth, and still no sign of them! Our risings will be wasted if they do not come soon.'

There was the sound of voices in the hall. The three men turned towards the door, which opened to admit a young man.

'What is it, Miles?'

'Two men from London, Your Lordship. They say that they are Generals Waller and Massey.'

'Waller and Massey? Are they not Roundheads?'

'They were, Thomas. But they are as disaffected with Parliament as the next man. They have been working to raise forces in London to support the King.'

'Then what are they doing here?'

'That is what I would like to know. And the only way to find out is to speak to them.' The Earl turned to Miles. 'Show them in.'

Two men, one much the same age as Sir Thomas and one somewhat younger, entered the room. They bowed low, offering their greeting in unison.

'Good day, My Lord Norwich.'

The Earl seated himself at his desk, indicating that the two men should take two vacant chairs. 'I had not expected to see you so soon. How goes it, Waller?'

'We were doing well, My Lord. Many diverse people in London are now coming out for the King – Royalists who had remained hidden until now; those who are disaffected with Parliament and the county committees; those who are unhappy with the burden of taxation. And others, such as ourselves, who were with the army but are no longer happy with the way Parliament deals with us.'

'So why are you here?'

'To counter our work, Parliament appointed Skippon as Commander of all the forces in London. We know him from the past as a man of integrity. Unfortunately, he seems to have changed and is carrying out his commission with ruthless efficiency. He has ordered searches for arms and horses. Many of our agents have been arrested. He has begun to build a circle of forts and blockhouses around the city and will soon have it sealed off. He makes no secret of the fact that, once any risings in the countryside have been defeated, he will crush any resistance in the city for ever. Those who support the King have been slipping away to Essex and Kent. Our hands are tied in the city so we have come to see if we can be of further use here.'

'Do you have any news of the Scottish army?'

'We received a message just before we left London,' Massey said. 'It seems that there are divisions amongst the Scots which have led to delays for the Engagers. It is likely to be the middle of next month before they cross the border, if not later.'

'Next month!' Norwich's face was white. 'Then all of our planning will come to nothing if we do not act carefully.' He was silent for a moment, chewing his lip whilst deep in thought. He nodded slowly as though coming to a decision. 'I will hold a meeting of the local gentry tomorrow. If we can lead a few demonstrations towards London that will keep some of the army pinned down here. We cannot allow them the time to march north and set up their defences against the Scots.'

***

On the urging of the Earl of Norwich, the gentry in Kent raised a petition against the county committee, with the intention of placing it before Parliament. The committee, which had been set up by Parliament to rule in place of the Royalist gentry, attempted to crush the petition by force. This was the catalyst which many in the area had been waiting for. The magazine in Rochester was seized, and the arms handed out to the

Royalists under Norwich. Little more than a week later, Simon and his father found themselves on the edge of London.

***

A horse galloped into the make-shift camp, its rider hauling on the reins to pull it to a halt beside the Earl.

'Your Lordship, the Kent militia has been defeated! There are no regular army to spare from London. Kent is now in our hands!'

Norwich smiled at the young man. 'Good. Now go and get something to eat.'

As the messenger rode away, Norwich turned to his companions. 'At least that has gone well. Unlike our situation.'

'You can hardly be blamed, My Lord. If Skippon had not fortified London Bridge, preventing Londoners from joining us, we could have a host twice this size by now!'

'If. You know as well as I do, Thomas, that skirmishes are not won on "ifs".' He looked across the open land towards the sprawling spread of London town. 'I see movement, but cannot make out the colours.'

'It is Fairfax, Your Lordship.'

The Earl looked at Simon. The young man wore a sword and pistol at his waist, trying to exude a feeling of ease, but Norwich knew better.

'Do not worry. We are safe enough back here. Fairfax's men will not reach us.' He indicated the river behind them. 'If the worst happens we can cross here, and the river will be a barrier to our enemy.'

'They certainly will not reach you, Simon. If they get close then you are to ride swiftly for Maidstone and wait for me there.'

'I will not leave you here, Father.'

Norwich nodded. 'Indeed. You will be safer with us than chasing across the countryside alone. What say you?' He turned towards Sir Thomas, who frowned.

'We will wait and see. That is all we can do.'

Suddenly, the morning air was rent with the sound of cannon fire from just outside the city walls. The three men swiftly mounted their horses. Prince danced in excitement and Simon fought for a moment to control him. This was the first taste of battle for both of them, and they were equally nervous. Norwich began to call out orders as Simon got his horse under control and sat quietly, waiting. From their position Simon could see the great gouts of earth thrown up by the artillery, but it seemed that few men had been hit and casualties were light. Their own few pieces of small ordinance, ranged ahead of the mass of men from Canterbury, fired in response. Part of the parapet at the side of the gateway collapsed. A cheer rose up from the throng, to be cut short as a body of infantry came into view and formed up opposite them.

'Stay here, Thomas. I shall command from the front. You are to direct the men to fill in any gaps which may open in our lines.'

'My Lord.'

Simon watched the Earl gallop away, shouting instructions as he rode. The front line formed up as he approached, muskets at the ready. They let off a thunderous volley, to be met by the same from the approaching enemy. Smoke and powder filled the air. There were cries of injured and dying men, but these were soon lost in the general noise of battle. Simon's mouth was dry and he licked his lips, afraid that the line would break. But it held.

'See, to the left of centre? That is Fairfax.'

Simon turned to his father. 'Does he not place himself in unnecessary danger?'

'No more than Norwich. In a small scale engagement like this they need to be in the thick of it. Things can change swiftly.'

'A small engagement?' Simon looked at the thousands of men who were now locked together in hand-to-hand combat. His hand shook on the reins and he fought to still it. Sir Thomas laid a comforting hand on his son's shoulder.

'Small in the scheme of things, but big enough for your first battle. Do not worry. We are safe here.'

'I am not worried.'

'Yes you are. And so am I. Only a fool would be unconcerned in a situation like this.' Sir Thomas turned his eyes back to the fighting as he spoke. The men were holding well where Norwich was, but the other wing looked like it might break. Sir Thomas turned to a messenger on his left.

'Ride to the cavalry. They are to circle to the left and take the enemy in their right flank.'

'Sir.'

The messenger galloped away. Moments later there was the thunder of hooves as a tidal wave of horses hit the wall of men. At first they surged forward, forcing the enemy back, but soon it became difficult for them to move in the press. They wheeled and rode away. But the line held. Simon watched as the main body of enemy musketeers took one step back. Then another.

'We are pushing them back!'

'I am afraid not, Simon. They are making room for the pikes.'

As he spoke a forest of pikes appeared at the forefront of the enemy line, marching relentlessly forward. The men of Kent tried to stand firm. They succeeded for a moment, but then began to retreat, slow step after slow step. The enemy pikes cut and thrust, leaving a mass of dying men on the ground. Simon felt sick. He hoped he would not disgrace himself.

'Can you send the cavalry in again?'

Sir Thomas shook his head. 'The horses would be gutted by those pikes. It is now a matter of numbers. And of skill. Fairfax has taken part in many battles, and his men are well trained.'

'Can we defeat them?'

'We shall see.'

The King's men fought fiercely for more than an hour, but lack of experience began to tell as Fairfax and his men pushed relentlessly forward. The enemy cavalry suddenly appeared on the right wing, wheeled round and attacked the weaker side of the Kentish forces.

'Cavalry! Engage!'

As Sir Thomas shouted out his orders their mounted men raced again for the enemy right flank, this time charging into the mounted Parliamentarians who wheeled to face them. Heavily outnumbered, the Roundheads traded swift sword strokes and disengaged. Once more the line held.

A rider approached rapidly.

'Sir Thomas, His Lordship says that we will not be able to hold. You are to lead the orderly retreat towards Maidstone.' Without waiting for an answer, he saluted and rode away again.

'Retreat?' Simon could hardly believe it. 'But we have just forced back their cavalry!'

'Only for a short time. If we retreat now we can do so in good order and re-form at Maidstone. If we leave it longer retreat could turn to rout.'

Sir Thomas wheeled his horse and began shouting orders. 'Get messages to Generals Waller and Massey. Their experienced soldiers are to cover the retreat of those who are fighting for the first time. Get the guns across the river behind us and have them set up on the far bank. The cavalry are to divide in two and take up position on the wings. They are to stop any interference by enemy cavalry as we retreat. Once across the river, the artillery and cavalry are to hold for as long as possible while the remainder march for Maidstone!'

Bugles began to call. Messengers galloped in all directions. Simon was stunned.

'What do we do?'

'Cross the river! Come on!'

Sir Thomas led the way down the bank and through the waters of the Medway, which were not deep enough to force the horses to swim, but did slow their movements. Once on the other side, they turned and watched the progress of the conflict.

Hundreds of barges had been held ready on the shore and these now began to ferry the fighters across. Some men, unwilling to wait for the barges to return, began to wade across. With muskets held above their heads and water to their chests, some lost their footing and were swept away, but most reached the other side safely.

'Make your way to Maidstone!' Sir Thomas called out to the officers who were gathering their men together. 'Make the fastest marching speed that you can, but do not run. This is to be an orderly retreat. Once at the city, man the walls and cover the retreat of those behind you.'

The soldiers began to march away down the road, others adding to their number as more barges grounded and troops disembarked. Simon watched them leave, then turned back to the conflict. The river was a mass of boats and men. Though they were dispirited, the crossing was swift and organised, hundreds reaching the near bank at a time before the vessels set off for the far bank once more. Simon's eyes followed them. On the other shore he could see the artillery pieces firing time and time again. They were only small, but the enemy were a large mass, and each shot brought down wounded and dead Roundheads. Between the guns and the enemy, Norwich held the more experienced troops together. They had formed up in a semi-circle to protect the embarkation point with musket and sword. For an hour they held, moving back a step at a time to take the place of those who had already made it to the other side of the river.

Suddenly, the sound of the guns stopped. Simon could see Norwich urging the artillerymen to load their pieces onto the barges, which were swiftly poled across. The horses which would pull them once they were on dry land again swam alongside.

'Do not wait for them all to get over. Make for Maidstone now!'

Simon turned to his father, pride in his gaze. It filled him with pride to see him so calm and controlled, ordering the men and holding them steadfast through the withdrawal. He found his back straightening. He would not let his father down.

His gaze travelled to the far bank once more. The entire ordinance had now been transported across the slow flowing river. Sir Thomas called to an officer, who had formed up his contingent of infantrymen and was ready to move out.

'Hold your men here! Form up into four ranks! You must cover the others as they cross!'

'Yes, sir!'

The musketeers formed up and began a steady, withering fire at the enemy on the other side of the river. The front rank fired, then knelt to re-load as the second took their place. Then the third. Then the fourth. Then it was time for the front rank to stand and fire again. Enemy soldiers fell, but there were always more to take their place. Simon could see Norwich with the cavalry turn and begin to swim their horses across as Waller and Massey urged their men into the barges. Enemy cannon began to fire. Some shot fell on the far bank, wounding their own men as well as those with Norwich. Some shot fell into the water, shattering barges and throwing men into the river. More shot began to rain down close to where Sir Thomas and Simon sat their horses.

'You need to ride for Maidstone. Now!'

'I am not going without you, Father!'

'Do not worry. I will be close behind.'

'Then I will wait!'

Sir Thomas glared at his son in frustration for a moment, but there was no time to argue. With an angry frown he turned back towards the river in time to see the Earl of Norwich urging his horse up the bank.

'Are you well, My Lord?'

Norwich nodded. 'Yes, Thomas. And I thank you for your handling of this retreat. Far more men would have been lost if not for your organisation. Now, be on your way to Maidstone.'

'What about you?'

'I am with you. The cavalry will form up as mobile protection for Waller and Massey with their men. We should all be within the city by nightfall.' The cavalry were already organising themselves. Massey and Waller were across and forming up their men as they came ashore. 'It is time that we were gone from here.'

Simon was glad to turn and follow the Earl away from the river, his father riding grimly by his side. For a time they rode in silence, passing men on foot who marched tiredly, helping the wounded on their way. At last Norwich broke the silence.

'We were not ready! If the Scots had come as promised, the people of London would have joined us. Fairfax would have had to send men to the north and would have had fewer to oppose us. We should have won that conflict! Damned Scots cannot be trusted!'

'They will come? Will they not?'

Sir Thomas turned to his son. 'They had better, my boy. If not then we shall be no more able to win this war than the last.'

'Then we hold out until they come.' Simon's smile was humourless. 'I may yet get to see action, after all.'

Sir Thomas was surprised. 'Have you not seen enough today?'

'Yes, if the truth be told. But I have not taken part.' He tried, unsuccessfully, to banish the day's experiences from his mind. Images of the dead and dying. The cries of anger and of pain. The sound of horses and musket fire. He looked around him. How could he forget, when he was surrounded by so many men retreating towards Maidstone. 'Although I am afraid, I am still willing to fight for our King.'

Shouts and the sound of musket-fire broke out behind them and the three men whirled round on their horses. A small troop of enemy cavalry had burst through the trees and were attacking their flank.

'They must have crossed further downstream!' Norwich drew his sword. 'Charge!'

Sir Thomas's response was instinctive as he drew his pistol and fired a single shot before thrusting it back into his belt, drawing his sword and racing after Norwich. Simon sat for a moment, too stunned to move. Prince reared up, excited and frightened by the noise. The need to control the horse freed Simon's mind. He, too, drew his pistol, took careful aim at a rider heading towards Norwich, and fired. The bullet hit the attacker in the shoulder and the man twisted with the impact, but it must have been a flesh wound for he continued on. Simon found himself drawing his sword and putting spur to flank.

'For the King!'

His heart was in his mouth. He had not felt so afraid since the attack on Marston; but he was older now, and felt he had a duty to take part in this skirmish like any other man. As he swung his sword at the closest horseman, he found himself thinking of Thomas. Was this what it had been like for him? The fear? The excitement? The sound of thundering hooves and blood pounding in his ears? He found himself screaming incoherently as he swung his sword, striking the man's arm raised to attack a soldier struggling to load his flintlock. Simon felt the blade cut through cloth, then flesh, then come to a jarring stop against the bone. The enemy screamed and dropped his weapon as Simon thundered by, the speed of his passing pulling the sword free. He turned in the saddle to see his father engaging a man, their swords flashing as their horses pirouetted and danced beneath them. Sir Thomas was obviously the more experienced and forced his opponent back. With a sudden cut, his sword was buried in the man's head and he fell, soundlessly, from the saddle. Sir Thomas whirled round, looking for Simon. Seeing him safe for the moment, he turned to his next opponent. Simon found himself on the edge of the road, breathing heavily after his first encounter. He felt sickened as he thought of his sword slicing the flesh of the enemy, and he did not want to do anything like that again. But the enemy troop was moving in on the men on foot, who were struggling to load their weapons. With an angry cry, Simon rode forward again. This time his opponent was ready, parrying Simon's attack and riposting swiftly. Simon countered, aiming a blow at the head of his assailant, who parried and cut towards Simon's unprotected chest. Simon knew that he would never be able to get his sword there in time, and wondered what it would feel like to die. Then a shot rang out and he saw a red stain spreading across the chest of the rider. The man looked down in stunned disbelief, giving Simon the split second he needed to swing his sword again. This time it caught his opponent in the head. The man slipped soundlessly from his saddle.

More shots began to sound around him as the men on foot finished loading. The small troop of attacking cavalry knew they could not stand against the gunfire and turned, disappearing into the trees as quickly as they had come. Simon turned breathlessly towards his father who trotted up to him, his face a mask of concern.

'Simon! Are you hurt?'

Simon shook his head. 'And you?'

'No.'

The Earl of Norwich approached as they were speaking. His sword was bloodied, and he wiped it with his sash before replacing it in his sheath.

'A flanking movement! If Fairfax has brought some of his cavalry over the river at another place, then who knows how many more men he has in the vicinity. We must move more quickly!'

The Earl pushed his horse into a canter and headed along the line of retreating men, shouting words of encouragement as he went. Simon watched him go. Now that the fight was over he was feeling weak. His hands shook, and he felt dizzy. Sir Thomas laid a comforting hand on his shoulder.

'Does it always feel like this?' Simon asked.

His father nodded, grimly. 'Yes. Although the first time is always the worst. Stay focussed and controlled and you will be fine.' Simon nodded, but said nothing as Sir Thomas continued. 'You did well, my boy. I am proud of you.'

With that, they turned and followed the Earl of Norwich towards Maidstone.

***

Norwich set up his command on Penenden Heath, deploying a detachment of three thousand men to guard the outskirts of the town, while barricades were built on all approaches. He kept his main force of seven thousand with him whilst waiting to see what Fairfax did next. He did not have long to wait.

As the afternoon drew on, Fairfax appeared at the head of his force, filling the open ground between the men on the heath and the town walls. The Earl frowned.

'So many.'

'But do we not outnumber them, My Lord?'

Norwich turned to Simon. 'Indeed we do. But the men with us here on the heath are untrained and poorly armed. Fairfax's men are veterans. New Model men who have fought pitched battles before. If we try to engage them here in the open without a clear line of retreat it will be a rout.'

'But what of the men in the city?'

'They will have to hold alone, Simon.'

The young man turned towards his father. 'Is that possible?'

Sir Thomas shrugged, his gaze bleak as he looked towards the river where Fairfax had halted his men, preparing to attack. 'It is unlikely. But we have to look at the broader canvas. Do we lose three thousand or ten thousand? Should we throw these inexperienced and ill-equipped men into a battle they cannot win, or do we retreat with them to a position where then can actually make a difference?'

Simon was silent. Ever since the attack on Marston Manor he had feared battle. He still felt weak at the thought of the men who had so recently lost their lives in front of him. He would not care if he never fought again. But what of the men who had been sent ahead to Maidstone? Could they really just abandon them? He found the prospect of turning and riding away more daunting than to ride forward and engage Fairfax. It seemed that Norwich could read his thoughts for he turned a sympathetic gaze towards the youngster by his side.

'I would ride to their aid if we had any chance of defeating Fairfax, but that is impossible. I have to do what is best for the King's cause, regardless of how it cuts my heart like a knife.' Pain filled his eyes, and Simon was glad he did not have to make such decisions.

The three sat their horses on the heath, watching the events unfold in the distance. It seemed that Fairfax had decided not to make a direct attack on the town. His forces surged forward in a flanking movement to take the outpost on the Farleigh Bridge, before crossing the river to the south west. There was fierce fighting for a time as the Parliamentarians forced their way forward.

'We had best retreat now, while we can.'

Simon turned towards the Earl. His shoulders were slumped as though he was exhausted, his eyes deeply sad. After a moment he straightened, issued his orders, turned and rode away. He did not look back.

***

It was three days since they had fought Fairfax at the Medway. The ride to Blackheath had been uneventful, the troops arriving tired but determined. They had been waiting for almost two days now, but only a trickle of men had come to join them from London. Sir Thomas spoke to the leader of the group who had just arrived.

'You say you come from Dorset?'

'Yes, sir. Ten thousand of us signed a petition, but only two hundred brought it to London. Although some have returned home, most are still with me.'

Simon watched the men being led away for a meal before being shown where they could camp. He turned back as his father continued to speak.

'What was the petition?'

'Much the same as all others which have been sent to Parliament this year. Or so it would seem.' Simon struggled to understand the man's heavy accent as he reported. 'We asked Parliament to make provision for His Majesty to come to London for negotiations.'

'How would that change matters? This has been asked often enough with no result.'

'Yes, sir. Which is why we asked that the current members of the Commons should be replaced by people who are more patriotic. People who want peace for the whole of England, not just some.'

'I doubt that they found that appealing.'

The man smiled grimly. 'Indeed not. But the people of Dorset feel betrayed by these men who have put themselves above the wishes of those who elected them.'

'What other demands were contained in your petition?'

'That representatives of all the religious factions should come together to find a solution to the problem of how we can have religious freedom for all. We asked for the county committees to be disbanded. Before this war our counties were led by families who had held those positions for generations. They may have let us down at times, but the good of the county was always important to them. These committees who now rule us appear to be there only for the gain that they can make for themselves.'

'Many of those families have lost land and property because of their loyalty to the king.'

'That is true, sir, which is why we have asked that these should be restored to them.'

Simon was thoughtful. 'I doubt that Parliament was happy with your demands. It seems to me that they are no different from the hundreds of demands which have been made over the last year or two. None of which the Commons were in the mood to accept.'

'Yes, that is so. But we did not know what else to do. The people of the west are so disillusioned by the way we have been governed by these people, and that damned New Model Army they are so reliant on. We had hoped that if enough people showed their dissatisfaction then something might come of it.'

'Indeed. It is what we all hope for.' Sir Thomas smiled grimly. 'I take it that your demands were rejected outright? There were no offers of compromise?'

'I am afraid so, sir.'

'Then you go and join your men. I will report to His Lordship. No doubt he will want to speak with you in the morning.'

'Thank you, sir.'

With that the young man turned and strode away.

Chapter 27

June 1648

More than a week had passed since the meeting on Blackheath. Although they had waited for as long as they dared, the hoped-for reinforcements from London had not come. Finally, the Earl had turned and marched his troops towards Braintree. En route they joined with Sir Charles Lucas, Lord Capel, Lord Loughborough and Sir George Lisle. As they rode together the following day, Norwich told Simon and his father what he had learnt.

'Sir Charles has brought the whole Essex Regiment with him, which greatly increases our number.'

'That is something to be thankful for.'

Although he said nothing, Simon agreed with his father. His first taste of action had left him feeling vulnerable, and he hoped that there would be greater safety in numbers for them.

Norwich nodded at Thomas's comment. 'Then you will also be pleased to hear that Colonel Farre has declared for the King. He brings the Essex Trained Bands with him.'

'Indeed! That is good news!' Sir Thomas smiled. 'Though I hardly think that Parliament will be pleased to hear it. They must have been counting on Farre to keep us contained.'

'How many men does he bring?' Simon asked.

'With his men, we now number around four thousand fighting men.'

'That many!' Simon looked over his shoulder at the snaking line of men who followed. He had not realised how many had come together in the last twenty-four hours. They must stretch for some distance behind them. He frowned. 'Will that not make us more of a target, and encourage Fairfax to try to take us?'

'Yes. Which is why we are marching to Braintree.'

Simon could see the town in the distance, no more than a ten-minute ride away. His brow was still furrowed by a frown. 'Why Braintree? What does it have to offer us?'

Sir Thomas smiled. 'Nothing, save for the county magazine.'

'You plan to take Parliament's munitions!'

'Indeed we do, young Simon.' Norwich smiled. 'As far as we know they are not expecting a large force such as ours, so it should be an easy task. The magazine is on the outskirts of town, not far from here.'

Simon nodded grimly. That would make sense. He had seen first-hand how much destruction could be wrought if anything went wrong. The thought of attacking the magazine brought back clear to his mind the scene of carnage at Norwich. He swallowed hard. He would not allow his fear to show. 'What is the plan of attack?'

The Earl inclined his head towards the leading troops, who were peeling away and heading for the magazine. 'We have five hundred there on foot. Far more than we need. We three will approach in their rear with a troop of cavalry. Our job will be to apprehend any who try to escape.'

'Yes, My Lord.' Simon wiped his sweaty palm on his trousers, then loosened his sword in its scabbard. He watched as a troop of cavalry wheeled out of line and fell in behind the swiftly moving troops, swords drawn.

'You stay behind me. Understood?'

Simon nodded to his father as the three men spurred their horses forwards. It seemed like no time at all before they were within reach of the walls, where they drew to a halt. The infantry were moving forward, muskets at the ready as they surrounded the stone building holding the magazine.

'I do not like this.' Sir Thomas frowned. 'They are less than one hundred yards from their objective, yet there is no sign of defenders. No musket fire.'

'Surely that is a good thing? We shall take them by surprise.'

'No, Simon. There should be guards. They know that there are Royalist forces in the area. What are they playing at?'

While he was speaking the leading men made their way cautiously into the building, still unopposed. Those following behind crowded in close.

'Dear Lord preserve us.' Sir Thomas whispered. 'What if it is a trap?'

'A trap? But how...' Simon's voice trailed off into silence. Of course. Draw them in, and then explode some of the munitions. He knew how devastating that would be. 'Should we tell them to withdraw?'

'It would be too late now.' The Earl sounded calm, collected. 'If that is their plan we could never get our men out in time. All we can do is hope and pray that they can take the defenders swiftly.'

The three men sat in silence for a moment. Simon itched to turn and ride away, further from any potential area of destruction. But his father remained calm, and he could not let him down. The tension mounted until he felt like a taut bowstring, ready to snap. His nervousness was transmitted to Prince, who began to stamp impatiently.

At last men appeared again in the doorway. Four of their own with someone else. A prisoner. Norwich and Sir Thomas urged their horses forwards into a trot. Simon was only a step behind. They drew up between the cavalry and infantry, arriving just seconds before the small group of men.

'My Lord, the building is empty.'

Norwich frowned at the soldier. 'Empty?'

'Yes, My Lord. This is the only man we found.'

'The munitions?'

'There are none, My Lord.'

Although Norwich's features remained calm, Simon saw the tension in his neck and shoulders as he turned to the captive.

'What were you doing in that building?'

The man stood straight and proud. 'Making sure that there was nothing of use to any Royalist.'

'What has happened here?' demanded the Earl.

The man was silent for a moment, then shrugged. 'There is no need for me to hold my silence, whether I speak or not will make no difference.' He smiled. 'You were beaten to the prize by Sir Thomas Honywood. He has seized the weapons for Parliament.' His grin widened. 'With luck you shall come across them in time. On the other side of a battlefield!'

The Earl sat silently upon his horse before barking his orders at the captors.

'Take this man to My Lord Lucas. He will want to question him. The rest of you, order the men to withdraw, leaving only one troop to check the building. When you have finished, report to me.'

'My Lord.'

The soldiers saluted before turning to do his bidding. With a face like thunder, Norwich turned and cantered away with Simon and his father in close pursuit. He had calmed somewhat by the time they re-took their place in the column. Simon took a deep breath before speaking.

'What happens now, My Lord?'

'We continue with Lucas' plan, though without the munitions we could have made such good use of.'

'Plan, My Lord?' asked Sir Thomas.

Norwich nodded. 'Fairfax has taken Maidstone and is not far behind us. We need to draw together as many men as we can. Then ensure that Fairfax remains here, rather than going north to meet the Scots when they come. That will require us to find a safe place where he cannot touch us. We march to Colchester.'

***

Simon looked down at the controlled activity. His position on the city wall offered a vantage point from where he could observe the preparations for the defence of Colchester. He could see the troops where they had taken up their positions in bushes and trees on either side of the Maldon Road. They were in the usual formation, infantry backed by pikes, and Simon could see where the cavalry mounts were tethered by the gates. He looked down the road to where he could see the approaching Parliamentary forces as a smudge on the horizon.

'Are we ready?'

Sir Thomas nodded. 'Yes. Twenty-four hours has been time enough to prepare the outskirts. Those on the walls are also ready to meet the foe.'

Simon looked around him. Father and son had been assigned positions close to the gate so that Sir Thomas would be able to report back to Norwich, and take charge if things became desperate. The walls were strongly manned. There were cannon and missiles which could be thrown down on attackers, as well as musketeers at regular intervals.

'I do not understand why our troops are out on the road when we have such strong walls. Surely they are vulnerable there?'

Sir Thomas nodded. 'To some extent, you are correct. But we need to keep Fairfax engaged. If we merely shut ourselves in the city he would leave a small force to contain us and take the remainder north to face the Scottish army. We have to make him realise that we will not sit idly. He has to know that we will take the battle to him from time to time. Then he will be forced to hold all of his men here.'

Simon nodded. 'I see.'

They watched in silence for a time. Fairfax had halted his forces out of range of the cannon on the walls, and they were spreading out on a front which stretched for half a mile. The defenders on either side of the road were ready. The cavalry soothed their excited mounts. The tension was palpable. Suddenly a voice rang out.

'Lone rider approaching!'

Sir Thomas looked along the road before calling down to those at the gate.

'One of our scouts! Let him through and escort him to my Lord Norwich!' He turned to Simon. 'Come on. Let us go and find out what news he brings.'

Fifteen minutes later they were with Norwich in the courtyard of the house he had appropriated as headquarters. He wasted no time in questioning the tired rider. 'The enemy force looks to be larger than we had thought. Who is there?'

'I waited as long as I could, My Lord,' the soldier began. 'Honywood has joined with Fairfax. As has Colonel Barkstead's Infantry Brigade from London.'

'How many men?'

'I would say more than five thousand. They all seem well trained and experienced. He also has over one thousand cavalry at his call.'

Norwich nodded his thanks, his face inscrutable. 'Thank you. Now go and join your unit.'

The soldier saluted, mounted, and rode away. When they were alone the Earl turned to Sir Thomas.

'They have the advantage of us when it comes to numbers.'

'But we are determined, and have the advantage of a highly defensible position.'

'Indeed. Now you and Simon must get back to your position on the wall. I have to take the news of Fairfax's allies to the others.'

With that he turned and walked away.

***

Simon had been back on the wall for an hour when his father clasped a hand on his shoulder and pointed down the road.

'There is a great deal of activity down there. I fear that Fairfax has decided to attack.' He squeezed his son's shoulder, his fingers conveying his tension as he spoke. 'This will be the first of many encounters over the next few days, Simon. It is unlikely that there will be fighting on the wall, but if there is...'

'I will not be sent away, Father.'

Sir Thomas looked at his son in silence for a moment. He nodded slowly.

'I see that. But you must remember that you are more than an ordinary soldier. The Earl will need you to keep records of what happens here, so you have a duty to protect yourself. Just as I have a duty to ensure that my life is not spent needlessly when it can be better used to further the King's cause in another way.' He looked out at the mass of soldiers approaching down the road. 'I will not ask you to leave the wall before me unless I need you to carry a message. If it does come to fighting here on the wall then keep your back to mine. That way we can protect each other.'

'Yes, Father.'

There was the sound of a trumpet calling the defenders along the road to be ready. From where he stood, Simon could see them load their muskets. Three ranks of musketeers were backed by a further three ranks of pike, hidden in the trees about two hundred yards along the road. About one hundred and fifty yards out, and blocking the road to the gate, was a troop of the King's musketeers. Behind these were the pike men, weapons firmly grounded. Simon realised that anyone who met that wall of steel would stand little chance of getting through alive.

As he watched Simon was taken by surprise by the thunderous roar of musket fire. Barkstead's attacking infantry had fired on the men in the road. Some of the defenders fell beneath the hail of shot, though their front rank calmly returned fire before moving back behind the pikes. The second rank followed the same manoeuvre as the advancing enemy fired again. Then it was the turn of the third defending rank to fire their one shot and retreat behind the pikes. Slowly, the whole body of men began to retreat towards the gate. It all seemed so orderly, so disciplined to Simon who feared that, if he had been amongst them, he would have turned and fled before the approaching enemy. When they saw the slowly retreating Royalists the attackers drew their swords and, with a cry of delight, broke ranks to race after the retreating men.

A sudden withering volley of musket fire came from the trees and bushes on either side of the road, taking the unsuspecting attackers in the flanks. Dozens fell dead and wounded as the Roundheads slowed their attack and turned towards the ambushers. With a cry the Royalist pike men in the road changed direction and rushed forward, cutting and thrusting into the men who now struggled to attack the musketeers who had ambushed them from the trees, at the same time trying to defend their now vulnerable front. As they moved forward, the enemy were met by more hidden pikes. Simon could see that they were now surrounded on three sides by the lethal weapons which held firm against Barkstead's men. He smiled grimly as the city's defenders began to slowly but surely push forward. Soon the fight became a brutal hand-to-hand combat of attrition. The cries of fighting men mingled with the screams of the injured and dying.

It was impossible for the men on the wall to do anything with the two sides so closely engaged, so Simon watched with a mixture of fear and frustration. He had no idea how long the conflict had been raging; it seemed to him like hours, but must have been much less than that. He marvelled at the courage and tenacity of the men, on both sides, in the face of such opposition. For a time he was not sure what the outcome might be, but then he saw that the attackers were being pushed slowly back along the road. Suddenly a trumpet called out the retreat. The Roundheads turned and ran.

A cheer went up from the wall as their troops who had been engaged stopped to rest for a moment, breathless but triumphant.

'We have won!'

'I am afraid not, Simon. We are still surrounded. I fear the enemy will merely re-group and make a second attempt on the gate.' Sir Thomas leant over the wall to call down to an officer inside the walls. 'Get our dead and wounded back inside the city!'

'Sir!' The man leapt to do his bidding.

'Captain Webb!' An officer looked around to see who had called his name. 'Up here! Join me on the wall!' Webb looked up. When he saw Sir Thomas he nodded and came running.

'Sir?'

Sir Thomas pointed out over the wall to where the unwounded defenders were re-grouping. 'Those men have done a magnificent job, but will find it hard to stand against a second attack. Get your men out there and take up positions either side of the road. Once you are ready you are to relieve those men and send them back into the city.'

Webb saluted. 'Yes, sir.' With that he turned and leapt down the stairs, two at a time, calling out his orders as he went.

Webb's men had been standing in reserve and were ready to go. Within ten minutes they were out on the road, and the weary but triumphant defenders marched back through the gates to the cheers of the men on the wall. Simon found himself shouting and waving along with the rest, proud of how well the men had fought. Yet, at the same time, he felt a knot of anxiety in his stomach. If Barkstead's men attacked again, they would not be taken by surprise this time. Casualties were likely to be higher. He turned towards his father, wanting to ask his advice, seek his comfort, but Sir Thomas stood proud and still on the wall, exuding an air of calm confidence. Simon was not sure if this aura was a true projection of his father's feelings, or a mask to encourage the defenders. He realised that he did not want to find out.

Three cannon had been brought forward from the enemy lines and suddenly began to fire. At first Simon thought that the attack was aimed at the wall but was falling short. Then he realised that they were aiming for the bushes on either side of the road. Hidden defenders fell. Simon felt sick as he heard the cries of the wounded.

'Return fire!' Sir Thomas called to the artillerymen on his right. 'We need to destroy those guns!'

The cannon on the wall began to fire. The first volley fell short of the enemy guns, but not by much. They were re-loaded and the muzzles raised before they fired a second time. This time the shot fell amongst the cannon, but it was too far to see if they had scored a direct hit. Then the enemy fired again. Only two guns this time. To Simon's right another cannon roared and he found himself covering his ears. Dust and earth was raised in huge gouts around the enemy guns. When it cleared he saw the enemy guns being pulled back.

'They have done their job,' his father said softly. 'There is no need for them to risk the guns being destroyed. Now that they have disrupted our troops in the bushes they will send in another attack on foot. See, here they come now!'

Simon peered down the road. The enemy were moving forward again, this time on a much broader front. The centre of the line was ten men deep, but on either side were extensive wings six deep. Following fifty yards behind them was another line of men who halted, ready to attack wherever the line was weakened.

The defenders had set up nearer to the wall this time, drawing the Roundheads even closer. At twenty yards there was the sound of musket fire from both sides, then a roar as the enemy charged forward. Simon could see the men on the road crash against the defending wall of pikes which shuddered under the impact, but did not break. It was not so easy to see what was happening on the sides of the road. Some of the men fought in full view, but others were obscured by trees and bushes, making it difficult for Sir Thomas to see what was happening. But this was no more difficult than for the enemy leaders who were unable to co-ordinate their attack. Although it was impossible to see the individual skirmishes, it was obvious that the defenders were struggling as the line of agitation in the trees moved ever closer to the walls.

'Cavalry!' The Commander looked up to where Sir Thomas stood on the wall. 'Lead them out in two wings. Bypass the fighting and take the reserve from either side. Then turn and take the attackers in the rear!'

'Sir!'

Simon watched as the cavalry trotted out through the gate before splitting and riding at a controlled canter around the fighting. At the sound of a trumpet the riders broke into a gallop, taking the enemy reserve in a tight pincer movement. Pistols fired. Swords flashed. In seconds the cavalry were through. They wheeled around and hit the reserve again. And again. And again.

'There is movement on the edge of the enemy mass!'

Sir Thomas tore his eyes away from the battle to look. More enemy troops were forming up ready to attack. He looked back to where the cavalry engaged the enemy, and smiled. 'Do not worry. Our men have seen them.'

Even as he spoke the Roundheads, who had been decimated by the cavalry, broke and ran while the horsemen turned and thundered into the rear of the forward battle line. Barkstead's men found themselves trapped between the defending infantry and the cavalry with nowhere to go. They fought bravely, but the battle was savage, their line too thin to adequately defend both front and rear. Within minutes, too soon for help to reach them, they turned and ran.

Sir Thomas once again re-organised the troops on the road, made sure the wounded were cared for, had the dead recovered. He and Simon took some bread and cheese up on the wall, not wanting to leave their post to take a proper meal. Simon had not thought that he would be able to eat after seeing so much death, but it had now been many hours since breakfast and the afternoon sun was low in the sky. After the first bite he found that he was famished and eagerly tore into the food.

While he was wiping the last crumbs from around his mouth, the warning trumpets sounded once again. This time the defenders were holding a solid line in front of the wall. Sir Thomas did not want to have his men inside the woods when darkness came. Being so heavily outnumbered, that would likely be a massacre. Simon watched the solid ranks of the enemy approach to just within musket range, then stop. Both sides fired volley after volley with hundreds of men falling to the shot.

'Enemy cavalry!'

On hearing the cry, Sir Thomas called down his orders to the defending cavalry who cantered away. Fairfax's horse, far outnumbering the Royalist, charged into the line of defenders, cutting a swathe of destruction as they came. They turned swiftly, re-formed and were about to take the defenders in the rear when the Royalist cavalry hit them. The fighting was fierce, men and horses slashing and kicking and trampling. The mounted Royalists fought well but it was obvious, even to Simon, that they could not win against such enormous odds. He was shocked to see that, while his attention had been on the cavalry, the enemy infantry had come on at a run. They were now hand-to-hand with the defenders, pushing them back against the city walls.

'Sound the retreat!'

As the trumpeter obeyed Sir Thomas's command, the defenders began to fall back in an orderly fashion until they were within the gates. The cavalry came thundering in behind them, the enemy hot on their heels. There was no time to close the gates and, within moments, the enemy infantry were inside the wall.

'Cannon! Fire on the approaching enemy! Musketeers! Face out and defend the wall!'

Simon picked up a musket and fired. As he reloaded he could hear the fierce fighting inside the walls. He desperately wanted to turn around and look. But it was his job to defend the wall. Taking aim again he fired into the approaching mass.

Suddenly the sounds behind him became even more intense. Cheers now mingled with the sound of clashing blades and cries. He took a quick moment to look over his shoulder, just in time to see a cavalry counter-attack coming down the main street. The Roundheads were slowed a little, but still continued to move forward under the press of more of their own men coming through the gates behind them.

'Well done, Webb!'

Simon turned at his father's words, and was in time to see Webb's men sortie from the side streets, taking the enemy in both flanks. Simon turned his back on the melee and fired down on the attackers outside the wall once more. The enemy cavalry were in the midst of the infantry, unable to move at speed. Simon could see that they were being picked off by the defenders. Obviously losing too many men and horses, the cavalry finally wheeled and rode away. The fire from the walls was withering. The attackers, unable to get through the gates for the press of their own men, began to fall back. Finally the Roundheads who had managed to get inside the city walls began to fall back too, until the only attackers left within the city were the dead or wounded. The defenders paused to take breath.

'I do not believe it. They are coming again!'

Sir Thomas looked out over the wall. 'I am afraid so. Fairfax knows that his only real chance of taking us is to push on today. If he leaves it until morning we will have all of our guns ready on the walls. He will never get in.'

'What do we do?'

'We kill as many of his men as possible.' Sir Thomas turned to Webb, who had joined them on the wall. 'You are to take two hundred men outside the walls. Form up in front of the gates to draw the enemy on. We will do the rest.'

The officer paled at the order, but saluted. 'Yes, sir.'

As he walked away Simon turned to his father. 'You are sending them out again?'

'Yes, but not far. The enemy can only meet them one on one, but we can take the enemy in greater numbers with cannon and muskets from the walls.' He met Simon's eyes. 'I will bring them in before it is too late. Do not worry.'

Simon nodded, but said nothing as the next wave of attackers charged down the road towards them.

***

It was midsummer and the daylight hours dragged on. As it began to get darker, Sir Thomas ordered the last of the troops into the city, and the gates closed with an ominously final thud. He had hoped that night would bring an end to the battle, but even when it became dark the attackers still continued to come. Torches on the walls were needed to enable the defenders to load the weapons, though that made them something of a target for the attackers. To even the odds, Sir Thomas ordered fire arrows to be sent out over the troops. Within minutes, the bushes in which the Royalist troops had hidden earlier in the day were afire, lighting up the enemy and offering targets for the cannon and muskets on the walls.

Simon was exhausted. The constant activity, the firing on living men, the fear of dying, all conspired to drain him of what little energy and emotion he had left until he was reloading and firing like an automaton. When he had a moment to spare to look at the other defenders, he could see that they felt the same. The exhaustion on the wall was almost tangible. Yet they continued to fight, hour after bloody hour.

Finally, as midnight approached, the sound of trumpets calling the retreat were heard as Fairfax finally acknowledged that the battle was lost.

As the Roundheads withdrew, the men on the walls raised a tired cheer. Sir Thomas ordered every fifth man to stay where he was and keep watch whilst the rest left the wall to take food and rest. Those who were chosen mumbled their displeasure as they stood to their post. Sir Thomas moved amongst them offering praise and encouragement, promising that they would be relieved within the hour. Simon, who followed close behind, was proud of the way his father led the men.

Finally, Sir Thomas had time to turn to his son. With a tired smile he led him from the wall to find food and a bed.

***

Two days had passed since the battle. The wounded were treated. The dead were buried. The defenders had now set up a routine of sentries on the walls, with hundreds of men waiting in the streets below to fight off any attack. But no attack came.

Simon was seated at a small desk, quill in hand as he made brief notes of the meeting. He would write them up neatly and in detail once Norwich and Capel had left.

'So, how many men do you think Fairfax has?'

Capel shrugged. 'It is hard to say. We estimate that he lost around eight hundred in the attack. Maybe as many as one thousand. That should leave him with more than four thousand but less than five, I would guess.'

'Much the same as our forces.' Norwich frowned thoughtfully. 'I assume that he is expecting reinforcements?'

'As far as we can find out, yes. There are a few detachments of the New Model locally, but nothing significant. Our spies in his camp have heard that he is waiting for more troops to be released after putting down other risings.'

'At least that means that we are not alone in this.' Norwich was grim. 'What I do not want is the King's men locally trying to do something on their own and wasting themselves. I have sent out men to negotiate on our behalf for support from Suffolk.'

'You think it will come?'

'Yes.'

Simon wondered if Norwich was as confident as he sounded. It was not his place to ask though, so he kept his head down and continued to make his notes.

'The Earl of Holland is mustering a relief force. He has the command of the Royalists in the south so will be able to bring us a goodly number of men,' Norwich continued. 'I am also in contact with the Suffolk Trained Bands. I believe that they will soon be with us.'

'If they do join us we are going to have trouble feeding everyone.'

Norwich turned to Capel. 'Only if we are holed up here for any length of time. Once the Scots come we will sally forth and hold Fairfax here.'

'But we need to supply ourselves until then. Now that Fairfax is building a circle of forts around the city, it is going to be difficult to get men and supplies in. And civilians out.'

Norwich's face was grim. 'We will find a way. No matter how many forts he builds, he cannot control every inch of land surrounding Colchester. We will find routes through when needed.'

There was a loud knocking at the door. Norwich looked towards Simon, who swiftly rose to his feet to see who it was. He was gone for only a moment before returning.

'A messenger from outside the walls, My Lord Norwich.'

'Bring him in.'

A man dressed as a civilian but obviously a soldier by his bearing, came in. He saluted and stood to attention.

'What news?'

The man looked from Norwich to Capel and back again, as though he did not want to speak. Norwich frowned.

'Out with it man!'

The soldier took a deep breath. 'Six companies of horse and dragoons have arrived in support of Fairfax, My Lord.'

Norwich and Capel were stunned.

'What! Where have they come from so speedily?' asked Capel.

'It is the Suffolk Trained Bands, My Lord. Fairfax has ordered them to move north and east to guard the bridges across the river Colne.'

A stunned silence met his news. Finally Capel dismissed the man with a wave of his hand. When the door was closed he turned to Norwich.

'You said that they had all but come out on our side! The traitors will live to regret this!' Norwich was silent. 'What say you, man?'

'Throughout our negotiations they have been asking my assurance that I will do everything to keep the fighting in Essex and away from their lands.' Norwich's voice was grim. 'It is my guess that Fairfax has promised them this, which is why he has sent them to the Colne. They will fight well there to protect their own.'

'Apart from the loss of their numbers, this makes things even more difficult for us.'

'How so, Capel?'

'The river mouth and harbour are already being blockaded by parliamentary forces. Our only hope of re-supply from that direction was across the river. That has now been lost to us.'

'Then perhaps we should send out the civilian population' mused Norwich. 'They were not happy to see us arrive, having been strong supporters of the King's enemies in the past. They are already complaining about having to feed and billet our men. We will be much better off without them.'

'Some have left, but the majority stay. I fear that they do not want to leave their property and possessions in our tender care!'

Norwich laughed. 'I can hardly blame them for that!' He was suddenly serious. 'With the Suffolk Trained Bands now lost to us, the civilians cannot hold their own food supplies any longer. I want all supplies of any sort – food, water, beer, fodder for the horses – to be collected and stored centrally. We need an inventory of what we have and how long it will last. We will also need to decide what the ration is to be. Make sure that the soldiers get the most. They will need their strength to fight. If the civilians do not like it, they can leave.' Norwich made his way over to the door. 'Come, Capel. We have work to do.'

As the two men left, Simon put down his pen. A dull fear settled in his stomach as he contemplated the weeks to come.

Chapter 28

Present day

Rob woke with a start. 'My God,' he thought, 'what are we to do? We can never hold out against such numbers! I'm caught in a siege and could die of starvation. If I'm not shot first.' His heart was beating rapidly, his mouth dry, he shook with fear and broke out in a cold sweat as he contemplated the future. A sudden ringing interrupted his thoughts, leaving him feeling disorientated. It rang again, and he realised what it was. His phone. But how did he know that that sound was a phone? And how could he have a phone in Colchester? No. Wait. He wasn't in Colchester. That was just a dream. He was in his bed at Marston. Yet it had felt so real, as though he had really been there. The incessant ringing of the phone finally helped Rob to concentrate, and he picked it up with shaking hand.

'Yes?'

'At last. You're a deep sleeper!'

'Who is this?'

'Jim. For goodness sake, man. Wake up!'

Rob struggled to focus. 'What's wrong?'

'There's something going on in the top field.'

'What?'

'Lots of lights. I can't be sure, but I think it's those damned travellers again. Hare coursing. I want you to come with me so we can get some pictures as evidence.'

'Okay. I'll be down in a minute.'

Rob switched off his phone, sitting in the dark for a moment as he tried to re-orientate himself. The dream had been so real, more real than any dream he had ever had before. He felt he could still taste the gunpowder, hear the clashing of blades, see the blood. But it was only a dream. It had to be. Rob shuddered. 'Pull yourself together, you bloody fool,' he muttered as he dragged himself from the bed and began to dress. Minutes later he met Jim in the courtyard.

'You ready?'

Rob nodded. 'Are you sure this is a good idea?'

'Absolutely. I may be wrong. But if I'm right this will be just the evidence we need to get rid of these thugs. Have you got your camera?'

Rob shook his head. 'It's in the car, but I've brought my phone.' He looked towards the fields where beams of flashlights could be seen weaving back and forth. 'Won't it be dangerous?'

'Not if we're not seen. And I intend to make sure we're not. Now, come on. This way.'

Jim led the way along the hedgerow, moving as quietly as possible, a crouching Rob following in his wake. After about a mile they came to the gate leading into the wide pastureland.

'Shit!' Jim slipped back behind the hedge. 'There must be fifty or sixty people there,' he whispered.

'Do you recognise them?'

Jim nodded. 'Most of the ones I can see seem to be from the campsite.'

Rob peered round his companion into the field, glad of the clouds which covered the moon, making it difficult for anyone to see him. He could make out shapes of all sizes. Adult men and women, teenagers, small children. It seemed to be almost a family outing. There was quiet talk, some subdued laughter; almost a festival atmosphere. As he let his eyes rove over the crowd Rob saw a group of men with six dogs. Lurchers he thought. Four of the animals had hoods on their heads and were lying on the ground, as though tired. The other two dogs were staring intently to their left, straining at their leashes. Rob could see a group of people moving slowly across the pasture, waving flags and stamping loudly as they came. Suddenly a small shape rose from its hiding place in the grass and dashed off.

Rob felt his pulse increase. 'A hare!'

'Get some photos.'

Rob shook his head. 'I can't. It's too dark. And we can't use flash.'

'Shit!' Jim moved closer and was in time to see the two lurchers loosed. They raced off, bunched muscles thrusting them forwards at a terrific speed. The terrified hare jinked and turned ahead of them, seeking escape. All the time the dogs drew closer, weaving rapidly to stay on the trail of their prey. There were shouts of encouragement from the crowd as the dogs raced ahead, the scene illuminated by powerful flashlights which followed the action. In a frantic effort to avoid the dog snapping close on its heels, the hare spun left, straight into the path of the second animal. Seconds later there was a scream, sounding almost like a child in pain. The sounds were drowned out by the crowd. Some cheering, some mumbling their disappointment. To his right Rob saw a group of men moving towards a dark figure who stepped into the torchlight. Cowan. In his hand he had a sheaf of money, which he began to hand out to the smiling men.

'The winnings.'

Rob nodded. 'The cruel bastards!'

Jim nudged him in the ribs. 'Look.' The owners of the two dogs which had so recently raced the course had retrieved their animals and were making their way towards the gate, one of them carrying the bloody remains of the hare. The chattering crowd was turning to follow them. 'I would guess that the other dogs have already had their turn. It looks like it's all over.'

'And we need to get out of here if we want to escape without a beating, or worse.'

Jim needed no second bidding. Without a word the two men swiftly made their way in the shadow of the hedge, back to the Manor.

***

Paul glared at the police officer.

'What do you mean, you can't prosecute? Hare coursing is against the law, isn't it?'

'Yes, sir.'

'Then get out there and do your job.'

Rob thought that the officer looked as though he was struggling to remain polite. He felt some sympathy for him. Jim had reported what they had seen as soon as they had returned to the Manor the night before but, as everyone involved had already left the field, the police had not come out immediately. When Paul had arrived that morning to be told what had occurred, he was seething. He immediately phoned the police and insisted that someone should come out. The officer who had arrived in response to the call tried to explain, once more, why he could do nothing.

'Hare coursing is illegal, sir. And, from what these two gentlemen have told me, I have no doubt that that is what was going on last night. It sounds like it was a low key affair and...'

'Low key?' Rob interrupted. 'There were at least fifty people there.'

The officer nodded. 'I appreciate that, sir. What I mean by low key is that it seems to be local travellers making small bets for fun. It wasn't one of the big events that draw people from across the country, and where thousands of pounds change hands.'

Rob looked surprised. 'That really goes on?'

'Yes. Organised crime is into this. And it seems to be spreading.'

'I'm not surprised, if you let them get away with it.'

The officer turned back to Paul. 'That isn't by choice, sir. We need hard evidence to be able to bring a prosecution. That means we have to be able to prove that there were beaters, that there were trained dogs which were released onto the hare, and that money changed hands.' He held up a hand to forestall Paul's next comment. 'Yes, I know that these men witnessed those things, but there is no evidence. We would need photos or video to prove it had taken place.'

'Surely you would be able to find some evidence where it happened? Sign of a struggle and some blood at the very least?'

The officer nodded at Jim's question. 'Yes. But it wouldn't prove anything. Without photos it could be argued that a pet dog, or a fox, took some animal in the field. And that's not unusual in the countryside, is it? Besides, we would still not be able to identify the individuals involved.'

'So what happens next?' Rob glanced at Paul as he spoke. 'Will you move the travellers on?'

'I'm afraid not. As there's no evidence, they would complain of discrimination.'

'For goodness sake! Why is it that these people get all the protection in the world and honest landowners like me get shafted!'

'I'm sorry you feel that way, sir.'

'I don't need your sympathy. I need those bastards moved on. And if you won't do it I will!'

'I'd advise you not to take matters into your own hands. I'm going down there now to talk to them, and I'll warn them that they will be moved on if they cause any trouble.'

'Good. Just make sure that you're ready to move them on when they do something else wrong. And they will.' With that, Paul turned and strode from the room. The police officer turned to Jim and Rob.

'Thanks for your report. Sorry I couldn't do more about it.'

'That's okay. Come on, I'll show you out.'

As Jim led their visitor towards the door Rob could see him visibly relaxing. The thought of a confrontation with Cowan was obviously preferable to the one he had just had with Hetherington.

***

'Hello, Rob.'

'Caroline! It's so good to see you!' Rob dismounted from Tully as he spoke. Draping the reins over one arm he embraced the woman. 'I've missed you.'

'And I've missed you, too. That's why I decided to take a long weekend and come to see you.' She kissed him passionately. For some reason Rob did not feel the upwelling of emotion that kissing Caroline usually gave him, and his response was half-hearted. Caroline drew back with a slight frown, although she didn't comment on his kiss. She turned and looked towards the house. 'This really is a beautiful place. It's no wonder you're burying yourself here.'

'I'm not burying myself. I just have so much work to do that it's hard to get away and…'

He was interrupted by Caroline's slightly forced laughter. 'Always taking the bait! I really should stop using my professional abilities to tease you!'

Rob grinned sheepishly. 'Caught me again! Will I never learn? Come on,' he said as he led the way towards the stables, 'I'll just see to Tully, then I'll show you round.'

Ten minutes later, with the horse happily rolling in the field, Rob began the tour. 'Let's start with the education centre, as we're already out here.'

'Isn't that where the fire was?'

Rob nodded. 'Yes, but it didn't take us long to clear up. We're now making good progress. Come and see.' He led the way into the old barn, which was undergoing a major transformation. 'This will be the dining room.' He indicated a large area to the left, well defined by stud walls which were in the process of being plastered. 'On the other side will be a resources room. We're going to put in some computers which will link to all sorts of web-based information on the civil war and life in the seventeenth century. There'll also be resources which I'm going to write, as well as worksheets for different age groups.'

'So your teacher training isn't going to be wasted?'

Rob smiled. 'No. To be honest, I'm really looking forward to that part of the work. I know I won't be staying on to teach after the project is completed, but I will probably come back to do a few lectures and workshops. It will be great if we can get colleges and universities to come here and use us as a resource.'

'You've really thought this through, haven't you?'

'Of course! It's my job!' Rob turned to meet Caroline's gaze. 'I'm one of the few lucky people who gets paid to do something he loves. Anyway, what do you think of the barn?'

'I like it. Once you decorate it in period fashion it will look great.' There was the sound of hammering from upstairs, and Caroline raised her head to look up at the ceiling. 'What's going on up there?'

'They're working on the bedrooms and bathrooms. Not much to see at the moment. Come on, I'll show you the Manor house.'

As they made their way across the yard Caroline took Rob's hand in hers. Her fingers were warm, caressing, but Rob found that they didn't excite him in the way they used to; not like Rebekah's. At the thought of Rebekah he frowned. What was happening to him? Why was he so attracted to that strange, enigmatic young woman at the expense of a relationship which, until he came to Marston, had been the very bedrock of his existence?

'What's wrong, Rob?'

He was startled by the question.

'What do you mean?'

'You used to call me at least once a day when we were apart. Now I can't remember the last time you called.'

'We spoke just yesterday!'

'Yes, but it was me who phoned you. And it has been me phoning you for the last week or so.'

Rob was thoughtful. 'Sorry. I hadn't realised. I suppose I've just been so busy with things that…' his voice trailed off.

'You've been so busy with things that you've forgotten about me.' There was an edge to Caroline's voice which Rob had not heard before.

'No! That's not true!' But, even as he said the words, Rob realised that it was true. Caroline had always invaded his thoughts in the past. Now his thoughts, and dreams, belonged to another.

'Okay.' Caroline's voice was conciliatory. 'Maybe you haven't forgotten me. But there is something wrong, Rob. Won't you tell me? Are you seeing someone else?'

'No.' Rob turned away for a moment, guilt washing over him. He wasn't seeing someone else, but that didn't mean he didn't want to. He was totally confused by his feelings. Caroline was still an important part of his life, in a way that Rebekah might never be, yet he could not stop himself wishing, hoping. He was not sure what he could tell Caroline when he was unable to understand his feelings himself. But he had to tell her something. He decided on part of the truth as he turned back towards her.

'It's the dreams.'

Caroline's face registered surprise. 'The dreams you told me about when you came home?'

He nodded. 'I'm still dreaming about life here at Marston in the seventeenth century. It all seems so real. So much so that when I broke my arm in my dream I could feel it when I woke up.'

'Are you serious?'

'Come on, Caroline. I couldn't make up something like that, could I?'

She was silent for a moment, then shook her head. 'No, I suppose not. You've never been one for a vivid imagination. Which means…'

'What?'

'Which means there's a psychological explanation. Are you still dreaming about the same people?'

Rob nodded. 'Yes. In my dreams I'm the youngest son of the lord of the Manor. I'm experiencing the war through his eyes.' For some reason he decided not to mention the fact that a girl called Rebekah featured in his dreams, and that she closely resembled a real life Rebekah that he had met. Somehow he did not think that Caroline would appreciate that in her present frame of mind. As it was, he feared that she would laugh at his dreams, tell him he was being a fool and to come back to reality. To his surprise, she seemed to be taking his dreams seriously.

'I can think of two possible answers to what you're experiencing.'

'Two? I'll be damned if I can think of one!'

Caroline's smile was more relaxed now that she felt she understood why Rob had been acting strangely. 'Yes. Two. First of all, you've found a personal connection here. It's your family home. The fact that you're so immersed in what this place was like during the civil war, and therefore how it affected your ancestors, could mean that all this stuff is coming together in your mind and you are processing it, filing it, while you're asleep.'

'That sounds logical. What's the other possibility?'

'It's a bit way out.'

'So are my dreams.' Rob smiled encouragingly. 'Go on, tell me. It can't be as bad as me thinking I'm going mad.'

Caroline took a deep breath. 'Have you thought about the possibility of past lives?'

'What?' Rob was astonished.

Caroline looked a little sheepish. 'You know. The idea that we have all lived many lives before, but don't remember them? Perhaps you're reliving a past life in your dreams?'

Rob laughed. 'Now I'm not sure if it's me who's going mad, or you! I don't believe in all that stuff.'

'I'm not saying that I do, Rob. It's not something I've ever really looked into. But if your dreams are so consistent, and so real, it could be a possibility.'

Rob was suddenly serious. 'You actually mean it's possible?'

'I don't know. But I'd be happy to do some research when I get home. If you like.'

Rob was thoughtful for a moment, then nodded emphatically. 'I don't suppose it can do any harm!' With a laugh he took Caroline's hand in his. 'Come on! Let me show you the rest of the family home!'

Chapter 29

June 1648

The roar of a cannon echoed in the enclosed streets. The walls of St Mary's Church shook as the huge gun placed on the nearby city wall hurled its load into the enemy camp. Simon smiled as he walked beside his father. 'There goes Humpty Dumpty!'

Sir Thomas laughed. 'I would love to know who gave it that nickname!'

'It does not matter who.' Simon laughed along with his father. 'The fact is that old Humpty Dumpty is something to set fear into our enemies' hearts. It has such a huge reach that they either have to endure the shot, or move further back. And to do that would open a gap for us to get through. They are a sitting target.'

'It is as much a weapon of the mind as a weapon of destruction', sighed Sir Thomas. 'With our limited ammunition for the gun, we can only fire a few times a day if we are to have enough to fight off any future attacks.'

'It little matters. Even knowing that it fires only three or four times a day must be frightening for the enemy who are within reach. And that pleases me.'

Sir Thomas cast a glance at his son. 'You are becoming hard, Simon.'

'Is that surprising, Father? Life is not easy for us here. What few sorties we have been able to send out for supplies have had little success. Rationing does not give us enough to eat. And I am not inclined to be friendly with those who are making me hungry.'

'We have supplies enough.'

Simon shook his head. 'You are not talking to one of the soldiers, Father. I write up the Earl's reports and so know what our true situation is. If only there were fewer civilians.' He sighed. 'Not only do they eat the food which could be better used for our troops, but they are starting to cause even more trouble now. Only this morning Webb had to deal with a large group of traders who were complaining about us taking their supplies. Even though he tried to talk them down, it came to blows.'

'That is the last thing we need. Soldiers and civilians at each others' throats.'

'I know. Maybe Lucas will be able to bring some supplies in.'

Father and son had reached the east wall and climbed to where they could look out over the open expanse of land around the city. Fairfax had completed his ring of forts, which stretched away to right and left. Any attempt to sortie from Colchester would be met by converging fire from the forts. Except for the stretch opposite the east gate. There the way was blocked by the Suffolk Trained Bands. At present some quarter of that force was arrayed in front of the wall, the remainder in camp at the rear, waiting their turn to go on duty. It was three weeks now since the opening battle, and the city's defenders had only gone out in small raiding parties to collect supplies. The Suffolk Bands were relaxed, not expecting any trouble now that the encircling of the walls was complete. Sir Thomas smiled grimly.

'Let us hope so.' He looked back inside the city walls. 'They appear to be ready to go.'

Simon looked down at the assembled troops who waited in silence, not wanting to alert the enemy to their presence. Six hundred foot were ready to sortie with four hundred horse behind them. The horses were stamping and champing at the bit, feeling the tension of their riders and eager to be off to battle. The men appeared less excited. Grim and determined faces turned towards the huge gates, which would be their exit from the besieged city.

Sensing that he was being watched, Sir Charles Lucas looked up at the wall. He smiled resolutely when he saw Sir Thomas and Simon, then turned back to his troops. Simon was too far away to hear the commands, spoken so that no shouts or trumpet calls would reach the enemy, but he saw the gates being unbarred and felt his shoulders tense. As the gates swung open and the infantry exited at a swift trot, he turned to look back over the wall.

The men had gone almost one hundred yards in complete silence before a cry went up from the enemy. The men from Suffolk quickly tried to form up into a defensive line, but they had left it too late. The cavalry galloped past the Royalist infantry, smashing into the enemy as they formed up, riding over the dead and wounded as they continued into the Roundhead camp. The swords of the mounted men were deadly, cutting and thrusting into the men who struggled to put on their armour and load their weapons. Behind the cavalry, the infantry had now reached the downed men, dispatching any who still tried to fight, though they were few in number.

Simon watched as small artillery pieces were hauled from the city to the former position of the enemy, where they set up and began to fire over the heads of their own men and into the fleeing mass. It was a rout.

After three weeks cooped up inside the walls, Simon knew how the men felt. He could imagine the excitement coursing through their veins as they pursued the Suffolk men, the men who were supposed to stand with them but had betrayed Norwich. For a moment he wished he could be out there with them. Chasing. Killing. He found that he was gripping the edge of the wall tightly, a grim smile on his lips as he watched the pursuit.

'Hold them, Charles. Hold them.'

Simon turned to look at his father who was muttering quietly to himself. 'Father?'

'They go too far. Too fast.'

Simon looked out again. The cavalry and infantry were still in pursuit of the enemy. The artillery fired repeatedly. The Suffolk Bands were being decimated. Massacred. He turned back. 'What is wrong?'

Sir Thomas drew in a swift breath between his teeth. 'That.'

Simon's eyes followed the pointing finger. His face paled, and his knees felt suddenly weak. On either side of the Royalists the enemy were forming up. In the distance he could see a troop of cavalry approaching. As he looked back at the skirmish he realised that their men had, indeed, gone too far. Instead of opening a breach in the defences and holding it, they had burst through to the other side. The enemy were moving into the gap, like waves covering a stretch of exposed sand. Within moments the artillery pieces were overwhelmed, the men with them swiftly put to the sword.

'Get hold of them, Charles. Bring them home.'

Sir Thomas's words were little more than a whisper, but it was almost as though Lucas heard him, for he turned in his saddle, shouting orders to his lieutenants. Trumpets sounded and the Royalist pursuit was halted. As the men began to make their way back towards the city their own artillery pieces were turned against them, bringing down men and horses. Simon felt sick.

'Will they be able to make it back?'

'I pray so, son.'

'Can we not help them?'

Sir Thomas shook his head. 'The enemy are out of reach of our guns on this wall. And there are no other troops ready to sortie. They are on their own.'

They watched in silence as Lucas drew his men together, sending his cavalry at the gallop to try to retake the guns and munitions. But the enemy had already got their pikes into position. To gallop into that wall would be slaughter for the horses, and for the men on their backs. The cavalry broke and rode back to Lucas, whose men were now running towards the gate. Orders were given, for Simon saw the king's cavalry split in two, protecting the flanks from attack by foot. But the enemy did not come in close. They did not need to. Musket fire was already taking its toll on the Royalists as they by-passed their taken artillery. As the Roundheads struggled to turn the guns round, hundreds of men were running to intercept the retreating infantry. Lucas rode in the middle of them, calling out encouragement, refusing to gallop away and leave them. He called over his shoulder to the cavalry.

As one, the cavalry wheeled to take the approaching infantry. Simon could see rider-less horses in their midst, the herd instinct drawing them on despite the loss of their riders. The depleted cavalry could not stop the counter-attack, but they slowed it enough to allow the infantry to get past. Suddenly cannon fired again. Simon looked to see their own artillery pieces turned and used against the fleeing men, firing into the backs of Lucas's infantry as they ran for the gate. No pretence at fighting now. Their only concern to reach the gate, and safety.

The cavalry held back to protect the vulnerable men for as long as possible, but as the cannon began to take their toll, Lucas called them to retreat.

'Yes, Charles. We can ill afford to lose our cavalry.'

Simon looked across at his father. His face was grim, but he stood straight and tall. Simon knew that it was an act, so that the men inside the wall would not know the despair that his son could see in his eyes as he forced himself to watch.

Simon turned back to look out over the wall. The cavalry galloped through the gate, closely followed by the first of the retreating men. Behind them came those who could not move as swiftly because of their wounds. Behind them, strewn across the summer grass, lay hundreds of their comrades.

'Can we not go out to them?'

Sir Thomas shook his head. 'The dead care not. And we will lose more men if we try to retrieve our wounded.'

'But...'

'In time, Simon. It may be that the enemy will take and tend to our wounded. If not, we will be able to go out in a short while under a flag of truce to bring them back. But that cannot happen until the fighting is over.'

He looked back over the wall. To be truthful, the fighting was already over. The cannon could no longer reach the few men who still ran towards the city, and the enemy wisely chose not to follow and bring themselves into reach of the defenders. It was only moments more before the last men were in and the city gates closed with a deadly finality.

***

It was early evening when the cannon fire began and Simon and his father made their way to their position on the wall. From where they stood they could see that the cannons, which had been placed by Fairfax in his new ring of forts, had opened fire. The barrage appeared to be focussed in their direction, at the only defences which lay outside the walls. Below him Simon could see the men in the grounds of St John's Abbey and the house of Sir Charles Lucas, cowering in what shelter they could find under the bombardment. Their small cannon were already firing back at the parliamentarian forces. The guns outside the walls were loud, but every few minutes they were drowned out by the roaring boom of 'Humpty Dumpty' on the wall by St Mary's church. Simon could feel the vibrations through the stones beneath his feet, through his very innards.

The enemy fire continued on into the evening, pounding the wall relentlessly. Sir Thomas was tense. 'This is likely to be a major attack. They aim to take out our artillery and then rush us.'

A cannonball hit the wall to their left, taking a piece of masonry with it as it flew on into the town. A defender had been brought down by its passage, and Simon watched as he was carried from the wall. He looked to his right and left. There was little for the men to do. The enemy was outside the range of anything but their cannon, so they could only watch. And wait. Simon was as tense as he knew they must be. To stand under such an attack and to be able to do nothing was a fearful situation. Another cannon ball hit, this time to their right, sending a shudder through to the very foundations of the wall.

'They are targeting Humpty!'

'It is what I would do.' Sir Thomas turned to Simon. 'If the enemy…'

There was another impact on the wall, but this time the vibrations did not stop. Instead they grew in intensity. A low rumbling could be heard as part of the wall began to collapse, hurling men down into the courtyard behind them. A cloud of dust stung their eyes, hiding what was happening from their sight. Another cannonball hit and the rumbling became a mighty roar, a scream of metal on stone, a crash which seemed to tear them apart, limb from limb.

There was a sudden, eerie silence. The clouds of dust began to clear and settle to reveal a gaping breach in the wall where the mighty gun had been.

'Dear Lord, preserve us!' Sir Thomas leaned over the wall to get a better view. The huge cannon lay still, barrel split and bent from its impact on the cobbles below, which were now little more than dust. Beyond the wall a huge cheer went up from Fairfax's camp. Trumpets sounded. An incoherent roar of voices rent the air. Sir Thomas turned his back on the cannon which had been their chief defence in this quarter. 'Here they come!'

It was difficult for Simon to see what was happening in the dark. Few cannons now spoke from the walls, many others had been taken when the big gun fell whilst the majority of those in the abbey had been crushed during the relentless pounding of the last few hours. From out of the dark

Simon heard musket fire, then the sound of steel upon steel as the attackers forced their way into the outer fortifications. Only where fires burned was Simon able to see the fierce hand-to-hand fighting which was taking place.

The defenders were tenacious, desperately trying to hold back the Roundheads who came forward in ever increasing numbers. It was a hopeless task. Minute by minute they retreated. Inch by inch the abbey and Lucas' house fell to the enemy. Slow step by slow step the Royalists withdrew. On the wall the defenders stood with muskets ready, only firing down into the mass below when they could identify a target. Simon found it infuriating. He wanted to do more. Shoot more. Kill more. This was not about the king. This was about defending men he had come to know, whose faces he recognised, whose voices had spoken to him. He felt powerless in the darkness of a night full of destruction. He saw a Roundhead clearly in the light of a burning building and fired. He knew that he had hit the man, for he saw him stumble and fall to his knees for a moment. When he rose again his arm hung limply from his side and he slipped back into the shadows. Simon reloaded and strained his eyes, seeking out another target.

***

A trumpet sounded from the enemy ranks. Moments later a single rider made his way forward at a slow trot. As he approached the city walls, he slowed his horse to a walk. The orange sash of the Roundhead officer shone brightly in the sunshine. In his hand he carried a pikestaff, the white flag tied to the blade fluttering in the breeze. The rider finally halted his horse close to the walls and looked up.

'Who holds here?'

Sir Thomas leant over. 'I do.'

'Well, I would speak with the leaders of this sorry band. Bring Norwich and Lucas here.'

Simon tensed in outrage at the arrogant rudeness. 'How dare he!'

His father held up a hand. 'Be still, my boy. He wishes to annoy us, so do not let him have the satisfaction of seeing that he has succeeded.'

Simon gritted his teeth but said nothing as Sir Thomas called down to the messenger. 'I will send for them. They will not keep you waiting over long.'

'I will not wait over long.' The lone man looked at the damaged walls, a smile on his lips. 'If they do not come soon then we shall resume where we left off last night!'

Sir Thomas turned to a soldier at his side, bidding him take the message to their leaders. When he turned back he saw a mix of emotions playing across his son's face.

'Simon?'

'I find that I cannot blame him for his arrogance,' he looked at the destruction all around them as he spoke. 'St John's Abbey. The home of Sir Charles. Our outer fortifications beyond the walls. All gone.'

His father nodded sadly. 'We lost heavily last night, both in position and men. But we are not defeated yet. Let us wait to see what this man has to say.'

As they waited for Norwich and Lucas, the sound of singing arose from the enemy ranks. It was a tune that the men on the wall did not recognise, and they struggled to hear the words. The messenger laughed.

'You hear that? That is the favourite song in the camp today!' He waited for the refrain to finish, then joined in with the voices which carried on the breeze as the singing began again.

'Humpty Dumpty sat on a wall,
Humpty Dumpty had a great fall.
Four-score Men and Four-score more,
Could not make Humpty Dumpty where he was before.'

Simon's mind raced back to the night before. The noise of battle. The confusion. The fall of the great cannon. The dead and dying. He found his hand tightly clasping the hilt of his sword. As he made to draw it, his father laid a restraining hand against his.

'Careful, Simon. He is here to parley. Do not raise a hand against him.'

'I can do nothing from here.'

'But drawing sword would be enough to offer offence.'

Simon turned to face the man who had spoken from behind him. 'My Lord Norwich. I apologise.'

'Do not worry, Simon.' Sir Charles Lucas did not look at Simon as he spoke, his eyes had sought out and found his home. His face was grim as he watched the enemy moving around within its grounds, setting up cannon. 'Let us hear what this man has to say. Then we can be rid of him.'

The rider must have seen the Commanders arrive on the wall, for he let his reins fall to the neck of his horse and raised a trumpet to his lips. He sounded a fanfare, then let the trumpet hang from its ribbon again as he took up his reins.

'Lucas! Norwich! My Lord Fairfax sends his greetings and his terms! The battle last night will have shown you that you cannot defeat us. You are held under siege. Your defences have been weakened. Food is running short. You cannot hold out!

'The terms offered are simple. If you open the gates to us today we will allow your men to disarm and disperse. You and your officers will be held at the pleasure of the Commons until the current uprising is supressed. If you then give your parole, you will be at liberty to return to your homes and families. These terms are most generous, and are not negotiable.'

Lucas looked down at the damage done to his house in the attack. His eyes narrowed and his mouth was a grim line. He turned back to the messenger.

'I see that I have little home to return to!' His angry words carried to the soldiers on the wall, who had been listening in silence to the ultimatum. 'Take my greetings to Fairfax and tell him that if he should send you here as his messenger boy again, he will spend the rest of this siege watching the crows pick your bones as you hang by your neck from this wall!'

A resounding cheer went up from the Royalist defenders as the rider, face red with anger, turned and galloped back to the Roundhead lines.

'Come.' Lucas led the way down from the wall as he spoke.

'Was that wise?' asked Norwich as he accompanied him. Simon and his father followed close behind.

'Wise? No, I think not,' said Lucas. 'But do you ask yourself why Fairfax urges our surrender, when all he needs to do is wait for a few more weeks until we are too weak from hunger to fight?' Simon looked quickly around to see if they had been overheard, but they were surrounded by armed guards who kept at a distance, and Lucas had spoken in a whisper. No one could have heard. Lucas continued. 'Only one thing could make Fairfax want to get this over with quickly. I pray that he wishes to leave here because the Scots have arrived at last, and he is needed in the north.'

'Do you think that is possible, My Lord?

Lucas smiled. 'Indeed I do, Simon. Which is why we will hold Fairfax here. You need to know', he said turning to Sir Thomas, 'that when we heard that Fairfax was focussing on this side of the city with his messenger, I ordered the cavalry to break out on the far side. If they get through they will ride north at all speed. One thousand cavalry should help the King's cause in the north.'

'And it will not hurt my task of making supplies go further. For man and beast!'

Simon laughed at his father's words, a lightening in his chest at the thought of the Scottish army. Could they be here at last? If so then he could soon be out of Colchester. The war could be over. He could go home.

Simon's exultant mood did not last for long. As they walked back towards the headquarters in the centre of the city, a tired and dishevelled man approached. He was filthy dirty and had the look of one who had not eaten in days. There was blood on his clothing.

'Massey? Is that you? Good lord man, what are you doing here?' Norwich could not hide his surprise. 'I did not expect to see you until His Lordship the Earl of Holland arrived with his relief force. Are they outside the city?'

Massey shook his head. 'I am afraid not, My Lord. They will not be coming.'

Norwich stopped walking. For a moment he did not speak, though he had no need to. Simon could see from his shocked expression and the anxiety in his eyes that this was not good news. The Earl finally found his voice.

'Has he gone over to the other side?'

'No, my Lord! Never that!' Massey was horrified at the suggestion. 'We were on our way here and had stopped at St Neots for the night. We had set sentries, knowing that Colonel Scroope was in the area. But we did not know how close.'

'What happened?'

Massey looked at Lucas. 'They attacked us during the night. An experienced detachment of the New Model. We fought hard, but were not able to hold them back.'

'Casualties?'

'Heavy, my Lord Norwich. Those not injured or wounded fled. My Lord Holland sent me here with his apologies that he cannot join you. I believe he intends to gather more men if he can, but he cannot guarantee that he will now be able to come to the aid of Colchester.'

Simon turned his worried gaze to his father. 'So what happens now?'

'We hold on. And pray that the Scots will soon have these damned parliamentarians on the run.'

***

Simon entered Norwich's office as the sun began to sink towards the horizon. He and his father had been summoned just as they were preparing to take dinner. Simon's stomach rumbled with hunger. A full day's ration in Colchester under siege was little more than he would take for lunch on a normal day at Marston. How he hoped they were here to receive good news. Maybe someone had managed to smuggle more supplies in. He certainly hoped so.

Norwich was sitting behind his desk reading a letter. He looked up when they entered.

Sir Thomas noted the grim expression. 'Bad news. My Lord?'

There was an imperceptible nod. 'The cavalry who rode out three days ago are back.'

Sir Thomas was shocked. 'But they had been gone so long that I had thought that they escaped?'

'As did I. And they almost made it. They were intercepted at Boxted soon after leaving here and have been fighting on and off all of this time. It appears that they held together well, but the enemy were just too great in number.' He sighed. 'It was a wise decision to preserve the cavalry and bring it back here. They could prove useful in the coming weeks. But it galls me that they could not get through and make for the north. Even more so now.'

'My Lord?'

Norwich lifted the letter. 'During their foray they met a man trying to sneak into Colchester.'

'That is a first.'

Simon smiled at his father's comment. Indeed, who would choose to make their way into a city under siege? He glanced at the letter in Norwich's hand, and hope blossomed in his chest. 'News, My Lord?'

Norwich smiled, something Simon had not seen for many days.

'News indeed! We all know that the Scots should have been here weeks ago to co-ordinate with our risings. The reason they were not is that there are divisions between the kirk and the nobles.' He held up the letter. 'This comes to me from the Duke of Hamilton, who leads the Scots. I know that His Majesty was hoping for a veteran army, but Leslie and thousands of experienced officers and men have refused to fight without the backing of the kirk. It is not the army we hoped for, but it is an army. And they entered England on the 8th.'

'Ten days ago!'

'Yes. And before you ask...' Norwich interrupted as Simon opened his mouth to say more, 'I know little else. The army is ill provided for, and are already plundering the countryside for supplies.'

'That will not go well with the northerners.'

'Indeed not, Thomas. But at least they are here.'

'Is there a parliamentary army to meet them?'

Norwich shook his head at Thomas's question. 'It appears not. Lambert is in the area, but his force is too weak to meet the Scots head on. It seems that they do nothing more than harry the flanks of the invaders.'

Simon tried to picture the disposition of the troops in his mind. 'What of the New Model, My Lord?'

'Bad news there, I am afraid. Cromwell has taken Pembroke at last. Some four days ago. He now marches north. It is my understanding from the messenger who brought this that Cromwell's men have not been paid. They are poorly supplied; many of them do not even have shoes. Yet they march with determination, seeing Hamilton's army as a foreign invasion, rather than their rightful King protecting his own.

'With Pembroke taken, the only other distraction for the New Model in the south is us. We have to hold out for as long as possible and keep Fairfax from marching. With Cromwell's men in such poor straits it will take them some time to reach the north. And every day is a day in which the Scots can further our cause. If any of the north rise to join them, then Cromwell will be hard pressed to defeat them.'

'So we can do nothing but wait?'

'It appears so, Thomas. Although I will try to get the cavalry out again. If they are swift enough they could harry Cromwell on his way north.'

***

Simon looked at the bowl of thin stew. A few vegetables floated in the broth and there was a piece of meat hiding in there, somewhere.

'Happy birthday, Simon.'

The sixteen year old looked up from his main meal for the day, and smiled. 'Not the sort of spread I am used to for my birthday!'

Sir Thomas smiled sadly. 'I know. I am sorry, my son.'

Simon felt guilty. 'That was not a complaint, father. I would expect no more than anyone in the town.' His stomach rumbled and he grinned boyishly. 'Although a joint of meat would be a most pleasant way of celebrating!'

His father laughed bitterly. 'Then it is a good thing that Gascoigne was able to break out with the cavalry at last. If not, you would probably be eating his horses by now!'

Simon spooned some of the stew into his mouth. 'Have you heard what happened to the cavalry?'

'It appears they got through the defences but then dispersed. I do not know if Sir Bernard plans for them to rendezvous somewhere, or if he is just waiting to see what happens in the north.'

'More forces joined Fairfax today, did they not?' Sir Thomas nodded, but said nothing as Simon continued. 'Then must we assume that things do not go well for our forces in the north? If they were causing too much trouble for Parliament then the reinforcements would have gone there, not to strengthen the ring around Colchester.'

'I fear you may be right.' Sir Thomas sighed, again. 'We estimate that Fairfax now has in the region of six thousand troops, while we have but three. And they are now hungry and weak. We must hold on though. My Lord Norwich received a letter from Langdale today.'

'The Commander of the northern forces?'

Sir Thomas nodded as he continued. 'Yes. He urges us to hold out, and promised to bring relief within two weeks.'

'Can we hold out that long?' Simon looked at his empty bowl as he spoke. He did not remember finishing the stew, indeed it felt as though he had had nothing to eat. His stomach still felt empty, and when he looked down at himself he could see that his clothes hung from his bony frame. He met his father's gaze, taking in the sunken cheekbones, the loose skin, the sunken eyes, the look of hunger. He knew that he must look the same. And that they were indistinguishable from everyone else held within the town by the encircling forts. Sir Thomas seemed to know what he was thinking, for a look of determination entered his eyes.

'Yes, Simon. We can hold out.'

Simon thought about the meat he had just eaten, and blanched. 'I assume that I will be used to the taste of dog and cat by the time we are relieved.'

'I know it does not taste good, son. But we need the meat, and there are few horses left.'

Simon shuddered. 'It is only those that belong to us amongst the leaders that now remain. All of the others have been eaten.' He thought of Prince. That noble steed was thin now, his coat lack-lustre, his breathing dry and hoarse. 'Even they would have been eaten if it were not for the fact that they might be needed.'

Sir Thomas sighed as he pushed his empty bowl away. 'If only we had been able to get rid of the civilians. We would then have twice the remaining supplies.'

Simon nodded. 'The civilians are for Parliament, so I do not understand why Fairfax would not let them leave.'

'Precisely because of the food situation. We have to feed them, which leaves less for ourselves. Fairfax would not listen to the Town Council, or Norwich, though it does his honour no good that he ordered women to be turned away from the gates with nothing, even though they begged for a little something to save the lives of their children.'

'The man is a monster.' Simon rose from the table. 'I cannot think of this tonight. I shall go early to my bed.'

Sir Tomas nodded. 'Good night, my son. Sleep well.'

Simon laid himself down, fully clothed, on the bed in the corner of their room. His stomach growled again, and he felt lightheaded. But what he felt most was fear. As the siege of Colchester dragged on, he wondered if they would be able to hold out until the Scots came south. And every day that passed he lost a little of the hope that had burned in his chest, beginning to sink into despair.

Almost a month had passed since Simon's birthday. The food supplies were so low that Sir Thomas had requisitioned all soap and candles, and people were desperate enough to eat them to assuage the pangs of hunger. As the morning sun rose in the sky he stood with Simon and Norwich upon the wall, watching their latest desperate attempt to get some supplies.

Five hundred starving women were waiting by the gates. Their clothes hung on them like sacks, their faces were hollow and sunken. Many of them were unsteady on their feet through hunger.

'I hope this works.'

Simon looked at the Earl. 'How could it not, My Lord? When Fairfax and his officers see the suffering of the civilians, they will have to give them some food.'

'Let us hope so.' Norwich turned to an officer beside him. 'Let them out.'

The man saluted, then moved quickly down the stairs. The gates were opened a fraction, and the women filed through before the gates shut behind them with an ominous thud. They stood still for a moment, then began to make their way over the sun-burned grass towards the enemy lines. Their progress was slow, but they finally reached their objective. Simon wished he could hear what was being said, but the distance was too great. It was obvious however that the women were begging for food, many of them on their knees. No one moved for ten minutes or more. Then a man on horseback cantered up. Fairfax.

There was a sudden sound of laughter from the enemy lines as the women struggled to their feet. They turned to make their way back towards the town, but soldiers moved swiftly to surround them. There were shouts, and more laughter. Simon struggled to see what was happening but could not. Then the ranks of soldiers parted.

'Dear Lord!' Sir Thomas's voice shook. Simon was not sure why and strained his eyes to see. Suddenly his eyes widened and he turned away in shock and embarrassment.

The women had been stripped naked. Without their clothing their starvation was even more apparent. Breasts which had been firm were now little more than pouches of loose skin hanging over ribs which stared out through their lily-white skin. The women began to shuffle back towards the town, hands and arms straining to cover themselves in their embarrassment.

'The evil bastards!'

Simon looked at Sir Thomas in surprise. Never before had he heard his father speak in such a way. He was always so polite, so calm and collected. But Simon could understand the reason for his anger, he felt it too and wished that there was something he could do for the women, something he could do to the enemy to make them pay for their cruelty.

No one on the wall spoke. The sentries turned their eyes from the women while civilians rushed to get blankets to cover them once they re-entered the gate. Simon wanted to run away, but he stood unmoving beside his father and the Earl. The attempt to appeal to the honourable nature of Fairfax had been their idea, and he knew that they could not walk away until the women were safely back and cared for.

At last the gate opened again. The women slipped through and the gates closed, sealing them in once more. Norwich continued to stand on the wall, brooding. His hooded eyes fixed on the enemy positions.

All of a sudden, cheers came from the enemy. At first it was in the section ahead of them, where Fairfax still sat his horse, but then the cheers spread until the whole city seemed to be surrounded by the sound, engulfed by it.

'What has happened?'

Sir Thomas turned to his son. 'I do not know, Simon. But I fear that it cannot be good news.'

Cannon fire broke out on the enemy lines, thundering volleys of sound, which echoed and re-echoed around the city.

'Is that a kite?' Norwich pointed a shaking finger at something flying in the air above the enemy lines.

'Yes. And there is another. And another!'

As Simon watched the sky was soon filled with kites, which floated towards the walls where they dropped on the defences and inside the city. One fell nearby and Simon rushed to pick it up. There were words written on it. When he saw them he blanched and began to shake.

'What is it?'

Simon looked at Norwich, and handed him the kite without a word. As the Earl read the words all colour drained from his face.

'The Scottish army has been defeated.'

The news was spreading swiftly through the town. Whispered words followed by a fearful silence. What would happen now?

As if in answer to the unspoken question on everyone's lips, a solitary rider made his way from the enemy ranks and stopped close to the city wall. His face was wreathed in smiles as he called up to the defenders.

'Send for your leaders! I have a letter for them!'

The Earl straightened to his full height, forced the fear and sadness from his eyes, and stood close to the parapet.

'I am the Earl of Norwich. Give your message to me and I will take it to the others.'

The gate opened; a soldier went out, took the letter and returned swiftly. He ran up the stairs and placed it in Norwich's hand. The Earl looked at the seal but did not open it. He turned back to the messenger outside the wall.

'We will discuss what is contained herein,' he called down. 'When we have an answer, I shall sound a trumpet and you may return to collect it.'

With that he turned and walked away.

The Royalist leaders stood in stunned silence. Simon watched from the desk where he sat with his quill poised to make notes of the meeting. Lucas finally spoke.

'Can it be true? Has Cromwell really defeated the Scots?'

Lucas looked at Norwich, who had asked the question. 'It would seem so.'

'But how do we know that Fairfax is telling the truth?' The two men looked at Sir Thomas who swallowed before continuing. 'I do not mean to be disrespectful, and up to this morning I would have said that Fairfax is an honourable man. But to strip the women like that! He would do anything to have this siege over. What if he is telling a lie, so that we surrender and he can go to the aid of the northern army?'

'I would say you could be right, if not for the enemy army.' Sir Thomas looked puzzled and Lucas continued. 'The cheering. Fairfax might have made an approach to us with false news of a victory, but he would have kept it from his men. To hear the cheers... It breaks my heart to say this but, yes, I believe that the Scottish army has been defeated.'

'So what do we do now?' Norwich's face was grey. 'Do we accept his terms?'

Lucas shook his head. 'I do not know. We must, at the least, consider them.'

'They are not favourable. All senior officers are to surrender to his mercy.'

'That is not unusual.' Sir Thomas looked from Norwich to Lucas, then back again. 'Surely we can accept that?'

'What is unusual is that he gives no guarantee as to how the officers will be treated.' Lucas looked worried. 'In all other such engagements, officers have been treated with honour and respect, their imprisonment suited to their rank. I cannot know what Fairfax plans for us.'

'Cromwell is an honourable man. He will not allow us to be ill-treated.' Simon could see the uncertainty in his father's eyes, and it seemed to him that Sir Thomas spoke with a confidence which he did not truly feel.

'You may well be correct.' Norwich sighed as he re-read the letter from Fairfax. 'It is not all bad. The common soldiers and junior officers will be granted quarter. We can order them to lay down their arms and go home. Let us be honest here, they are in no condition to fight. Most of them are little more than skin and bones. They have served their purpose in keeping Fairfax here and there is no fight left in them. We cannot hold out for...'

Norwich stopped speaking and listened. The sound of someone running across the courtyard could be heard. Few men had the energy left to run and he feared the worst. There was a knock at the door.

'Enter.'

A breathless aide entered, bowing low. 'A message from the north, My Lord.'

A young man entered hard on his heels. His clothes were torn and bloodstained, which spoke of battle. But a battle won or lost? Simon looked into the man's eyes. He did not need to ask the question. A tense silence descended on the room as Lucas held out his hand and took the letter without looking at the messenger.

'Wait outside.'

The two men left, the door closing softly behind them. Lucas opened the letter and began to read. His face paled and his hand began to shake.

'Charles?'

Lucas looked up at Norwich, then began to read the letter out loud, his voice full of emotion.

My Lords,

When the Scottish army crossed the border it was our hope to raise more men from the north. They fought well for the King before, but few came to our call this time. It seems that their love for His Majesty is out-weighed by the hatred of the Scots. Indeed, one can hardly blame them, for once the army had crossed the border they began to plunder the surroundings as they were so ill-supplied.

All appeared well when the Duke of Hamilton arrived with his army on the eighth of July. Cromwell was still besieging Pembroke, while Rossiter was at the gates of Pontefract and Scarborough in the north. Lambert was with his horse at Penrith, Hexham and Newcastle. Fairfax was, of course, busy with you at Colchester.

I led the advance guard to Carlisle and we daily expected reinforcements from Ulster. But none came.

As we marched, Lambert harried us along the way. His force was too weak to bring us to battle, but they still caused damage and disruption, slowing our advance skillfully. Then, as you know, Pembroke fell and Cromwell began the long march north. His men were ill-supplied, but picked up shoes and stockings as well as food as they marched. I must say, My Lords, that they marched with greater speed than any had expected. Cromwell collected local levies on his way and arrived at Doncaster just one month after Hamilton had crossed the border. For all our efforts in that time, we had made little progress southwards.

There was disagreement as to where the army should march, giving Cromwell the opportunity to approach even closer. He moved to attack us in the Ribble valley with some eight and a half thousand men. We had more, perhaps nine thousand, but they were spread out to make it easier to gain supplies, which left us vulnerable. I found myself protecting the left flank. Cromwell attacked us on the eighteenth. I had only three thousand foot and five hundred horse at my disposal as he hit us on Preston moor. My men fought hard and with great honour, but we were out-numbered. After four hours we were driven back to the Ribble.

Baillie attempted to come to our aid, holding the bridges at Ribble and Darwen, but Cromwell forced his way through. After two days the battle was lost.

It is my sad duty to inform you that, although the Scottish army still fights in defence, they retreat steadily northward. I do not think that they will make it to the border before they have to lay down their arms and surrender.

My Lords, you should seek whatever terms you may from Fairfax. The war is all but over and we cannot win.

Let us pray that there will be a future victory for our king, and that he will soon be back upon his throne.

Your humble servant,
Marmaduke Langdale

No one spoke. No one could find the words. It was all over. They had lost.

Chapter 30

Present day

Rob dug the fork into the soiled straw, lifting a load and depositing it into the wheelbarrow. He had come to the stable to keep himself busy, to keep his mind occupied. But mucking out required little concentration, and he found his thoughts straying back to the moment he had awoken. He had been exhausted. All he had been able to think of was the hunger and deprivation. His stomach growled and ached, his whole body feeling weak from lack of food. He had lain for a time, unmoving in his fatigue. Gradually, as the minutes passed, Rob had felt his strength returning and been able to sit up. It was then that his mind turned to the defeat. The surrender. His hands shook and his body was wet with sweat. What would happen to them now? What would happen to the king?

It was some time before his thoughts returned to the present. The dream had been so real, more real than any that had gone before. That in itself did not worry Rob, what scared him was the way that the dream continued to have a hold on him after waking. How was it possible for the hunger and exhaustion created by his imagination to pursue him into his everyday life? Rob knew that he could not hide from his fears any longer. Something was seriously wrong. Either he was going mad, or Caroline was right about his dreams being a reflection of a past life. He was not sure which he feared most. With an angry curse he threw the pitchfork onto the wheelbarrow, turned and strode from the stall.

The temperature plummeted. The hairs rose on the back of Rob's neck. There was a movement in the corner, an indistinct shape detaching itself from the deeper shadows, moving forward. The figure which stepped into the beam of sunlight entering from the loft window caused Rob to stop in his tracks.

'Something troubles thee, Hardwycke. Thou art confused and afraid, and thy feelings have drawn me to thee.'

Rob retreated until his back was pressed against the wall of the loosebox and he could go no further. He felt that he was in the presence of evil.

'What do you mean? How can my feelings have anything to do with you?'

'Thou art everything to me. I wouldst not be here if not for thee.' The old woman smiled. 'Thou canst not know how much it pleases me to feel thy pain and confusion, though it is but a beginning. I know thy dreams, Hardwycke. Thou seemest to have forgotten thy history; the years have wiped thine own story from thy mind. But I bring thee dreams. Through them thou shalt remember all that thou hast been, all that thou hast done. Then thou shalt pay for thy crimes.'

'Leave me alone!' Rob's words were little more than a whisper, as though he withdrew within himself and was unable to confront the hatred and evil which seemed to emanate from the woman. 'I have done nothing wrong! I have done nothing to you! Leave me alone!'

Harsh laughter rang out. 'I shall leave thee alone, Hardwycke. But not until thou dost beg for mercy from me. Mercy which thou shalt not receive, just as it was denied to me and mine!'

'Enough!'

The voice which spoke that one word was strong and clear, like the sound of a church bell on the summer breeze. Rob forced his head to turn towards the person who had spoken. Rebekah.

She stood in the doorway, surrounded by sunlight which caused her hair to shine like a halo around her head. Her eyes flashed with anger, but there was also a strange sadness in their depths as she stepped forward.

'I say enough. Trouble him no further.'

Fearing for the safety of the young woman, Rob forced himself away from the wall and stepped forward. 'Get back, Rebekah! It's not safe!' He tried to step towards her, but something seemed to hold him back and he found himself unable to move. To his surprise, Rebekah smiled.

'There is nothing to fear, Robert. She cannot harm you.'

'But Rebekah...'

The young woman ignored his words and turned towards the apparition. Her voice, when she spoke, was filled with a strange mixture of anger and compassion. 'Leave him. He is not the man you seek. That person exists no longer. Any harm he did to you is long dead. Leave Robert alone, and go.'

'And leave him with thee?' The older woman shook her head. 'You cannot understand the danger that thou art in when thou art with him.'

'He will not harm me.' Rebekah stepped forward, her hand outstretched until it almost touched the ghostly figure. 'Leave him in peace, and seek peace of thine own.'

There was a softening in the gaze of the old woman, a warming of the air as her outline began to waver. Whatever held Rob transfixed began to loosen its hold, and he stepped forward. At his movement, the air around him suddenly froze again. The dead eyes hardened as they turned back to him. Rob found himself unable to move once more.

'No, child. I cannot seek peace until he pays. And peace can never be mine whilst you defend him.' She turned to the younger woman. 'How has he deceived you so?'

Rebekah smiled sadly. 'It is not I who is deceived. Go now. Please. Leave him in peace until the story is told and he has a chance to redeem himself.'

The old woman seemed unable to retain her anger in the face of Rebekah's calm certainty. The ghostly form seemed to waver for a moment, then was gone. Whatever had held Rob immobile was there no longer, and he rushed to Rebekah's side.

'Are you alright?'

Rebekah smiled, an expression which warmed Rob's heart. 'Yes, Robert. I do not fear her. She cannot harm me.'

'But she is a ghost! And she wants to hurt us!' He frowned. 'No. She wants to hurt me. Why is all that hatred and anger directed at me?' Rob was frightened and confused. 'What does she mean when she says that she has sent me my dreams?'

'I believe that she wants you to understand a story from the past. Her story. I believe that if you can understand that story then she will find peace.'

Rob ran his hands through his hair. 'This is impossible! You are saying that a ghost is using my dreams of the past to try to get some sort of closure? But why me?' He turned to Rebekah. 'Do you really believe that she is a ghost?'

'How can it be otherwise? You saw that she is a spirit in the way she disappeared.'

'Then why are you not afraid?'

'She will not harm me.'

'But she wants to hurt me!'

'Perhaps, when the story is told, she will no longer feel that way.'

'I can only hope that you're right. I wish I had your certainty, Rebekah.'

The young woman reached out, laying a comforting hand on his arm. 'I am certain enough for both of us.'

She held Rob's gaze with her own. In her eyes he could see strength, confidence, sureness. And love.

Rob felt his heart swell in his chest. This woman, little more than a girl, loved him. Somehow he knew that her love would protect him and see him safely through whatever lay ahead. His fears subsided, and he smiled.

Rob did not know who moved first, but seconds later they were in each other's arms. Her head rested against his shoulder so that he could feel the softness of her hair brush his cheek. Rob closed his eyes.

He felt as though he had come home.

Chapter 31

September 1648

It seemed strange to be back at home again. The house was the same. Nothing had changed. Yet everything had changed.

Simon knelt on the floor of his room, throwing back a rug before lifting a loose board. Reaching into the dark space beneath, he searched for a moment, then withdrew his diary. Slowly rising to his feet, the young man carried the book across the room and placed it carefully on his desk. He opened it to his last entry, made months before. He had hidden the diary on the morning of their departure, afraid to take it with him on his journey in case it had fallen into the wrong hands. Now he had to bring the events in it up to date. He opened the book to a new page and stared at it for a few moments, lost in thought. He was not sure that he would be able to find the words. The page began to blur as tears filled his eyes. Brushing them angrily away, Simon walked over to the window, drawing calmness from the familiar view. As he stood there he let his mind travel back over the events since Langdale's letter had reached them in Colchester.

Fairfax had refused to negotiate the terms, leaving the Royalists no choice but to accept. Norwich continued to worry about what kind of imprisonment awaited the leaders, and had tried to persuade Sir Thomas to play the part of an ordinary soldier to enable him to take Simon home. He had refused. Simon had felt pride in his father's stand, but also a cloying fear about what his future might hold. In the end Lucas had ordered Sir Thomas to leave with the common men. At least one of their number needed to remain free to aid the king in whatever way they could. Lucas, Norwich, Capel and Lisle would have to remain. Fairfax knew they were there so escape would be impossible. But, as far as they were aware, Fairfax did not know that Sir Thomas was inside the walls. He must be the one to escape.

Simon had watched the next morning as the Royalists laid down their arms and opened the gates. He had watched as Fairfax entered the city at the head of his troops. He had watched as the house belonging to Lord Lucas was ransacked. And when the soldiers found nothing of value he had watched as they broke into the vault and dismembered the bodies of Lucas' wife and sister. Simon still felt sick as he thought of that. But not as sick as he felt when he thought of what followed.

The common soldiers had been disarmed and forced to swear an oath not to take up arms against Parliament again. They were too tired and dispirited to do anything else. Passes of safe conduct were handed out and the soldiers left. Sir Thomas had refused to take the oath, so the two of them had dressed as civilians and hidden openly in the crowd, which silently listened to the final terms of Fairfax. Simon's heart wept for the town's people, most of whom were Parliamentarians and had been trapped with their enemy for months, enduring starvation and deprivation through no fault of their own. Now they were to pay fourteen thousand pounds to protect what was left of Colchester from pillage. The hatred which smouldered in Simon was fanned to a weak flame by that. Then came the military court, and his hatred rose to a burning fire.

The Lords Norwich, Capel and Loughborough were to be sent to London where Parliament would decide their fate. Fairfax ordered that Sir Charles Lucas, Sir George Lisle, Colonel Farre and Sir Bernard Gascoigne were to be treated as traitors. He argued that Lucas had executed Roundhead prisoners in cold blood, had broken his parole given at the end of the first war, and had forced the people of Colchester to fight on in an indefensible position.

No one had really expected the sentence to be carried out. Fairfax commuted the punishment for Gascoigne when he learnt that he was an Italian citizen, and Farre escaped. But Lucas and Lisle had been shot.

Simon still could not believe it. Every time he thought of the executions his heart beat wildly, his mouth went dry and he thought he would pass out. He felt deeply for the men he had known and lost. But even more so for his father. What would have happened if they had not been ordered to leave? Would his father be dead now? He consoled himself with the thought that his father had never given his parole, so perhaps Fairfax would have been more lenient; but he doubted it. Every day now he prayed for the souls of the martyred men. And he thanked God for the order from Lucas which had saved his father's life.

Simon turned his back to the window and looked at this diary on the desk, waiting for him. It would be hard to write the words, but the story must be told. Perhaps the telling would ease the pain in his heart.

***

Simon sat on his horse on the edge of the clearing, looking at the woodman's cottage. The thatch was thin in places, the walls peeling. Just another victim of the war. Everything was so different from the first time he had been there, the day he had met Rebekah and her family. So much had happened to them all. So much pain and suffering.

He saw the door open, and Rebekah came out. She had grown, no longer the little girl who had found him when he fell from his pony. The teenager was thin as a willow, but moved with a grace which he found appealing as she made her way towards the well. Somehow she must have sensed that someone was watching, for she turned quickly, a look of fear in her eyes. Simon urged his horse forward.

'Rebekah! It is only me! I am sorry if I startled you!'

Her eyes widened, the fear replaced by recognition. Her face broke into a smile.

'Simon! I did not recognise you. You look like a man full grown.'

Simon laughed as he reined his horse in and dismounted. 'I am sixteen years old now.'

'A man indeed!'

Simon laughed. 'It is good to see you, Rebekah.' Indeed it was. Seeing her here lifted his heart, made him feel as he had when he had returned to Marston. It was almost like coming home again. Suddenly unsure of himself, Simon did not know what to say. He fell silent under Rebekah's quick, intelligent gaze. She frowned as she saw how his clothes hung from him. Her frown deepened as she saw his hollow cheeks and the black rings under his eyes, which stood out starkly against his sallow complexion.

'You are so thin! What has happened to you? Have you been ill?'

Simon shook his head. 'No. I was at Colchester.'

Rebekah's face paled. She had known hunger in her life, but she was old enough to know that the hunger of a siege went far beyond anything she had ever experienced.

'The Lord preserve us! If I had known that you were there I would have been so worried about you. What was it like?'

Simon shook his head. 'I do not want to talk about it. Not yet.'

Rebekah's nodded, understanding and sympathy in her steady gaze. 'You will tell me when you feel the time is right. Come.' She took his hand and led him towards the house. 'Let us sit here and talk a while.'

Her hand in his felt good, comforting. Simon fought to hold back tears which a man should not cry. Leaving go of her hand, he swallowed hard as he tied his horse to a tree, struggling for control.

'Where is Prince?' Simon shook his head, unable to find the words. Rebekah understood and laid a hand on his arm, her touch more comforting than any words. 'Come, let us sit.'

As they sat side by side, Simon remembered the first time he had sat there, when Henry Sawyer had spoken with him, trying to help him to understand what was happening in a world going slowly mad. That all seemed so long ago, like a half remembered dream. Henry was dead now, leaving his family to struggle on as best they could with no one to protect them.

'How is your mother?'

Rebekah smiled. 'She is well, thank you. There is always need for her healing skills, so we do not go hungry.'

'Indeed.' Simon thought back to the winter when his niece had been born. He still felt sick with fear every time he thought of what would have happened if Ann had not gone to the Manor with him. Thoughts of little Ann brought a smile to his lips. 'Did you know that my niece is named for your mother?'

Rebekah's eyes widened. 'No. Is it really true?'

Simon nodded. 'My sister wanted to show her gratitude to your mother for saving them both.'

'It is what she does. There is no need of thanks.' Rebekah smiled. 'But she will be so happy to hear that!'

'Where is she now?'

'In the village, attending an old woman. But where are my manners!' Rebekah jumped to her feet as she spoke. 'Mother would be ashamed of me if she knew that I had not offered you a drink!'

'I need nothing.'

Rebekah's eyes roved over the thin frame. 'That is not true, is it. You need plenty of food and drink before you are yourself again.'

'That cannot happen in an afternoon, so do not worry about it.'

Rebekah ignored his words as she made her way towards the cottage. 'I will not be long.'

Simon sat back, allowing the afternoon sun to warm him as he listened to the girl moving around in the cottage. For some reason he felt more relaxed here than he did at home. Perhaps it was the simple acceptance he found here, so different from the guilt his father had unsuccessfully tried to hide since their return. Simon had told him that he was not responsible for what Simon had seen and endured at Colchester, it had been his own choice to leave Marston Manor. It made no difference. He knew that Sir Thomas would always regret that he had not left Simon at home, and that Simon had needed to grow up too fast in those dark days under siege. His sister, too, made him feel uncomfortable. Mothering him as she had when he was a small boy; finding him tasty things to eat as she tried to build up his strength; saying in actions, if not in words, that she too regretted what he had been through. Simon had felt smothered, glad to be at home but also desperate to get away. He felt that his family treated him like a small boy, while he felt like a grown man. The situation was frustrating. He sighed.

'Is something wrong?'

Simon had not noticed Rebekah in the doorway, and shook his head. As the young girl placed a platter of bread and two mugs of small beer on the table, she frowned. 'That was a deep sigh if there is nothing wrong.'

Her honesty brought a smile to his lips. 'I was thinking of my father. At Colchester he treated me as an adult, as an equal. Now it is as though the last year has not happened and I am a boy again.'

'That is understandable.'

Simon was surprised. 'I may not look fully like a man yet, but I am certainly no boy!'

Rebekah laid a calming hand on his arm. 'That is not what I was saying. I am sure that you know why he does this, do you not? It is understandable because he feared that he would lose you, and he wants to continue to protect you.'

'But I can protect myself.'

'Of course you can; and your family must surely know it. But for a time let them look after you. As you regain your strength, I am sure that they will see in you the man you have become.'

'How do you know me so well, Rebekah?'

She shrugged. 'I do not know. All I know is that you do not need to tell me how you feel, because I can see it in your eyes.'

'No one else can read me like that. Only you.'

'And no one understands me as well as you do. Perhaps it is because we have been friends from childhood.'

'Yes, you are right.' As he said the words, Simon felt that it was more than that, but could not quite define the way she made him feel. Feeling confused, he reached for his beer and took a drink.

'It confuses me, too.'

Simon looked up and caught her eyes. How could she have known that he was feeling confused? Suddenly they both laughed. Simon realised that it was the first time that he had truly laughed since Colchester. It felt good.

Chapter 32

January 1649

Simon looked at the food on his plate. Just a few months before, while in Colchester, he would have given anything for so much food. Now he felt that he could not eat, would not be able to swallow if he put any of the food in his mouth. He sighed heavily.

'What is it, son?'

Simon looked across the table at his father, who seemed to be having equal difficulty eating his own dinner.

'I find myself too worried to eat.' He sighed again. 'My stomach is making as many twists and turns as my thoughts!'

'Then share those thoughts with me. Perhaps it will help.'

'I was thinking of what happened after we left Colchester. The New Model thought themselves untouchable. Even Parliament seemed unable to challenge their position and so turned again to negotiations with the King. I thought then that it was all over. The King would come to agreement. We would have peace.'

'How many times have we thought that? And still it happens not.'

'But it felt so close then!'

'Yes. If His Majesty had agreed with Parliament that would have been the end of the New Model, and the King would have been back on his throne. Instead...'

'Instead, he let us down again.'

'Simon!'

'I am sorry, Father, but it is true. What is more, you know that to be so.'

'Yes. Although it pains me to admit it.' Sir Thomas pushed his plate away in exasperation. 'Why does he find it so difficult to negotiate honestly and openly? You know how his actions frustrated me.'

Simon nodded, but said nothing. He remembered too well his father's anger towards the King; something which he had never seen before. It had been anger born of frustration, true, but it had still caused Simon to fear what the future might bring. And he had not been wrong.

'I can understand why the Levellers and New Model thought that the King should accept their demands. They wanted what the first war had been fought for, and could not see why they could not have it. After all, they had won and the King had lost.' Simon's voice was bitter. 'Perhaps they were right.'

'But we all knew that His Majesty would not agree.'

'Indeed, Father. How was it that the King's loyal supporters could see that his only hope was to negotiate in good faith with Parliament, yet His Majesty remained blind to the fact? Why did he act so?'

Sir Thomas shrugged. 'I know not, Simon. Maybe it was his innate character which caused him to hold out. Or perhaps his deeply-held religious beliefs. Whatever it was, the King had been a prisoner on the Isle of Wight for the whole of the second war. He had not seen the suffering of Colchester, nor the loss of the battle in the north. Perhaps he convinced himself that, somehow, he was invincible and would finally win.'

'But surely Parliament's actions would have disabused him of that?' Simon shook his head. 'To transport so many of the King's men to the West Indies! That is a punishment for common criminals, not the lords of England!'

'That indeed was a dark moment. Even if they had given their parole at the end of the first war the punishment was too severe. I believe it broke the King's heart. He values so much the loyalty of his subjects. That they suffer so because of him is something that I believe will always be a burden to him.'

Simon nodded. 'You cannot begin to understand how glad I am that you never gave your parole. At the time I was hurt, thinking that you neglected us at Marston. But now...' he paused for a moment. 'To think that you could have been sent to those hateful isles as a common criminal!'

Sir Thomas nodded. 'Though my refusal to give my parole had never been about my own safety. It had been, and always will be, about my loyalty to the King.'

'But having seen the harshness of those punishments, surely His Majesty should have made haste to compromise when they began to accuse him of being the greatest traitor of all?'

'It would seem to have been the most sensible course. But the King could never see himself as a traitor to England.' Sir Thomas sighed. 'It takes us right back to the start of all this, does it not?'

'Yes, but at the start we would never have imagined that an army would take over Parliament, leaving but a small number of the Commons and Lords to rule.' Simon was silent as he remembered the fear the move had caused. The military had taken over. Far from seeking freedom from the King and true representation through an elected Parliament, their sudden move overturned everything that both sides had fought for. The army had been in control.

Sir Thomas nodded. 'No one understood the danger, for how could such a small number, the minority of those who legally represented the people, believe that they could run the country?'

Simon smiled for the first time that evening. 'Do you remember how people called those few left in Parliament "The Rump", the backside of Parliament?'

Sir Thomas nodded. 'Yes. Even in Oxford boys were running around shouting "kiss my Parliament!"'

'But it turned out not to be a joke after all.' Simon's expression became serious once more. 'We all hoped that, paradoxically, it would turn things in the King's favour. Yet here we are.'

'Indeed. It was only a small number who wanted to put the King on trial. So many wanted to continue to negotiate.'

'Yet His Majesty refused. Again.'

'He thought he had the upper hand, Simon.'

'But how so? We had lost the war!'

'I know. I know.' Sir Thomas shook his head sadly. 'I wish I could have been here in London with the King. Maybe I could have helped persuade him. Oxford was so far away.'

'But we are here now.' Simon remembered how his father had finally decided to go to the capital, in the hope that he would be close on hand should he be needed. It had taken Simon many hours to persuade his father to take him with him. After what had happened at Colchester Sir Thomas did not want to put his son in danger again, but Simon was persuasive, and his father finally agreed. They travelled to London just before Christmas, in the hope of being close to matters, maybe trying to influence the king, but he was being held in close seclusion and they could not see him. As the year drew to a close, and the King still refused to agree to anything other than a return to how things had been before the war, they were at a loss as to how matters could be reconciled. Neither of them expected what happened on the first day of the new year.

'I still find it hard to believe that Parliament passed a bill to try the King for treason.'

Sir Thomas nodded. 'Surely the treasonous ones are Parliament, for making war against their divinely appointed King.'

'I do not know where we can go from here, Father. Surely the rumours that the King could be executed cannot be true?'

'I do not believe it is possible. The King is naïve, living in a dream world, but he will surely come to agreement before we reach such a position.'

'Perhaps he should abdicate?'

Sir Thomas nodded slowly. 'I never thought I would agree with that. But my loyalty to the monarchy as an institution must outweigh my loyalty to the King. However much it pained me, I would support one of the King's sons on the throne in order to save the throne itself.' He sighed. 'It goes against us that His Majesty's two older sons are abroad and the third in the custody of Parliament. That plan will not work in the foreseeable future.'

'So we find ourselves here. I tell you, Father, I am as much afraid here as I was in Colchester. Maybe even more so.'

'It is the same for myself. The worse for knowing that I can do nothing.' Sir Thomas sighed. 'All we can do now is wait to see what tomorrow will bring.'

***

Simon and his father stood at the back of Westminster Hall, silent in their attempt to remain unnoticed in the crowd. All around them people were calling out, many of them in favour of the King, while the judges sat silently, nervous tension evident on their faces.

'Why are there so many empty chairs?'

'It appears that only about half the judges named to sit have come here today. Perhaps to judge the mood of the crowd first.' Sir Thomas looked around. 'It certainly seems that more of the crowd are for the King than against him.'

Simon nodded. The crowd were unruly, shouting out that the King should not be treated in such a manner. One of the judges turned and spoke to an officer, who nodded and departed. The judges continued to sit in silence, waiting. The wait was not long. There was the sound of marching feet, and Simon blanched as he saw two hundred soldiers enter the hall. They quickly ranged themselves around the walls and behind the judges. Their fearsome appearance had the desired effect. The shouting slowly died, and an uneasy silence settled on the hall. To Simon the atmosphere felt like the air before a summer storm, as though lightning would strike at any moment. The judge turned and spoke to another officer, who saluted before leaving to carry out his orders. Moments later, those closest to the doors began to whisper amongst themselves. Heads turned and people strained to see what was happening. Then the diminutive figure of the King appeared.

'Long live the King! Long live His Majesty!'

Charles nodded his head and waved a hand in recognition of the adulation. The soldiers stepped forward threateningly, pikes at the ready, and the shouting ceased as the King made his way to the seat which had been prepared for him. As he reached it, a lone female voice cried out.

'What you do here today is illegal! This court has not been called by Parliament in its fullness, but by a mere Rump!' There were cheers and cries of encouragement as the veiled lady stepped closer to the bench. She called out something else which Simon could not hear. Obviously others wanted to know what she said, for silence returned to the hall. 'This court is also illegal as it defies the Magna Carta! That document was written to protect all citizens of the country, and it says that no man shall be imprisoned without the lawful judgement of his equals.' She pointed to Charles. 'There stands your King. Your king! Who amongst you is his equal? No court comprising men of England can sit against him. The only court that could try him would consist of other crowned monarchs, but I see none here!'

There were more cheers as soldiers surrounded the woman and she fell silent.

Simon found himself cheering too, then turned to face his father.

'How courageous! And what a clever argument! She is right, is she not?' Sir Thomas nodded but did not look at his son. He stared at the woman, a look of surprise on his face. Simon's eyes followed his father's gaze. 'Do you know her?'

Sir Thomas nodded. 'Her face may be well hidden, but if I am not mistaken that is Lady Fairfax.'

Simon's eyes widened in surprise. 'Lady Fairfax? But what will her husband say?'

His father's gaze was thoughtful. 'I would not be surprised if he knew that she was here. Like Sir Francis he felt that the King was abusing his power, which is why he sided with Parliament. But for all that, he is still a Lord. He still owes some allegiance to the King. He would not believe that this court is legal.'

'And he would not be able to speak out against it without endangering himself. But his wife...'

'Indeed. I believe that is the way of the matter.' Sir Thomas turned back to the bench as he spoke. 'Perhaps such an open display will sway the judges to do what is right, and halt this sham of a trial before it begins.'

Sir Thomas's hopes were immediately dashed as the judge in the centre rose to his feet. His face was stern as he addressed the King.

'Charles Stuart, you are charged with treason.' A murmur came from the crowd, soon silenced by the menacing pikes. 'You are charged that, although you were trusted with limited power to govern by and according to the laws of the land, you ruled as a tyrant, traitor and murderer, and were a public and implacable enemy of the commonwealth of England.'

Simon looked at his father, who was shaking.

'How can they say such a thing?' he whispered.

Sir Thomas shook his head. 'It is they who are treasonous, not His Majesty.' He looked towards the King. 'He must now plead guilty to a few specimen charges. It is likely that they will then give him a nominal punishment. This court is merely here to make him acknowledge that he was in the wrong, and that he will give up some powers to them.'

'How severe might the punishment be?'

Sir Thomas frowned. 'At worst? They could declare him deposed in favour of one of his sons. I do not know...'

He fell silent as the King looked boldly into the eyes of each judge before turning to their spokesman.

'I do not accept the authority of this court. What authority do you have to try me?'

There was a stunned silence before the judge spoke again.

'Charles Stuart. You are charged with treason. How do you plead?'

'I plead not. If power without law may make laws, may alter the fundamental laws of the kingdom, I do not know what subject he is in England that can be sure of his life, or anything that he calls his own.'

Sir Thomas groaned. 'Oh, Your Majesty! In God's name, do not do this!'

The King was unable to hear Sir Thomas, but Simon realised that it was unlikely that he would take note in any case. As the day passed, and the judges spoke and presented evidence, the King had nothing to say, save that he did not recognise the authority of the court. He refused to answer to a court which he said had not been legally constituted. As the day wore on the crowd became more vocal and cries of 'God save the King!' were frequently heard. The soldiers did not know how to respond, and as long as no one approached the bench or became violent they did nothing. Even when Lady Fairfax began to call out again, denouncing the Rump as unrepresentative of the people, they did nothing. It was obvious that the judges were as unsure as everyone else, disagreeing on what they should do next. Finally, the court was dismissed for the day and the King led from the hall.

'Is it all over?'

'I am afraid not, Simon. The court will sit again tomorrow, by which time I assume that they will have orders from their masters.' His voice was full of anger. 'What in God's name does he think he is doing?'

Simon was puzzled. 'Who? Ireton?'

His father turned to him and Simon was shaken by the fierceness of his gaze. 'No. The King! Does he think that this is just one more negotiation? The fact that this court is illegal is irrelevant! He must plead and take a punishment. Heaven knows what will happen if he does not!'

With that he turned and stormed from the hall. After a moment of stunned silence, Simon followed him.

***

Simon found himself in the same place in Westminster Hall for the fourth day of the trial. The second and third days had passed in much the same way as the first. The court had presented evidence that the King had actually made war against his own people, leading traitorous armies and even bringing foreign forces into the land. They said that there was no doubt of his guilt, yet Simon thought they were wrong. Yes, it was true that he had done those things, but that did not make the King guilty. He was the monarch, after all! He ruled this land! Simon had stood for hour after hour, unable to comprehend that the King should be treated in such a way. And all the time the King said nothing about the charges. He spoke, always eloquently and, Simon noticed, without his usual stutter, but all he was prepared to say was that he did not accept the authority of the court. The Scottish Parliament sent a protest, and an embassy arrived from Holland, but they were not allowed to speak in the court. The time for diplomacy now seemed to have passed. Simon could see the frustration on the faces of the judges slowly replaced by anger. He also noted his father's anger. Deep inside himself he felt confusion, and fear. Three days. Three days of the court sitting and getting nowhere. Three days of impasse. Even he knew that this could not be allowed to go on, and he feared the consequences. As the King entered the court on this fourth day, Simon felt his fists clenching and he prayed silently that the King would prove less stubborn today. The judge rose to his feet.

'Charles Stuart, this court has heard evidence of your crimes and finds you guilty of leading war against your people.' Simon took his father by the elbow to steady him as he swayed on his feet. The judge continued. 'In our mercy we ask you again. How plead you?'

Simon looked at the King. He stood straight, regal in his bearing. There was no fear in his eyes as he spoke.

'I do not recognise the legality of this court. I will not plead before it.'

Simon felt his father's weight lean against him as an agonised whisper escaped his lips. 'Oh my King, my King! You must see where this leads! In God's name plead! Plead guilty, Your Majesty! Plead guilty!'

Simon was stunned. Never before, not even during the darkest days at Colchester, had he seen his father so close to despair.

'Father! What is wrong?'

'They must sentence him now.'

'Yes. I see that. But if they send him into exile we shall place one of his sons on the throne. You said yourself that the monarchy must survive!' Sir Thomas straightened, drawing on all his strength to stand tall in the face of what he feared was coming. 'Father?'

'Common Law.' He whispered. 'If they use the Common Law we are lost!'

'Charles Stuart.' Simon and his father turned towards the bench as the words continued. 'You have been found guilty by this court of being a tyrant, traitor and murderer. You have refused to plead, even after we have urged you to do so many times. Under the Common Law of this land, the punishment for refusing to plead is death.' The groan which escaped Simon's lips was lost amongst the collective groan which came from the crowd. 'For the crimes contained in the charge, you shall be carried back to the place from whence you came, and thence to the place of execution, where your head shall be severed from your body.'

The King looked around himself as though in a daze. He stepped forward, opening his mouth to speak, but the judge held up his hand.

'You have been given chances unnumbered to speak to this court and have declined. You are now to be taken from this court to prepare for your punishment. May God have mercy on your soul.'

There was uproar in the Hall. People were shouting, crying. As the King was dragged past them, Simon heard him calling out 'I am not suffered to speak! I am not suffered to speak!' The soldiers laughed, blowing gunpowder and smoke into his face as he was taken away.

Simon turned towards his father, stunned by what had happened, seeking confirmation and comfort. Sir Thomas stood, still as a rock, tears falling like rain.

***

Simon shivered and pulled his cloak closer around himself. It kept out the bitter cold of January, but failed to warm his heart, or to banish the chill of a dread which reached deep to his bones. From their position at the top of a flight of steps leading to a shop, he and his father looked out over the silent crowd. No one moved. No one spoke. All eyes were focussed in one direction. Simon did not want to look, but could not help himself. His eyes turned slowly towards the raised scaffold with its block. He turned to look at his father. Sir Thomas stood straight and still, outwardly calm, although Simon could see the tension in his clenched jaw and the nervous twitching of one eye. Turning back towards the scaffold, the young man thought back to the time the King had visited Marston Manor. They had felt so sure of victory back then. No one could have predicted that things would end in this way.

The crowds thronging Whitehall stood silent and still around the black draped scaffold, come to see the execution of their King. Simon was glad that they had got there early and were close to the block. Not that he wanted to see what happened in detail, but he knew that his father wanted to be able to offer comfort and strength to the King, if at all possible. They had tried so hard to get to see him after sentence had been passed, but had not been allowed. Sir Thomas had ranted about the unholy actions of the Rump, called down all kinds of curses upon the heads of Cromwell and Ireton, threatened revenge for the cruel way the King had been treated. But as the hours passed he had calmed, accepting that what was now ordained was inevitable, wishing only to say goodbye and take an oath to his sovereign that he would continue to support the Stuart cause. Such a meeting would have been an equal comfort to himself as to the King. The denial of access had wounded him deeply.

There was a low murmur of anguished voices as all heads turned towards the Banqueting House. The execution party had arrived.

The King, wrapped warmly against the bitter January morning, was flanked by a bishop and his executioner. He said something in a quiet voice to the bishop, who nodded. The King stepped forward. Simon was unable to hear the first words the King spoke, and leant forward to listen more intently. Due to the soldiers who stood between him and the crowds, Charles's voice did not carry far, but Simon and Sir Thomas were able to make out what he said.

'For the people, truly I desire their liberty and freedom as much as anybody whomsoever. But I must tell you that their liberty and freedom consist in having of government, those laws by which their life and their goods may be most their own. It is not for having share in government, sirs; that is nothing pertaining to them. A subject and a sovereign are clear different things. And therefore until the people have the liberty of good government, as I say, certainly they will never enjoy themselves. Sirs, it was for this that now I am come here. If I would have given way to an arbitrary way, to have all laws changed according to the power of the sword, I need not to have come here. Therefore I tell you, and I pray God it be not laid to your charge, that I am the martyr of the people.'

Simon was impressed by the calm assurance of the King's voice. As with his trial, there was no trace of the stammer which usually marked his speech. As he spoke in those final moments of life, he was truly a monarch to be proud of.

The condemned man turned to his executioner.

'I shall say but very short prayers, and when I thrust out my hands...' The executioner nodded, no further words were needed. Charles turned to the bishop and asked for his cap, which he placed on his head before turning back to the axeman. 'Does my hair trouble you?'

'It would be best, Sire, if you placed it all beneath the cap.'

The King nodded and proceeded to do so, aided by the bishop and executioner. Simon found it hard to believe that this was all real. The King behaved so calmly, spoke so calmly. The execution party was polite. The crowd restrained. It felt to him like play acting, as though the scene would soon be over to loud applause, and the actors leave the stage. But no. The reality continued as the King spoke again.

'My Lord Bishop, I fear not. I have a good cause, and a gracious God on my side.'

'There is but one stage more, Your Majesty, which, though turbulent and troublesome, yet is a very short one.' Simon could hear the catch in the man's voice, as though he struggled with the words. It was obvious that the man was not comfortable with his task and wanted to do all that he could to aid the King. 'You may consider it will soon carry you a very great way; it will carry you from earth to heaven; and there you shall find to your great joy the prize you hasten to, a crown of glory.'

The King nodded. 'I go from a corruptible to an incorruptible crown; where no disturbance can be, no disturbance in the world.'

'Indeed, Your Majesty. You are exchanging a temporal for an eternal crown. A good exchange.'

Simon stole a look at his father. Sir Thomas stood calmly, his gaze sure as he kept his eyes on the King's face. For a moment he caught the condemned man's eye. There was recognition in Charles's eyes, and gratitude for a faithful servant who had dared to come forward to offer his support. He inclined his head slightly in acknowledgement. Simon heard a deep intake of breath from his father as he fought to control his emotions, focussing on giving all of his strength to the King, who now turned back to his executioner.

'Is my hair well?' At a nod from the man he removed his cloak, which he handed to the bishop. His hand went to his neck, to the jewelled pendant of Saint George, symbol of the Order of the Garter. He held it in his fist for a moment, as though reliving in his mind past days of glory. Then he removed it and handed it to the bishop. Next came his doublet and waistcoat before he put the cloak back over the crisp white shirt, as though to lessen the impact of the bright flow of blood which must soon cover it. He breathed deeply and held his hands out in front of him.

'When I put out my hands this way, then.'

The executioner nodded.

The King of England stood for a moment, his lips moving in silent supplication, his eyes lifted towards heaven. Then he knelt and laid his head on the block. After a moment in which he composed himself, the King held out his hands.

The heavily muscled executioner raised the axe above his head. It held for a moment at the apex before he brought it down with all his might. With one blow, the King's head was severed from his shoulders.

Simon found himself trembling, his knees weak, his stomach wanting to disgorge his breakfast as the head fell to the wooden boards with a thud. Bright blood fountained from the neck and began to pool as the body slipped to the side, an arm still twitching. He looked at his father and took strength from the way he stood, unmoving, seemingly unaffected. Simon straightened and turned back to the block in time to see the executioner pick up the severed head and hold it for the crowds to see. There was no cheering. No sign that this execution was the will of the people. Instead a collective groan went up, like the sighing of the wind before a storm. Only the soldiers cheered, and this seemed to Simon to be more out of a sense of duty than from the heart.

Two soldiers stepped forward and lifted the King's body, placing it in a coffin. The executioner placed the head with the body and the coffin was covered with black velvet. More soldiers stepped forward, lifted it to their shoulders and carried it solemnly back into Banqueting House.

Simon and his father stood unmoving. Unable to move. They watched as people came forward, soaking handkerchiefs and pieces of cloth in the King's blood. No doubt some did so as tokens of their wish to see the King dead, but they were few. Simon could see by the reverent, tear-stained faces that most people took the blood to cherish it as the sacrifice of a martyr, as a blessing from a divinely appointed monarch who now wore his incorruptible crown.

England no longer had a king.

Chapter 33

Present day

Rob dragged himself from his bed and across to the washbasin where he was violently sick. He could still hear the sound of the axe as it cut through flesh and bone, the thud of the blade as it buried itself in the block. He could still see the blood spurting from the severed neck as the head fell to the wooden scaffold, dead eyes staring. As the retching began to subside, Rob stood with eyes closed for a moment, using his hands on the sink to support himself. When he finally opened his eyes, it was to see his hands red with blood. Then he remembered. The King was dead. He and his father had made their slow, reverent way through the crowd to the foot of the scaffold. There they had each torn one of the lace ruffs from their sleeves and soaked it in blood. The King's blood. Rob turned on the tap, roughly rubbing his hands together to rid himself of the blood, but he could not rid himself of the hollow feeling inside. The King was dead. He had watched as the martyr's head had been struck from his shoulders. What hope was there for anyone in England now?

Rob watched the water running over his hands. They were still red, although the colour was fading fast, but the blood was not being washed away by the water. That was still flowing pure and clear. Where had the blood gone? Rob turned off the tap and looked at himself in the mirror. Slowly his thoughts returned to the present. He had not been there when King Charles lost his head. It had all been part of one of his fantastically realistic dreams about Simon. But what of the blood? He looked down at his hands. No sign of blood there now.

Rob stumbled back to his bed and sat down, head in hands. It had all been so real; the smells, the sights, the sounds. He knew that it had all been a dream, yet he had felt so clearly the horror and sadness which Simon had felt, his fear for the future now that the King had been murdered. Rob now felt a similar fear, but this time for himself. What was happening to him? Why did these dreams haunt him? How could he make them stop? Then he remembered Simon's notebook. At the beginning of his dream Simon had taken his diary from its hiding place beneath the floor of his room. This very room. Rob stared at where the loose board had been. Had Simon really hidden his deepest thoughts there? Was the book still beneath the floor? Within his reach?

Rob closed his eyes. Of course not. How could it be? It was just a part of his vivid imagination. Yet... He opened his eyes. He knew that he would not be satisfied until he had at least taken a look. Rising unsteadily to his feet, Rob made his way over to the place where he had dreamt the loose floorboard to be. Kneeling down he leant his weight on it; gingerly at first, but more firmly when it moved. Suddenly the board twisted beneath him until one corner was raised. Heart beating wildly, he pulled the wood up to reveal a dark space beneath.

Rob sat back on his heels, fighting to control his breathing before reaching into the darkness. At first he felt nothing. Relief began to wash over him and he smiled. What had he expected? It was only a dream, after all. Then, as his questing fingers searched the hidden recess they brushed against something bulky. Rob allowed his fingers to close around the object and pulled it out. Whatever it was had been wrapped in cloth, dusty now with age. As he carefully unwrapped it Rob felt a wave of dizziness overwhelm him.

In his hands he held Simon's diary.

***

Rob sat in the kitchen, an open whisky bottle on the table and an empty glass beside him. He had not had time to read the whole diary, he would do that later. But he had, in his careful turning of the pages, been able to follow Simon's experiences, exactly as he had dreamt them. The last entry had been a description of the execution of Charles I. Nothing more had been added. Nothing to say what had happened to Simon and his family after that momentous event.

He had also found, tucked into the back of the book, a delicate piece of lace. It was yellow with age, where not stained brown with some substance. Rob did not need to get it analysed to know what it was. Blood. It was part of Simon's shirt which had been bathed in the blood of the king.

Hands shaking, Rob poured himself another whisky and drank it down in one go. How on earth could this be possible? There was no doubt now. He had been reliving Simon Hardwycke's experiences of the war through his dreams. Everything he had seen and felt had been true. Rob could not explain what had happened, just thinking about it filled him with fear, but as he turned again to the last page he felt a semblance of peace. The diary recorded what had happened to Simon from the outbreak of war to the bitter end. He had not written in his diary again. His story was over. Perhaps that meant that the dreams were over too. Rob hoped with all of his heart that was true.

But if so, why had he been haunted by the ghost? What was it that she blamed Simon for? There had been no indication in his dreams that Simon had ever harmed any woman. To the contrary, he had seemed a caring and honest young man, compassionate and just. What could he have done to cause such anguish that a spirit could not rest in peace?

Rob leant forward and rested his head in his hands. Did he really believe that he was being haunted by a ghost? He had tried to convince himself that his dreams had been nothing more than that, and that the ghost was not real. But now… He raised his head and looked at the diary resting on the table in front of him. Slowly he picked it up and began to turn the pages. He could not deny to himself that the ghost resembled Rebekah's mother. Was it her restless spirit? If so, would she now leave him in peace?

Feeling a sudden chilling of the room Rob looked over his shoulder, but saw nothing. Wanting to escape his nightmares Rob re-wrapped the book in its ancient cloth and swiftly left the kitchen.

***

Tully stood quietly, head held low in relaxation, tail swishing to keep the flies away. Unable to calm his mind, Rob had made his way out to the pasture where he now stood with the horse. His arms circled the graceful curve of the neck; his forehead rested against the warm hide. Breathing deeply of the sweet scent of horse, Rob felt himself beginning to relax at last. He sighed deeply.

'What ails you, Robert?'

Startled, Tully raised his head then, as Rob stepped back, the horse turned and trotted away.

'Robert?'

Rob felt a gentle peace enfolding him as a hand was laid on his arm. He turned to face his companion.

'Rebekah.'

'You look so weary, Robert. What is it that ails you?'

Rob wanted to talk to Rebekah about his dreams, and the diary, and the ghost. But, even though he felt closer to her than anyone else he had ever met, he felt that he could not. He did not want her to think he was foolish. Or mad. Besides, she had already seen the old woman, the ghost, and he was certain that she would tell him everything she knew about it in her own time. Rob found himself smiling at Rebekah. 'Nothing's wrong. I'm just a little tired, that's all.'

Rebekah smiled as she withdrew her hand. 'Perhaps you will feel better after a good sleep this night.'

'I hope so. A good night's sleep has been sorely lacking of late.'

'What do you mean?'

Rob shrugged. 'I've been dreaming a lot, that's all. But I think that must be over now.'

'Why do you say that?'

'Just a feeling. But, enough about me.' Rob smiled. 'I'm very glad to see you, Rebekah. I was just thinking about you.'

'And what is it that you were thinking?' Rebekah returned his smile and Rob felt a deeper calm, as though nothing could hurt him now.

'I was hoping that I might see you again. To ask you about your family.'

'My family?'

'Yes. You are always alone when I see you. Does your family live close by?'

'My mother and myself are all that are left of my family. Our home is not far from here, in the woods.'

'Have your family always lived here? I know that this was once the home of my ancestors and I feel very close to them here. Is it the same for you?'

Rebekah shrugged. 'This has been the home of my family for as long as can be remembered. It is the only place I think of when I think of home.'

'And your mother?'

'What of her?'

'She has always lived here?'

'Yes, Robert.' Rebekah frowned. 'My mother suffers somewhat. Life has not always been good to her.'

'Is there anything I can do to help?'

Rebekah's gaze was serious. 'It is sadness which causes her to suffer. A feeling that she had been misused. It is not the truth, Robert. The person she believes to have hurt her did not do so. But her mind tells her otherwise. I hope that, one day, she will see the truth and find peace.'

'I know someone who might be able to help her. A psychologist.'

'What is that?'

'A doctor for the mind. Perhaps, if your mother was to see her and tell her her problems?'

Rebekah shook her head. 'I think not. At least not for the present. My mother already seeks the path to her peace. I pray that she will find it soon.'

'But if not, the offer still stands.'

'I thank you, Robert, for your kindness.'

'It's nothing. No thanks are needed.' Rob smiled. 'Unlike your mother, I think I have found my path to peace.'

Rebekah raised a quizzical eyebrow. 'And what is that?'

'You, Rebekah. I always feel at peace when I am with you.'

'Then I will stay close by.'

'Good. Don't think I've forgotten that I offered you a job at the Manor. Once that is sorted out we'll be able to talk whenever we want. If you would like that?'

Rebekah's eyes met his, and he thought he would lose himself in their depths.

'Yes, Robert. I would like that very much.'

Chapter 34

February 1649

Simon sat on the wall surrounding the orchard. The branches of the apple trees were bare; it would be two months before they were once more clothed in green, and the delicate white blossom unfurled. In the past Simon had always been impatient for the spring, for its promise of new life, of a warm summer, of barns filling with the harvest. He could not feel like that today. For him there seemed no bright future, only one filled with uncertainty and fear. He watched as drops of moisture from the early morning rain fell from the branches. It seemed somehow fitting that the days should be dull grey, damp, monotonous.

'Hello, Simon.'

The young man started at the sound of the voice and turned round, his face breaking into a grin.

'Rebekah! What are you doing here?'

She smiled as she climbed up onto the wall beside him. 'I heard that you had come home, and so came this way in the chance that I might see you. I was worried about you.'

'Worried? About me?'

She nodded. 'Of course. I had heard that you were in London with your father when...' her words petered out. For the first time since he had known her, Simon sensed an uncertainty in Rebekah.

'You mean that you had heard that we were at the King's execution.' He still found it difficult to say the words, as though not speaking them would deny the reality of what had happened. But then he only had to close his eyes to see again the spreading pool of blood, and the King's head held high for all to see. No matter how much he tried to deny it to himself, he would have to face the fact that the war was over and the King was dead.

'What was it like?'

Simon frowned as he turned to Rebekah, thinking that she was ghoulish in her curiosity. But then he saw the concern in her eyes. She may now be fourteen years old, on the brink of becoming a woman, but she was still the little girl he had first met who cared more for others than for herself. He sighed.

'Everything seemed so unreal, from the trial to the execution. I kept hoping to wake up and find that it was all a bad dream. A nightmare. But it is all too real, and I fear that the nightmare has yet to begin.'

'What do you mean?'

Simon looked away, unable to meet Rebekah's gaze.

'Do you think your father would have wanted things to end this way?'

'No.' The response was immediate, firm, uncompromising. 'My father wanted things to change. He wanted a better life for people like us. But he would never have dreamt that Parliament would take the life of the King. I know that he would have hated that.'

'Yet he supported Parliament.'

'As did many others. Your father's friend, Sir Frances, for one. Did he want to see the death of the King?'

'You are right, as always. When the war started I do not believe that anyone would have entertained the idea that this could happen. But it has, and now I am afraid of what the future will bring.' Simon smiled sadly. 'That does not make me sound very brave, does it?'

Rebekah laid a comforting hand on his arm. 'If you are not afraid, you are likely to be the only person in England! Everyone is fearful of how things will turn out. But at least the fighting is over, so perhaps there is hope.'

Simon nodded. 'We two are friends; and if that can be so when our families fought on opposing sides, then perhaps there is hope.'

'Your father must find this very difficult. I know from what you have told me that he was fiercely loyal to the King.'

'He is very bitter. I feel that something has broken deep inside him that cannot be mended. But I hope that he will be able to pick up the pieces of his old life again in time.' Simon's eyes strayed from the orchard to the fields beyond. The sheep were heavy with their young, a new flock of lambs to be born and bring renewed life to the Manor. 'I think that taking back control of the estate will provide the healing that he needs.'

'What of your sister's husband? Was he not running the estate for the last few months?'

'Yes. But now that the war is over he has gone home. His father was killed at Oxford, so he has his own estates to run now Parliament has handed them back once more.' He gave a rueful shake of the head. 'It seems strange that Elizabeth has been married to Benjamin for three years, but this is the first time she has ever been to his home.'

'It must be difficult for her.'

Simon smiled at Rebekah. 'You always understand others so well. Your father always admired that in you, did he not?'

Rebekah nodded. 'He has been dead for so long now, but I still miss him. I do not believe that there have been any real victors in this war.'

'I believe you are right. Does your mother feel the same? How is she?'

'She is well. She still misses Father, of course, but she no longer has the old hatred for the Royalists. I believe that helping your sister with her delivery, and the naming of your niece after her, helped a great deal.'

'She is a wise woman. Does she still use her knowledge and potions to heal the sick?'

Rebekah nodded. 'It is who she is. She knows nothing else. Although we miss the money that Father made, people pay us in kind for Mother's treatments, so we are able to survive.'

'You know, I have not really thought about how you and your mother live. I have been so involved in this war that I have not given the thought to you that you have always given to me.'

'It is no matter,'

'It is indeed a matter that I should pay attention to.' Simon was silent for a time, deep in thought, finally he smiled. 'Would you like me to give you a job, Rebekah?'

She frowned. 'A job? What work could I do for you?'

'Perhaps you could work in the dairy? You would then earn a little something to help your mother and we...'

'We what?'

Simon fell silent again. What had he intended to say? Perhaps that it would be a way that they could continue their friendship? But as he looked at Rebekah, realising that she was growing into a beautiful young woman, he had the sudden feeling that it was more than that. There was her open, expressive gaze, her concern for him and his family, her intelligence, her developing beauty. Simon felt the heat rising in his cheeks. He was still only sixteen, but his experiences over the last year had turned him from a boy to a man, and he realised that he wanted more from Rebekah than the friendship of childhood. But did she feel the same? Was she not still too young? And how deep did his feelings go? He felt flustered, unsure. All he knew was that he wanted Rebekah to be close by so that he could talk with her whenever he wanted to. He realised that Rebekah was still looking at him, her face puzzled. He cleared his throat.

'We ... er ... we could continue our friendship. You do not appreciate how much I enjoy talking with you.'

Rebekah smiled shyly. 'I think I do.'

Simon felt himself grinning like a love-stricken swain. 'So you will take a job as dairy maid at the Manor?

'If my mother agrees then, yes, it would please me greatly.'

The two young people smiled at each other as they sat in companionable silence. Perhaps there was hope for the future after all.

***

August 1649

Simon sat straight-backed in his chair, trying to portray an air of maturity. As a child he had always loved the harvest celebrations, the food and drink, the music and dancing, the laughter. He had loved to dance with the estate workers and play with the children, but things had changed since then. As a young man, and heir to the estate, he could no longer act with such abandon. He sighed as he watched the children clamber over the bales of hay, or dodge between the legs of the huge shire horses tethered outside the barn. Some of them chased around the roaring fires where hogs were turning on spits, or created their own wild dances to the music. Many were hungry, unable to wait for the feast, and were munching on apples and slices of bread as they ran and played. How he wished he could join them.

Simon turned his attention from the children to the adults. As he watched them dancing, he was amazed at their energy. It was something he had never thought about in the past, but having watched them working twelve hours a day to bring in the harvest, he had expected the farm workers to be exhausted. Yet here they were, looking as though they could dance all night long.

'I wish I did not have to sit here and behave in such a reserved manner.'

Sir Thomas laughed. 'Believe me, Simon, I feel the same! I remember you at these celebrations as a boy. So much like I was at that age.'

'Did you use to play with the estate children?'

'Of course. I was once a child too, you know. Losing that innocence, losing the simple friendships of childhood, they were some of the most difficult parts of growing up for me. When I was old enough to wander by myself, I became friends with the wool merchant's son. My father was not too happy as they were beneath us, but at least I was not friends with one of the peasants, so it was acceptable.' Sir Thomas chuckled. 'I have always suspected that Father had his own friends in the village as a boy, though he never admitted it. But you,' his smile faded, as he looked at his son, a shadow of sadness in his eyes. 'I wish you had had the same opportunity to have a boyhood friend, but by the time you could go about by yourself the war had come and it was not safe. Just one more thing that the war took from you and you can never have back.'

Simon was thoughtful. His father was right, he had missed out on the youthful escapades of boys together. For a short time that role had been filled by Thomas, then he had gone away to war never to return. But he had a friend. Rebekah had been a part of his life for years now, only seen infrequently but a friend he could trust nevertheless, someone he could be himself with. His father's words now made him think more seriously about that relationship. He was sure that Sir Thomas would not approve of a friendship with a peasant. That the peasant was a girl would have made it all the more unacceptable. He frowned, wondering if he would lose Rebekah from his life, just as his father had eventually had to lose his friend, the wool merchant's son.

'Why the frown? This is a celebration!'

'I was thinking of Thomas.' It was only a small lie. He had been thinking of Thomas and could only say that name, for he could not bring himself to speak to his father about Rebekah. He did not need to say more, however, for Sir Thomas's eyes became distant, as though seeing past harvest celebrations, in a time now gone for ever. After a moment he re-focussed and rose to his feet.

'Come, Simon, let us get the serious business out of the way.'

As father and son stepped forward, the estate manager rushed over to the musicians to stop their playing. The dancing stopped a moment later, and the children ran to find their parents. A quiet crowd soon gathered in front of the great barn doors, where Sir Thomas climbed up onto a bale of hay so that he could be seen by everyone. He perused them silently for a moment, before speaking in a loud voice.

'In a manner, it only seems like yesterday when we last celebrated harvest together like this. Yet again, it feels like a century. Seven years. Seven of the worst years of all our lives.' His gaze travelled across the uplifted faces. 'I see men here who fought with me. I see others who were against us on the battlefield. I see your wives and children. Your mothers and fathers. I also see those who carry the wounds of war. And I do not see...' he paused for a moment, struggling to go on. 'I do not see many who should be here with us. Your husbands, and fathers, and sons. My son.

'It is a changed world we live in. A world which none of us yet fully understands. A world where we must work hard to make sure that nothing like this happens again. Never more shall Englishman take up sword against his neighbour, his brother. But as I look at you here tonight, hope flares in my heart. We have worked together this year to plant and harvest, as our families have done for centuries. Parliamentarian and Royalist worked the plough together, stood shoulder to shoulder as they scythed the crops, threshed and winnowed, baled the hay. We have worked peacefully together. We have come home.'

There were murmurs in the crowd and he waited, giving the people time to turn to others; past friends, then enemies, now friends once more. He could see that, despite the difficulties, despite the deaths and woundings, the people of his Manor were healing. If it was like this in most other communities, then there was hope for England. He smiled sadly as he continued.

'In the past, now would be the time when our priest would step forward to bless our crops, to bless our cattle and horses, to bless our workers. But tonight I am breaking that tradition. Many of you would find my priest too formal, many others would find the Puritan words to short and informal. We have come together as one, so I will let nothing divide us. In place of the blessing of my church, I give you my thanks, each and every one of you. Thanks for your hard work. Thanks for your tolerance of each other. Thanks for the way you have brought peace to this Manor. And with my thanks I ask God to bless us all as we face the future together.

'Now, instead of the prayers that we would have shared together in the past, I ask that you take some time this evening, between food and dancing, to give your own personal thanks to God for the good harvest which we have brought in, our healthy cattle and horses. Take a moment to ask Him to protect us in these times, which are still unsettled. When we ask Him humbly, He will give His blessing to us and heal our community.' Sir Thomas smiled at the crowd. 'Now, this is our first celebration since the end of the war, so let us enjoy it!'

There was a rousing cheer as the music started once more, and the crowd made their way to the feast, led by Sir Thomas and Simon. Food was served to them on simple wooden platters. Steaming slices of succulent pig whose juices ran pink, soaking into the large chunk of bread. Carrots and beans. Shiny red apples and crisp green pears. The wealth of the harvest, washed down with flagons of beer.

As Simon and his father sat at their table, their plates empty and their stomachs full, Sir Thomas sighed. 'So different from a year ago.'

Simon nodded. 'When I close my eyes I can almost feel the hunger, smell the filth, hear the roar of the cannon. I do not think that I will ever wish to visit Colchester again.'

'I know how you feel. After the travels I had, and now living in such a changed world, I do not think that I will ever seek to leave Marston again.'

'I may avoid Colchester, but I do not think that I will spend the rest of my days at Marston and never travel.'

Sir Thomas laughed. 'That is as it should be! You are a young man with your whole life before you! There is so much for you to see and experience, so many new people to meet. When you reach my age, with your wife and children beside you, then you may begin to feel differently.'

'Wife? I am not ready for that yet!'

Sir Thomas laughed at the expression on his son's face.

'Of course not! I wish you a few years to be at peace and find out who you really are before we settle you down with a wife!'

Simon laughed as he rose to his feet. 'Thank you, Father. Until I find a woman such as you found in Mother, marriage is not a thing that will trouble my mind!' With that he turned and made his way towards the barn. He stood for a moment, stroking the face of one of the gentle giants who pulled the plough, using the shire horse as an excuse to be away from his father and closer to the activity. He watched the crowd. As had been happening all evening, his eyes were constantly drawn to the slim figure of a girl who sat beside her mother, and he smiled.

Rebekah had been working in the dairy for more than six months now, and rarely a day went by when he did not find an excuse to go there. They often talked for a while, about everything and nothing. Sometimes he could not remember what had been said, but he always cherished the feeling of comfort and companionship from their meetings.

His heart always felt light when he saw her, and tonight was no exception. She looked so animated, laughing at something which someone in their group said. He wanted to talk to her, to see her laughing like that for him, but even in his inexperience he knew that he could not make for her directly. He gave the horse a final pat and made his way over to where a half-eaten pig was still turning on the spit. Many people came to take more, and he joined them, taking a piece of the skin. He took a bite and smiled. It was crisp, salty, dripping with fat. Delicious. As he chewed on the crackling he slowly made his way from one group of people to another, stopping to speak, to ask after their families, to wish them well. He heard the adults speaking kindly of him as he passed, saying that he was so like his father and would make a good lord of the Manor one day. He felt guilty, knowing that his kindness to them was, in part, a ruse so that he could get close to Rebekah.

As he drew nearer he noticed that there was more than one young man in the group who was paying attention to Rebekah, listening to what she had to say, laughing at her words, and he felt his heart skip a beat, the breath catch in his throat. When one young man reached out and took Rebekah by the hand, the crackling in Simon's mouth seemed to turn to wood. It was too dry to chew or swallow. He felt a sinking feeling inside, angry that the young man should touch her. Rebekah laughed at something her companion said, and Simon felt a flash of jealousy. He wanted her to look at him like that. To smile and laugh for him. As the young man led her onto the dance floor Simon took a step forward, then halted. What right had he to go to her? What would his father say if he danced with the dairymaid or, the Lord forbid, fought the young man to stop him dancing with her? As the young man slipped his hand around Rebekah's waist, Simon could stand it no longer. He turned away, throwing the remains of his food to the ground as his appetite disappeared. He knew from what his father said that a friendship with a peasant was not acceptable, yet he wanted to be with Rebekah. He felt a sudden hollow feeling inside as he contemplated life without being able to talk to her. As he strode towards the Manor house, he did not see Rebekah turn to look in his direction with a frown, he was too engrossed in his thoughts, wondering why he felt so jealous, and fearful of exploring the answer.

***

Simon stood in the doorway and watched Rebekah as she worked. She was sitting on a low milking stool, her back towards him as she worked the full udder. The milk came out in steaming jets, which hissed as they hit the bucket. He could smell the rich, creamy odour from where he stood, a comforting reminder of childhood. Rebekah's head was pressed against the flank of the cow, and her hair hid her features from him. He wanted to go to her and brush the hair away from her face, but resisted the temptation.

At last the milking was finished. Rebekah moved the bucket away so that the cow would not kick it over, then stood up. She arched her back as though to stretch out her tired muscles, and rotated her head to loosen her neck. Bending down to pick up the three-legged stool Rebekah turned, a look of welcome on her face as she saw Simon.

'How long have you been standing there?'

Simon shrugged. 'Not long. I was enjoying watching you work.'

Rebekah smiled. 'I am not sure why that would be. You must have seen hundreds of cows being milked.'

Simon did not reply. He did not really want to talk about milking. He wanted to ask her who the young man was whom she had danced with at the celebration. Had she spent the rest of the evening with him? Did she like him? But he could not find the words. Even if he could, he did not know if he had the right to ask such questions of her. Rebekah seemed puzzled by his silence.

'Are you ill? You look as though you did not sleep well last night, even though you left early.'

'No, I did not sleep well. But how do you know when I left?'

'I saw you go.'

'I am surprised. You seemed to be enjoying yourself dancing. I did not think you had seen me.' Simon was surprised by the harshness of his own words, and could see that they troubled Rebekah as well.

'Of course I was enjoying myself. It was the harvest celebrations. Everyone was enjoying themselves!'

'Not me.'

Rebekah frowned. 'What is wrong?'

Simon shrugged. He felt that he was behaving like a child, but could not stop himself. But at least thoughts of childhood gave him something to say rather than ask the questions racing around inside his mind. 'I used to enjoy the celebrations, but now I cannot. I have to act like a man and keep my distance. I wanted to join in with the boys, like I did as a child. And I wanted to join in the dancing.'

'Being the heir to the estate is not easy, is it?'

'No.' Simon smiled ruefully as he made his way across the straw littered floor to stand beside Rebekah. 'But I suppose part of the problem is that I still have some growing up to do. At the moment I am betwixt and between. Neither child nor adult. And I do not really belong in either camp.'

Rebekah nodded and smiled. 'It is the same for me. I remember the games from my childhood, but last night all the boys wanted to do was dance with me!'

Simon felt his jealousy rising again and fought to control it. 'Did you spend all evening dancing with the man I saw you with?'

Rebekah shook her head, her eyes dancing. 'No. He was just one of many.'

Surprisingly, Simon found that he preferred that answer to her saying that she had spent the evening with just one person. He smiled sheepishly.

'You work hard Rebekah, and you deserve to enjoy yourself at the celebrations. I am glad that you enjoyed the dancing.'

'I had hoped that you would dance with me.'

'Father would not have approved. He does not believe that there was anyone there equal to my station.' Simon saw the hurt in her eyes and inwardly cursed himself. 'I am sorry Rebekah. I did not mean to speak cruelly to you, but that is how my father thinks.'

'It matters not. I know that I am just a poor girl whilst you are a rich young man. I had just hoped that could be forgotten for one night of the year.'

Simon looked into her eyes and saw reflected in them the same attraction and confusion he felt. He had lain awake for most of the night, wondering about his mixed emotions, wondering what they said about his feelings for Rebekah. He had come to the conclusion that she meant more to him than just a friend. But how much more, and where that would lead he could not tell.

'Perhaps it can. Next year, Rebekah. I will dance with you at the next harvest celebrations. If you still want me to.'

Rebekah smiled. 'Yes, Simon. I think I would like that.'

Sensing a subtle change in their relationship Simon reached out and took her hand in his, a smile of happiness lighting his face.

***

December 1649

The drawing room fireplace was decked with holly and ivy. A huge yule log glowed redly in the hearth. On a table to one side was a bowl of hot punch and a plate of sweet cakes. Sir Thomas was smiling happily.

'It will be good to see them again. Marston does not feel like home without Elizabeth.'

'I know. I cannot remember a time without her. She has always helped and advised me.'

'Indeed. I am not sure how well I would have done all that was needed when you were a small child without Elizabeth's help. She cared so well for you in place of your poor mother, God rest her soul.'

'I was lucky to have such a sister.' Simon warmed his hands at the fire. He grinned. 'You know, Father, I feel like a little boy again waiting for her! I am so glad that they are able to join us for Christmas; I would have missed her dearly.'

'Yes. Regardless of the restrictions placed on us by the Puritans, I intend to make this a happy Christmas. Like the ones we had in the past. Before the war. Before…'

The two men, father and son, looked up at the portrait above the fireplace. Neither said anything. No words were needed. Sir Thomas could see the features of the young man in the painting reflected in those of the young man by his side. He sighed sadly. Christmas would never be the same without Thomas.

The sound of a carriage on the gravel outside drew their melancholy thoughts back to the present.

'Here they are!' Simon rushed into the hallway and on out of the front door, which was swung open by the butler. 'Elizabeth! Welcome home!'

As he opened the carriage door his sister alighted, her bearing calm and collected, the epitome of a married woman visiting the family home. Simon stilled for a moment, but then noticed her eyes laughing gaily.

'Happy Christmas, Simon. It is good to be home.'

The two young people embraced as Benjamin dismounted from his horse and threw the reins to a waiting groom.

'Good afternoon, brother. Merry Christmas!'

The two shook hands as Sir Thomas came out of the house at a more sedate pace than Simon, though his delight in seeing his daughter was no less evident.

'Welcome home, my dear.'

Elizabeth made her way to her father, gave a curtsy, then kissed him on the cheek. A smiling Sir Thomas took her in his arms.

'No formalities, my dear child. Marston has always been your home, and always shall be.' He bowed his head to his son-in-law. 'It is good to see you again, Benjamin.'

'And you, sir.'

Sir Thomas looked around, then at the coach, his eyes questioning. 'Surely someone is missing? Where is my granddaughter?'

Elizabeth smiled as she turned back to the coach. 'She feels nervous of meeting her grandfather. She has spent so little time with you, and it is ten months now since she last saw you.'

'But does she remember me?' Simon stepped forward as he spoke.

Benjamin laughed. 'Of course she remembers the uncle who was more like a father to her for the first year of her life.' He reached into the coach and lifted down his daughter.

Simon was surprised at how much Ann had changed. Her face had matured from that of a baby to a young girl, and when Benjamin placed her on the ground in front of Sir Thomas she stood steadily, without wavering. Her chubby little fists were clenched at her sides as she stared up at the large man before her.

'Heyo, Ganfava.'

Sir Thomas smiled as he crouched down to her height. 'Hello, my darling. Welcome to Marston.'

The serious gaze met his for a moment before glancing around. Suddenly the features broke into a radiant smile as she saw Simon.

'Ucle Si! Ucle Si!'

Simon opened his arms and the child ran into them. He picked her up and swung her round. 'My, my. How big you have grown!'

Ann laughed gaily as she threw her chubby arms around his neck. 'Appy Cismus, Ucle Si!'

As Simon hugged his niece, Sir Thomas turned towards the house.

'Come inside out of the cold. We have refreshments waiting for you.'

As the family made their way up the wide steps Simon knew that it would be a very 'Appy Cismus' indeed.

**

Ann had been tucked up in bed since six o'clock, her maid in attendance, leaving the adults to enjoy a leisurely dinner. As they sat around the table, enjoying a dessert of sweet apples, stored from the harvest and served in a delicate custard, talk turned to Elizabeth's new home.

'The farmers on Benjamin's estate tend to grow grain,' she explained to her brother. 'It is a very different annual cycle from Marston. We have little to do at the moment. We are waiting for spring to come so that we can plant and sow, but you must be busy with the sheep and cattle.'

Simon nodded. 'The dairy herd is doing well. We have hardly lost a beast this year, and the number of calves has been excellent. Over-wintering them will not be too onerous a task, as we had a good harvest.'

Sir Thomas nodded. 'As usual at this time of the year, our focus is on the sheep. Thankfully it is a mild winter so they are still out in the fields, but we will soon need to start bringing them in ready for lambing.' He smiled. 'All the ewes look healthy and we hope that we will not lose too many.'

'It must be difficult to adapt to a whole new way of farming.'

Benjamin nodded at his brother-in-law. 'Yes, but Elizabeth has managed magnificently. I am an extremely lucky man.'

Elizabeth lowered her eyes, a blush shading her cheeks at the praise.

'I am not surprised.' Simon smiled warmly at his sister. 'While you and Father were away I was supposed to be in charge here, but the estate would not have survived so well if not for Elizabeth.'

'It was a team effort, brother. You did more than you realise, although I was happy to help you. It was a strange time for me, to be married but without a husband. Helping you look after Marston stopped me feeling sorry for myself.'

Benjamin put down his spoon and reached out to take Elizabeth's hand in his. 'I am sorry about that, my dear. I…'

Elizabeth was horrified. 'No, Benjamin! You must *never* apologise for being away! You did your duty, and while I would have preferred to have you with me, I was so proud of you, and the way you supported the King!'

There was silence for a moment. Despite the fact that almost a year had passed since the execution of Charles, they still found it difficult to speak about him. Doing so not only filled their hearts with sadness, but also with anxiety for a future which was still uncertain. Sir Thomas changed the subject.

'Married life certainly seems to agree with you, my dear.'

Elizabeth's smile lit up her face. 'Indeed it does, Father. This last year has been the happiest of my life.' Her smile faded. 'Oh! I did not mean that my life here was not happy, but…'

Sir Thomas laughed. 'You do not have to explain. I was married too, all be it for all too short a time. You speak of a different, more mature happiness.'

'You do understand.' Elizabeth giggled, an almost girlish sound. 'Now there is only Simon left to find out what we are talking about!'

Simon dropped his spoon. 'What? Me? What do you mean?'

'You are a young man now. It will soon be time for you to settle down, get married and produce the next generation of men to inherit Marston!'

Simon paled. 'But I am far too young for that!'

'Why do you say that? You know how to run the estate, you have even been to war. You are no longer a child, Simon, and must think about settling down!'

'But…but…' Simon struggled to find the words, turning to his father for support. 'I am not ready yet! I have not met anyone I would like to marry!'

Elizabeth could keep a straight face no longer and burst into peals of laughter, joined by Sir Thomas and Benjamin. Simon realised that he was being teased and grinned sheepishly. 'Well done, Elizabeth. You certainly caught me there!'

'Do not worry, my boy', said Sir Thomas with a smile. 'You can count on a year or two more of freedom before I fetter you to some empty-headed girl for the rest of your life. Just as I gave Elizabeth to poor Benjamin.'

'Father!' Elizabeth was horrified, but Benjamin laughed all the more.

'You tease your brother with impunity, wife, but cannot take the teasing when it comes back to you!'

The four people around the table laughed together. But when the laughter stopped Simon was quiet, his thoughts turned inward. Why, he wondered, when talk had turned to marriage, had his thoughts turned to Rebekah?

***

Simon rode his new horse slowly through the woods. The animal was large, a charger in its prime, yet the young man controlled it with ease. He smiled, remembering the first time he had met Rebekah and her mother; he was unlikely to take such a tumble from his mount now. As he rode along the same track, allowing the horse to pick its own way between the muddy puddles, he wished it was Prince. He still deeply regretted taking the horse with him when he journeyed with his father. If he had not done so, the poor beast would not have been slaughtered to feed the starving soldiers in Colchester.

Simon was so engrossed in his memories that he almost missed the small path to the Sawyers cottage. It had been many months since he had visited. Now that Rebekah worked in the dairy he could see her whenever he wanted and, he realised with a shock, it was nigh on ten months since he had ridden this way. The bushes on either side brushed his legs. Since the death of Rebekah's father there had been no carts removing the wood, and he would not be surprised if the last horse to walk the track had been his own. Life had been hard for Rebekah and her mother since Henry had died. He was glad that the job as a dairymaid was helping them to make ends meet.

Simon saw Rebekah as soon as he rode into the clearing. She was sitting at the table wrapped in a thick woollen cloak. Her long hair hung loose, framing her face with the lively brown eyes and sensitive smile. For days now, ever since Elizabeth had jokingly spoken about marriage, Simon had been seeing that face in his dreams, both waking and sleeping. As she rose to greet him with a wave, he felt a tenderness which was new and he realised that, sometime during the past months, his feelings for Rebekah had changed from those of a friend to something more. Unsure of himself, he said nothing, but waved in return as he dismounted. How strange that he had not noticed the change until Elizabeth had spoken of marriage.

Simon took a few moments to untie the bundle from his horse. By the time he turned again he had his expression, if not his feelings, under control.

'Happy Christmas, Rebekah!' He looked around as he spoke. 'Where is your mother? You did tell her I was coming?'

Rebekah nodded. 'Yes. But I am afraid that she has been called away to the village. It is always the same in the winter. So many people suffer from the cold and damp, especially the children or elderly. Her potions are always useful.'

'The village are lucky to have her as a healer.'

'That is true. Now, come and sit. I will fetch you a beer.'

Rebekah disappeared into the cottage for a moment as Simon made his way across the clearing, placed his bundle on the table and sat in a chair carved from a single piece of wood. He recognised it as Henry's work and smiled.

Rebekah noticed his expression as she came back out with two leather flagons. She passed one to Simon. 'What are you smiling at?'

'I was just thinking of your father. He was always so kind to me, answering the questions of a little boy who was probably something of a nuisance.'

'No, he never thought of you like that. He always felt honoured that the son of the lord of the Manor would seek his advice and opinions.'

'I was the one who was honoured. He always had such sound, well thought out opinions.'

'He was just an uneducated man.'

'He may have lacked an education, but he was a wise man. I believe that if he had been born to a different station then he could have done great things.'

'He always hoped that things would change after the war so that people would be judged on their merit, not on their station in life.'

'So far that does not seem to have happened.'

Rebekah sighed. 'So far much of what he hoped for has not happened. I think he would have been saddened by the way the war went. I know he would have been horrified by the King's execution. That was something he could never have imagined.'

'And what about life under the Puritans? Is it what he would have hoped for, do you think?'

Rebekah took a sip of the small beer. Her brow wrinkled into a slight frown as she thought. Simon found it endearing. After a moment's silence she answered his question.

'I think he would have said that one tyrant had been exchanged for a handful of tyrants. I do not think he would have liked all the restrictions placed upon us. His hope had always been that all men should be treated equally, and have the freedom to worship as they choose. Now the Catholics and the followers of the English church are forced to follow Puritan ways; and many Puritans do not like the severity of the rules imposed on us.' She shook her head sadly. 'I do believe that if he were here now he would say that what we have now was not worth fighting for.'

The young people sat in silence for a moment, thinking of those they had loved and lost, the wasted lives; the wasted years of their childhood. Simon finally spoke.

'Enough of that!' His voice was brisk. 'The war is behind us and we can do nothing to change it. What we must do now is look forward. It will be up to our generation to make sure that what your father and my brother died for can become a reality. Now,' he indicated the bundle as he spoke, 'here are your Christmas gifts. I had hoped to give my greetings to your mother, but perhaps you can do that for me?'

'Of course, but you did not need to bring us anything.'

Simon smiled warmly. 'I know, but I wanted to give you something. It is little enough. Just some cloth for you and your mother to make some clothes, a couple of blankets and some food.'

'You are too kind to us.'

'It is nothing.' Simon did not feel it was a kindness. He was not doing something for them as the heir to the Manor, but as a friend. Perhaps more than a friend.

Rebekah must have seen something in his expression, for she tilted her head to one side, a movement Simon found endearing.

'What are you thinking, Simon?'

He was silent for a moment, struggling to find the words, fearful of how she might react. Should he tell her about his changed feelings? Would it be better to act as though nothing had changed?

'Simon?'

He put down his tankard and met her gaze. His words were hesitant. 'Do you think of me as a friend, Rebekah?'

She was horrified. 'Of course I do! Surely you know that! In fact, I would say that you are my best friend. You seem to understand me in a way that others do not.'

'Exactly!' Simon stood as he spoke. 'That is how I feel about you! I can talk to you about anything and know that you will understand. You have always been there for me, and never had an unkind word. After the attack on the Manor and the death of Thomas we should have been enemies; yet you were there for me. It was always you who helped me.'

'Then why the question?' Rebekah stood too, and moved around the table until she was standing in front of Simon. The puzzled frown was back on her face. 'Why ask that question now?'

'Because...'

Rebekah did not say anything, waiting for him to finish. Simon searched her face for a hint of how she might react. He saw nothing there but puzzlement. He took a deep breath.

'Because I have realised that you are more to me than a friend.' The words came out in a rush. He stood, tense and still, awaiting her reaction.

'What has made you realise that? And what do you mean when you say more than a friend?' Rebekah's words were hesitant, almost defensive. Simon swallowed hard. He could not tell her that he had realised how much she meant to him when his family had been discussing marriage. He shrugged.

'Nothing specific has changed me. It is just that, since you have been working in the dairy we have become closer. I find that my day does not seem complete if I have not been able to see you. When I say that I think of you as more than a friend, I...' he lowered his eyes as he spoke. '...I would like to walk out with you.'

They were silent for a moment, then Rebekah reached out tentatively and placed a hand on his arm. Simon felt the warmth of her touch but dare not raise his face in case the warmth was not reflected in her eyes.

'Simon?'

Finally he looked up. Rebekah looked nervous, questioning, maybe a little afraid. But there was no rejection in her eyes. Simon found that he could breathe again.

'Surely you do not mean that? I am the daughter of a woodcutter. You will inherit the Manor. How can we walk out together? That is not something I thought that your class of people did anyway. I thought that it was only something we villagers do?'

Simon nodded. 'Maybe that is because it is rare for people like me to meet people like you. But I care for you, Rebekah. And did we not just say that it is up to our generation to change things?'

'Yes. But perhaps not such great things. And not so quickly.'

'That is something we may have to face in the future. All I am asking now is that you will walk out with me. Do you want that? If not then we can remain as friends and I will not mention it again.'

Rebekah smiled, and Simon's heart raced.

'Yes. I also think of you as more than a friend. I had not thought that you could too, as I am so far beneath you. I had not dared to hope. But I would be honoured to walk out with you.'

Simon was smiling happily as he placed his hand over Rebekah's where it still rested on his arm. 'The honour is mine.'

His eyes danced with delight, although the brown ones he gazed into were more cautious.

'We may believe that the war has changed things, Simon, but many people will not agree. We must be cautious. We cannot walk out in public. We cannot be seen. It would not be seemly.'

Simon nodded. 'I know. But for now, I care not!' He leant towards her and hesitantly placed his lips against hers, which were warm and inviting. As they shared their first tender kiss, Simon felt that his heart would burst with happiness.

Chapter 35

Present day

Rob recognised the number of the incoming call and made the connection. 'Caroline?'

'Hello, darling. How are you?'

'Fine thanks. And you?' Rob settled himself in an armchair as he spoke.

'I'm okay. A bit tired though.'

'Busy?'

'Yes. You know how it is.'

'Of course. Working for the NHS is always pressured. Why don't you get a job in the private sector?'

'Because I enjoy what I'm doing. Just as you enjoy your work, no matter how busy you get.'

'Touché.'

'Have you been sleeping well?'

Rob knew that, even though she had not mentioned his dreams, this is what Caroline was referring to. He was not quite sure what to say.

'Rob?'

He was afraid of his dreams, afraid he might be going mad. Part of him wanted to bury it deep; yet another part knew that if anyone was able to help him, it would be Caroline. With a deep breath he plunged in.

'I've been dreaming again. I dreamt to the end of the war. To the execution of the King.' He shuddered as he thought of it. It had all seemed so real. 'I was really scared, Caroline. Then...'

'Then what?'

'In my dream I dreamt that I ... Simon ... kept a diary. I dreamt where he hid it and...'

'And...?

'And I found it.'

There was silence from the other end of the phone, then. 'What? You mean you found the actual diary?'

'Yes. And it was so accurate. What I dreamt really happened, Caroline. I can't explain it. And that scares me.'

'Perhaps I can help. I...'

'I don't think psychology can help here. It was real. Don't you understand? What I dreamt actually happened and...'

'Calm down, Rob.'

Rob leapt to his feet. 'Calm down! Do you have any idea how frightening this is!'

'Yes. As a professional I can make a pretty good guess. So let me help.'

'How? Can you make the dreams go away?'

'Didn't they end with the death of Charles?'

'No. I've had another.'

'About what?'

'Simon. His life after the war.'

'The same characters?'

'Yes. Simon's family. And ... Rebekah.'

'That's the girl he met, right?'

Rob nodded, then realised she could not see. 'Yes. Do you remember that I said she looked like a younger version of someone here at Marston?'

'Yes.'

'Well, the girl in my dreams has grown up. And she's identical. She seems to be the same person. But that's not possible. Is it?'

'I don't know, Rob. It's likely that you're just putting her features on this imagined person.'

'But it feels so real!'

'Then perhaps it is.'

Rob was stunned. 'What do you mean?'

'I've been talking to someone. A colleague.' Caroline gave a nervous laugh. 'It doesn't mean I agree with her, Rob; but hear me out. She thinks you could be experiencing a past life through your dreams.'

'What?'

'It's her speciality. She thinks that you could have lived before. Been this Simon. The memories were dormant, but with you going to Marston Manor and burying yourself in the civil war, they are surfacing through your dreams.'

'And you believe this rubbish?'

'Not really; no. But it is a theory.'

'I don't believe in re-incarnation, Caroline. We just get one go at life, and this is it for me.'

'Okay.' There was a pause, then... 'She did have another theory but that was ... bizarre.'

'And past life memories aren't? This must be really whacky!'

'She mentioned something called the akashic record.'

'The what?'

'Akashic record. The theory is that everything that happens – past, present and future – leaves a record which we can access.'

'A record? Where?'

'On the astral plane. Some people can access this and see what happened in the past.'

'Or in the future? This is mad, Caroline!' Rob's laugh was almost hysterical. 'If that's the only option, then I'll have to believe I'm reliving a past life. And so is Rebekah! Unless you have another explanation?'

'Well...'

'You're kidding! What now?'

'I have just one other theory, Rob. My own this time.'

'This had better be good.'

'If your dreams really are showing you what actually happened in the past...'

'They must be. The diary proves that.'

'Then what if Rebekah is a ghost? Maybe she is trapped here for some reason? Perhaps she needs to tell someone her story before she can ... move on?'

'And she's chosen me?'

'It's possible.'

Rob was silent for a moment. He sat down again, feeling drained. He sighed deeply.

'I suppose it's possible. It seems the most likely explanation of the three.' He gave a strangled laugh. 'How mad is that? Saying that a ghost is telling me her story through my dreams is the most likely explanation for what is happening to me?'

'But you think it might be possible?'

Rob closed his eyes. Imagining the Rebekah that he had met in the woods. Remembering the kiss they had shared.

'I'm not sure, Caroline. She's so real. Flesh and blood.'

'How do you know?'

Rob remembered the touch of his lips on hers. Her hand on his shoulder.

'I don't. It's just that I can't see through her. She must be real.'

'It's something to think about.'

'Okay.'

'Whatever happens though, don't worry, Rob. They are only dreams. And dreams can't hurt you.'

'That's easy for you to say.'

Neither of them spoke for a moment. Somehow it didn't seem right to talk of mundane things after the conversation they had just had. It was Caroline who eventually broke the silence.

'I worry about you Rob. As I said, just think about it. I'm sure it will make you feel better. I love you, darling. I'll call you again in a few days.'

'Okay. Take care. And thanks for calling.'

Rob disconnected the call without the usual endearments, but he did not notice. He made his way over to the window and gazed out across the courtyard, his mind a whirl of jumbled, conflicting thoughts, and his stomach a tight knot of fear. When he had met Rebekah in the stable, she had also said that a ghost was trying to tell him its story, but then she was referring to the apparition of the old woman. Although it went against all logic, he had come to accept that the ghost had some sort of message for him. But what of Rebekah? Was she also a ghost? Did she have some sort of message for him too? Despite his fear, Rob hoped that he would have another dream sometime soon. Anything to get to the end of the story. Anything for some peace at last.

***

'So, what do you think of them?'

It was the morning after his phone call with Caroline, and Rob was feeling more at ease. He had rejected the past life theory, and had never given any consideration to the idea that he had been accessing some vague ethereal record of the past. The only other theory was that Rebekah was a ghost. He knew that this was not true, so all he had to fall back on was his imagination. That is all that it was. His dreams were his mind playing tricks on him. He refused to listen to the small voice, which told him that this was not possible.

Turning his attention back to the field, Rob let his eyes rove over the cows. They were a striking white colour, with upright ears, smaller than the cows he was used to seeing in the fields, a little slimmer too.

'Very attractive. Are they typical of cows at the time?'

Jim nodded. 'There are a few herds which have been preserved. I've just taken the six for now. Once we get set up properly with someone to look after them, I'll get a bull as well.'

Rob grinned. 'I think I can help you there. I've met a local girl who would be keen to work in the dairy.'

'A local girl? Where does she live?'

Rob shrugged. 'I'm not exactly sure. I've only met her a few times, walking on the estate. At first I thought she was with the travellers, but apparently not. I got talking to her and she says she can make butter and cheese, and would love to work in the dairy here.'

'Sounds perfect! Get her to come and see me and I'll set it up.' Jim turned a speculative gaze towards Rob. 'Have you met many of the locals?'

Rob shook his head. 'No, she's the only one I've seen on the estate, and I don't tend to visit the village much.' He frowned. 'She's a strange one, Jim. Very nice but a bit other-worldly, as though she doesn't really belong here. Yet she seems to belong more than anyone else I know.'

'A bit of a contradiction there.'

Rob nodded. 'Too right. I'm not sure who she is, but I do think she would be perfect for the job.'

'Okay, introduce us when you get the chance.'

Rob found himself thinking that this would prove that Rebekah was a living, breathing woman, not some ghost. 'Sure.'

'Good. I look forward to meeting her.'

Rob tensed and glanced across at Jim. He wondered why he suddenly felt so jealous.

Chapter 36

August 1650

It was harvest time again. It had been a good summer and the barns were full. Simon was thankful that Oxfordshire had not endured the heavy rains of the eastern counties, which had caused mildew on some of the crops. As he looked around himself, he could almost have believed that no time had passed since the last celebration. The same people, the pigs roasting on spits, the music and dancing. One thing had changed, though. This year the prayers had been conducted by a Puritan minister and, while they appreciated the thanks that were given to God, Simon noticed that his father did not seem relaxed. He sat stiff and upright, far too formal for such a festive occasion. Simon did not need to ask to know that Sir Thomas resented the fact that he could not use a member of the clergy from his own church. The Puritans now had complete control over what could, and could not, be done in regards to worship. The Hardwyckes were not the only ones who felt uncomfortable with the informality and lack of ritual, but for the sake of peace nothing had been said.

Once the prayers and exhortations were over, the crowd had made their way to the fires to help themselves to food. Simon and his father now sat together at their table, enjoying the traditional meal of pork with fresh local vegetables. Sir Thomas smiled as he cast a proprietorial eye over the gathering.

'We are lucky, son. A good harvest and no problems in the village. I would not like to be in the east this year. There is talk of a poor harvest; and more tales of witching.'

Simon turned uneasily towards his father.

'Are they having problems with witchcraft again?'

'I am afraid so.' Sir Thomas took a sip of beer to wash down a mouthful of food. 'Let us hope that the situation does not get as bad as during the war. Those two years after Naseby were troubled times for Huntingdonshire and the eastern counties.'

'Indeed. I wonder if the fear of the war was what made those witches cast more spells?'

'That could be so, although it is strange that the worst troubles were confined to that small part of the country. Maybe it was because Cromwell is from that area and has a strong following. People did not go openly against him. Maybe those who could not use weapons to fight him chose sorcery instead.'

'Or perhaps it was because of the Witchfinder General.'

Sir Thomas turned a puzzled frown towards his son. 'What do you mean?'

Simon was hesitant, choosing his words carefully. 'Well, which came first? Was there a great outbreak of witchcraft and then Hopkins came forward to deal with it? Or did Hopkins seek it out? Did his actions make things worse?'

'How so?'

'Perhaps not all of those who were tried as witches were guilty? What if Hopkins, and others like him, used the witches as an excuse to target the King's men? Surely so many witches could not have suddenly appeared in one area?'

Sir Thomas sighed. 'We both know that witches live in every community, they just keep to themselves so that there is little need to confront them. Indeed, why would anyone want to harm a white witch? Their potions and spells are often the only help that the poor get when they are ill.'

'Yet Hopkins was able to find so many whom he considered to be practicing sorcery.' Simon looked enquiringly at his father. 'I hear that he paid people for denouncing witches. Perhaps he was so vigilant, and so keen to prosecute, because it made him a great deal of money.'

'The Reverend Gaule agrees with you there. In his pamphlet he denounced Hopkins for persecuting unfortunate people, so that he could make money from the fears of their neighbours. And it is true that the numbers of witches who were denounced dropped dramatically after Hopkins' disappearance.'

'What do you think happened to him?'

'I do not know. The common understanding is that he fell ill and died.'

'I wonder if one of the witches put a spell on him?'

Sir Thomas shrugged. 'It may have been the only way that they could protect themselves. If so, I doubt that we shall ever know the truth of the matter.'

'I am so glad that we do not have such troubles in our community.' Simon pushed his empty plate away from him as he spoke.

'Indeed. The villagers seem to be enjoying themselves.'

Simon looked out over the gathering, his eyes automatically seeking out Rebekah as they had done since his arrival earlier in the evening. As during the previous year's harvest celebrations, she was with a group of young people, a number of them young men who vied for her attention. Simon felt jealous, but not the consuming jealousy of twelve months before, when he thought that she might be interested in one of the young men. This time it was because the young men were able to spend the evening with her while he was not. The fact that he had seen her almost every day since Christmas should have helped, but did not. He was used to seeing her, talking with her, spending time privately together. Each day he would see her at the dairy, or in the orchard, or on her way home. And each day he had been able to kiss her goodbye. How he wished he did not have to keep his relationship with her a secret. He wanted to be with her tonight, talking and laughing. Dancing together in front of the huge bonfire. Instead he watched as others danced with her and held her hand, and his heart ached. Over the months, Simon had come to realise that what he felt for Rebekah was not just a passing fancy. He loved her.

As the evening light finally began to fade, Simon rose to his feet and stretched.

'I think I will just take a short walk before returning to the house.'

Sir Thomas nodded. 'Perhaps I will join you.'

For a moment Simon was lost for words. That had not been his plan. He had arranged to meet Rebekah in the orchard, indeed he could see her slipping away at that very moment. He could not let his father accompany him.

'One of us should remain here. It is our duty to have a presence. If you would like to take a walk then I shall stay here.'

Sir Thomas looked at his son and smiled. 'You are right. I will remain. Enjoy your walk. I used to enjoy a walk with a pretty girl after the festivities when I was your age.'

'Father?' Simon's heart was beating wildly. Had his secret been discovered? But his father did not look angry, and Simon realised that Sir Thomas thought he was just engaging in the typical behaviour of a young man of his age and station. It would not be unexpected for him to meet with a village girl from time to time, just as long as it was nothing serious. In fact, his father would never dream that it could be serious. A village girl would be so far beneath Simon, and she would know her place. If the relationship progressed to something physical and the girl was with child, then it would not be acknowledged, although a gentleman would provide for its means. Simon realised that there was a huge gulf between what he wanted and what his father would expect of him. With a sigh and murmured thanks he turned and walked away.

Rebekah was waiting for Simon in the shadows cast by the apple trees. When she saw him she stepped out into the moonlight, her face lit by a smile which took his breath away. He leant down to kiss her tenderly. After a moment they broke away and he smiled wistfully.

'I have been watching you all evening. So many young men danced with you and I could not.'

'I saw you watching.'

'Was it that obvious?'

'Only to me.'

'I hated seeing you dancing with someone else, but could not look away. I wanted you to be in my arms. I wanted to hold you and dance with you.'

'Well, I am here now.' Rebekah smiled.

'Will you dance with me?'

Without a word. Rebekah took his hand and he drew her to him. She was warm and yielding in his arms as they moved to the rhythm of the music, its sound softened by distance. Simon felt as though he were in heaven, that his heart would burst with happiness. He rested his cheek against her soft hair, breathing in the scent of lavender.

'I love you, Rebekah.' His words were soft, whispered; but she heard them. Rebekah's feet stilled and she pulled away from Simon so that she could look up into his face. Her eyes were shadowed, and Simon felt his heart lurch, his breath catch in his throat.

'I am sorry, Rebekah, I had not meant to say that. But it is true. I love you. Why do you pull away from me? I thought you felt the same?'

Rebekah shook her head sadly. 'We cannot speak such words. We are from different worlds, you and I. There is no hope for a love between us.'

Simon felt that he could breathe again. 'Do you love me Rebekah? Forget that I am who I am. Do you love me, Simon, who you have known since I was a boy?'

Rebekah lowered her eyes. 'It is wrong.'

'No, Rebekah. Nothing has ever felt more right to me.' He placed a hand beneath her chin and gently lifted her face so that she looked into his eyes. 'Do you love me?'

Rebekah was silent for a moment, her eyes searching his. A slow smile spread over Simon's features. No matter how wrong she felt it to be, she could not deny it.

'You do love me, do you not?'

Rebekah nodded slowly. 'Yes, Simon. I believe that I have always loved you, from the very day that we met, when you fell from your pony.'

'You have been special to me since that day, too. I did not realise that it was love. All I knew was that you were my best friend and I could not live without you. I still feel the same, only the feelings are deeper. We belong together, Rebekah. Though you say that it is wrong, I believe that it is right and we will find a way. God will not let our love be denied.'

'But what of your father? I can never be accepted by your family.'

'We are young. We have plenty of time to resolve those problems.'

'I do not know, Simon. Perhaps it would be better if...?'

'Do you not want to see me again?' Simon interrupted.

Rebekah shook her head. 'I could no more stop seeing you than breathing. But...'

'No buts, we will work this out.'

Simon ended her protests with a kiss.

Chapter 37

December 1650

Another year had passed, a year in which Ann had grown into a charming little girl who chattered incessantly. The depth of her love for her 'Ucle Si' knew no bounds, and she spent every possible moment of the Christmas holiday with her chubby little fingers holding tightly to his hand as they explored the estate. Simon adored the child, and hoped that he would be equally close to her sibling, who was due to be born in the spring. Elizabeth was glowing with health, although her back ached at times with the weight of her unborn child. She was sitting in front of the fire, fingers busy with her embroidery, when Sir Thomas joined them in the drawing room.

'Well, my dear', he warmed his hands at the fire as he spoke, 'I suppose that Benjamin is happy with the prospect of another child?'

Elizabeth nodded. 'Yes. He hopes for a boy to inherit, but if it is another girl then it is no matter. We both love Ann, and a sister to keep her company would be welcome. We can always try again for a boy, if necessary.'

Sir Thomas laughed. 'I am sure that that will not be an onerous task.'

Elizabeth lowered her eyes to her sewing, a blush staining her cheeks. 'I have been lucky in my marriage, Father. You chose wisely for me. So many people in our station have loveless marriages, and I pity them. Benjamin is my best friend as well as my husband.'

Simon grinned. 'What about me? I thought I was your best friend?'

'You were always my best friend as children,' Elizabeth laughed, 'but this is different. One day you will understand what I mean.'

Simon said nothing. He already knew what she meant. Rebekah was his love, his best friend, his soulmate. When he thought of the possibility that he might not be able to spend the rest of his life with her he was breathless, his heart paining him so that he felt he might die. How he wished he could tell Elizabeth about Rebekah, but would she understand? Simon realised that this moment was fortuitous. Perhaps he could use talk of Elizabeth's marriage to find out what she, and their father, thought.

'Would you have married Benjamin if you had not loved him?' His words were tentative. Rebekah looked up and met his gaze.

'Of course I would. In fact, I hardly knew him when we married and our love did not grow until later. I trusted Father to choose the right person for me.'

'But what if you had already known Benjamin and fallen in love with him, but Father chose someone else for you? Would you have married the other man?'

Elizabeth was thoughtful. 'I suppose so. I would have found it difficult, but I would have done my duty.'

'If that had been the case, then I hope you would have spoken to me.' Sir Thomas smiled indulgently. 'Although certain considerations of rank and politics have to be taken into account when finding a husband, Benjamin would have been most suitable and I would have taken your wishes into account.'

'But what if he had not been suitable?'

Sir Thomas turned to look at his son. 'Then I would not have given my consent. Although I love Elizabeth dearly, there are rules which we must abide by in society.'

'Have those rules not changed since the war?'

'To some extent, yes. But there are barriers which it would be impossible to cross.'

'Such as?'

'Such as station in life. I would have let Elizabeth have her choice of noblemen of our class, but a merchant, no matter how rich, would have been beneath her.'

Simon felt his heart plummet. A rich merchant would not have been good enough. So how would his father feel about a penniless dairymaid? Simon did not really need to answer the question. He had known that Rebekah would be considered unsuitable, but it hurt to hear it put into words. He sighed. Somehow he needed to bring his father round over the next few years so that, when the question of his marriage arose, he would be more amenable.

'Why the heavy sigh?'

Simon turned to his father and shrugged. Elizabeth laughed.

'I know what troubles him! He hates the talk of marriage! Poor Simon is afraid that you will tie him to some spinster old enough to be his mother, in return for her rich estates!'

Simon paled. Could that happen?

'For goodness sake, child! Will you cease from teasing your brother!'

Simon looked up and saw the delight in his sister's eyes. A sheepish grin spread over his face. 'You have me again, Elizabeth. It is unfair. You are married and understand all this, it is so unkind of you to tease me when my marriage is years away yet!'

'Years away? But you will need to provide an heir to follow after you and Father!'

'I am eighteen, Elizabeth! There are years a plenty before I need to worry about that, are there not, Father?' Simon turned to look at Sir Thomas.

'Indeed, son. I plan to live a good many years yet, so the heir can wait.'

Simon should have felt comforted by the words, but he did not. There was a slight frown to his father's brow and his eyes were thoughtful. Perhaps he considered eighteen old enough for him to begin to look for a bride for his son.

***

Simon entered the dairy, seeking respite from the bitter wind outside. The heat from the animals ensured that the temperature was more pleasant, although their breath still showed as steam from their nostrils. The low mooing of cows waiting to be milked was comforting. The whole scene created a feeling of warmth and calm, something which Simon did not feel himself. He sat on a bale of hay, waiting for Rebekah. After a few moments he stood and began to pace, his restlessness not allowing him to sit for longer. Where was she? At last he heard the swishing of her skirts as she entered. He turned and rapidly enfolded her in his arms.

'Oh, Rebekah! I am so pleased to see you!'

Rebekah laughed. 'What is the matter? You are all a tremble as though something is wrong. Or is it just the cold?'

'It is more than the cold. I have just come from a conversation with my father and sister.'

'That does not surprise me. After all, she is only here for a few weeks.'

'It is the topic of the conversation which troubles me.'

Rebekah frowned as Simon pulled away from her and began pacing the barn. 'What were you discussing?'

'Marriage.' He turned to meet her questioning gaze. 'We talked of Elizabeth's marriage, and she teased me. She said that I would soon have to marry to provide an heir!'

Rebekah smiled. 'She was only teasing.'

'At the time, yes. But then the conversation took an unpleasant turn.' Simon told her of how his father had spoken about the type of person he considered suitable. He shook his head sadly. 'Father would never let me marry you, Rebekah.'

She was silent for so long that Simon was worried. At last she spoke. 'Would you want to marry me, Simon? You have never asked.'

'I am sorry! I just took it for granted!' Simon took her hand in his. 'You know I love you, and I want to spend the rest of my life with you.' His voice softened. 'Will you marry me, Rebekah?'

Rebekah's eyes became bright with unshed tears as she shook her head. 'You cannot ask me, Simon. We both know that it would be impossible.'

Simon felt the bottom drop out of his world. 'Then why have you been spending time with me? I thought you loved me?'

Rebekah placed a comforting hand on his shoulder. 'I have been spending time with you because I do love you, with all my heart. But marriage is nothing more than a dream. Your father will not allow his estate to pass to the children of a peasant.'

'They would be my children, too.'

'That is naïve of you, Simon. We know that it would be impossible for such a child to move in the correct circles in society. You and your children deserve more than that. Your father would see you marrying me as a disaster. He would never allow it.'

Simon was exasperated. 'Then what was the war for? Your father fought for more equality for all.'

'But he would never have expected this. The son of a lord to marry his daughter? Change cannot come that quickly, Simon, war or not.'

Simon felt a deep resolve building inside him as he reached out to take Rebekah in his arms again.

'I do not care what father thinks now. We have a year or two at least before the question of my marriage will be raised, and in that time I will make him see our point of view. Somehow.' He held her gaze with his. 'We will be married Rebekah, come what may. We love each other. Nothing and no-one will part us.'

Chapter 38

Present day

Rob stared at the smoking ruin.

They were lucky that the cows had been out in the pasture. And that no one had been hurt. When Rob thought about what could have happened if Rebekah had started her job and been working in the barn when the fire broke out, he felt sick.

When he had first arrived at Marston Manor he had fallen in love with the place, with the feeling of home which it engendered in him. He had believed that he could be happy here. But now he was haunted by his dreams, and by the ghost of a woman who wanted to harm him. And the project was jinxed. One fire was unlucky; but two? It could not be co-incidence. Someone wanted to stop this project. A knot of fear formed in his stomach as his thoughts whirled. Were the two things connected? Had the ghost caused the fires? The one in the barn conversion had caused little damage, but this? The dairy had been completely destroyed. All that remained now was a smoking ruin.

'Your insurers are going to be asking some pretty stiff questions about this.'

Rob turned to face the leading fire officer as he spoke. 'Why?'

'Are you joking? Two fires in such a short time will be considered suspicious. Either they will think it is an insurance scam and won't pay out. Or they will assume negligence, and again won't pay out.'

'Paul Hetherington won't like that.'

'Well, you can't blame the insurers, can you?'

Rob shook his head. 'I guess not.' He inclined his head towards the devastated building. 'Any ideas how this started?'

'Not yet, I'm afraid. A preliminary look doesn't seem to show an accelerant. But don't quote me on that.'

'Paul is going to be livid.'

'You mean the owner?'

'Yes. He's so keen to get everything ready for a start next spring. This is really going to set us back. Though I think we can cope.' He was thoughtful for a moment. 'The cows are okay outside for the time being. If we haven't rebuilt by the time the bad weather comes, I'm sure we can find a local farmer who can take them in on a temporary basis.'

'Looks like you're about to find out how he feels.' The fireman indicated the swiftly approaching jeep as he spoke. 'If I'm not mistaken, that's Mr Hetherington. If you'll excuse me?'

Rob nodded. 'Of course. Best to stay out of his way if possible.' He watched the man quickly stride away, then turned to face a furious Paul as he climbed out of the jeep.

'This is the last straw!' He gazed in seething anger at the pile of rubble, small fires still burning in pockets. 'Cowan has gone too far this time!'

'You can't be sure it was him.'

'Shut up, Jim! Who the hell else could it be?'

'It could have been an accident.'

Paul turned an incredulous face towards Rob. 'An accident, my arse! That man is out to get me!'

'But why? I'm not making excuses for him, Paul. But why would he want to do this? I can't see that he'd have anything to gain.'

'There's only one way to find out!' Paul turned back to the jeep and jumped in.

'Now hang on! Don't do anything hasty!'

Jim climbed in after Paul, quickly followed by Rob as the engine was gunned into life and Paul threw the vehicle into first gear and onto the drive.

Moments later the jeep pulled into the travellers' camp. There was no one there. The vehicles had gone, as had the caravans. The washing lines had been taken down. There were no dogs. No horses. The place was deserted.

'Where the bloody hell are they?' Paul was furious as he climbed out of the jeep. His eyes took in the piles of rubbish, a still-smoking campfire, the churned up earth. 'This is all the evidence I need. The bastards can't face the police and have buggered off.'

'Or they're innocent and have left so they don't get the blame?'

'Bloody hell, Rob! You're such an old woman! Don't you care that they're trying to destroy this project?'

'That's just it. I don't know why they'd want to do that. Do you?'

'Sheer bloody-mindedness.'

'Or a way at getting back at Paul for the earlier confrontations.'

Rob turned to Jim. 'So you think it was them as well?'

'I don't know. But who else could it be?'

'It could just be another accident.'

'They say accidents happen in threes. God only knows what else we'll have to face if that's the case!'

Rob said nothing. He knew that the travellers had not done this. And he feared it was no accident. But what did that leave? A vengeful ghost? No matter how much he wanted to talk to someone about this, he knew that Paul and Jim would not believe him. As he followed his two companions back to the car, Rob knew that he would have to follow the dreams to their end if he was to find any solution for Paul. And any peace for himself.

***

Rob ran his hand gently over the warm leather. The embossed letters felt good beneath his hand, exuding a sense of timelessness. Opening the Bible to the front page, Rob looked again at the names, the family history. Simon Hardwycke. Rebekah. He needed to know the truth.

Although he was nervous, fearful of what might happen, Rob closed his eyes and focussed on the names.

'Okay. Tell me more.'

He felt slightly dizzy but continued to focus on the past, desperate to reach the end of the story, and sanity.

Chapter 39

April 1651

Simon put down his pen and rubbed his forehead, leaving a dark smudge of ink above one eye. He sighed as he read what he had just written.

I had thought that I would write no more after the end of the war and the death of the King. I had thought that all of our troubles would be over, but that is not so. I seem to see trouble on all sides, and do not know what to do about it. It was finding myself in such a situation, back in the year of our Lord 1642, which led me to first write my diary. It seems fitting that an unsettled mind is what urges me to pick up my pen once again.

I had hoped that the New Model would be disarmed and disbanded once the Scottish army had returned home and the King been defeated, but that did not happen. They fight still, now in Ireland and Scotland. Catholics and those who supported the King continue to be persecuted. They fight on, but are in need of a figurehead if they are to avoid defeat. Father and I hoped that His Majesty, the second King Charles, would take the lead. It saddens us that he has failed to do so. Although he has not been lawfully crowned, we call him 'King' when we are in private. He is the legitimate heir of the martyred monarch and our rightful leader, no matter what Cromwell says, or does. I know that Father would take up arms in an instant if the exiled King were to return to England. And though fear fills my heart at the thought, I would also follow his banner, wherever that might lead.

I struggle to know what to make of Cromwell. The enlargement of our navy was something I had not expected of him. I had thought his focus would be on England, with a necessary eye on Ireland and Scotland, but he has given us a strong presence at sea once more. Not since the time of the last King Henry have we been able to face the great naval power of the Dutch on equal terms. We are once more a major military force to contend with in Europe, and I cannot deny that the self-confidence and prestige of the people of England has grown hand in hand with this. It makes me proud to be English, but also sad, as such a force will be used against we Royalists, should the King come.

It frightens me that the military success which has been achieved in little more than a year has not been reflected on the political scene. Although it was the army who brought about the trial and execution of the King, many members of Parliament opposed it. Even within the Rump there were few who wholeheartedly supported the actions of the army, even fewer who would go as far as them in pursuing godly reform. The Council of State, set up by the Rump to rule in place of the King, holds many members who have not taken the Engagement; they will not pledge to a government without a king or House of Lords. But where does that leave us? Those in power who voted for the execution of a king do not want government without one, yet they support an army that continues to grow in strength and will fight the new king should he return.

If only the army were not so strong. I fear that its demands could bring this country to yet more grief. Why do they continue to demand religious reforms? Have things not been changed sufficiently for them? How will the clergy survive if we abolish tithes? How long will the Catholics and followers of the church of King Henry sit quietly by while all their practices are banned and they have to worship in such a bland way? I do not know what will happen if the government cannot stand against the army's continued threats to the clergy, lawyers and gentry. I pray God that they do not have their way and end this present parliament so that they can fill a new one with their new 'godly' members; those who seem to know nothing of the love of God, the love of neighbour.

At least within the counties things have returned more to their normal course from before the war, which is something for us to be thankful for. The county committees, which were so hated during the conflict, have been wound up, their powers returned to the Justices of the Peace. Many moderate parliamentarians now hold this position, and I have even heard that some sons of Royalist supporters of the King have been appointed. I fear that Father's role at the King's side was too great, and he will not again be offered his seat as a Justice of the Peace. If I were older, or if Thomas had not died, then maybe one of us would now hold that position. As it is, Sir Francis now presides over the area which encompasses our lands, though that is not a bad thing. He may have fought against us, but he has always proved himself to be a true and loyal friend. So far his actions on the bench have showed him to be honest and fair. That, at least, is one good thing to come out of the whole sad situation.

Distressing though I see the political situation, I wish it were the only thing to plague my mind and take away my peace. I have one thing far dearer to my heart, worries far more painful. My Rebekah. With each day that passes I love her more. I know that I cannot live life without her. Yet I cannot see a way to live life with her. That she loves me is my one consolation in these troubles. My heart is only ever light when I am with her. My happiness is complete when she is by my side. I love her dearly and wish to take her to wife. And it is for that reason that I have not allowed our relationship to move on. Although I think about her all the time and want to love her fully, I cannot let that happen. Should a child result, my father would have her dismissed and we could never be together. My only hope is to wait until I have Father's blessing, however long that may take. I will only have Rebekah when our future together is assured and any child will be recognised as mine, and inherit accordingly.

It is hard for me to hold back with her, and although I have not told her my reasons she is loving and gentle and kind, and never remonstrates with me to love her in a way that we both desire so much. It only serves to make me love her more.

Rebekah is so strong, so mature for her age. In her shadow I am a coward. I have not yet found the courage to talk with Father; I do not know when I shall be that brave. In three months I shall have my nineteenth birthday. Perhaps that will be the time that I will face my problems as a man. But each time I think of it, I am so afraid of Father's reaction and feel like a little boy again.

I pray that God will give me the strength to stand firm. With that strength, and the love of Rebekah, I believe I can do anything!

Simon sighed. Yes, when he was with Rebekah he did believe that he could do anything. But when he was alone...

Simon's eyes rested on the sheet of paper in front of him, though he did not really see it. For all the words he had written he felt no less confused, saw his way no more clearly. Still, whatever the future brought could not be worse than the years of war he had lived through. With a decisive gesture he folded the paper, determined that by the time his twentieth birthday approached the matter would be resolved, and Rebekah would be his wife.

***

July 1651

'Well, son, how does it feel to be nineteen years old?'

'Little different from yesterday when I was eighteen!'

Sir Thomas laughed as he reined in his horse, Simon halted beside him. 'That only goes to prove that you are a man! As a child you would always say that you felt bigger, more grown up each year. Now you are like any man, trying to forget that the years fly by too quickly!'

'Hardly that! I am still young enough to have a great deal to look forward to!'

'While I have only my dotage ahead of me?'

Simon laughed. 'I did not mean that, and you know it!'

'Indeed. I may be getting old but I still look forward to Ann and little Charles growing up.' He smiled indulgently. 'Elizabeth may have said that she did not care if this new baby was a girl, but I know that both she and Benjamin are delighted to have a son and heir.'

'And you are equally delighted to have two such fine grandchildren.'

'Yes. I did not dream that they would take a hold on my heart so quickly. In my eyes, the more grandchildren the merrier!' He smiled at Simon. 'But less of this! We should be celebrating your birthday. For all our merriment, nineteen is a turning point in life for young men. Time to think about the future. What are your plans?'

Simon urged his horse into a walk, creating distance between himself and his father to give him time to think. Surely his father only asked about his plans for Marston? Surely he was still too young to think of marriage? Sir Thomas kicked his horse into a trot and caught up with his son.

'Well, Simon?'

'There is little to say, Father. I think you can guess my plans. I intend to work beside you and learn all there is to know about running the estate. Then one day, a day which I hope is many, many years away, I will take over the running of Marston.'

Sir Thomas nodded. 'That is why we are out riding the boundaries today.' The horses had reached the top of an incline and the two riders stopped again, gazing out over the vast area of land which belonged to Marston Manor. 'All of this will be yours one day, Simon. It is time that you thought of the future.'

'I do, Father. Often. I have seen that the dairy herds are flourishing and would think that we could expand them, still keeping the sheep on the rougher grazing. As for crops, although you grow plenty of feed for the animals in winter, I wonder if we might not try turning some of the land over to other crops? I think beans would do well, and the price we could get for them would pay for winter feed while leaving a tidy profit.'

Sir Thomas nodded thoughtfully. 'I see that you have put a lot of thought into this, and am glad that you take your responsibilities seriously.'

'I do. But I know so little of farming in comparison to you. Perhaps any changes I suggest should only be applied to small areas first, to see if they work.'

'As you say. The fact that you have already begun to makes plans encourages me to give you twenty acres next year to try your beans. How does that sound?'

Simon smiled broadly. 'Splendid! Thank you, Father. I will not let you down. I promise!'

'I know you will not. But enough about the land. There are other aspects of your future which we need to think about.'

Simon's heart plummeted. 'Such as?'

'We have already spoken of grandchildren. I wish to hold yours in my arms before I die, as well as Elizabeth's.'

'Nineteen is too young for me to think of children, Father.'

'Maybe. But not too young to think of marriage.'

Simon found his eyes straying towards the woodland, to where Rebekah lived. 'I do not think that I am ready for marriage yet.'

Sir Thomas nodded. 'I know. And if circumstances were different I would not mention it for a year or two.'

'Then why now?'

'Because the land is not yet settled. The Rump still tries to make trouble for us, we cannot worship freely, the New Model is still strong.'

'What has that to do with me getting married?'

'Who knows how things will fare for we Royalists over the next few years. It would be better if we were to guard our backs.'

'I do not understand.'

'An alliance, Simon. That is how things are usually arranged between families such as ours. A marriage with the daughter of a prominent Roundhead, whose character is beyond reproach, whose actions during the war showed his loyalty to Cromwell. If you were to marry the daughter of a man like that, then Marston should be safe, whatever turn the politics of this country takes.'

Simon was stunned. 'I never thought to hear such a suggestion from you!'

'It is not so surprising.' Sir Thomas smiled. 'If there had been no war, it is just as likely that I would arrange the same union for you.'

Simon was not sure that he was hearing correctly. His mind seemed to swirl with thoughts, but only of Rebekah. He wanted to marry her. How could he ever contemplate someone else? The daughter of an enemy?

'What do you mean, Father?'

'I mean that you should marry the daughter of Sir Francis. As my oldest friend I would have suggested a union between our two houses anyway. But he would also be able to protect our family from Cromwell and his cronies. And he was good to you and Elizabeth while I was away. We owe him a debt of gratitude for that.'

'And you will pay that debt by giving him Marston as a wedding gift to his only daughter?'

Sir Thomas turned angrily on is son. 'Such words do not become you!'

Simon had the grace to lower his head sheepishly. 'I am sorry, Father. It is just that this is all so sudden. I did not think I would be considering marriage for two or three years yet.'

'I know. But nothing is as we would have it be. If Thomas had lived...' He paused thoughtfully for a moment. 'If Thomas had lived, then I would be proposing his marriage to Abigail. I would have taken time to seek for someone suitable for you, and you would still have years left to sow your wild oats.' He turned to his son. 'I assume that you are spending time with women? If not, then perhaps you should think of having those adventures now. I doubt you will see twenty before you are wed, and such goings on would not be wise when making a marriage to protect our family and lands.'

Unable to find words, Simon turned his horse back towards the Manor, his father close behind.

Dear Lord in Heaven! What an utterly disastrous birthday! Father wants me to marry Sir Francis's daughter!

I do not believe that I have seen her since I was four or five years old, and she younger. Who knows what she is grown into. Probably plain, verging on ugliness, with rabbit's teeth and the mind of a child!

That was unforgiveable of me. It is not her fault that our fathers have decided on this union. She may well be as averse to it as I. Though if she is anything like Elizabeth, she will be willing to do her father's bidding.

But what about me? Does no one think to ask what I want in this matter?

Simon rose angrily from his desk and began to pace the room, his mind in turmoil. He felt trapped. Whichever way he turned there seemed no escape. His life appeared to be planned out for him and he could do nothing to gainsay it. With a sigh, he sat down, picked up his pen and continued writing.

I suppose that it is as Elizabeth once said. We have to follow our parents' wishes. She was lucky to be given to Benjamin, to fall in love with him and he with her. But I know that cannot happen for me with Abigail. I love Rebekah with all my heart. No-one can take her place. Yet I also have a duty to Father. I cannot go against his wishes. Yet I cannot give Rebekah up.

It would break Rebekah's heart if I were to tell her that I am betrothed to another. It would be cruel of me to tell her that until I have found a solution to this problem.

I shall say nothing to her for now. But I will speak to Father. He says that I have a year before my marriage. I will speak to him in the next few weeks, tell him that I cannot marry Abigail, that I must have Rebekah. He is a good and honest man. I know that he wants the best for me. I know that he loved Mother, as Elizabeth loves her husband. I do believe that, with time, he will come to see that I cannot marry Abigail if I do not love her.

Chapter 40

August 1651

Sir Thomas looked out of the window and sighed.

'Raining again! These last few weeks, when our crops should have been ripening in the sun, have seen more rain than should be expected.'

'How bad is it?'

Sir Thomas turned to his son. 'Bad enough. Although it could be worse. The rye is mildewed, but I believe that we can save much of it.'

'And the hay?'

His father shrugged. 'If it stopped raining now and we had sun for a few days, then maybe the meadows would dry and we could cut the hay. We can but pray that God sees fit to send us good weather.'

'If the rain continues? How will that affect us?'

'It may well be a lean winter, but we will not starve. Perhaps we will have to sell a few more cattle and sheep than intended so that we can buy grain and fodder, but we will survive. It is not unusual to have a bad year. Let us hope that next year will be better.'

Simon said nothing, merely staring out of the window in the direction of the dairy. He could not see it through the steadily falling rain, but he knew that Rebekah was there. He just needed an excuse to go out and see her. Attempting to appear nonchalant, he turned to leave the room.

'I'll just go and check on the dairy; make sure that the water is not getting in. We do not want the cows to develop problems with their feet.'

'That will have to wait. We are expecting visitors, and I do not want you greeting them covered in mud and smelling of cows!'

'Visitors? Who would be coming to see us in such awful weather?'

'Did I not tell you? I am sorry; it must have slipped my mind. The arrangements were made days ago, when I last visited Sir Francis. He is coming here today; with his daughter, Abigail.'

Simon felt the blood drain from his face, and heard a rushing noise in his ears as though he were drowning in a fast flowing stream.

'Are you ill, Simon?'

The young man turned towards his father, his face pale. 'I am sorry. I had not expected to be introduced to her so soon.'

Sir Thomas laughed. 'Goodness me, Simon! I never thought that you would be so afraid of meeting a young woman.' He put his head to one side thoughtfully for a moment. 'It is not the thought of meeting any young woman, is it? It is the thought of meeting *this* young woman.'

Simon said nothing. His mind was in a tumult and he could find no words at all.

'For goodness sake, boy. Calm down!' Sir Thomas was still grinning. 'You will only be meeting her today. It is not as though you will getting married this afternoon.'

Simon swallowed hard. 'I know. It is just that…'

Sir Thomas crossed the space between them and laid a comforting hand on his son's shoulder. 'It is just that you feel too young for marriage and all the responsibilities which come with it. Never fear. You and Abigail will be given time to get to know each other over the next few months. You will not be such complete strangers when you marry.'

When we marry! Simon thought that his knees would give way at the thought. He had never felt so helpless or afraid in his life, not even during the dark days in Colchester. How he wished that he had spoken to his father in the weeks which had passed since his birthday. Perhaps he could have forestalled this meeting. Once they met, though, it would be harder for him to persuade his father to agree to a marriage with Rebekah. He silently cursed himself for his cowardice. Simon felt the need for space, a few moments' quiet to collect himself and his thoughts, time to prepare himself.

'When will they be here? Perhaps I should go and change?'

'No. They are already half an hour late. I would think that the rain has held them up.' There was the sound of a carriage on the drive, and Sir Thomas smiled. 'Ah, that must be them now.'

'Does she know?'

Sir Thomas was puzzled. 'Does who know what?'

'Does Mistress Morrison know that you and her father have … have arranged our marriage?'

Sir Thomas nodded. 'Yes, she has been informed. But we will not talk of that today. This morning is just an opportunity for you to meet each other again, and begin to get to know each other.'

As Sir Thomas finished speaking, his friend was ushered through the door into the withdrawing room.

'Francis! It is good to see you again!'

'And you, my dear friend.' The two men shook hands before Sir Francis turned to the younger man. 'Good day, Simon.'

'Good day to you, Sir Francis.' He bowed his head in respect.

'Well, well. Look who is here!' Sir Thomas's eyes fell on the demure young lady standing a few paces behind her father. 'Step forward, Abigail. You do not need to hide behind your father.'

The young lady stepped forward and made a deep curtsey. 'Good morning, Sir Thomas.'

'Do you remember my son, Simon?'

Abigail shook her head. 'I am afraid not. I cannot have been more than three years old the last time we met. I only remember a boy who had no time to spend with a little girl.'

Sir Thomas laughed as he turned to his son. 'Well, here is the little boy grown into a man.'

Abigail curtsied again. 'Good morning, sir.'

'Well, are you not going to greet my daughter?'

Sir Thomas grinned. 'I think he has been struck dumb by her beauty!'

Indeed, Simon was at a loss for words. He was not sure what he had been expecting, but certainly not this. Abigail was beautiful. Each time she curtsied her golden ringlets bobbed, brushing the pale skin of her cheeks. Her vivid blue eyes, whilst held demurely low, held a glint of mischief. Her frame was slight, though with the curves of a young woman. She was a woman who would take any man's breath away, let alone that of a youth of nineteen. Simon stepped forward and bowed, taking her extended hand in his and brushing the back of it with his lips.

'Good morning, Mistress Morrison. I am happy to welcome you to our home. I promise that I will not slight you this time. I have learnt some manners in the years since we last met.' Abigail smiled as Simon led her towards a chair beside the window. 'Would you care to be seated? I would ask that you enjoy the view, if it were not for this dreadful rain which blots our estate from sight.'

'It is no matter, sir. I have come to meet with Sir Thomas and yourself, not gaze out of a window.'

Sir Francis was smiling indulgently. 'She is so much like her mother, is she not?'

Sir Thomas nodded. 'Indeed she is. Not only in her looks, but in her confidence and wit.'

Abigail raised a hand to her lips. 'Sir, you make me blush,' she said coyly, although it was obvious that she was pleased with the praise.

'Then I will ask Father to make you blush again, it suits you.' Simon could hardly believe the words that came from his lips, but they were true. Her cheeks were the colour of roses of the palest pink, and he felt that he wanted to reach out and touch them. Turning to take a chair on the other side of the room, Simon tried to gather his thoughts together. He was captivated by Abigail. She had the classical beauty that one saw in portraits, a look which would make Rebekah seem plain if they were to stand together. He frowned slightly, feeling guilty at his perceived betrayal of Rebekah, but when he turned back to the other three occupants in the room and sat down, his frown was gone and he was smiling again.

While the two young people were introducing themselves Sir Thomas had sent for refreshments, which now arrived. As the small cakes and glasses of Madeira wine were handed out, Simon turned to Sir Francis.

'How goes it with you, Sir Francis? Will it be a poor harvest this year due to the rains?'

'Indeed, but we will survive. As we have survived these many years. Have we not, my dear?' He turned to Abigail as he spoke. She nodded.

'Indeed, Father, although it is not the harvests that we have had to survive in the past. I thank God that the war is over and we have peace again.'

'Was it difficult for you during those years?'

Abigail turned to the young man. 'It was difficult for us all, although I would think that my lot was better than yours.'

'And why is that?'

'Because we sided with the Parliamentarians, of course. I did not have to endure my father being away and not knowing where he was. I was lucky enough to have him here for most of the time during the years of conflict. Whereas you...'

'I...?' Simon was intrigued. Abigail seemed to be intelligent and thoughtful, where he had thought that she might have no understanding of life and politics. But then, perhaps his prejudice was due to the fact that he had never wanted to meet her. If he thought about it, she was very much like his sister, Elizabeth. Calm, self-assured, intelligent. Simon felt relaxed and able to talk to Abigail in a way that he had not anticipated. At the same time he felt guilty for taking some enjoyment in their conversation when he would rather be with Rebekah. He put thoughts of Rebekah to the back of his mind and focussed on what Abigail was saying.

'You, sir, had to grow up quickly in order to take charge of your father's estates. From what my father told me, you were a boy doing a man's work, and did it better than any would have anticipated. I congratulate you.'

This time it was Simon's turn to blush. 'Thank you. But I was only doing my duty.'

'I have told my daughter how impressed I was with you, Simon.' Sir Francis was smiling, pleased to see how well the young people seemed to be getting along. 'Your father is lucky in his son.'

'Indeed I am. I...' The sound of galloping hooves caused Sir Thomas to halt in mid-sentence. Although the war had been over for more than a year, the sound of swift riders still filled everyone with fear. Somehow, they always expected bad news. There were sounds of muted conversation in the hallway and Sir Thomas excused himself to find out what was wrong. The three remaining in the drawing room were silent, unable to pretend to conversation until they knew what was happening. When Sir Thomas returned his face was troubled.

'I am needed in the village.'

'A problem?'

Sir Thomas nodded at his friend. 'Yes. Witchcraft.'

There was stunned silence, a palpable feeling of fear in the air. Simon saw that the blush had left Abigail's cheeks, leaving them pale and wan. He turned to his father.

'Witchcraft? In what way? What has happened?'

'I am not sure. I have just received a garbled report of demonic possession. I must go and investigate.' He turned to Sir Francis. 'I am sorry, but I must leave you. Perhaps it will be best if you take Abigail home now?'

Sir Francis shook his head. 'No. With your permission, she will remain here, where it is safe. I will come with you to see what is happening.'

'As will I.' Simon rose to his feet as he spoke.

Sir Thomas was quiet for a moment, then nodded. 'Come, we must be away.'

With that, the three men turned and left the room.

***

The mill was surrounded by a small crowd of people. The rain had stopped, but their feet churned up mud as they shuffled uneasily. There were fearful mutterings as they stared at the building.

'What has happened?'

A middle-aged man turned towards Sir Thomas, his eyes full of fear, his hands shaking. 'Witchcraft, sir.' He crossed himself as he spoke.

'Witchcraft? But what...?' Sir Thomas's question was cut off by piercing screams from the mill. The villagers fell to their knees in the mud, beginning to recite the 'our father'. Simon blanched as the screams were interrupted by the desperate shouting of a man, the words too garbled to hear properly. Sir Thomas tightened his grip on the hilt of his sword. 'I think we had better take a look.'

Simon and Sir Francis said nothing as they fell in behind Sir Thomas, entering the living accommodation attached to the mill. The interior was dark, and for a moment Simon could see nothing. As his eyes grew accustomed to the shadows, he saw the miller standing to one side, his brother with him. They seemed petrified by the small group of people on the other side of the room. Simon could just make out the miller's wife and his three children, huddled in a corner. They were all scratching madly at their skin. The miller's wife screamed again.

'Make them stop! Make them stop!'

'In God's name, what is going on here!'

The miller turned. When he saw Sir Thomas he rushed across and fell to his knees.

'Please, sir, I beg of you. Please help them!'

'How? What is it she is saying, man? Make what stop?'

'It started nigh on two hours ago, sir. I was working in the mill when I heard my children beginning to cry. My wife did nothing to stop it, so I came to see what was wrong. I found them like this. She says that there are beetles crawling under her skin. The children say the same.' He looked across at his son and two small daughters. 'They just tear at themselves, trying to rip the insects out. In God's name, sir! Please help us!'

Sir Francis laid a hand on Sir Thomas's arm as he took a hesitant step forward. 'Is it wise to approach them?'

'I do not know, Francis. But we have to do something.'

As Sir Thomas took another step forward the young boy began to scream, waving his arms in front of himself as if to ward off some kind of demon.

'What is wrong, boy?'

'The wolf! He is biting me! Make him stop! Make him stop!'

Simon could see nothing in front of the child. His tiny arms were waving madly at empty air as a look of horror filled his eyes. Simon began to shake with fear as he took a step backwards. He halted. It would be cowardly of him to leave his father and Sir Francis to deal with matters alone. Steeling himself, he stepped forward, hand gripping tightly to his sword hilt. 'What do we do, Father?'

'I do not know.'

'I have sent for the minister.'

Sir Thomas turned to the miller. 'A wise move. No doubt he will be here momentarily. Perhaps, for now, we should wait and do nothing.'

As he spoke the miller's wife began to tremble, then her body broke into fits and convulsions. Her arms and legs beat the air wildly, her head banging against the wall, although she seemed to feel no pain.

'In the name of sweet Jesus, what do we do?' Sir Francis moved forward as he spoke. 'If we do nothing she will cause herself harm!'

'Come, brother.' The miller stepped hesitantly forward. 'Help me to hold her.'

His companion reluctantly followed his lead. Seconds later they reached out to hold her, gripping her arms and legs, but she fought wildly. The two men were thrown from side to side, crashing into the walls as they struggled with the demented woman. Simon felt sick with fear. What would happen if she escaped? Clearly she was possessed by the devil. He had never been so afraid in all his life, yet knew that if they stood and did nothing then it could be the death of them all. Looking wildly around Simon spied a coil of rope in the corner, grabbed it and rushed forward.

'We must tie her down!'

His two companions joined him as he began to wrap the rope around the woman's ankle. It took the five men all of their strength to hold her and tie her to the bed. Still she continued to throw her body around, convulsing in pain; she almost broke the wooden frame of the bed with her violent actions. The men stepped back, fighting for breath after their exertions, their ears ringing with the curses which poured from the woman's lips. In the corner, the children were still tearing at themselves, their bodies bloody where they had broken the skin, tearing it away in their attempts to get at the insects which they said were crawling beneath. The three men from the Manor crossed themselves, then turned and left.

The air outside seemed fresh and clear after the stink of sweat and fear inside. Simon felt that his knees were about to give way and wanted to crumple to the ground. But as he saw the expectant faces of the villagers, he knew that he could not. He had a position to uphold. God only knew what would happen if he and the others gave way to their fear. He looked across at his father. Sir Thomas's face was white, his eyes haunted, but he stood straight and tall as he addressed the crowd.

'It appears to be witchcraft. There is little that we can do. This is a matter for the minister, who is coming. I ask you to go home. Go home and pray for the poor souls in this house. Pray that God will protect them, and drive this evil out.'

'Are they possessed?'

Sir Thomas looked at the man who had spoken, then nodded. 'It appears so.'

Simon watched as people began to look fearfully around them. He knew what they were thinking; he was thinking the same thoughts himself. Where was the witch who had called up the devil and his demons? Did they need to be close to keep the spell strong? Was the person looking at him the witch? The feeling of fear intensified as people began to slowly slip away, heading for home and the hope of safety from the evil which had so suddenly invaded their village.

***

Sir Thomas stayed at the mill when the minister arrived, while Simon accompanied Sir Francis back to the Manor. After a fortifying brandy, Sir Francis left with Abigail. As he watched them go, Simon realised that he liked Abigail. She was beautiful and witty and intelligent. She would make a perfect wife. But he did not love her. Yes, he had been captivated by her, but as he stood here alone, there was only one person he wanted to be with in his fear. Simon went back into the study and sat at the desk, his knees too weak to stand. His hands shook as he poured himself another brandy and drank it swiftly. He closed his eyes, but could still clearly see the scene in the miller's home, feel the all-encompassing fear of the presence of evil. He shuddered. He did not want to be alone with his fears. Rising to his feet, he went outside and made his way over to the dairy.

Rebekah was feeding the cows when he arrived. She smiled happily as she went over and kissed him. Simon lost himself in the sweetness of her lips, allowing them to soothe away some of his troubles. As the kiss ended and she pulled away, Rebekah was still smiling happily. Simon realised that she had not yet heard about the possessions in the village. He was glad. He needed to talk to her about Abigail without anything else to distract them. Taking her hand in his he led her outside.

'Where are we going?'

'To the orchard.'

'But it has been raining! We will be much more comfortable in the dairy.'

Simon's gaze was serious as his eyes met hers. 'We need to talk.'

The smile left Rebekah's eyes as she walked by his side into the seclusion of the trees.

Water was dripping from the leaves, the grass was wet and muddy. It seemed such a melancholy place, which suited Simon's mood to perfection. He took Rebekah to the far side of the orchard, where they could not be overheard, and began to speak.

'We had visitors this morning.'

'Yes. I heard that Sir Francis was here.'

'Did you also hear that he brought his daughter with him?'

Rebekah shook her head, her eyes troubled. 'What is wrong, Simon?'

'My father and Sir Francis have arranged for me to marry his daughter.'

All colour fled from Rebekah's face. 'When was this decided?'

'He told me on my birthday.'

'On your birthday?' Rebekah's eyes were puzzled. 'Surely not? You told me nothing about it.'

'I know. I did not know what to say.' He hung his head sadly. 'You know that I love you, do you not, Rebekah?'

'Yes.' Her voice was soft, filled with sadness. 'I love you, too. But we both knew that this day would come. Although I had not expected it so soon.' For a moment Rebekah was silent. When she spoke again her words contained a hint of anger. 'I wish you had told me on your birthday. It was cruel of you to keep silent.'

Simon looked into her eyes. The hurt he saw there almost broke his heart. 'I am sorry. I just did not know what to do, or say. I was going to discuss it with Father, but I left it too late. Now Abigail and I have been introduced, and she knows that she is promised to me by her father.'

Rebekah turned away, her shoulders tense, unhappiness evident in her movements. 'Then this is goodbye.'

'No!' Simon took her by the shoulder and turned her back to face him. 'I have to make a choice, and I choose you! I want to marry you, Rebekah. I will talk to Father and we will work it out. Somehow.'

Rebekah shook her head sadly. 'Those are the thoughts of a boy, Simon. You are a man now. You know that you have a duty to your father. Even if this marriage had not already been arranged, you know that he would not allow you to marry me.'

'But I cannot live without you!'

'Then you will not have to. Marry Abigail. Do your duty. Have a family with her. We can continue to meet in secret, as we do now. Nothing need change.'

'That sounds so heartless!'

'Heartless? Oh, Simon, you do not know how it breaks my heart to say the words!'

Simon felt angry, bitter. 'They seem to fall easily from your lips.'

'Only because I have known that this day would come since the first time you kissed me. Each night I have lain in my bed thinking of this day, and what would happen. I have practiced these words a hundred times, a thousand, but they still tear my heart to pieces!'

'Then take the words back! I will not accept them! We love each other and I will not have that kind of relationship with you.' His eyes clouded. 'And I could not bear to think that you would marry someone else if I were to wed Abigail. I cannot live with the thought that you will be another man's wife, bear his children. You are mine, Rebekah. You belong to me. We belong to each other!'

'It can never work, Simon. We both know that!'

Simon pulled her towards him, enfolding her in his arms as he rested his cheek against her wet hair. For a moment he wondered if it had started to rain again, then realised that it was his tears which wet her beautiful locks.

'It will work. I do not know how we shall accomplish it, but we will be together. I will never let you go, Rebekah. Never!'

***

Sir Thomas's face was haggard when he returned to the Manor. Throwing his cloak onto a chair, he poured himself a large measure of brandy.

'Do you want a glass?'

Simon shook his head. 'No, thank you. I have already had sufficient. It has calmed my nerves somewhat.'

Sir Thomas's hand shook as he lifted the glass to his lips. 'I pray that it does the same for me.' He drank the brandy swiftly, then placed the empty glass on the desk. 'The minister came, but he could do nothing.'

'Nothing at all? What about prayer? Could he not cast the demons out?'

'He tried, but nothing seemed to work.'

'Are they as bad as before?'

'Worse.' Sir Thomas sank into his favourite chair beside the empty hearth. 'They still scream about the insects beneath their skin. But the children are having convulsions too, as though they are trying to cast out the evil. And now they are all seeing the wolf.'

'Is that the witch's familiar?'

'I do not know.' Sir Thomas leant forward and rested his head in his hands. 'It may well be, for no one else can see this creature that they are so afraid of.'

They were silent for a moment, each deep in their thoughts and fears. At last Simon spoke.

'What do we do?'

'Nothing at the moment, save to pray. The minister is with them and I pray that he will be able to cast out the spirits.'

'But what if he cannot?'

'We wait a day, two at most, to see what transpires. But if our village is not healed in that time, we must send for a witchfinder.'

Simon was silent for a moment. Everyone feared the witchfinders, and Simon had doubted their honesty when talking to his father on the topic. But now he found that he would welcome them to Marston. Anything to heal those poor people. And maybe to drive the terrible scenes from his mind.

Sir Thomas sighed as he leant back in his chair. 'This should have been a happy day for us. Indeed, Francis and I were pleased with how well you and Abigail were getting on. I hope that the appearance of witchcraft at the time of your meeting does not bode ill for your future together.' A slight smile curved his lips. 'You seemed to take to her well.'

Simon fought to find the right words. 'Yes, Father. She is everything that a man could hope for in a wife.'

Sir Thomas nodded. 'She is indeed. I knew that it would go well. Once we have found and dealt with the witch, we can arrange another meeting between the two of you.'

Simon swallowed hard. 'Perhaps she will not want to come to Marston. The fear of witches is strong in us all.'

'I know. That is why we will wait until it is safe for her to come here without fear of bewitchment.'

Simon was full of fear about the witchcraft, but he wondered if it might be fortuitous for him. Could he use it to make his father change his mind about Rebekah? He took a deep breath.

'But what if you are right, Father? What if this is a bad omen? There has never been witchcraft here before, yet it suddenly arises when you introduce me to Abigail. Perhaps our union is not meant to be, and will not be blessed.'

Sir Thomas frowned. 'I do not think that likely. It is nothing but an unlucky co-incidence. If there were evil intent to end your marriage to Abigail then I would expect either her, or you, to be bewitched. But that has not happened. As I said, a sad and unlucky co-incidence, but you need not fear that your marriage will be called off.'

Simon took a deep breath. 'I do not love Abigail, Father.'

'I know. How could you after such a short acquaintance? But love will grow, likely as not.'

Simon licked his dry lips. He realised that this was the time. If he did not speak out now the opportunity would be passed and he never would.

'Love will not grow, Father. I am in love with someone else.'

Sir Thomas's mouth dropped open, his eyes widened in surprise. 'What? Someone else? Why did I not know? Who is she?' He frowned angrily. 'No doubt this is just some infatuation with a woman you have seen from a distance. It will not interfere with our plans for you and Abigail.'

'No. It is not an infatuation. I have known her for many years. I know that I love her. And she loves me. I cannot marry Abigail.'

'Cannot? Do not be foolish, boy! You know that I want to unite our two houses. And you know that this is politically the right thing to do.' His voice was angry. 'You will marry Abigail, and no more will be said on the matter.'

Simon stood and began to pace the room as he spoke. 'Do you not see? Those who fought us in the war wanted to bring more freedom. I do not say that they were right in what they did, but we would both agree that there were flaws in the way the King ruled.'

'Simon. Tread carefully.'

The young man looked at his father. Never before had he seen him so angry. His hands were clenched tightly to the arms of the chair, as though to prevent himself rising, or to stop him striking out at his son. Simon felt deep shame at upsetting his father so badly, but alongside the shame was a deep burning love for Rebekah. He knew that, regardless of the consequences, he could not stop now.

'We lost the war, Father. And the world has changed, whether you like it or no. I believe that in this changed world I should have the right to choose my own wife. Maybe it is part of God's plan for me, which is why this ill-omened witchcraft appears today.'

'Do not blaspheme, Simon! Who are you to know the plans of the Lord!' Sir Thomas stood, glaring angrily at his son. 'Who is this woman anyway? How did you meet her?'

'Her name is Rebekah. She is the daughter of Master Sawyer, who helped me back from the woods when I was a boy. She works in our dairy.'

'In our *dairy?*' Sir Thomas could hardly comprehend what he was being told. 'You would turn your back on a marriage to the most eligible young woman in the county, a woman of beauty and intelligence, to marry a *dairymaid?*' He stepped closer to his son, finger poking angrily at his chest. 'For all his faults, Cromwell never would have imagined an England where such a thing could happen. He would be the first to prevent his son from marrying a woman so far beneath him. You will never see this woman again. No more will be said on the matter.' He turned away, his face ashen. 'The Lord help us if Francis ever finds out that you contemplated marriage to such a whore.'

'She is not a whore!' Simon spoke through gritted teeth. 'She is chaste. Still a virgin. How dare you speak of her like that!'

'How dare I? *How dare I!*' Sir Thomas turned angrily. 'Have you no shame? Do you think so little of me? Of your family? Of your home? Do you place a peasant above the daughter of my best friend? A man who stood by you and did all that he could to keep you safe when I could not? I do not know how I can have raised such a man!'

'You raised me to be honest and true!' They were both shouting now. 'I am who I am because of you. So it is because of you that I feel I must remain true to my heart. I will marry Rebekah, and there is nothing that you can do to stop me!'

'You think not, boy?' Sir Thomas voice was hard, and it tore at Simon to think that he had driven such anger between them. Yet, deep inside, he felt that he was right. He drew strength from this feeling as his father stepped closer, until their faces almost touched. Sir Thomas stopped shouting. His voice was icy, his eyes filled with pain and anger as he spoke. 'If you persist in this wild imagining, you shall be dis-inherited. You will leave my home and never return. Marston will go to Elizabeth and it will be as though you had never been born.' There were tears in Sir Thomas's eyes. 'How I wish that Thomas had lived to marry Abigail. I would never then have needed to know this shame in my other son.'

Simon reached out a hand to his father. 'Surely there is no shame in love, Father?'

Sir Thomas roughly brushed the hand aside and turned away. 'What do you know of love? You are a mere boy still.'

'No, Father. I am a man. And I can make a man's decisions for myself.' There were tears in his eyes, too. 'We are both angry, Father. And the fear of the sorcery we have seen still haunts us. Perhaps we need time to calm down before we speak again. Perhaps we should wait until the situation in the village is resolved.'

'Maybe.' Sir Thomas was thoughtful. 'There is little to be done in regards to your future until the witch is caught. We will not speak of this matter again until then. I pray that it will give you time to come to your senses.'

'Thank you, Father. I believe we both need time to reflect. But I know that it will not alter the way I feel about Rebekah.' Simon swallowed hard, his heart tearing in two. 'If, when we talk again, you still feel that I should choose between marrying Abigail or leaving Marston for ever, I will make the right choice. For me.'

Without another word he turned and left the room.

***

Simon scribbled hurriedly. His writing was untidy, very different from his usual neat letters. There was a small blot of ink at the lower edge of the page, but he did not seem to notice it.

What am I to do?

I never thought that speaking to Father would be so difficult. I thought that he might at least listen to what I had to say. Maybe even meet with Rebekah. I know that, if he did, he would realise why I love her, and perhaps support us in our marriage. But there is little chance of that now.

I know I should have spoken sooner, before Sir Francis brought Abigail to call. But it is no use crying over spilt milk, although perhaps today was not the day to do it. We were both so full of fear about the witchcraft that any confrontation was bound to be exaggerated. It hurt so deeply to have Father say such things to me. To call my dear Rebekah a whore! To say that he will disinherit me! I never thought that a father and son who love each other as we do could fall so far apart.

After I spoke with Father I went to see Rebekah. I thought that she would understand and support me, but I was wrong about her, too. When I told her I was prepared to give up Marston so that we could be married she was, at first, comforting in her attempts to get me to change my mind. Then she got angry. I have never seen her so angry before. She says that I will never be able to live in poverty, and that any children I sire would deserve better. I agree on the latter point, I do not know why any children that Rebekah and I might have should suffer because of my father's prejudices. But I cannot agree on the former. I have seen Rebekah's home in the woods, seen how her family live, and I know that I could do it if I must. I admit that it would be difficult, but I survived Colchester and could survive as a poor man. I told her that I could work.

Maybe as an estate manager, or a clerk. Maybe I could study law. But Rebekah still insists that it would not work. She still says that the best plan for both of us is for me to marry Abigail, and continue to see Rebekah in secret. I do not think that I could do that. I believe that it would break my heart. And, in time, break Rebekah's too.

Now I find myself in conflict with Rebekah as well as my father. But I will not give in. If I insist that I am going to marry Rebekah, Father may change his mind. I know that he loves me and wants me to take over Marston. I am sure that I can persuade him. If not, if he insists on disinheriting me, then Rebekah will have no reason to refuse me. She is too loving and kind to allow me to give up everything for nothing. I believe, deep in my heart, that she only makes her suggestion because she loves me, and wants the best for me. Wants me to keep my birthright, and to continue my relationship with Father just as it was before. She has always been so intelligent, so mature in her thoughts. I am sure that she sees this as the logical thing to do. But our love is not built on logic. It is built on the feelings of our hearts. To me, Rebekah is my soulmate. I cannot live without her by my side. I am sure that she feels the same.

I want to settle this as soon as possible, but I think that Father is right. With the fear and tension of the witchcraft, things will only go from bad to worse. Let us settle that before I speak to him again of Rebekah.

In the meantime I will show her that I am sincere, and that we will marry. Come what may.

***

Simon was surprised to see Sir Francis when he entered the study three days later. He quickly looked over at his father. Had he already spoken to his friend about Abigail and Rebekah? Sir Thomas must have registered his questioning surprise, for he silently shook his head.

'Sir Francis has kindly returned to try to help us with the witchcraft problem.'

Simon turned to their visitor. 'That is most kind of you, sir. But what of your daughter?'

'Do not worry. She is safe enough at home. If, the Lord forbid, the problem should spread out of Marston, then my manager is instructed to take her to my brother's estates in Gloucestershire. She will be safe there.'

'Are the miller's family still possessed?'

Sir Thomas nodded at his son. 'Yes. But now other families, too, are seeing the visions. They appear to have been bewitched by the same spell, for they all complain of insects or other such creatures beneath their skin, trying to eat them from the inside. Men, women, children. The affliction appears to know no bounds.'

Simon shuddered. 'Why would someone do something like that? Although one could never condone it, it is possible to imagine that a witch could cast an evil spell such as this on someone they feel has wronged them. But women and children too? That is almost beyond belief!'

'Perhaps someone who feels wronged by the miller has paid the witch to cast the spell.'

'Are all of those who are afflicted connected to the miller in some way?'

Sir Thomas shook his head. 'I think not. The only thing that binds them is that they live on my estates.'

'Is that coincidental, my friend?'

'I believe it must be, Francis, for I have done nothing to offend anyone since the war ended.'

Simon nodded. 'I cannot believe that anyone would deliberately set out to harm you, Father. Although we will know soon enough, once the witchfinder arrives.'

Sir Francis looked surprised. 'You have sent for someone?'

'Yes. William Lewes. I expect him later today.'

'I have had his quarters made ready, but I do not know how many men he may have with him. I have ordered arrangements to be made for ten.'

Sir Thomas nodded. 'Thank you, Simon, that should be sufficient.' He turned and made his way towards the door as he spoke. 'If you would like to come with me, Francis, we will speak once more with the minister, before Lewes arrives.'

The two men departed, while Simon remained in the room. His father had not excluded him from their foray, but neither had he included him. Before their confrontation about Rebekah Simon would automatically have joined them, but things had been difficult for the last few days. His father had only spoken to him occasionally, and then only enough to convey something regarding the running of the estate. Their usually even-tempered relationship no longer existed, and Simon knew that his father wished to avoid his company whenever possible. Perhaps he was afraid that he would not be able to keep his temper if they should begin to talk of more personal things.

At a loss as to what to do, Simon turned and made his way to the kitchens, ready to check once more that all was in order for the arrival of the witchfinder.

***

It was late in the afternoon when Lewes arrived with a party of six soldiers and a clerk. As Simon watched them ride up to the house, he was reminded of the attack on Marston during the war. It seemed strange that people in the same uniform now came to the aid of his family.

Lewes dismounted. He was a tall man, thin as a rake, his long hair hanging unkempt around his face. Above his aquiline nose a pair of brown eyes burned fiercely. He shook dust from the folds of his black cloak. 'Sir Thomas Hardwycke?'

Sir Thomas bowed his head. 'That is I, sir. Thank you for coming so swiftly.'

'I could do nothing else. God has called me to root out the works of the devil, and I shall take no rest until I have done so.'

'Can I show you to your quarters, sir?' Simon stepped forward as he spoke. 'You must be tired and wanting to refresh yourself.'

Lewes eyes burned into him. 'Who are you?'

'Simon Hardwycke, son of Sir Thomas.'

'Well, young sir, I mean what I say. I have no time for rest. Maybe a swift bite to eat and something to take the dust of the road from my throat, then we must away to the village. I wish to get a feel of what is happening today so that I can plan our actions for tomorrow.'

It was a scant half hour later that the party set out for the village. Sir Thomas and Sir Francis rode beside Lewes, with Simon and the clerk behind, the soldiers bringing up the rear. As they rode into the village the aura of fear was palpable. Few people were on the street, and those who were hurried quickly about their business, eyes darting rapidly in all directions as if afraid that some evil would pounce on them at any moment.

Sir Thomas led the party to the mill, where it had all begun. The miller looked haggard, far beyond tired, as he watched over his family. They were quiet now. The insects seemed to have left them and they no longer tore at their skin, but, from time to time, they still saw evil creatures and would break out into screams and cries once more. Lewes looked and asked questions, but offered no remedy.

From there they visited the homes of the cooper, a seamstress, the carter. In each one the story was the same - a family, no different from any other, torn apart by fear. Each person who had been bewitched called out in terror and pain, offering curses to those who did nothing to help. By the time the group left the last house Lewes was grim.

'This is worse than I feared. So many possessed by the devil. There must be a powerful witch indeed on your lands, Sir Thomas.'

'But what would bring them here? Why would they do this?'

'That is what I must find out. For without that knowledge I may not be able to eradicate the evil swiftly.'

'Perhaps the minister...'

Sir Thomas's words were interrupted by a savage snarling from the shadows to their right. The men turned fearfully towards it. Slowly emerging from the shadows was a great grey wolfhound.

'That is our dog.' Simon rode forward. 'What are you doing here, boy? Come on, let us get you home.'

The dog growled deeply as it crept forward, head low to the ground, teeth bared and dripping saliva. Simon slowly drew his horse to a halt.

'May I suggest that you move back, carefully. Do not turn your back on the hound.' Lewes spoke softly, though his voice was commanding. 'Gently, boy.'

Simon slowly reined back and squeezed with his knees so that his horse took a hesitant step backward. Then another. The dog crept closer, keeping pace with him. Suddenly, with no warning at all, the animal leapt forward. Simon's horse neighed shrilly as it reared up on its hind legs, front hooves flailing at its attacker. Simon struggled to control his mount as the wolfhound leapt upwards, teeth snapping closed on the horse's throat. The early evening rang to the growls of the dog, the screams of the horse, the cries of the men. Then a shot rang out. The dog loosed its grip and fell. There was stunned silence, broken when Simon's horse stumbled to its knees and he leapt from its back.

'You say that this is your dog?'

Sir Thomas nodded. 'Yes. But he has never behaved like this before.'

Lewes frowned. 'It is exceedingly rare, but there are occasions when animals, too, suffer from bewitchment.'

'But why would someone want to bewitch my dog?'

'I do not know, Sir Thomas. But I mean to find out.'

Simon had encouraged his horse to its feet and was examining its wounds whilst the others spoke. He turned to his father. 'The bites are not deep, but I think I should take him back to the stables to be tended to.'

His father nodded. 'Do so. Sir Francis will accompany us to the minister. We will see you back at the Manor later.'

Simon nodded and began to lead the horse away. Behind him he heard Lewes voice again.

'Fine shooting, soldier. But we do not know what evil possessed this dog. Take it and burn it somewhere outside the village.'

***

It was a damp morning. A thin mist hung low to the ground. Simon shivered. His father had returned the previous evening with no deeper understanding of what was happening. Although he and Lewes had talked to the minister it seemed impossible to identify who, or what, was casting evil spells in the village. With such a lack of knowledge, Lewes had ordered all of the bewitched brought to the tithe barn for questioning first thing in the morning.

A long table had been set up. Seated at the center was Lewes with Sir Thomas and Simon on his right. On his left were Sir Francis and the minister. Two of Lewes' men stood in the main body of the barn, halberds at the ready as they waited for the first of the bewitched to be brought in. When the miller and his family arrived, Simon felt a shiver of fear. The man seemed to have aged years in the last few days. He was thinner, as though he had been unable to eat, and his hollow eyes held a haunted look. With him came his wife and children, hands tied in front of them. They were led forward by two more of the soldiers who had accompanied the witch-finder.

Simon listened intently as the miller described what had happened to his family, the details exactly as Simon remembered. When he had finished speaking, Lewes began his questioning.

'Have you done evil to any man to make him cast spells on your family?'

'No, sir.'

'You have not lied, or cheated? Given poor measure?'

'No, sir. I have always been honest in my dealings.'

'Has anyone given strange foods for your family to eat?'

'No, sir.'

'Have you eaten the same as them?'

'Always, sir. Although little food has passed my lips in the last few days.'

'Understandable.' Lewes frowned thoughtfully. 'Have your prayers for them had any effect?'

'I feel they may have done, sir.' The miller rubbed his tired eyes. 'The rest of my family have been praying constantly since this began. My wife and children are now calmer. They do not feel the insects beneath the skin, or see the wolf. The great shakes which took them have diminished. I can only put this down to prayer and the power of the almighty.'

Lewes beckoned to the miller's children who stepped forward.

'Can you understand and answer my questions?'

Three frightened children nodded.

'Do you see the devil or his familiar?'

The children looked puzzled. Sir Thomas leant forward over the table.

'Is the wolf still here?'

The children shook their heads.

'What about the insects?' Sir Thomas continued. 'If we were to unbind your hands would you still feel the need to tear them out?'

The children shook their heads. Sir Thomas turned to Lewes. 'What do you suggest?'

'It seems to me that this family are victims, not witches.' He turned to the wife of the miller. 'How say you? Are you in league with the devil?'

The woman threw herself to her knees. 'No, sir! I am an honest, God-fearing woman! This is not my doing. Someone else has cursed my family!'

'You say that the evil in you is diminishing?'

'Yes, sir. I awoke this morning feeling better. Although what I have seen and felt still fills my mind with fear, I see and feel it no longer.'

Lewes turned to the minister. 'Do you feel the presence of evil here?'

'No, sir.'

'Sir Thomas?'

Sir Thomas shook his head at the witch-finder's question. 'No. There is fear here, but I do not feel the evil that was present at the mill.'

Lewes sat in silent contemplation, fingers drumming on the table top. Finally, he spoke.

'Victims.' He turned to the soldiers. 'Unbind their hands.'

'Is that wise?'

Lewes turned to Simon. 'We shall see. But fear not, my men will be able to bind them swiftly should that be needed.'

There was a fearful, expectant silence in the barn as first the woman and then the children had the ropes binding them cut free. They stood, quietly rubbing their wrists, their eyes fearful. Lewes watched for a time before turning to the soldiers.

'Take them to the barn we have readied. Keep them there under guard but do not bind them again. Send someone to me immediately if they show more signs of bewitchment.'

'Sir.'

Simon watched as they were led away. 'Does this mean that the witch is gone?'

Lewes shook his head. 'I doubt it. For some reason the witch has cast a spell on this family and then moved on. The spell now seems to have weakened and released them. We need to question all others who have been bewitched. I pray that the evil is also leaving them, and that someone may be able to point us towards the witch. Until he, or she, is found no one will be safe.'

***

The morning passed slowly. The families of the cooper, seamstress and carter were brought before the witch-finder. Each person was questioned. Each answered in the same manner as the miller's family. The evil spell which had been cast seemed to be diminishing, the families improving. All of those who had been affected were taken to the barn. Most had the ropes tying their hands removed, although some who had been bewitched for a shorter time and still felt the insects beneath their skin remained bound. Lewes appeared puzzled.

'This is a strange case indeed, Sir Thomas. Why does the witch cast an evil spell then release the victims? Whatever the purpose, I pray that it is over. That these few poor souls are the only ones who have been bewitched and that the power of prayer has overcome the evil in your village.'

'Indeed. Perhaps it was fear of your arrival which has driven the witch away?'

'Or into hiding?' Lewes frowned. 'Perhaps the evil waits only for me to leave before returning with a vengeance?'

'I fear you are wrong.' Sir Francis rose unsteadily to his feet as he spoke. 'What is that noise from outside?'

There was the sound of shouting and cursing. The door to the tithe barn shuddered as something heavy struck it, then it was thrown open by two soldiers. Each held a rope and between them they half led, half dragged the village blacksmith into the barn. When he saw the people gathered there he began to shout and curse.

'Damn you! Why do you just sit there? Help me! The spiders are in me and will not let me go! The devil rides my back! I am bewitched!'

Simon, his father and Lewes all rose hurriedly to their feet as the blacksmith leapt forward, dragging the soldiers with him. Simon's heart was beating so rapidly that he thought it might burst. Sweat broke out on his brow and his hands shook. As he looked fearfully at his father and Sir Francis he could see that they, too, were shaken by the scene. Only Lewes seemed to stand calmly, un-affected by what was happening. The minister was still in his seat, calling on God to protect them. The blacksmith continued to scream and curse.

'In God's name, find the evil one who has done this to me! I see his dog snapping at my heels. Do not let him eat me!'

'We cannot question him in this condition. Guards! Take this man and confine him alone. Stay close. If he subsides, if the devil leaves him, send for me.'

The soldiers complied, dragging the hulk of a man out of the door and across the yard, screaming as he went. There was a deathly silence in the barn, finally broken by the minister who rose shakily to his feet.

'I will go and pray over him.'

The others watched him leave before giving in to their weak knees and sitting once more.

'I must speak more with the families of these poor people.' Sir Thomas shivered as he spoke. 'They are my responsibility, although I doubt I can do anything for them.'

Lewes nodded. 'It is a wise thing to do. I will come with you. There must be something common between them. The witch has to have had contact with them all to cast this spell.'

'But why these people?'

Lewes shook his head at Simon's question. 'I do not know. But I intend to find out. And when I do we will deal with this witch and free all those who are under his spell.'

'Shall I come with you?'

'No. You should return home and wait for us there.'

Simon was puzzled. There was something strange about the tone of his father's voice, but he could not say what it was. He was looking at him in a strange way, too, as though he almost feared Simon.

'Is there something wrong, Father?'

Sir Thomas quickly shook his head. 'No. Just return home; the farm must not be neglected whilst we deal with this. We three will see what we can find out.'

With a puzzled frown, Simon turned and left the barn.

***

Simon paced the length of the study and back again, time after time. Where was his father? It had been almost three hours since he left the tithe barn and he had heard nothing. What was happening? At last he heard the sound of the front door and rushed out into the hallway. Sir Thomas had just entered, his face haggard.

'Father? What is wrong? Has something happened.?'

Sir Thomas gave his son a pained, almost fearful look, before entering the study and pouring a brandy. He drank it swiftly.

'Father?'

Sir Thomas placed his glass carefully on the table before turning to face his son.

'We believe that Lewes has found the answer, in part.'

'What do you mean?'

'He believes that I am the target of the witch. These people have nothing in common but that they live on my estates.'

'But why would the witch target you?'

'Perhaps to punish an imagined wrong.'

'I do not understand. What wrong have you ever done to anyone? Is anyone else bewitched?' Simon took a step towards his father as he spoke, only to see him tense, fear filling his eyes. He was stunned. 'Surely Lewes does not think that I am the witch?'

Sir Thomas shook his head, holding his hand out in front of him. 'No! Not that!' He took a deep breath before continuing. 'He thinks that you may have been bewitched as well.'

Simon felt that he could not breathe, his hands began to shake and he felt weak at the knees.

'Me? Bewitched? But I have no signs!' He shook his head in disbelief. 'I do not see hounds or wolves; there is nothing beneath my skin.'

'Not all bewitchments manifest in the same way.' Sir Thomas took a deep breath. 'Lewes believes that a love spell has been cast on you, so that you will marry that dairymaid; her mother will then have my estates in her hands.'

Simon could not believe what he was hearing. 'That is ridiculous! No one has cast a love spell on me! Even if they had, how could that be linked to the bewitchings we have already seen?'

'All hurt me in some way, Simon. All will affect the income from the estate. And it makes sense. Why else would you want to marry that ... that girl.'

'Because I love her!'

Sir Thomas nodded slowly. 'You say that, and it may well be true. But Lewes says, and I agree with him, that you would not love her if you had not been bewitched. You would not even have spoken with her save for the spell which is cast over you.'

'That is not true, Father! You knew that I spoke with her family when I was a child and...'

'But I did not know that you continued to visit that family! They have had countless opportunities over the years to cast spells on you. So many years that the spells would only need to be small. No one noticed the way they were getting control over you.'

'But it still makes no sense, Father! If it is as you say, why would they bewitch others now?'

'Because they have found out that you are to marry Abigail. Their long plans to take my estates through you had failed and so they now try fear instead.'

Simon was speechless, struggling to comprehend what his father was saying.

'You believe that Rebekah and her mother are the witches? That they are casting evil spells throughout the village just because I am to marry Abigail?

Sir Thomas nodded. 'Lewes thinks that is the case. And I agree with him. He is very experienced in these matters.'

Lewes! Simon's face paled. Standing here, listening to his father, he had forgotten about Lewes.

'It was you who told him about Rebekah, was it not?'

Sir Thomas nodded. 'He wanted to know of everything strange that had happened recently.'

'What will he do?'

'Is that not obvious? The witches will be arrested and tried.'

'When?'

'Lewes goes to their home as we speak.'

'No!' Simon turned and rushed for the door. 'This cannot be happening. Rebekah is innocent!'

Sir Thomas took hold of his arm. 'Stay, Simon. You can do nothing. Let justice take its course.'

'Justice? You call it justice to accuse the woman I love of witchcraft just because you do not like her?' He shrugged off his father's hand. 'I must go to her!'

'Then I am coming with you.'

Sir Thomas followed his son out of the house and across to the stable. Simon was saddling his horse swiftly. Sir Thomas called to his groom.

'Get my horse ready!'

***

Simon almost missed the turn to Rebekah's home in the gathering dark. Reining in his horse he forced it round, almost bringing it to its knees. He had to move at a slower pace along the track, careful of overhanging branches and potholes which could trip his mount. As he rode into the clearing he was speechless at the sight which greeted him. Lewes sat his horse outside the hut, two of his soldiers flanked him, carrying flaming torches which lit the gloom. There were shouts from inside, followed by a scream.

'Rebekah!'

Simon flung himself from his horse and rushed forward. At a signal from Lewes the two soldiers dropped their torches to the ground and took hold of Simon, preventing him from entering the hut. Behind him he could hear the sound of more hooves, and knew that his father had arrived. Moments later Sir Thomas had his arms around his son.

'Leave it, Simon. Come away, son.'

'No!'

Simon struggled as he saw Rebekah and her mother being led from their home, a soldier on either side. They came quietly, as though they knew that it was useless to fight. When Ann Sawyer saw him she spat in Simon's direction. Rebekah reached out a hand towards him, but was pulled back.

'Simon?'

'I did not know they were coming! I swear!' His voice was filled with anguish. 'I will not let them hurt you. I promise!'

Ann Sawyer looked up at Lewes where he sat his horse. 'What will happen to us?'

'You will be held close tonight. Tomorrow you will be tried as witches.'

'But it is not true! They have done nothing wrong!'

Lewes turned to Simon. 'Be careful young man. You have been bewitched, but I do not consider you dangerous. Do not get closer to these women. Do not stand with them. You can be saved from their evil if they have no further chance to harm you.'

Simon knew that Lewes would not listen. He struggled again, desperate to reach Rebekah. His father and the two soldiers held him firm as he watched the women being dragged away.

'Do not worry, Rebekah! I will be there at the trial! I will save you!'

Rebekah turned to take one last look before she was dragged from the clearing. As she disappeared from his sight Simon slumped, as though all of the energy had gone from him. There were tears in his eyes as he turned to Sir Thomas.

'This is wrong, Father. They have done nothing evil.'

'Then that is what shall be discovered at the trial.' Sir Thomas looked at Simon with eyes, which held more love and compassion than Simon had seen since he had first spoken about Rebekah. 'We only seek the truth, my son. And healing for the bewitched, whoever they are.'

'I am not bewitched.' Simons voice was soft, exhausted.

'You say that. Yet look how you have calmed now that the women have gone. It is as though their presence inflamed you.'

Simon turned to Lewes. 'No, it was the presence of your soldiers which inflamed me. You cannot use that excuse to keep me from their trial.'

'On the contrary. I truly believe that they have cast spells upon you, Master Hardwycke. And I will therefore require you to be at the trial. You will have your chance to present your evidence. Maybe I will be proved wrong. If so, we still have witches to find.' The witchfinder's eyes were filled with compassion as he looked first at Simon and then Sir Thomas. 'Go home. Rest. No harm will come to those women tonight. You have my word.'

Chapter 41

Present day

Rob stumbled, almost falling. With a groan he made his way over to a chair and sat down heavily. His heart was beating rapidly and his hands shook. When he had tried to force a waking dream, he had never imagined that it would be so terrifying. Witchcraft! Poor Simon. Poor Rebekah. Rob felt the icy finger of fear trace his spine. And Ann Sawyer. He had no further doubt that the ghost which had haunted him since his arrival at Marston Manor was that of Rebekah's mother. Was this the wrong she spoke of? Had Simon been unable to save her? Did she somehow hold Rob responsible for that?

Or had she been a witch? Had she really cast a spell on the villagers? And on Simon? Did that mean that she was responsible for the fires at the Manor? Was she trying to destroy the project because of her hatred of Simon? A hatred that spanned more than three hundred years and now focussed on Rob himself?

Rob felt exhausted, drained, as though he had used up every ounce of energy to conjure up the dream. He knew that he would not be strong enough to do that again for a few days. If he ever had the courage to try again. No matter how much he wanted to know what happened, the thought of facing such open hatred and fear and ... evil ... left him almost unable to move. Was this what had really happened, or was it his imagination? He knew that his dreams of Simon's experiences during the war were true, the diary proved that. But the diary had ended with the death of the King. Was this continuation of his relationship with Rebekah also true, or nothing more than a dream? Knowing that he would not be able to face another vision of the past until he felt stronger, he decided to try to find the notes which Simon had written in this last dream. With deep trepidation Rob stood and made his slow way up to his bedroom.

***

Back in the library some thirty minutes later, Rob pulled a box file towards himself. He had not been able to find Simon's latest notes hidden away in the space beneath the floor where the diary had been concealed, but he did have other evidence to what had happened after the war, after the end of the diary. Rob slowly reached inside the file and took out the page he had found hidden in the family Bible. The ancient paper was encased in plastic to preserve it, but he was still able to read every word.

He scanned it carefully, certain phrases seeming to jump out from the page, to imprint themselves on his mind.

...Today is the day on which my life should have begun anew, my life with thee forever beside me...

...I must take another to wife...Abigail is a good woman...but how can I give myself to her knowing that it is thee I cherish...

... I know that if not for me thou wouldst still be here...

...I pray that you were able to forgive me my love...

...My guilt will haunt me until the day that I shall meet with my Maker...

...My darling Rebekah, this is the goodbye I was never allowed to speak. Forgive my past deeds and my betrayal of you as I now take Abigail to wife...

So, Simon had married Abigail. Something, somehow, had happened to prevent him being with Rebekah. Something he regretted. Something so momentous that he had been unable to say goodbye, and which had left him with no prospect of speaking to her ever again. Rob tried to imagine what that might be, but found it impossible. He knew that the only way he would find out was by following the dreams to their conclusion. But he could not face that. Not yet. He still felt exhausted from his last dream, needed to recover before allowing himself to try once more.

Rob looked around him. The library was unchanged, yet he no longer felt so at ease here. He imagined that Simon hid in the shadows, waiting to continue his story, that the ghost of Ann was watching him, waiting to reveal herself once more. With a shudder Rob replaced the paper in the file and stood up. He had to get away from Marston for a time. He needed to find out more about the witchcraft in order to feel more prepared if ... when ... he dreamed again. His eyes fell on his computer on the desk, but he did not want to use that for his research. He needed somewhere else, somewhere where he could feel at peace. Rob remembered his days in Oxford, where he had done his teacher training. He had enjoyed his time there. The place held no negative connotations for him. That was where he would go.

***

Rob had sought out Professor Jane Rutherford, whose speciality was sixteenth and seventeenth century English history. He had seen her at a couple of conferences but had never had the opportunity to talk with her for long. Now they were seated opposite each other over a cup of coffee. Jane smiled.

'So, to what do I owe this pleasure? I didn't know you were in Oxford.'

'Well, I'm not in Oxford as such. But I am working in the area.' He quickly explained the project at Marston before steering the conversation towards witchcraft. 'I want to include something about witches at the Manor and wondered if you can help with some information?' he asked.

'Specific or general?'

'How do you mean?'

'Well, there were cases of witchcraft in the area in the 1660s, but I don't have many details.'

'Really?' Rob felt a frisson of fear, which he pushed to the back of his mind. 'Were there any witches at Marston?'

Jane shrugged. 'I don't know. Theoretically it is possible, although I've never come across it in my research of witchcraft in Oxfordshire. You could try to find out, I suppose. Where I think I can be of most help would be in general terms. Just some background on witchcraft. Would that be okay?'

Rob nodded. 'Yes, please. It's not something I've looked into before. My focus has been more on war, and the social and economic background. Religion and superstition have never really grabbed me, so to speak.'

'Well, who's to say it's superstition?'

'What? You mean that you actually believe in witches?'

Jane smiled. 'Not witches per se, but you're a historian. You know that stories are often based on fact.'

Rob nodded. 'True. So what facts do you have about witchcraft?'

'Well, as you know, many illnesses in the Middle Ages were blamed on witches. If you had a fever, it was a witch. Sick animal? A witch. Dying child? A witch. Between the fifteenth and seventeenth centuries there was an epidemic of witchcraft outbreaks. Over forty thousand men, women and children were executed as witches.'

Rob was astounded. 'That many?'

Jane nodded. 'One witchfinder in England took two hundred and fifty people accused of witchcraft before the courts in just two years.'

'Were all the cases similar?'

Jane shrugged. 'They varied. For example, in 1589 the five little daughters of the Throckmorton family, who lived in the Manor house at Warboys, near Cambridge, were struck with a strange illness. And so were seven of their maidservants. The father called in a number of doctors and clergy, who all had varying ideas as to the cause. Most put it down to witchcraft.'

'What were the symptoms?'

'Classic for demonic possession. Visions of wild animals trying to eat them, violent fits. It was believed that witches sent out their animal familiars to trap the weak into making a pact with the devil. As usual, it was some poor local misfit who took the blame. In this case it was a woman called Alice Samuel. The poor woman was scratched to draw blood on a number of occasions.'

'Why?'

'They thought it would relieve the suffering of the people she had bewitched. But there were other forms of torture as well. Anything was considered acceptable, as long as it helped to relieve the suffering of the people under a witches spell.'

'The end justifies the means.'

'In the case of witches, yes. Alice was interrogated for a year before she finally confessed. She was hung. Along with her husband and daughter.'

'The poor woman.' Rob took a sip of coffee. 'It wasn't just England though, was it?'

'No. There were problems with witches all over Europe. And America, too, of course. I'm sure you've heard of the Salem Witch trials?'

'Yes. Wasn't that one of the bigger episodes?'

Jane nodded. 'One hundred and fifty two people were accused of witchcraft and imprisoned. Nineteen were executed, although none of them confessed.'

'Sounds like mass hysteria to me. What caused it all?'

'Similar physical symptoms to those at Warboys. Eight little girls said they had been bewitched, and for a year they testified against other people in the town.'

'Was it a deliberate attempt to cause trouble? It sounds so strange.'

'Some people think that, but others believe that the girls had experienced something and were very frightened. So they struck out at anybody, and everybody.'

'But to execute so many, on the say-so of a group of children who were not behaving normally. Why would they do that?'

'You're thinking in modern terms, Rob. Back then they truly believed that the devil was responsible. To blame witchcraft was just as likely as blaming anything else.'

Rob shook his head sadly. 'It's all so long ago now. I don't suppose we'll ever know what caused it all.'

Jane smiled, as though she had a secret she was dying to share. 'Oh, I don't know about that. We do have some theories, partly derived from the last case in Europe, when a bishop was called out to do an exorcism because a witch had cast a spell on a whole town.'

'When was that?'

'1951.'

'*1951!*' Rob was incredulous. 'Are you serious?'

'Of course. Let me explain. It should be very useful for your information centre at the Manor.'

'I'm all ears!'

Jane settled herself comfortably in her seat. 'Ever hear of Professor Linnda Caporael?' Rob shook his head, and Jane continued. 'I'm not surprised, it's not really your field. She's a behavioural psychologist.'

'What does that have to do with witchcraft?'

'She researched what happened at Salem. Initially she believed that the girls had made it all up. But the deeper she dug, the more she began to feel that most of what they experienced had not been faked, particularly the severe convulsions. The fact that many other people in the village, not just the girls, reported similar visions made her think that there must be something else involved. It wasn't confined to children, men and women were also affected. It was when she was reading one particular account that Linnda noticed its similarity to the effects of LSD.'

'LSD?' Rob was incredulous. 'You don't mean acid, do you?'

Jane nodded. 'Yes. LSD, a popular hallucinogenic drug from the 1960s.'

Rob shook his head. 'That seems a bit way out.'

'More way out than witchcraft?'

'Sorry, I didn't mean to offend but ... *LSD!*'

Jane was smiling. 'No offence taken. But think about it. People who have taken LSD say that they have incredibly vivid hallucinations, like living nightmares. The way they describe them is very similar to the accounts that bewitched people gave at Salem. And at Warboys.'

'But I thought LSD wasn't invented until the 60s? How could it be linked to things that had happened three hundred years before?'

'It was actually invented in 1943. Though invented is not really accurate. Like most drugs, it is derived from nature. A Swiss neurophysiologist, Albert Hoffman, experimented with a natural fungus called ergot whilst looking for medical applications for naturally occurring drugs. He made an extract from the ergot fungus and spilt some on his hand. Within hours he began to get terrible hallucinations. When he had recovered, he derived LSD from the extract.'

Rob frowned thoughtfully. 'So, theoretically, something like LSD could be produced naturally?'

Jane nodded. 'Linnda began to take a closer look at ergot poisoning. The descriptions of hallucinations and physical discomfort in the medical books matched the symptoms from Salem. Her next question was simple. How had the settlers come into contact with it? She re-read the primary source accounts. It wasn't only the settlers who were affected, but their animals as well. A number of cattle died of no natural causes, even more acted very strangely. Linnda began to wonder if the cause could have been a food source common to both humans and animals. So she began looking at grain. The dominant crop in Salem was rye. The next step was to find out how ergot could have got into the rye fields. It was Professor Maurice Moss who came up with the answer. He is a fungal toxicologist who has made an intensive study of fungi.'

'Mushrooms?'

Jane shook her head. 'There's more to fungi than just mushrooms and toadstools. A fungus contaminates its host and gradually replaces the original seed with its own material. If the rye in the fields at Salem was contaminated then the bread would have been contaminated too. Moss explained that the nerve toxins contained in the bread would account for all of the symptoms of people who were thought to have been cursed by a witch. The hallucinations; the pin pricking sensations; the feeling of insects crawling beneath the skin; the powerful fits which meant that the sick people could barely be held down by their friends and family.'

'The stuff is really that powerful?'

'Yes. Ergotamine has been used in Holland to treat migraines. It has to be used carefully as it has constrictive powers which can lead to convulsions, and to the blood draining from the skin causing pricking sensations.'

Rob's mind was a whirling combination of the information which Jane had given him and images from his dream. All the symptoms she described, every one, had been a part of his dream. But how could that be? How could he have imagined this, unless it was all true? The fear which he had been holding at bay crept closer. The more he learnt, the more he was convinced in the reality of his dreams. But that meant that Rebekah and her mother had been accused of witchcraft, blamed for casting spells when it was nothing more than a natural phenomenon.

Rob took a deep breath. 'So you think ergot poisoning is the answer to witchcraft?'

'It goes a long way to explaining things. And I certainly prefer it to thoughts of the devil.'

'But why would it only happen at certain times? If ergot is present in rye then there should be even more cases.'

'Ergot thrives in wet, damp soil. In 1691 the Salem crops had been planted in low marshy ground. For a mass infection of the harvest to take place it would have needed a warm, wet spring and summer. The spring of 1691 was stormy and wet and was followed by a wet summer. The crop grown was rye. Most of the sickness was on one side of the village. The side where the homes backed onto the farms with swampy marshlands.

'Rye was also the staple diet in Europe in the Middle Ages, which could explain the witch persecutions which took place so frequently. The poor peasant classes were hit most, and rye was their staple diet. I don't know if you've heard of Mary Matossian, she's a historian who has mapped outbreaks of witch trials which were localised in Britain. Most, but not all, were in Essex and East Anglia. These were the main rye growing regions. Also the weather conditions at the time were different to today, and were ideal for the formation of ergot on rye.'

Rob was impressed. 'Pretty compelling evidence.'

'There's more. So far we have evidence from psychology, neurophysiology, toxicology and geography, but archaeologists have also provided evidence in support of this theory.'

'Archaeology? I'm no scientist, but surely no physical evidence could survive for any length of time?'

'Ever hear of the peat bog man of Grauballe?'

Rob frowned thoughtfully. 'I think so. Wasn't a body discovered in the 60s in Denmark?'

'Close. It was 1952 actually. But you're spot on with the country. The body had been buried in a peat bog during the Iron Age. The man had been murdered with a knife and club, then dumped naked into the bog. His throat had been cut from ear to ear. A blow to the right temple had fractured the skull.'

'Gruesome.'

'Yes. But this was often done if someone was thought to be possessed by demons. It would allow the demon to escape, in effect freeing the man. It could be viewed as an act of kindness. A post mortem was carried out on the body. His stomach contents showed that his last meal had been full of ergot. The poor man would have been hallucinating and convulsing. Local people would have thought that he was a witch and killed him to protect the village.'

'Poor man. At least we can be thankful that this doesn't happen anymore.'

'I think you've forgotten the date I mentioned earlier. The last example I'm aware of was in 1951, just one year before the Grauballe man was discovered.'

Rob's eyes widened. He had been so focussed on how this evidence might explain what had happened in his dream that he had completely forgotten the more recent outbreak. 'Of course! What happened?'

'It was in Pont St Esprit, in France. An entire village suffered ergot poisoning caused by poisoned bread, in August 1951. Two hundred and fifty people. Several people were taken to hospitals and psychiatric asylums. They were sick, had stomach cramps, couldn't sleep, suffered from violent convulsions and terrifying hallucinations. Many had to be strapped down to stop them trying to jump out of windows to escape. At least five people died. A dog which had been fed on scraps of rye bread ran in circles and was biting at rocks until it broke its teeth on them. Then it died. After much investigation it was finally found that they were suffering from ergot poisoning. Many people didn't believe the explanation and the Bishop of Nimes was called in to exorcise the devil from the bakery.'

Rob shook his head. 'This is all so incredible! Not what I was expecting at all when I asked to meet you!'

Jane laughed. 'Don't you just love the way science keeps finding out answers to our questions from the past?' Rob was silent, his mind replaying information from his dream. The wet summer. The rye crop damaged. Simon's dog which had gone mad. The mill which had ground the rye being the source of the outbreak. 'So,' Jane continued, 'do you think this information will be of any use to you at Marston?'

Rob nodded slowly.

'Yes. More than you could ever know.'

Chapter 42

August 1651

Simon lay in his bed but could not sleep. Every time he closed his eyes he saw Rebekah and her mother being taken away, heard the scream, and Rebekah's questioning voice as she spoke his name. He tossed and turned for a while, unable to relax. Finally, in exasperation, he threw back the covers and rose from his bed. He looked out of his window at the stables, and the dairy in the distance. Everything looked so peaceful, so calm. Surely it was all a nightmare and he would wake soon to find no evil spells in the village, no witches. Just Rebekah by his side as his wife. How he longed for it all to be a dream, a nightmare from which he could awaken. But he knew that it was not. At that very moment Rebekah was being held by the witchfinder. And, if Simon could not help her, she and her mother would be condemned.

He wanted to do something, anything, to help, but his every word and action would be construed as that of a man bewitched. He turned away from the window with angry frustration, driving his fist into the wall. The flash of pain helped a little, focussing his mind on the knuckles which would be bruised by morning. But it did not really help. Nothing could drive thoughts of Rebekah from his mind.

When Simon turned back to the window, his forehead creased into a frown. Perhaps he had slept after all, for the pale red light of dawn was already bathing the distant dairy with its light. But the sky was still dark, clouds scurrying across the face of the moon and the thousands of stars which twinkled down. He looked back towards the dairy, his eyes widening as realisation dawned upon him.

'Fire.'

The word was soft on his lips, and he stood rooted to the spot for a few seconds before turning and throwing on a pair of breeches and picking up his boots. He made his way to the door, hopping on one leg as he struggled with his footwear. Finally he was outside his father's room and began to hammer on the door with his fists.

'Father! The dairy is on fire! Come quickly!'

He had just finished pulling on his second boot when the door opened and Sir Thomas emerged.

'What is all this shouting about? Why are you not in bed?

'The dairy! It is on fire! Come quickly!'

'Fire?'

'Yes! I saw it from my window!' Simon ran towards the stairs, shouting back towards his father. 'I will raise the men! Hurry!'

Sir Thomas needed no second bidding and returned to his room for clothes. By the time he had on breeches and jacket, Simon was rushing through the servants' quarters, raising everyone with his cries of alarm.

Less than five minutes after seeing the first flames, Simon drew to a breathless halt outside the dairy. He could hardly believe that the fire had taken hold so quickly. Flames licked the sides of the building and smoke billowed, thick and bitter to taste. He found himself coughing as he turned towards the men and women who began to arrive.

'Bring buckets and water! Douse the walls!'

Frantic bellowing came from the beasts trapped inside the barn. As Simon moved towards the doors he felt a hand on his arm and looked down.

'You cannot go in there, sir, it is too dangerous!'

Simon roughly shook off the groom's hand. 'We must save the herd!' With no more thought he rushed towards the building. The door was hot to the touch, but he gritted his teeth and dragged it open. The interior was lost in the billowing smoke from which the flames were eerily reflected in red and yellow. The sound of burning wood and falling timbers was all around him, yet this was almost drowned out by the bellows of fear and pain from the trapped animals. Simon began to cough as the smoke filled his lungs, but he forced himself to move forward. On his right the bulk of a cow in the side pen appeared through the smoke. He turned towards it, throwing open the gate. 'Out! Get out!' But the cow was too afraid. Instead of passing Simon and moving out into the fresh air, it backed away. With a muttered curse Simon followed. Getting behind the beast he drove her forward and was relieved to see her finally move in the right direction, towards the door. Thankful that the cows were herd animals, Simon got behind the rest of them, driving them forward, watching them rush past the men who now struggled to enter the burning building. They joined Simon and opened more pens, driving the animals out. All the time the fire roared, the smoke billowed ever more thickly. Simon's eyes burned, his throat was raw from the smoke and his coughing. But he forced himself on until he felt a hand on his arm. It was one of Lewes's men.

'Do not go further! It is not safe!'

Simon shook his head. 'I must! There are more animals back there!'

As he spoke there was the sound of cracking timbers. Seconds later a section of the roof fell in front of him, covering him in a shower of burning embers. Taking a deep breath Simon stepped forward again, only to be halted by a more forceful hand on his arm.

'Sir Thomas would rather lose his cows than his son. We must get out of here!'

Simon looked to where he could hear the trapped beasts bellowing in pain, and was thankful that he could not see them through the thick smoke. Already the smell of burning flesh was tainting his nostrils, but he knew how important the animals were. He took another step forward, just as more of the roof came crashing down. One of the huge beams caught him a glancing blow to the shoulder and he fell to his knees. He struggled to his feet again, and Simon saw the fear in the soldier's eyes as he took his arm.

'Come on!'

Realising that there was nothing he could do to save the trapped animals, Simon turned and left the building in a stumbling run.

***

It was dawn before the fire was extinguished, leaving a smoking ruin where the dairy had once stood. The rescued cows had been let out to pasture, as far away from the fire as possible. Simon was thankful that they had managed to save most of the animals, but even so some ten beasts, including the prize bull, had been lost. It was a devastating blow as they faced the coming winter months.

Feeling utterly exhausted, Simon and his father washed the dirt and smell of the fire from their bodies, before donning clean clothes and making their way to the tithe barn where the trial of the witches was to take place. They sat to one side, close to the table where Lewes was seated. At the rear of the barn were silent villagers, afraid of what they might see yet hopeful that whatever happened would expose the witch and bring an end to the fear which gripped their village. Simon had barely taken his seat when there was the sound of approaching footsteps as Rebekah and her mother were led in. Despite the soldiers who flanked the two women, the villagers cowered back, crossing themselves and muttering prayers.

The two women looked tired as they stood, heads bowed, before the witchfinder. Their hands were tied behind them, and each had a rope around her neck which was held by one of the soldiers. Simon made to stand up, angry at their treatment, but felt his father's restraining hand on his arm.

'Be still, son.'

'But they are being treated like animals!'

'Until we know that they are not witches, we must be protected. If things are as you believe, then they will be free before this morning is out.'

'And if not?'

'We must wait and see.' He glanced at Lewes, who was frowning. 'Now be still.'

Simon sank back into his seat as Lewes stood and began to speak.

'I need say nothing about the evil which has taken hold here, for you have all seen it.' He looked at the villagers at the back of the barn. 'You have been living in fear of the witches who are amongst you. I am here to end the fear. These two women,' he pointed at Rebekah and her mother as he spoke, 'are accused of witchcraft. I have questioned those who have suffered bewitchment, and their family and neighbours. All the evidence I find points to their guilt.'

'No!'

Lewes turned angrily towards Simon, who had leapt to his feet in protest. 'You will have your chance to speak. As will they. But first you must hear the evidence.' Simon reluctantly sat down as Lewes continued.

'The evil is confined to Marston. All those in the village who have been bewitched work for Sir Thomas. Sir Thomas's dog was bewitched and tried to attack its owner. All this led me to believe that Sir Thomas is the target.

'I searched for someone who might bear ill feeling against Sir Thomas. Mistress Sawyer was heard to say, many times, that she blamed him for the death of her husband in the war. What better way to punish him than to instil fear into his villagers, so that they turn against him. I believe that it was her aim to do this, so that his son would replace him.

'That was the beginning of the plan, and it was accomplished by giving potions to the unfortunate ones who have been bewitched, all of whom have recently sought help from Mistress Sawyer for minor ailments. She, and her daughter, then bewitched Simon Hardwycke so that he would fall in love with Rebekah. He would marry her and Marston Manor would come into the hands of their family, thus completing her revenge.

'Her plan has been thwarted by Sir Thomas, who came to me for aid. The women were arrested yesterday evening then, during the night, there was a fire at the Manor which destroyed the dairy and many fine animals: fire caused by these angry witches!'

He pointed to the two women as he spoke. The villagers shrank further back, crossing themselves to ward off evil as Simon leapt to his feet.

'It is not true! The fire was just a coincidence!'

'You say so, but I believe you to be bewitched.' Although his words were harsh, Lewes' eyes held some compassion for the young man. 'Be seated. I will give the witches a chance to speak. Then it will be your turn.' Reluctantly, Simon sat beside his father as Lewes turned back to Ann Sawyer. 'What say you?'

Ann kept her eyes lowered, her body shaking in fear. For a moment she said nothing, but then she straightened her back a little and lifted her head. Her words were soft, but all in the silent barn could hear what she said.

'My daughter and I are not witches, just honest folk. It is true that I have treated many with herbs, but I have been doing that all of my life, as has my daughter. They are just simple remedies to help the suffering. I have never made potions or cast spells to bewitch people.'

'But you did say that you blamed Sir Thomas for the death of your husband?'

'When I heard that my husband was dead I was heartbroken, and angry. I wanted to blame someone, so I blamed the only man I knew who had been in the battle on the side of the enemy. I blamed Sir Thomas's eldest son. But as my grief began to subside, I realised that such thinking was foolish.' She looked across at Simon and his father. 'I do not feel any ill-will towards Sir Thomas, and I have not used witchcraft against him or his family.'

'But you used witchcraft last night to fire his dairy.'

'That is not so!' Ann raised her voice in indignation. 'You had us confined. How could we have set the fire?'

'Just before the fire broke out, two crows were seen flying from the window of your prison. You had changed yourselves and flew to the Manor.'

'No! That would be evil magic! I only work with what is pure and good to heal people. I do not know how to turn into a crow! Or fly!'

There were murmurs from the people at the rear of the barn. Lewes looked at them, then back at Ann.

'It seems that your neighbours believe that you could do that. They fear having you living in their midst now that you have revealed yourselves.'

Ann hung her head once more. 'What you say is not true. But you have made up your mind to the matter and what I say will not influence you.'

'You are right to say that the words of a witch will not influence me, save that they are a renunciation of all that is evil. But you will not go undefended if there is but one person to speak on your behalf.'

Simon stood up, his voice ringing out across the barn. 'I will speak for them.'

Lewes nodded. 'I knew that you would wish to do so, and I will let you have your say. But I will finish the evidence against these witches before you speak in their defence. Sir Thomas,' he turned towards the man as he spoke. 'Will you stand and give your evidence of the evil that these women have done?'

'Father?'

Sir Thomas laid a hand on his son's shoulder. 'I must speak the truth as I see it, Simon. As must you. It will be for Lewes to find the truth of the matter.' Taking a deep breath, Sir Thomas began to give his evidence.

'On the day that the miller's family were first bewitched I was with my son, Simon, Sir Francis Morrison, and his daughter, Abigail. It was the first meeting of the young people after we had agreed that they should be married. That meeting was interrupted by a message to say that there was witchcraft in the village. Later that day, after we had carried out what investigations we could, and the Morrison's had returned home, we spoke of the evil. My son suggested that the appearance of witchcraft at the very moment when he was introduced to his future bride could not be a coincidence. I have to agree with him.' Sir Thomas looked sadly towards Simon. 'My son has told me that he does not wish to marry the woman of my choice. He would rather marry that girl there.' He pointed to Rebekah as he spoke. Those who had come to watch whispered amongst themselves in disbelief. 'My son first met this family when he was a child. On the very first day he was given salves and potions for his injuries after a fall. Every time he visited them thereafter he took food or drink. All through those years I believe they have been casting their evil spells against him. I do not know if they had a plan in mind at the beginning, but after the death of her husband Mistress Sawyer would have done anything to get revenge against my family. Since the end of the war the girl has insinuated herself further into my son's affections, even going so far as to obtain work in our dairy so that she could be closer to him, to cast her spells little by little. A small spell cast daily, would not be noticed. In that way she, and her mother, gained control of Simon so that he wants to marry her.'

'Father, you know that is not true.' Simon's voice was soft, but his words carried to Sir Thomas who shook his head sadly.

'I am sorry, son, but I do believe that it is true. This pair both cast spells on you, one to win your love, and one to gain revenge. Do you not see? They blamed your brother for the death of Henry Sawyer. What better way to be avenged than to drag down the brother of the man they believe responsible, to steal the lands of his father. To raise themselves up in place of those they hate, so that Henry Sawyers' grandchildren would one day be the owners of Marston Manor. It is a powerful reason for what they have done.'

'But what of the possessions? How could that have helped them to gain what they wanted?'

'In no way at all. But, having found out that you were to marry Abigail, they sought revenge on our family another way. They tried to hurt us by hurting those who work for us, causing fear so that people would eventually leave Marston. No one would come to work here for fear of witchcraft. We would lose everything.'

Simon turned his disbelieving gaze towards Sir Francis. 'Do you believe this, too?'

'Yes. When your father told me that you said you loved the dairymaid I knew that it could be nothing but witchcraft. I went with him to denounce these evil women.' He laid a comforting hand on Simon's arm. 'Do not worry. We will break the spell they hold on you, then you can marry Abigail in peace and safety. I will not hold this against you, for none of it is your fault.'

Simon angrily tore his arm away. 'I respect you greatly, Sir Francis. But I must tell you that in this you are wrong. I...'

'Enough!' Lewes spoke loudly, and all eyes turned towards him. 'I see the logic in what Sir Thomas and Sir Francis have to say. They believe that these women are witches. They are not angry with you for choosing this girl above the daughter of Sir Francis, for they know that you would never have done so if you had not been bewitched. They know also that Mistress Morrison will see this too. They agree that there will be no impediment to your marriage, once you have been released from evil. You have heard the arguments for those who speak against these women. You may now speak in their defence, Master Simon Hardwycke. But take note. I will not be swayed by words of emotion; they can too easily be the result of spells cast against you. If you have evidence to the innocence of these women, if you can give as clear an argument for what has happened here in their defence as your father has in his condemnation, then I shall consider it. So, tell us all now, why you do not believe these two who stand before us are witches.'

Simon stood, his hands gripping the edge of the table so that none could see how they shook. His mouth was dry, and he was afraid that he might not be able to speak. So much hung on his words. What could he possibly say to counter his father's arguments? Looking across the space between them he caught Rebekah's gaze. He could see fear in her eyes, but also love. Her strength reached out to him and he felt comforted, calmed. He took a deep breath and began to speak.

'I do not agree with what my father and Sir Francis say, although I do accept that their argument is sound, or would be so if Rebekah and her mother truly hated us. But that is not so. It is argued that Mistress Sawyer seeks revenge for the loss of her husband. Her words at the time of his death would seem to prove that. But how many of us have uttered such words in the last few years? War has devastated our lives and our communities. And where people lose a loved one, they seek to reach out and blame someone for their hurt. When I heard about the death of my brother, Thomas, I would have killed any Roundhead that I could in my anguish. But I have come to terms with my loss. I know that I cannot blame an individual for what happened on the field of battle, and I believe that Mistress Sawyer feels the same.' Simon let his gaze rove over the assembled villagers, the soldiers, Lewes. 'How many of you lost family and friends during the wars? You cannot deny that you felt the same. But wanting to lash out in your hurt and anger does not make you a witch. And you have put that hurt behind you to try to build a new life.' He looked back at the accused. 'These two women have done the same. You cannot use words spoken years ago in a fit of grief to accuse them of witchcraft today.'

Lewes nodded, his gaze thoughtful, but he said nothing as Simon continued.

'It is also argued that Ann Sawyer cast her spells over the villagers because she treated them for their illnesses. But she has been doing that for years. Never once during all that time has there been a bewitchment in our village. Yes, her salves and potions are something that the poor people who have been bewitched have in common, but so do many others who have not been possessed by evil. You could equally argue that all those who have suffered ate bread baked from flour ground at the mill. Does that make the miller a witch? Casting his spells through the flour he provided? Indeed, the evil began in his own family, so why not say that it comes from the mill?'

'Because, as you say, the first victims were his family, people he loved. He would not harm them.'

Simon nodded towards Lewes, who had spoken. 'Yes. But I would also argue that Rebekah loves me, and that she and her mother could not harm me because of that love.' He held up a hand as his father made to speak. 'I know that you would not agree with this, Father, but it is what I feel and what I believe. And if you look into your heart, I am sure that you will see that these women do not wish to harm our family. Look at them.' He pointed at Rebekah and her mother as he spoke. 'Those are the two women who came out in some of the worst weather we have seen for many a winter to help my sister, your daughter, through a difficult birth. She would have died if they had not come. Surely, if they hated us so much they would not have helped. Look at Mistress Sawyer.' He pointed at her again. 'She saved the life of your daughter and your granddaughter. The child is even named for her. Surely you cannot believe that she is evil?'

Sir Thomas frowned thoughtfully, as though weighing the argument. 'You argue well, Simon. But you do not answer all of the questions that have been raised in my mind.'

'Indeed,' Lewes was nodding in agreement. 'There is much more to this than you say. Even your actions here today make me wonder at their guilt.'

'How so?' Simon was puzzled. 'You said that I might argue in their defence, and I have done so. In what way have I done wrong?'

'It is not your words, but your actions.' Lewes was thoughtful. 'You were angry, impatient, uncontrolled even, whilst listening to your father. But then you stood to give your evidence. We all saw the young woman catch your gaze and hold it. We all saw you calm before it. We all saw how you suddenly found the words for their defence and spoke strongly and confidently for them. Was not that, too, an example of the evil influence they hold over you?'

Simon was shocked. 'How could you think such a thing? You take my words and actions, whatever they may be, and use them against me, and against these innocents. If I am angry, it is their spell. If I am calm, it is their spell. If I struggle for words, they are to blame; likewise if I speak eloquently. How can I defend them if you use each of my words against me?'

'Fear not, your words have a sense to them and I shall weigh them in my judgement. I intend to be fair in this matter, for if these women are not witches them there are others who are, and we must find them.' Whilst Lewes was speaking there was the sound of voices outside, then a man entered, flanked by two soldiers. 'You may be seated. There is one other who would speak for these women.'

Simon recognised the man who entered and sat down, perplexed, as Doctor Morton made his way towards the table where they all sat. Morton inclined his head towards the assembled group. 'Good morning, sirs.' There was a chorus of replies as the doctor took his place in front of the witchfinder.

Simon turned towards his father. 'Who has called him here?'

'I did. Despite what you think, I too want to get to the truth of this matter. You spoke well in defence of Mistress Sawyer for what she did for Elizabeth, but I do not know whether that was skilled healing or witchcraft. That is why I sent for the good doctor.'

'Then you do not know what he is going to say?'

'No more than you.'

Simon swallowed hard. Did the doctor realise just how much hung in the balance of his words?

Lewes rose to greet his new witness. 'I thank you for coming, doctor. I will not keep you overlong. Please just state clearly for me what happened at the birth of Sir Thomas's grandchild.'

'I know little enough about the birth, save what has been told to me by those who were present, but I do have my tale to tell.' Morton paused for a moment, took a deep breath and began his evidence.

'Sir Francis asked me to care for Mistress Elizabeth whilst she was with child, a duty I was happy to perform. There were no problems, and I expected the birth to be easy. However, the child presented incorrectly and she had a difficult time. To make matters worse there was a great blizzard so that Simon could not send for help. By the time he sent for me things were critical. He decided to bring in these two women to help, based on Ann Sawyers' reputation as a healer. I can say now that I do not believe that either mother or child would have survived if not for the help provided by the two accused.'

Lewes nodded. 'So I have heard tell. And none can fail but to be grateful for what they did. My question to you, though, is this. Was she able to help because of her knowledge of herbs and healing, or because of witchcraft?'

'I would say both.' There was a sharp intake of breath from Simon. Morton turned to him, and the young man felt calmed by the compassion in his gaze. 'I say both because we all know that there are white witches who use their powers for the good of others. They use God's gifts of healing herbs, and the skills which God Himself has given to them, to work good in this world. I believe that Ann Sawyer is one such. Mayhap her daughter is also, but I cannot give evidence to that.'

'So you believe that at least one of the accused is a witch?'

Morton nodded at Lewes' question.

'Yes. But as we all know, being a witch in this country is not a crime. What is a punishable crime is to use the power of witchcraft for evil.' He turned to look at Rebekah and her mother. 'I have only met these two women once, and I am willing to swear on God's holy word that, on that occasion, they used their powers for good and not evil.'

'Thank you, sir.'

Morton turned to Simon. 'I say nothing but the truth.'

'And your words give me cause to think.' Lewes rested his elbow on the table, chin in hand, as he thoughtfully perused the two women. 'I feel it is certain that Mistress Ann Sawyer is a witch. You have given evidence that she is good. A white witch. Maybe that is so, but that still leaves us with no one else on these estates who has shown that they can practise the magic arts. It is not unheard of for a white witch to use her powers for evil if she feels thwarted in any matter. As for her daughter...'

Simon was tense. He felt that he might be sick at any moment. What of Rebekah?

'...As for her daughter,' Lewes continued, 'I find it hard to judge. Maybe she is a white witch like her mother. Maybe she practises the evil arts as well. Or maybe she is a pure innocent. Although the evidence presented here today has been clear in both accusation and defence, I do not believe that it can clearly show the guilt or innocence of either party to the charge of witchcraft. I will not convict without being certain.' Simon felt relief flood over him. The witchfinder would not convict! Rebekah and her mother were saved! But his relief was short-lived as Lewes continued. 'My uncertainty means that I need more proof, one way or the other. The two accused must suffer trial by ordeal.'

Rebekah and Ann had been standing straight, giving the appearance of aggrieved innocence, but at the words of the witchfinder they slumped, as though all fight had gone from them. Simon groaned as he looked despairingly at Rebekah. The trial would be so hard for her to bear. Even if she were found innocent, the ordeal would scar her for life. He began to rise from his seat to go to her, to comfort her in whatever way her could, but he felt a restraining hand on his arm. He looked down at it, then up into the face of the man who held him.

'Do not go to her, Simon.' His father's words were gentle, compassionate. 'We have to let this play out. But you may take comfort in the fact that the witchfinder cannot immediately find them guilty of black witchcraft.' He frowned. 'If they are found not guilty, then I do not know where we stand with regards to your marriage. Please, be still. Let matters take their course. You can see that Lewes is a fair man.'

Simon reluctantly took his seat. Indeed, the witchfinder had shown far more intelligence and compassion than Simon had dared hope for. He thanked God that Lewes was not a man like Hopkins. But until the verdict was given, Rebekah and her mother were still in danger. He turned towards Lewes, who had risen to his feet.

'It is my judgement that these women should face Almighty God,' he began. 'God will judge their innocence or guilt through the ordeal of swimming. The trial shall take place immediately.' Without further words he turned and strode decisively from the barn.

Chapter 43

Present day

'God, Rob! You look awful!'

'Thanks for that.'

'No. I mean it.' Caroline let her gaze rove over the tired features, the black shadows beneath eyes which held a haunted look. 'What's happened to you?'

'The dairy has burnt down.'

'Yes, I know. You told me on the phone. That's why I took a couple of days off. I thought you could do with some support.'

'The same building was burnt in my dream.'

'What? What are you talking about?'

'I've had more dreams. And in one that same building was destroyed by fire.'

'That's just coincidence, Rob. What on earth is wrong with you? You don't seem to be thinking straight.'

'How can I possibly think straight! I'm dreaming of a past that really happened. And you said that it was possible that the Rebekah I've seen here is a ghost telling me her story from the past! How can anyone think straight with all that going round his head!'

'It was just a theory, Rob. I didn't say it's what's actually happening.'

'It's either that, or I'm going mad.'

'I've been thinking about that.'

'You think I'm mad?'

Caroline laid a comforting hand on his arm. 'No, Rob. Never that. I can't explain how your dreams were so close to what you read in this Simon's diary. But now that the story of the diary is finished maybe the haunting, or whatever it is, is over.'

'But I'm still dreaming!'

'Maybe your imagination is taking the story further. If you let me counsel you, we might be able to get to the bottom of it. Bring your imaginative story to a conclusion. Stop the dreams.'

'But perhaps I'm still dreaming the same story. Maybe Simon didn't write it down. Or I haven't found everything that he wrote. Maybe I have to find out what happens in the end for the dreams to stop.'

'What's happening now in your dreams?'

'Rebekah and her mother have been accused of witchcraft.'

'Witchcraft?' Caroline held Rob's gaze. 'This is going too far, Rob. I really do think you need help. Take a few days off. Come back home with me. I'll treat you. Or I'll recommend someone else, if you think I'm too close.'

Rob pulled away. 'No.'

'Why not?'

'I can't leave Rebekah! She needs me!'

'What are you talking about? She lived hundreds of years ago. You can't help her now.' Caroline's brow furrowed into a deep frown. 'You are talking about the Rebekah in your dreams, aren't you? Not the woman you met here?'

Rob was silent for a moment, trying to analyse his feelings. Yes, he wanted to save Simon's Rebekah. He wanted to go back and make sure that whatever happened in the trial, she was safe. He had no idea how he could do that. But he did know why he had to try. Because she was just like his Rebekah. The girl he had met on the estate. He had no idea how she could have taken such a hold on his emotions so quickly, but he knew that he loved her. Loved her in a way that he had never loved Caroline. The realisation made him feel guilty. Angry. Scared. He rounded on Caroline.

'I have no idea what you're talking about!'

'Come off it, Rob! Ever since you've met her you've been acting strangely. I'm not stupid, you know! I can tell that you're holding something back from me when we're together. And when we're apart, I don't think you even remember that I exist!'

'I can't do this, Caroline! Not now!' They were both shouting now.

'Not now? Then when? When you've dreamt a whole new life with this woman?' Suddenly Caroline went quiet. A look of understanding, pain and rejection suffused her face. She spoke quietly now. 'That's it. Isn't it? All this stuff about your dreams is just a load of rubbish. You've met someone else and haven't got the guts to tell me.'

Rob shook his head. 'No. That's not it. The dreams are real.'

'Come off it, Rob. I'm a psychologist. Remember? You can't play mind games like that with me and expect to win.'

'You're wrong. You mean as much to me as you ever did.'

'But not as much as her?'

Rob was silent. No. Not as much as Rebekah. Not the past Rebekah. Nor the Rebekah he had met in the present. He did not know where the sudden understanding came from but he knew, beyond all reason and all doubt, that Rebekah was the woman he loved. The woman he wanted to spend the rest of his life with. He turned back to Caroline.

'This is getting us nowhere. I think it might be best if you went home. I'll come later. When I've sorted out my dreams.'

There were tears on Caroline's face as she nodded. 'Yes. I'll go. But this isn't the end, Rob. I love you, and I have no intention of giving you up. I'll find a way to help you through this. Okay? I know we can work this out. What we have is too precious to lose for the sake of a dream.'

Rob said nothing, just turned his back. Without another word Caroline turned and left the study.

Chapter 44

August 1651

Lewes led the small group from the barn towards the duck pond, closely followed by the silent crowd of villagers. This was something which all had heard about, but none had experienced. It was with a mixture of trepidation, fear and hope that they gathered around Lewes, the soldiers and the two accused.

'Strip them.'

'Simon...' Sir Thomas laid a restraining hand on his son's arm as he made to step forward. 'You must let this run its course.'

'But Father, how can we allow them to be shamed so? Do you not remember the starving women of Colchester who were stripped by the enemy? We turned away and allowed them their dignity; we treated them with compassion. But here...' his eyes roved over the crowd of people he had known since childhood, 'these people will watch Rebekah and her mother being humiliated. If it must be, then why not in private?'

'Because all must see that justice is done, my son. Then no-one can question the result.'

The two men fell silent as soldiers stepped forward and began to pull at the women's clothes. Ann held up her hand in protest. She turned her searching gaze towards Lewes.

'Must this be?' At his silent nod tears filled her eyes. 'Then I beg you, allow us some dignity. We will disrobe ourselves.'

Lewes signalled the soldiers to step back as Rebekah turned towards Ann.

'Mother?'

Ann struggled to hold back her tears, to be strong for her daughter. 'I am sorry, Rebekah, but we must.'

The young woman's tears began to fall silently as she removed her clothing, never taking her eyes from her mother, as though seeking strength from her. Simon bowed his head, ashamed of what was happening, but knew he could not intervene. Though convinced of the innocence of the two women he knew that, if it had been someone else accused of witchcraft, he would not have objected to what was happening. When he finally looked up the two women were naked, struggling to cover themselves with their hands yet failing to preserve their modesty, eyes turned to the ground as they hunched over. He wanted to catch Rebekah's eye, to let her see that he loved her and did not doubt her, but she did not raise her eyes. Simon could not stop himself looking at Rebekah. He had never seen her unclothed before. He had always dreamed that the first time he would see her naked would be on their wedding night, when he made love to her. His heart cried in anguish to see her like this, the eyes of the village on her breasts, her womanhood.

Sir Thomas's grip tightened on his son's arm. 'Simon?' At first the softly spoken word went unheard. 'Simon.' This time a little louder, more forceful. Simon dragged his eyes from the two women to look at his father.

'Perhaps it would be better if you were not here?'

'I cannot leave. She must know that I am here to support her.'

Sir Thomas's eyes were filled with compassion, and he nodded. 'And despite everything, despite what you think of me and what I have done, I am here to support you. I only did what I believe was right. We have to know...'

'Perhaps you need to see this to know the truth, but I do not. My heart tells me what is true.' Although his words were harsh Simon felt comforted by his father's presence, finally accepting that his father did not do this out of hate or spite but to protect his home, his family and his estates. Their eyes held for a moment, then they turned to Lewes as he spoke.

'Do you women have familiars?'

The women shook their heads. Ann spoke for them both.

'No, sir. We are not witches. We wish no one any harm and do not consort with the Devil.'

'What of the crows which flew from your window last night, before the fire?'

'They had nothing to do with us, my lord.'

'They had not come to feed? To drink your blood?'

'No, sir.'

Lewes turned to his soldiers. 'Search them carefully for the Devil's mark.'

Four of his men stepped forward, two going to Rebekah and two to her mother. The women stood silently as every inch of their bodies was searched. Rough hands roamed over their faces and heads, hands and arms, their backs, probing between their buttocks. The first hands of a man which ever touched Rebekah's breast did not stroke them softly, but roughly sought any sign that she had been succouring a familiar. The women's legs and feet were examined, and between their legs. Sir Thomas tried to turn Simon's face away, but he refused. There was nothing he could do to stop what was happening, but he was determined that at least one pair of eyes filled with love, not fear and hatred, would watch. Finally the soldiers stepped back and whispered quietly together.

'Anything?'

Their spokesman stepped towards Lewes. 'Yes, sir. The old woman has a mark on her arm which could be where her familiar drinks. The younger, a scar on her leg which could be the mark of the Devil. We believe that they are the witches we have been seeking.'

At these words the villagers crossed themselves and shuffled back, further away from the women who, it now seemed, really were witches. Ann shook her head wildly.

'No, my lord! They are wrong! See here.' She raised her left arm as she spoke, revealing a dark mole on her underarm. 'I have had this mark since birth. I swear by Almighty God that I do not have a familiar, and that no evil creature has ever fed from me. As for my daughter,' she turned towards Rebekah as she spoke, 'the scar on her leg is from a cut she received as a child. We live in the forest, sir, and it is all too easy to be cut by branches or tree roots.' She looked wildly around her, first at the witchfinder and his men, then Sir Thomas and Simon, finally her fellow villagers. 'Which one of you does not have a scar? Which of your children has never cut themselves and left a mark? I beg you all, do not hold these marks against us for they are innocent. As are we.'

Simon stepped forward. 'She is right. I have scars from childhood falls. And what man amongst us who fought in the war does not carry a scar, great or small? You cannot condemn them for these marks!'

Lewes nodded thoughtfully. 'It is true. There may be innocent explanations for these marks. Yet they may also be the mark of the Devil. To be absolutely certain we must proceed to the swimming.'

The soldiers, now convinced of the guilt of the two women, roughly dragged them to the ground. Tears flowed from Rebekah's eyes. 'Please, sir, be merciful.'

Her words were little more than a whisper, but Simon heard them and tears filled his own eyes. 'Is there nothing we can do, Father?'

'No, my son. But be still for just a little longer. If they are truly innocent it will soon be over. Then we will have to continue our search for the evil doers.'

'But how can we trust the trial? Those soldiers are wrong about the marks which Rebekah and her mother bear.'

'The trial will be in God's hands, Simon. He will judge their innocence or guilt.'

As the two men spoke softly together the soldiers roughly tied Rebekah's right thumb to her left big toe, then her left thumb to her right big toe. After doing the same to Ann they tied two ropes around the women's waists. Lewes finally stepped forward. His eyes roved over the assembled crowd for a moment. Then he spoke.

'We all know the evil which has troubled your village over the last week. We are here today to find out if these two women are the source. I entreat you all to pray most fervently whilst the trial is conducted. Ask our Merciful Father to pass his judgement.' He signalled to the priest who stepped forward. 'Let it begin.'

The priest began to recite the Lord's Prayer as the two soldiers holding the ropes around Ann's waist took position on opposite sides of the pond.

'Our Farther, who art in heaven…'

Lewes signalled to two other soldiers who lifted Ann and threw her into the water.

'…hallowed be thy name…'

'Mother!' Rebekah's frightened scream was drowned out by the voice of the crowd, which now joined the priest in his prayer.

'…Thy kingdom come…'

The two soldiers pulled on the ropes, dragging the bound Ann to the surface, where she struggled to raise her head and take a breath.

'…Thy will be done…'

'Hold her loosely!' called Lewes. 'She must float or sink by the will of God, not the strength of your arms!'

The soldiers seemed to loosen their grip slightly on the rope. Ann sank beneath the surface, then rose again.

'…On earth as it is in heaven…'

'Do they hold her up, Father?'

Sir Thomas shrugged, not answering as he continued to pray along with the rest.

A second time the ropes were loosened and Ann sank. A second time she rose to the surface.

'…Give us this day our daily bread. Forgive us our trespasses as we forgive those who have trespassed against us…'

Ann struggled to lift her head above the water, drawing in quickly-snatched breaths as the soldiers held her in the centre of the pond.

'…Lead us not into temptation. Deliver us from evil…'

The crowd crossed themselves at those words, staring fearfully at the woman in the water who refused to sink though her hands and feet were bound.

A third time the soldiers loosed the ropes. A third time she came back to the surface.

'…Thine is the kingdom, the power and the glory…'

'Mother!' Rebekah turned her tear stained face to Lewes. 'Sir, I beg you! Be merciful!'

Lewes nodded grimly. 'It is over.'

'…Amen.'

As the prayer ended the two soldiers dragged Ann to the edge of the pond and hauled her out. Lewes strode over and gazed down at her, his eyes harsh.

'The water has rejected you.' He paused for a moment as the woman coughed and spat out water, then... 'Leave her tied.' He turned towards Rebekah who was shivering with fear. 'Do you now freely admit your guilt?'

Rebekah shook her head. 'I cannot! I am innocent!'

Lewes signalled the soldiers who held her. 'Throw her in.'

'No!' Simon stepped forward, only to be restrained by two of the soldiers as Lewes turned towards him.

'Be still! She must undergo the trial! If you interfere then you, too, must be considered a witch and treated the same.'

'But she is innocent!'

'That is for God to judge, not I.'

'Simon! Please! Help me!'

Simon's face was anguished as Rebekah called out to him. He struggled against those who held him, but could not break free. 'Rebekah!'

The two soldiers lifted the naked young woman and threw her into the water. She sank, and for a moment Simon prayed that she would not surface, just for a short time. Not long enough to harm her, but enough to prove her innocence. The crowd were praying again, but Simon could not hear their words. The blood pounding in his ears threatened to deafen him, his knees felt weak and he was afraid that he might vomit.

Seconds after being thrown into the pond Rebekah surfaced. The crowd groaned. Simon watched as Rebekah fought to keep her head above the water, unable to swim because of the ropes which bound her, hand and foot. The soldiers relaxed the ropes around her waist and she sank a second time. It seemed like only seconds later that her head broke the surface, her shoulder, the curve of her breast. As the crowd continued to pray Rebekah was lowered into the water for a third, and final, time. When she surfaced, seemingly without the aid of the soldiers on the ropes, Lewes signalled for her to be dragged from the water. The young woman lay on her side in the mud, retching, gasping for air. She struggled to roll over, to hide her nakedness, but was unable to because of the ropes which bound her. Lewes' fiery gaze fell on the two women as he passed his judgement.

'You have been tried by water, the purest of elements. God would not allow this purity to be sullied by evil. Thrice was each of you offered to the pure embrace of the water. Thrice you were rejected and rose to the surface.' He lifted his eyes to the crowd of villagers, gathered silently in front of him. 'Almighty God has spoken! We have found our witches!'

'No!'

Sir Thomas laid a hand on his son's arm. 'Simon, be still.'

'But, Father! It is not possible! They are good, decent people!' He turned back towards the women as Rebekah struggled to speak between her sobs.

'But I am innocent, sir!'

Ann raised her eyes, seeking those of the witchfinder. When he looked into them he saw anger and hatred. He hurriedly crossed himself and took a step back as Ann began to speak.

'This is not the judgement of God, but of men. God will judge us innocent, but you he will find guilty.'

Lewes turned away, fearful that she might curse him, or put a spell on him. Raising his eyes to the crowd he spoke again, his voice commanding.

'It is written in the book of Exodus "Thou shalt not suffer a witch to live." These two women are found guilty. They will be put to death. Sentence shall be carried out tomorrow, before they have time to do more evil amongst us. Take them away.'

'No!'

Simon's cry was the only sound to be heard, save for the weeping of Rebekah. As the young man fell to his knees in despair, the soldiers lifted the still naked and bound women and carried them away.

Chapter 45

Present day

Rob's face was wet with tears. He struggled to focus on the library. The desk and chairs. The shelves of books. The bible. As the present day became clearer, he found himself wanting to go back again. What he had just seen and experienced left him feeling bereft. Poor Rebekah. He had to do something to help her. Never mind that it had all happened three hundred years ago, for him it felt real, the present, today. Never mind that the thought of facing the fear and hatred of the witch trial and its consequences filled him with dread. Rebekah could not be left to face her punishment alone. He had to be there for her. No matter what the cost to himself.

'Robert?'

That voice. A voice which he loved. A voice which seemed to reach to the very heart of him. For a moment Rob thought that he was back in his dream. But if so, why was she not calling him Simon? He turned towards the door.

'Rebekah?'

'Oh, my dear Robert! What ails thee? Why do you weep?'

'I was dreaming of the past and...' His voice trailed off. What could he say to her that would not sound crazy? Rebekah took a step towards him.

'The past? Did you dream of me?'

Rob looked into her eyes. Eyes full of love and compassion. He had seen those eyes before. In his dreams. He nodded.

'Yes. You are in my dreams. Or it seems to be you.' He took a deep breath, then rushed on. 'In my dreams I love you, Rebekah. I love you with all my heart and soul. And you love me.'

'Yes, my Robert.' Rebekah stepped closer as she spoke. 'We love each other. We have always loved each other. You are a part of me as I am a part of you. I have waited a long time for you to return to me, my love. When you first came and remembered me not, it was hard. But now you truly see me. I am your Rebekah. And you are my Simon. Together at last.'

Rob's mind was in a whirl. It all sounded so strange, so impossible. Yet felt so true. He nodded.

'I love you, Rebekah. Now as in the past.' He closed the space between us. 'Do you know how Simon felt? At your trial? His heart was breaking. My heart was breaking. And I could do nothing.'

'There was nothing you could do.'

'Then why have you been showing me this? Surely now that I know what happens I can change it?'

'You have seen Simon's story. But have you been able to influence him? Change his actions?' Rob shook his head as Rebekah continued. 'The past is the past, my love. It cannot be changed. What happened happened.'

Rob was afraid to ask the question. But even more afraid not to.

'What did happen, Rebekah?'

Rebekah reached out and took his hand in hers. The room began to fade as Rob felt himself being pulled back into the past once more.

From the doorway Caroline watched as Rob and Rebekah stood, still as statues, barely breathing.

'Rob?'

There was no reply.

Chapter 46

August 1651

An early morning dew lay upon the grass. The sun had risen into a cloudless sky, holding the promise of a hot summer's day. Birds were singing. Simon noticed none of these. All he could see were the two gibbets which had been hastily erected by the witchfinder's men the evening before. The shadows of the scaffolds stretched out before them on the grass, like evil hands reaching out. Simon shuddered. He could not believe that this was really happening, that Rebekah and her mother would die here within the hour. Surely something would happen to prevent it? Some sign that they were not witches? Maybe Lewes would commute the sentences? Simon closed his eyes and prayed harder than he had ever prayed in his life.

There was the sound of footsteps and Simon turned to face his father. Sir Thomas said nothing. His eyes were filled with sadness and compassion as he took his place beside his son, and he watched in silence as the villagers began to gather on the green.

There was little sound. A few murmured words, a prayer, but nothing more. These were people who had lived with Ann and Rebekah all their lives, had relied on Ann for help and healing, now they believed that for all that time they had been harbouring witches. Fear vied with anger in their hearts as they came to see justice done, to see the threat to their families removed for ever.

There was the sound of a horse's hooves, the animal moving at a steady walk as it approached Simon and his father from the rear. Simon clenched his fists in anger, but did not turn. He could guess who it was, and he was not sure that he would be able to control his feelings, or his actions. Sir Thomas, however, turned to face the approaching rider. The sound of hoof-beats stopped. There was a muted thud as the man dismounted.

'Lewes.'

'Sir Thomas.'

The witchfinder tied his horse to a tree, then stepped forward so that he was facing the younger man.

'Simon.'

Simon swallowed hard, fighting to keep the anger from his eyes, though not succeeding. 'Lewes.'

The witchfinder's eyes held a gentle kindness which Simon found hard to reconcile with the role the man was about to play. Lewes understood this. His voice was soft as he spoke to the young man.

'You truly believe yourself to be in love with this girl. I know how you feel, for I watched my loved one die, though for her it was disease not...' He was silent for a moment, then continued. 'These women have been found guilty. For years they have had you under their sway so the spell will not be easily broken. Their deaths will sunder the link betwixt and between you. It may be that there will be some small evil remaining, but fervent prayer will heal that. Of this I have no doubt. You must believe this, too, for your life to be healed.'

For a time Simon said nothing. He could not think of himself or his future. All he could think of was Rebekah, his love who was going to die this morning. Right here, in front of him. He closed his eyes and took a deep breath. When he opened them, it was to see Lewes looking at the gallows.

'Will it be quick?' Simon's words were soft, but his companions heard them. Lewes nodded.

'As swift as possible. I seek the Lord's justice, not vengeance.'

'It will be over soon, son. Have no fear.'

Simon turned to his father.

'Have no fear? How can you say that? You, who watched the King die, then wept with grief? How can you expect me to face this without fear? Or anger? Or hatred?'

'I cannot, Simon. You know well the pain in my heart at the King's execution. All I can offer you is my love and support, as I offered them to him that day. And as you must offer them to ... the witch.'

'Can you not say her name, Father? Just once? Can you not acknowledge her?'

Sir Thomas sighed. 'You must be strong. You must not shed a tear, but hold yourself straight and true. Hold Rebekah's eyes with your own and help her through her ordeal.'

'You seem to have softened to these witches, Sir Thomas.'

Sir Thomas turned to Lewes. 'They are children of God, just as we all are. Though they may have gone astray we must acknowledge their humanity.'

Lewes nodded. 'Justice and compassion.'

'And mercy?'

Lewes turned to the young man. 'Yes, Simon. Mercy. If they should confess.'

The strange conversation was interrupted by a rising murmur from the crowd as the two condemned women were brought forward. Rebekah's eyes darted wildly around, seeking a way of escape, but there was none.

Finally her gaze found Simon's. Two pairs of eyes reflecting fear, horror … and love. As they looked they seemed to draw strength from each other. Simon straightened his back and stood tall, willing his strength to leave him and go to her, to help her through the ordeal which lay ahead.

Lewes strode forward to stand in front of the two women. 'You have a final chance to confess to your sin of witchcraft.'

'What would happen if we do?'

'You would be imprisoned. The evil forced out of you. Maybe one day, if you are no longer considered a threat, you would be released.'

'Impossible. We cannot confess to something we have not done. We cannot spend the rest of our lives in your hands whilst you seek to drive out an evil which does not exist.'

'And do you speak for your daughter?'

Rebekah shook her head. 'I speak for myself.'

For a moment Simon hoped and prayed that she would confess. The thought of her being held in prison filled him with loathing, but at least she would still be alive. Perhaps he would be able to help her. But Rebekah spoke, and his hopes were dashed.

'I am an innocent. I place myself in the hands of Almighty God, who is my Lord and my Judge. He knows the thoughts and actions of my heart and soul. Though I am afraid of death, I know that it will lead to a purer life for me. An eternal life, with no pain, no suffering.'

'Father. Will he show compassion? Surely no one who was a witch could speak such words?'

Sir Thomas shook his head sadly. 'I am afraid not, my son. It is confession or…'

He stopped speaking so that they could hear Lewes' words.

'They have had their chance. Take them.'

The soldiers roughly dragged the two women onto the scaffold where they were helped onto two stools, their balance hindered by their hands tied behind their backs. Their hair had already been braided into thick plaits, which hung down their backs against the rough homespun cloth in which they were dressed. A soldier lifted the hair so that a noose could be placed around their necks, close to the skin. Simon could see Rebekah shiver at the touch. As the soldiers stepped back, Ann lifted her eyes towards the Hardwyckes. Simon recoiled at the hatred in them and crossed himself, which did not go unnoticed by his father.

'Simon!' Ann's voice rang out clearly. 'It is not we who are evil, but you! Your family has taken my husband from me, now you take my life. I could bear that. But to take my daughter? You profess to love her, yet have done nothing to protect her. You have an evil heart. I curse you!' The crowd crossed themselves and hurriedly stepped back, murmuring prayers for protection. 'You will know no peace in this life. You will have no peace in death. I will seek you through all eternity and make you pay for this, Hardwycke! What you do to us today will be a stain on your soul for all eternity!'

To silence her Lewes gave a signal and the two stools were kicked away.

Simon saw Rebekah fall. There was a snapping sound as, mercifully, her neck was broken. Tears filled his eyes as he watched her body swing at the end of the rope. Her open eyes seemed to accuse him. He pulled his own eyes away only to see Ann kicking and struggling at the end of her rope.

The knot had not been correctly positioned and her neck remained intact. As she slowly strangled, struggling for each gasping breath that she took, her eyes sought his and held them. With a supreme effort of will she spoke again.

'I curse you. I curse you.'

The struggling body convulsed. The face turned a vivid shade of blue for lack of breath. The eyes began to start from their sockets. As Simon watched the convulsions diminished until, with one final twitch, Ann Sawyer was dead.

***

Simon laid down his pen and sat, staring at the paper in front of him. His face was pale, black rings beneath eyes which were red-rimmed from crying. But there were no tears now. His jaw was set in a grim line as he picked up the paper and folded it carefully. Slowly rising from his seat, he made his way over to the large family Bible. He ran his hands over the smooth, warm leather before opening it and reading the front page.

Thomas Hardwycke married Mary Sutter this day 24th October 1623.

This Bible shall be the record of our family over the generations. I pray God's blessing on our marriage and our future life together.

Though the house is not yet complete it is our wish that our children be born here. For that reason we lived in the finished rooms for some weeks until the good Lord blessed us with the safe birth of a son and heir.

Thomas Hardwycke born this day 15th January 1625. The Lord be praised for his goodness.

Simon continued to read. Here was his family history. The names of his siblings who died in childhood; the births of Elizabeth and himself; the deaths of his mother and Thomas; the marriage of Elizabeth and Benjamin. He touched the blank space beneath. Here was where his own marriage would be written. It should be Rebekah's name written there, but that was a dream lost as so much mist is burned away by the morning sun. Later that day his name would be written there, next to that of Abigail, and the family history would move on, unrolling over the years from their union.

Simon gently kissed the folded paper in his hand before carefully sliding it inside the spine of the Bible. He closed the book, checking carefully to make sure that his letter could not be seen. Placing his hand on the warm leather, he closed his eyes as though in prayer. His words, like his dreams and his love, were now buried. With a hardened face, and a hardened heart, he turned and left the room.

Chapter 47

Present day

Rob opened his eyes. For a moment he thought that he was still dreaming. In front of him stood Ann, her face blue, her hate filled eyes bulging from the sockets. But, no, this was no dream. This was real. This was the spectre that had haunted his first night at Marston.

'So, Hardwycke. Now you remember.' Her voice was harsh. 'Now you remember what you did to me. And to Rebekah.'

'But it wasn't me!' Rob was confused, not sure of where ... or when ... he was. 'It was Simon who loved Rebekah then. And he would have done anything to save her!'

'Liar!' Her voice was filled with venom, causing Rob to take a step back in his fear. Then he realised that he was not alone. Someone was holding tightly to his hand. He turned his head to see Rebekah standing next to him. She returned his gaze with a quiet confidence.

'Do not worry, Robert. All will be well.' She turned to the apparition. 'Enough, Mother! Leave him be! Have we not all suffered enough?'

'No! Never!'

A fierce wind sprang up from nowhere, tearing the books from the bookshelves and flinging them around the room. Rob raised his arms to protect his head. The wind died as suddenly as it had started. When he raised his eyes and looked around, Ann had gone.

'What on earth just happened?' Caroline took a hesitant step into the room. 'Did I really just see a ghost?' Rob nodded. 'And who is this?' She continued.

Rob looked down to where a small hand was still entwined with his.

'Rebekah.'

Caroline frowned. 'You mean...?'

'What the hell is going on here?' Paul strode into the room, his voice loud and angry. 'What's all this noise? And what's happened to all my books?'

Rob was not sure what to say, where to begin. He took a deep breath.

'Remember the ghost you saw? Well, it was her. She did this.'

'Rubbish! That was just my imagination.'

'No. I saw her too.' Caroline's face was pale, her hands shaking with shock. 'She was here. For some reason she hates Rob. That's why she did this.'

'And that is why she set the fires.' Rebekah spoke for the first time, and Paul turned towards her.

'*She* set the fires? Not the travellers?'

Rebekah nodded. 'Her hatred is such that she wishes to destroy Robert, and this place with him.'

'Why?'

Rob turned to Paul. 'It's a long story. I'll tell you the details later.'

'Who is this girl?' Paul looked at Rebekah as he spoke. 'What has she got to do with all of this?'

'My name is Rebekah. The ghost is my mother.'

'This is ridiculous! You're not a ghost! Is this some kind of joke? If it is, I can tell you right now that I'm not laughing.'

'This is not said to amuse you, sir. She is filled with hatred and cannot let it go.'

'Wait!' exclaimed Rob as he turned to Rebekah. 'She hates me because of what happened to you. Right?' Rebekah nodded. 'She thought I ... Simon didn't love you and didn't try to help?'

'Yes.'

'But I can prove he did!' Rob dashed over to the table and rummaged amongst the scattered books until he found the folder he was looking for. He opened it swiftly, then carefully took out the letter which he had found in the bible. 'We must show this to her!'

Paul turned to Caroline. 'What is he talking about?'

She shrugged. 'I have no idea.'

'Rob...?'

'Not now, Paul! I'll explain later. Right now, I've got to put a stop to this!' He grabbed Rebekah by the hand again. 'Come on!'

'Where are you going?'

'Outside, just in case this goes wrong.'

'I'm coming with you.'

'No, Caroline. This is something between the ghost, and Rebekah and me. You and Paul would only be in the way.'

'I'm not sure that I understand any of this.' Paul's voice was hard with anger. 'I'll play along for now, Rob. But then you explain everything if you hope to keep your job.'

Rob nodded and, without another word, he and Rebekah left the room.

***

Five minutes later they were in the orchard. Rob turned to Rebekah.

'Can you summon her?'

Rebekah nodded and closed her eyes. Moments later Rob saw a shimmering of the air in front of him. Slowly, from nowhere, the apparition of Ann materialised.

'What is this, child? Do you stand with him against me?'

'No, Mother. Not against you. But I do stand with him. You knowest that I love him. That I have loved him since first seeing him hundreds of years ago.'

'Even knowing what he did to us?'

'That was when his spirit was Simon. It was not this Robert whom we knew then. But even so, I would stand with Simon. I know that he loved me and would never have harmed me.'

'But he did nothing to save us.' Ann turned her angry gaze on Rob. 'Thou knowest now why I hate thee. Why I must have my revenge.'

Rob nodded. 'I know why you hated Simon. But he didn't deserve it. That's why I asked Rebekah to bring you here. To show you this.' He held up the letter. 'These are Simon's words, written on the day that he married Abigail. Will you let me read them to you?'

'I knowest not what thou might say to allay my anger. But read it. Then I shalt take my revenge.' The air around the ghost seemed to crackle with electricity, as though a summer storm approached.

'Mother, please listen with an open heart. Father would not have wanted you to judge without first hearing what Robert has to say.'

A sadness filled Ann's eyes. 'How I have missed your father. The centuries have been long without him by my side.'

'Please, Mother? It may be that these words can bring an end to your hatred. It may be that you will find a way back to Father when your heart is filled with love.'

There seemed to be a softening of the air around Ann. Although still filled with fear, Rob felt that there was a lessening of the hatred, a chink in Ann's armour.

'I found this hidden in the family bible at the house.'

'So thou sayest.'

'It is true, Mother. I held his hand as he saw again what Simon had done. I saw Simon writing these words, although I couldst not read the words any more than thou can, and do not know what this paper says. But I saw Simon write it and hide it in the bible. These are his words.'

Rob licked his lips, then began to read.

My darling Rebekah, today is that day which I long hast dreaded. Today is the day I should have walked with thee into the church and made thee mine own in front of God and of witnesses. Today is the day on which my life should have begun anew, my life with thee forever beside me through the long years that lie ahead. But those years shall be long indeed, longer than I canst imagine, for I must take another to wife this morn, another shall walk beside me through all my days, and she shall be one with whom I can share nothing of my heart and mind as I have shared them with thee.

'Abigail is a good woman, Rebekah, and if I had known thee not then perchance we could have been happy together. But how can I give myself to her, knowing that it is thee I cherish? Thee, whom I crave during each long and lonely night?

'Oh Rebekah! How my heart weeps! How it breaks! For not only have I lost thee, my one true love, but I know that if not for me thou wouldst still be here. If not for the foolishness of my youth thou wouldst still live close by, we would still be able to share our love, though it be secretive and hidden from the prying eyes of those who could never understand and could only condemn.

'I pray that you were able to forgive me my love, for I shall never be able to forgive myself. My guilt will haunt me until the day that I shall meet with my Maker and seek his pardon and forgiveness for my wrongs. But know ye this, every day that I live shall be a penance, every hour I will try to live my life as thou wouldst have me do, every minute I shall think of thee.

'My darling Rebekah, this is the goodbye I was never allowed to speak. Forgive my past deeds and my betrayal of you as I now take Abigail to wife. There is nothing else that I am able to do, and so I shall live the remainder of my days in utter hopelessness...

There was silence as Rob finished, though he sensed a shifting of emotions, a deeper change in the atmosphere. He turned to the young woman at his side. Tears filled her eyes and traced delicate pathways on her cheeks.

'Rebekah?'

She lifted her eyes, filled with love, to meet his. 'You truly meant it when you asked me to be your wife?'

Rob felt a strange dislocation, himself yet at the same time, Simon. He nodded. 'You were the only one I ever loved. If I had been older and handled things differently, perhaps I could have saved you and your mother. It was the foolishness of youth which made me declare my love for you to my father. If not for that...'

'If not for that we would not have been condemned as witches.'

Rob turned to meet Ann's accusation. 'Yes. I freely admit that. But it was a mistake out of ignorance and love, not out of hatred. Can you forgive Simon ... me? The child you helped, the child who thought of you as the mother he had never known? I wish you peace, Mistress Sawyer. Peace to be again with your husband.'

The hatred seemed to die in the eyes which held his, then moved to meet those of her daughter. 'Rebekah?'

'Yes, Mother. Be at peace.'

Ann stepped forward. Still fearful, Rob forced himself not to step back, not to show his fear. But Ann's attention was not focused on him. She reached out a hand to gently touch the cheek of her daughter.

'It has been so long, my child.'

'But it is over now. Rest in peace.'

Ann turned once more. This time Simon saw no hatred in her eyes.

'I have misjudged thee, and for that I am sorry. Be well, Simon. I hope that, one day, thou wilt find the happiness which has eluded thee.'

There was a shimmering in the air. The outline of Ann began to fade. Then she was gone.

Rob stood quietly for a moment, trying to untangle his thoughts and emotions. He knew that he was Rob, but at the same time he felt Simon's emotions, remembered every detail of his life. Somehow, he did not know how, he was both of them in one body. It was Rebekah's voice which helped him to refocus on the present.

'Her spirit has been unable to rest for so long. Thank you, Robert.'

He turned to meet her steady, loving gaze. 'The words that Simon wrote. They are as true of my feelings today as they were for him then. I love you, Rebekah.'

'And I love thee.'

'Will you stay with me while I finish my work here? Then come with me when I leave? We can spend the rest of our lives together.'

'Thou forgetest thyself, my love.' Rebekah's eyes were filled with sadness. 'I am not of thy time. Simon lived his life and died. His spirit has been reborn in you. But my spirit has had no rebirth. For three hundred years I have waited here. It is now time for me to move on.'

'But I don't understand? Your mother was a ghost, each time I saw her she was insubstantial. But you are real. I can touch you and feel you. Why can't you stay?'

'I am as much a ghost as my mother. When I am not with thee I am as insubstantial. It takes more energy than thou canst imagine for me to appear real to thy touch. I am no more than a spirit.'

'Why was your spirit held here? You weren't filled with hatred like your mother. What held you?'

'She did. I love her. I could not leave her soul in torment here alone.'

'But what happens now?'

'I move on. It will be hard, knowing that I have found thee again, but my spirit can no longer remain.'

'I don't think I can bear to live without you, Rebekah!'

'Thou must. Remember this, my love. I have waited three hundred years for thee, knowing each day that I could not be with thee. But now my spirit is free. We belong together, and I believe that we will be together someday.'

'But not in this life?'

'No.'

'Then this is goodbye?'

'Yes, my love. Until we meet again.'

Tears filled Rob's eyes as he leant down and placed a gentle kiss on Rebekah's lips. For a moment they were soft and yielding beneath his, then there was nothing.

Rebekah was gone.

***

'So, you're telling me that this Rebekah was actually another ghost?'

The couple stood on the driveway in front of the Manor house. Rob knew that he needed to talk to Caroline in private, but could not face taking her to the orchard. That place was too special now. Rebekah's. He nodded at Caroline's question, but said nothing as she continued. 'And these two ghosts both haunted you because of something that you did in a previous life?' Another nod. 'I'm not sure I can believe this!'

'But you saw them yourself.'

'True. And...' Caroline struggled to find the words, '...and you loved Rebekah in your previous life?'

'Yes.'

'What about now?'

'Rebekah and I are soulmates. We belong together. But that's not possible.' Rob couldn't meet Caroline's gaze. 'I love her. But I love you too. What I felt for you before I came here hasn't changed.'

'You mean you want us to stay together?'

Rob nodded. He had thought long and hard about this. If he couldn't have Rebekah, then there was no one he would rather be with than Caroline. 'I know it won't be easy. We have a lot to talk about. But I think we can talk through this. And when we come out the other side we will be stronger.'

'You really believe that?'

'Yes, if you still love me.'

'Oh, yes, Rob. I still love you.'

'Good, then...'

Caroline held up a hand to quieten his words. 'I still love you. But this is the end for us.'

Rob was thunderstruck. 'Why?'

'Oh, come on. You don't think you can tell a woman that you are only with her because you can't be with someone else and expect her to be happy with that.'

'But Rebekah isn't here...'

'No. She was a ghost. She was never real to you in this life. Yet you still love her more than me. How do you think that makes me feel? Coming second to a ghost?'

'I'm sorry, Caroline. When you put it like that...'

'Yes. When I put it like that. But there's something else, Rob. You say that you and Rebekah are soulmates. You hope to be with her in another life. If that's the case, then I must believe that I have a soulmate too. Someone I belong to in the same way as you and Rebekah belong together.'

Rob frowned thoughtfully. 'I hadn't thought of that.'

Caroline smiled ruefully. 'No. I didn't think you had. But you know what that tells me? Just as your love for me is second best, maybe my love for you is too.'

'What?'

'Who's to say that my soulmate isn't out there somewhere, waiting for me?' Caroline waved a vague hand in front of them as she spoke. 'Why should I settle with second best? With you? I intend to go out there, Rob, and look for the man who is meant for me. Okay, I might not find him in this life, just as you won't have your Rebekah, but how can I not take that chance?'

Rob was quiet for a moment, then gave a sad, slow smile. 'You're right, of course. I wish you luck, and hope you find him.'

The couple embraced for a moment, a moment when their emotions shifted from love to a deep abiding affection which they both knew would last for the rest of their lives. As she drew away Caroline was smiling.

'Good luck, Rob. You deserve it.'

With that she turned and made her way back into the Manor house. When she was gone Rob sat on the low stone wall beside the driveway. The avenue of trees stretched before him, like arms opening wide to encompass the gentle Oxfordshire landscape. He breathed deeply, enjoying the scent of the trees, feeling at home once more.

After a while a new feeling of peace seemed to enfold him. An acceptance of what had been, and what would be. Knowing what he would see, Rob turned his head to where a young woman stood at the tree-line, watching him. Her face was framed by chestnut hair, a smile played on her lips, and love flowed from her gaze. Their eyes held and, in that moment of time which seemed to stretch for an eternity, spoke of love and hope, and a promise for the future.

Then Rebekah turned to walk away. As Rob watched her image faded. And was gone.

THE END

Other books by Dorinda Balchin

Heronfield

Amidst the bombs and bullets, the fear and confusion, sometimes it's the battles within our hearts which leave the deepest scars.

Experience a sweeping saga set in war-torn Europe during the desperate years of the Second World War. At its heart is a cast of characters who draw us into their lives from the defeat of Dunkirk to final victory:

Tony, a young man barely in his twenties who experiences the horror of Britain's first defeat and offers his unique talents to the war effort, only to find that his secret work threatens his relationships with those he loves. David, Tony's elder brother, fighter pilot and hero of the Battle of Britain. Sarah, whose work with the VAD's brings her into contact with so many, forcing her to choose between a man with loyalty and honour or another with all the characteristics of a coward. Bobby, a young American GI for whom a posting to England brings love and hope. And at the centre of it all, Heronfield, the manor house set amongst the gentle rolling downs of southern England, one time home for Tony and his family and now a war-time hospital.

Heronfield, witness to six long years of loyalty and love, anger and hatred, loss and betrayal.

Praise for Heronfield

'It is difficult to set Heronfield down. An Amazing read.' – Historical Novel Society

'Heronfield is a fictional story with accurate historical events that made for a superb book. I cannot recommend it highly enough.' – Reader's Favorite

'The raw emotion grabbed at me and didn't let go, even after finishing the book. I've never read a story that's taken me by the soul and stayed with me quite the way Heronfield has done...An absolutely amazing story that needs to be read.' – Whispering Stories

The Guardians

The gold of El Dorado belonged to the Aztecs. Their gods will do anything to protect it.

It is all too easy to lose focus on what is really important in life when surrounded by the pressures and demands of modern living. It can take something extraordinary, something out of this world, to re-focus us on life's priorities.

For archaeologist Rick Gibson the priority is to discover a 'great find' which will make him a household name, and he is prepared to sacrifice everything – his home, his wife, his son – to achieve this. After years of disappointment Gibson's luck changes with the discovery of an ancient manuscript detailing the hiding place of the Aztec treasure of Montezuma. Gibson leads a dig to Mexico to uncover the famous treasure of Eldorado, but it is not as easy as he had assumed for the treasure is guarded. 'The Guardians' come from the world of the dead to protect the treasure and, one by one, the members of Gibson's party suffer the consequences.

The suspense builds from a gentle beginning in suburban England to a terrifying climax with supernatural forces of good and evil battling for supremacy. Woven skillfully into the narrative are the questions which all humans face, and the answers to which will bring life, or death, for Gibson.

Meet the author

Dorinda Balchin, a voracious reader since childhood, writes historical novels set during periods of war and conflict. She loves the detailed research necessary to create books which have a real feel for the period; her debut novel, Heronfield, was described as 'an amazing read' by the Historical Novel Society. Heronfield was followed by a supernatural thriller, The Guardians. Dorinda is now working on a series of novels featuring a war correspondent.

After a career teaching in England, Dorinda and her husband suffered a 'mid-life crisis' which took them to India where they spent seven very happy years running a guest house in a remote rural location. The couple have returned to the UK, where Dorinda continues to write her historical novels. She spends her spare time painting, fencing and riding.

Connect with Dorinda Balchin

Please feel free to contact Dorinda through any of the following channels:

www.dorindabalchin.com

www.facebook.com/DorindaBalchin

www.twitter.com/DorindaBalchin